DOUBLE DUTCH

RAY SCOTT

Publisher: Silverbird Publishing
Ray Scott
website: www.raycwscottwriting.com.au

First published in Australia 2019
This edition published 2019
Copyright © Ray Scott 2019
Cover design, typesetting: WorkingType (www.workingtype.com.au)

Scott, Ray
Double Dutch
ISBN- 978-0-6485298-7-3

pp374

ABOUT THE AUTHOR

Ray Scott was born in Kent in England and lived and worked for over 30 years in the Midlands near Birmingham. After National service in the Royal Navy he joined the insurance industry and was employed for many years in Birmingham and Wolverhampton. He and his wife Mary and their two boys immigrated to Australia in 1970 and have lived since then near Melbourne where he again joined the insurance industry, while Mary rejoined the nursing profession.

Ray has been writing for many years. This is his fourth venture into publishing, the others being *"The Fifth Identity"*, *"Cut to the Chase"* (also a paperback) and *"The Wimmera Shoot"*, all thrillers.

www.raycwscottwriting.com.au

*To my wife Mary for her never-ending support,
and also my severest critic when my knowledge
and use of grammar has been sadly lacking.*

CHAPTER 1

Francis Burton, the Director General of ASIO, consulted a file before him. Seated opposite was his colleague Alan Kelsey.

'Strictly speaking, Alan,' Burton began. 'This doesn't relate to anti-terrorism within Australia, but our colleagues at ASIS have discerned internal rumblings in the state of Taranga which indicate all isn't well below the surface.'

'I thought Taranga had settled down after the coup that toppled that bloody incompetent Communist regime.'

'Regrettably other factors are at play,' Burton replied. 'I agree the Leader, Colonel, Prime Minister, President — Great Leader and Teacher — De Souza, call him what you will, appears firmly in the saddle. The Reds are finished, nobody wants them back; but other groupings are jostling.'

'You're talking fundamentalists?'

'I am,' Burton agreed. 'They want a new constitution and the introduction of Sharia law, which De Souza is resisting, he's Catholic so you wouldn't expect much else. I believe he's also a democrat at heart, though that will take time.'

'Difficult to introduce something you've never had.'

'Amen to that! There's another complication.'

'As if one wasn't enough. What's that?'

'There's another grouping, an influential and militant one, that wants Taranga incorporated into Indonesia. There's support for that in Jakarta.'

'Even after what happened with East Timor?'

'Even after that!'

'I presume we're talking oil?'

'You're ahead of me,' Burton said ironically. 'Yes, we are.'

Kelsey sat back and considered. Taranga was an independent island state in the Timor Sea, originally colonised by Portugal, who abandoned it in the early 1800's, deeming it uneconomic. The Dutch later colonised and exploited it more skilfully, with oil discovered offshore before World War II. The Japanese then invaded, after liberation Taranga obtained independence from the Dutch.

A democratic constitution was imposed by the Allied powers but this was negated by Maoists who won the first democratic election and made sure there weren't any more. The resultant Maoist Communist Government was in power for over thirty years.

After years of unrest a group of army officers led by a colonel named Juan De Souza seized control in a coup d'état.

Despite civilian trappings the military were never far from the seat of government, but lip service was paid to democracy and there were reforms. Some new Ministers had no military connections and the country appeared to be moving slowly away from rule by gun and bayonet. Elections were hardly on Westminster or Canberra lines; cynics hinted the Taranganese

Government preferred to have an inkling of an election result before calling one. Yet the process of government appeared to be moving, albeit slowly, in a democratic direction, although some ministers ran their portfolios like personal fiefdoms.

An extreme Muslim faction rioted occasionally because they wanted government according to Sharia law, while Christian factions demanded seat quotas in the predominantly Muslim Cabinet. Marxists were still prevalent, but had little influence after the incompetent Maoist government was sent packing and the subsequent Soviet Union collapse.

The oil field was located on the south east of the island, the far side from Indonesia, attempts by Jakarta to claim sovereignty over it had been brusquely rejected. Since the military coup, Taranga had resisted offers by Indonesia and China to develop the oilfield, they preferred to negotiate with Australia, which had no territorial ambitions.

'How does this affect my area?' Kelsey asked.

'ASIS have detected underground groups in Taranga with contacts leading back to Sydney and Melbourne. They believe people enter Australia on tourist visas from Indonesia who then move onto Taranga. Taranga conducts close checks on anyone from Indonesia for obvious reasons, but are less cognisant of trouble makers entering from here, although we've warned them.'

'Have we any idea who's passing through Australia to reach Taranga?'

'ASIS suspect dissidents and hired mercenaries have already reached here and established themselves.'

'How long have they known that?'

'I suggest you liaise with Colin Minton at ASIS, he will be able to fill you in.'

'It seems to me ASIS were trying to handle it on their own!'

'Cool it,' snapped Burton. 'I've already covered that point with ASIS and the last thing we want is inter-departmental bickering. Our object now is to locate these bastards. We know they're undercover here and it's up to us to find them. They could have various half way houses anywhere in town or country areas. I want no inter-departmental squabbles hindering the process — got that?'

CHAPTER 2

The whole affair, as far as Douglas Van Ekeren was concerned, began with a summons from Bill Flowers, Melbourne manager for Harwood, Larbalestier & Luck, a firm of Lloyds insurance brokers. Looking back, that interview seemed innocuous, yet led to the worst few weeks of his life.

Douglas Van Ekeren, aged 28, had been born in New South Wales. His father, Willem, was born in Queensland, and Van Ekeren's grandfather, Henricus, had been born in Eindhoven in Holland before immigrating to the former Dutch East Indies and then Australia. Henricus lived in Sydney and still talked of his family's former large plantation in what is now Indonesia. Henricus spoke Dutch fluently, his first language, and Portuguese. His son had been christened Willem, but by the time Douglas Van Ekeren and his brothers arrived the family had become Australian by birth and outlook so the offspring were named in succession Douglas, Geoffrey, Norman and Neville, although their second names retained Dutch connotations.

Van Ekeren and his brothers all spoke fluent Dutch and were often called on by their employers to communicate with clients of Dutch or Portuguese extraction. When selling Life Insurance years before to Dutch immigrants from The Netherlands and the former East Indies this linguistic ability had been invaluable.

Flowers ran his hand through his spiky grey hair and eyed Van Ekeren levelly.

'We've been asked to investigate a recent warehouse break-in in Taranga. Because of the high value of the goods taken, and suspicious circumstances, our Taranga representative insists the investigation be done from here, which means you.'

'Why me?'

'You've been there before; you speak Dutch and some Portuguese.'

Van Ekeren considered, an overseas trip wouldn't come amiss but he could think of better places to go.

'How long will it take?' he asked, a tactical error as it indicated tacit agreement.

'About a week. Ten days at the outside.'

'Hmm!'

'In part it's routine, we usually send someone senior there this time of year to sniff around and discuss company policy. But there is sensitivity about overseas multi-nationals in Taranga right now. We had to register and incorporate that broking company in Taranga and channel business through that instead of transacting direct from here.'

'Yes, we appointed local directors and had to have a Taranganese government official on the board.'

'I'm one of the directors,' said Flowers. 'The others are Willemsen — he's bloody useless but has useful contacts and Heeremans, who knows the difference between a good risk and a bad one. We recently appointed this fellow Roberto Lopez as General Manager.'

Van Ekeren nodded. He knew Heeremans slightly but not Willemsen nor Lopez. The pause extended, he knew Bill Flowers' tactic of maintaining a silence which the other party had to break. Despite his determination to remain silent, he succumbed.

'You mentioned a warehouse claim. What's the problem?'

'We insure Taranganese Industries, the industrial combine. Their Government has a majority shareholding. Insurance coverage is through the Australian market and some is held by Lloyds. The government wants the bulk of the risk covered through their local government-controlled insurer in Taranga City.'

'Which is financially suspect,' Van Ekeren interjected. 'We checked their balance sheet last week. Their underwriting practice is dicey. Their reserve for unexpired risk is woefully inadequate. They reduced it and appropriated the cash.'

'Raided would be a closer description,' commented Flowers. 'Aside from that, there's this break-in at the Taranganese Customs warehouse. We've had a request from Lopez, at HLL Insurance Brokers in Taranga City, for somebody from here to investigate it.'

'Can't they do it?' protested Van Ekeren.

'It exceeds their limit, but only just. Any claims over $80,000 Australian must be handled from here according to the terms of reference and the claim is approximately $AUS90,000. We instructed him to investigate but Lopez refused and insisted we send someone.'

'Tell him to get stuffed and get on with it.'

'I've done that, not the words you used, but he refuses and insists.'

Van Ekeren grimaced. Lopez was insisting on applying rules and regulations the firm itself had drawn up.

'It looks as if I'm stuck with it,' he said resignedly. 'The trip is just to investigate this warehouse break-in is it?'

'Not entirely!' Flowers shook his head. 'We're not keen on the Taranganese national insurer being included, even to a minor degree, on the Taranganese Industries schedule of insurers. We want that message rammed home.'

Van Ekeren nodded. Large risks were never covered by a single insurer, the leading office would offer parts of it to other insurers to avoid having too many eggs in one basket. Insurance brokers often negotiated this apportionment or schedule, but no insurance brokers worth their salt would ever place their clients' business, or part of a schedule, through suspect insurers likely to go bankrupt. In that event Harwoods could be sued for professional negligence.

'We informed the Taranganese Government, and Taranganese Industries, if they insist on including their national insurers on the schedule we'll pull out. After a long argument, everything was placed through the Australian market, who nearly buggered things up by increasing rates in view of claims experience.'

'How did Taranganese Industries take that?'

'Badly, usual inspired arguments about wicked foreign capitalistic imperialists grinding the faces of the poor, but the current insurers have said take it or leave it. We need someone with experience to help Lopez resist government pressure to place part of the Taranganese Industries insurance schedule with their nationalised insurer. He's handed us a pretext to visit Taranga with this burglary claim.'

'All right,' Van Ekeren said grudgingly. 'Guess I'm the fall guy!'

'It rests on you, Doug,' Flowers replied.

If he had to go overseas, a trip to Taranga was not unattractive, situated in the Timor Sea, between Timor and Melville Island off northern Australian and in the same time zone. It sounded like a short trip which suited him.

'Taranganese Industries recently had a fire in one of their processing plants,' Flowers riffled through a file. 'It was placed with a local assessing firm who did a reasonable job, but despite the more enlightened regime, government interference is still rife. If assessors do the job impartially, they fear they'll offend some desk bound bureaucrat and won't be on the approved list the following year.'

'Did they send a report?'

'It's here,' Flowers tossed it over. 'According to their surveyor everything in there was imported equipment of the latest state of the art. More than can be said for their taxi cabs!'

They both examined the file.

'Well, that's the background. Maybe Lopez is emphasising he's keeping his hands clean. Anyway, that's for you to decide. You'll be leaving in a few days.'

CHAPTER 3

Valerie Andrews leant out of bed and ran her finger nails over the floor.

'What are you looking for?'

'My "T" shirt,' she said coldly. 'I have to visit the bathroom and don't want to freeze to death.'

'It's over there,' Van Ekeren pointed in the direction of the window.

'How did it get over there?'

'I threw it there.'

'Then perhaps you'd be good enough to fetch it.'

'What! Like this, I'll freeze to death.'

Valerie lay back and sighed.

'We seem to have reached an impasse,' she said. 'What if I cook bacon and eggs for breakfast, if you fetch it and turn the heating on at the same time.'

He considered the point, and nodded.

'It's a deal.'

Valerie Andrews and Van Ekeren had been co-habiting for 8 months; they met while working at Carpenter Locke, an insurance broking firm. Van Ekeren had left and joined Harwood Larbalestier & Luck about 6 months previously for the usual reason...more money!

Further, Van Ekeren's estranged wife was known to and friendly with some of the hierarchy and female staff of Carpenter Locke so liaison with Valerie could have caused problems, despite the marital separation occurring long before Valerie's arrival on the scene.

After moving to Harwoods those problems evaporated as nobody there knew either Catherine, his first wife, or Valerie. Van Ekeren had his own flat in South Yarra, but his divorce was taking time and he didn't want anything to prejudice it. As far as he knew Catherine was unaware of Valerie's existence.

At breakfast they discussed Van Ekeren's coming trip to Taranga. Valerie wasn't keen on it but was mollified that Taranga was only a few hours by air.

'When do you go?'

'Day after tomorrow,' he replied. 'It seems straightforward, a dicey fire claim to be checked, and a warehouse burglary that exceeds the limit of the local incumbent.'

'Fairly routine then?'

'Looks like it.'

The irony of that casual statement would come back in later days to haunt him.

Val left the apartment first.

'What are you doing for lunch?' she asked as she left.

'The hotel next door to the office,' he said. 'I'll be with Bill Flowers but he won't mind if you butt in.'

*

The first sensation on disembarking at Taranga City Airport

was the heat. It slammed into the tarmac, bounced up and hit new arrivals between the eyes. Most passengers were Australian and not overdressed, but had to walk from the aircraft to the airport buildings and were perspiring freely when they reached it.

Van Ekeren had previously visited Taranga and remembered the drill. The Customs officials were not overpaid and not averse to receiving voluntary donations, while supervision from above was lax. He sandwiched a $20 bill within his passport but not too obviously, it was just peeping out from the back cover. He was eyed keenly as the Customs man casually drew a chalk mark on the case. His passport was returned minus the bill, the sleight of hand very impressive. The following passenger didn't profit from Van Ekeren's example and was given a rough ride. He had to open all his cases.

Van Ekeren passed through but waited for Westerman, the other passenger. They had been in neighbouring seats on the aircraft and in animated conversation since leaving Sydney, it would have been churlish to abandon him.

'Bastards!' Westerman was furious as he emerged.

'Tipping is endemic here,' Van Ekeren said. 'Sorry, I should have warned you. It's surprising what $20.00 can do. You haven't been here before?'

'No! And I don't want to come again,' Westerman sniffed although his good humour re-asserted itself while they hailed a taxi. As they drove off, he began to chuckle. 'I thought they were going to make me take my jocks off.'

'If you'd been a woman they probably would.'

'Where are you staying?'

'The Republic Hotel'

'So am I,' Westerman looked pleased. 'There's a coincidence.'

'Not if your firm booked you in,' Van Ekeren commented.

'Every hotel in town with one star has rotten plumbing, two stars have an eccentric chef and any with three stars have contracts with the local brothel.'

'The Republic is three stars then is it? Jolly good!'

'No,' Van Ekeren smiled. 'Five stars! It's just one of four in town.'

'Pity, I liked the sound of the three-star,' said Westerman.

Westerman was a civil engineer. His firm was erecting a bridge over a busy intersection and a railway track to relieve traffic congestion in the city centre. During the flight Westerman said in his view it would relieve the congestion for about a week and then move the traffic jam two city blocks further west, making it even more difficult to sort out the next traffic problem.

'I pointed this out to them,' he said during their conversation on the aircraft. 'But the buggers wouldn't listen because the plan was sanctioned by their Minister of Works.'

'It could have benefits for you,' Van Ekeren had commented. 'You may have to build another bridge.'

'There's a thought,' Westerman had waved both hands in the air. 'Then another and another!'

'There you are, you see,' Van Ekeren clapped him on the shoulder. 'Your future employment is assured!'

On arrival at the Republic Hotel they were greeted by a doorman who graciously opened the door for them and assumed it was his right to be tipped by the two of them separately, a point of view they didn't share. Van Ekeren was the fall guy and slipped him a tip, the doorman looked grateful and yet slightly disapproving. He was put out when Westerman walked past him without a second glance, but another taxi drew up whose occupant sported a white Stetson hat and he hastily resumed his position.

They tramped to the lift with their cases, but the porter staff were busy elsewhere. Van Ekeren wasn't unduly worried, he usually travelled light on these occasions but Westerman had two heavy cases plus his document case. He gave Westerman a hand, but they were both perspiring freely when the lift reluctantly wheezed to a halt and they clambered in.

'What are you?'

'Fifty-seven.'

'Fifty-two,' Westerman checked his key. 'I'll see you later.'

They left the lift and walked in opposite directions to their rooms. Remembering what he had said about the one-star hotel standard of plumbing, Van Ekeren hoped the five-star Republic hotel would pass muster as right now a shower was a necessity.

As Van Ekeren entered, there was a note on the floor, obviously pushed under the door. It was addressed to 'Mr Van Elderen'. His surname of Van Eckeren was generally misspelt, mispronounced or mangled in Australia so he could hardly blame a Taranganese for getting it wrong. He opened it.

'Greetings Brother,

The final planning Conference agreeing our rightful demands and plan of action will be held within the week, we shall be in touch when we have arranged the place and time.

We shall be in touch with you.'

JL

He turned it over but there was nothing on the back. It seemed odd, but he knew the penchant of the average Taranganese for drama, they loved expansive gestures. The conference in question was presumably about the burglary claim; his main raison d'être. As for 'Greetings Brother', it made him feel like a Trades Union delegate. He assumed it was from Mr Lopez, although he was uncertain of the man's first name. He wasn't sure what was meant by 'demands', presumably to do with the claims negotiations.

He felt refreshed after showering, although he was caught under an icy downpour several times when a hot tap on another floor was turned on, and nearly scalded when someone flushed a toilet. The toilet also bubbled menacingly occasionally which indicated fellow guests were queuing up somewhere on the sixth floor. He wondered what the plumbing was like in one-star hotels.

Later he and Westerman went for a stroll, it was almost impossible to hold a conversation against the incessant honking of motor horns. The average Taranganese motorist drove under the impression he and his vehicle had a divine right of way at a constant speed, constantly thumbed his horn and shouted abuse at anyone, motorist, pedestrian or street vendor, who got in his way.

They saw many near misses during their stroll, one resulted in a shouting match that nearly came to blows but the combatants hastily resumed their place in the traffic flow. Whether compulsory Third-Party insurance applied in Taranga Van Ekeren wasn't sure, but a Motor Assessor's task looked simple, merely assume the loser of the fist fight was liable.

'Reminds you of Melbourne, doesn't it?' Westerman grunted which caused them both some amusement.

The haggling in the stalls and shops was much the same, Westerman was locked onto by two aggressive stall holders when he casually picked up a shirt from a stall to examine it. Van Ekeren hastily steered him away.

'Don't ever pick up anything off a stall like that,' Van Ekeren said. 'You of all people should know better, you've been to Hong Kong and Singapore. These buggers won't let you go until you buy it, they could accuse you of shop-lifting!'

'Shop-lifting!' Westerman exploded.

'It happened to a friend of mine, Clive Passey, only last year. All he did was pick up a shirt and look at it. They tried that on him, charges were dropped eventually but it was a nasty business.'

Westerman paused by another shop window but hastily moved on as scurrying footsteps headed in their direction from within. They felt like flies on the edge of a spiders' web.

They drifted through the rancid smelling market, the smell put them both off buying anything remotely edible. The stalls area was crowded with women haggling with stall-holders, hands on hips or arms waved skywards, until terms were agreed.

'Watch for pickpockets' Van Ekeren cautioned as they headed for a crowd around a large stall. 'Keep your hand on your wallet.'

Westerman muttered but did so and Van Ekeren kept his hand in his own pocket wrapped around his banknotes. They were jostled once or twice, but no pickpockets were in evidence, if they were they failed to make an impact.

*

Van Ekeren slept soundly that night and was woken in the morning by the phone.

'Hallo!' he answered sleepily.

'Mr Van Ekeren?'

'Speaking'

'My name is Lopez...did you sleep well?'

Lopez? Lopez? It was a few seconds before it registered. Lopez was general manager of HLL Insurance Brokers (Taranga) Inc., the man he had come to see. He recalled Bill Flowers' run down on Lopez.

'Nice chap, if you don't cross him, a little nationalistic but no chauvinist,' was Flowers' brief summation, just before Van

Ekeren departed. 'He's a bloody cold fish, very intelligent, and a humourless bastard. But don't underestimate him.'

'Mr Van Ekeren!'

Van Ekeren realised Lopez had been patiently waiting whilst he was replaying his conversation with Flowers

'Good...Good morning,' he replied. 'How are you, Mr Lopez?'

Apparently, Lopez was well, Van Ekeren replied in like manner. They covered the weather, and the trip from Melbourne. Having disposed of the niceties Lopez came to the point.

'I would like to see you this morning, Mr Van Ekeren,' Lopez' voice sank to a purr. 'You will be available?'

'Why yes. Just give me time to have breakfast and I'll be with you.'

'No need to hurry,' Lopez radiated benevolence. 'Make it 10 o'clock.'

'Very well,' and they uttered their farewells. After some thought he decided to risk the shower again.

*

The HLL Insurance Brokers were situated in a large office block in the middle of Taranga City, near the hotel so no need to risk life and limb in a taxi, but there were considerable perils in crossing the street. The routine appeared to be for any group of pedestrians to gather in a tight knot at any likely crossing point and brave the bitumen when they deemed numbers were sufficient. It was similar to scenes in American Grid Iron football, the teams conferred as to the plan of action before making the move. In the pedestrian group, a decision maker emerged; the group would step into the carriageway assuming numbers guaranteed safety. It usually did, there was a cacophony of horns as they bulldozed their way across, drivers shouted abuse which the pedestrians returned with spirit and they successfully attained the safety of the other side, miraculously with no injuries.

Objective being achieved, what had been a small disciplined army then disintegrated and evaporated into thin air. There were smiles as they separated, for a period they had been comrades in arms, their mission now accomplished.

Van Ekeren headed for the HLL offices on the seventh floor. A notice on the door said 'Please Enter' in Dutch, English and Taranganese.

A dusky, dark-haired receptionist was sitting at right angles to the door, she was facing him as he entered. She gave him a spontaneous smile which seemed to fill the room with sunlight and caused tremors to go down his back, through and into the soles of his feet. She was one of those people who, when she smiled, clearly meant it.

'Good Morning,' she said in accented English, having clearly established his nationality in her mind.

'Good morning!' it was indeed.

'Can I help you?'

'Yes!' he replied brightly and hoped she couldn't read his thoughts. She fired another smile at him and waved him to a chair. 'I've come to see Mr Lopez'

'You're Mr Van Ekeren?'

'Yes.'

'I'll tell him you're here,' she said. 'Would you like some coffee?'

'Yes, thank you.'

'How do you like it?'

He asked for milk and no sugar. She rang Lopez and told him Van Ekeren was waiting, then went to a coffee machine in the corner. The coffee was good; it was the best he had tasted for a long time. He was glad Lopez kept him waiting for those few minutes, it enabled him to drain the cup and be offered another.

Lopez finally indicated he was ready, she showed Van Ekeren into his sanctum.

CHAPTER 4

Lopez relinquished the document he had been reading; it looked like a Lloyds Marine policy form, and held out his hand.

'Mr Van Ekeren?' he said. 'Welcome.'

'Thank you, Mr Lopez,' Van Ekeren was guarded as he sat down.

They regarded each other for a few seconds. Lopez could only be described as dapper, he had a hawkish face, was very slim in body, with slim hands and long tapering fingers, what Van Ekeren's mother would have described as pianist's fingers. He was average height, about 5'8' (or 173 centimetres), had dark hair parted on one side and swept back in a large quiff, an olive skin and tight thin lips. His eyes were blue, and piercing.

Yet Van Ekeren assessed that although Lopez was of slight build, he was not an insignificant man. There was a look in his eye of cold steel and he had the appearance of a man who could give a good account of himself verbally if it came to the crunch.

'Your journey was pleasant?'

They completed a repetition of the earlier phone pleasantries, Van Ekeren added his journey to the office and the road crossing episode as a postscript. Lopez permitted himself a smile at the description of the pedestrian phalanx.

'An elementary lesson in self-defence, it evolved from necessity,' he observed. 'There is a bill in our Parliament to introduce pedestrian crossings.'

'A wise move,' Van Ekeren said with feeling.

'In the long run ...yes,' Lopez smiled again. 'But I anticipate difficulties in the short term. Motorists will no doubt ignore them, you have observed they tend to become very macho behind the wheel with scant regard for anyone else. I don't doubt when heavy fines have been imposed and some licences suspended, they will have some effect. Pedestrians will initially consider them as bridges, inviolate rights of way across the road. In early days I fear they will be sadly disillusioned.'

The next hour was spent discussing various aspects of the Taranganese insurance market, and the Government's desire for Harwoods to direct more insurance lines to the Taranganese National Insurance Corporation. They touched briefly on the pending claims and Van Ekeren requested confirmation of data relating to the fire claim. There was also mention of the goods stolen from the bonded warehouse.

Van Ekeren asked Lopez why he had insisted on Australia investigating this particular claim when the fire claim, which had been for a larger figure, had been handled locally. Lopez brought himself under control with an effort. It appeared there was more to the claim than met the eye.

'The fire claim was straightforward, the burglary claim was not,' he replied. 'I have a problem. I am one of the part owners of the warehouse building. Consequently, I preferred it be handled by a disinterested party.'

'Were you responsible for selecting it for the storage of the stolen goods?'

'Yes and no,' his eyes wandered to the ceiling and he didn't appear at ease. 'The eventual owners of particular items of incoming stock insisted we stored the complete transaction when it arrived from Jakarta.'

'Is that usual?'

'No, it isn't,' he still looked uneasy. 'It was requested by addressees at this end so we acquiesced. I didn't like it and with the subsequent result you can appreciate why.'

'Why did they insist you stored them, even if temporarily?'

Lopez forbore to answer; he merely shrugged and spread out his hands. Van Ekeren wondered if there was something going on in the background here, someone profiting from the value of the goods and the insurance moneys with a phoney burglary, an occurrence not unknown in Australia. Yet, if that was the case, why would Lopez insist Harwoods handle the claims assessment? If he was involved in an insurance scam he would be only too anxious to handle the claim himself.

Lopez changed the subject.

'You are aware there is considerable pressure to transfer all Taranganese Industries business insurances to the national insurance office?'

'I had heard.'

This would be coming up again and again. Van Ekeren wasn't altogether unsympathetic. Recently there had been criticism within Australia about multi-national companies having too much of a foothold in Australian industry and controlling too much of the national economy. Foreign based insurance companies had come under fire.

'Parsimony on behalf of Australian insurers will make it more difficult to resist pressure to place the business locally. I am anxious to retain the status quo.'

'Of course,' Van Ekeren replied. 'I can only adjust the claim as I see fit. But if the national insurer is in the habit of paying all claims and accepts all articles as new and/or lost or stolen without investigation, I fear for their financial stability. They have had a history of financial instability; practices such as these could have been the cause.'

Perhaps he had gone too far on such a short acquaintance, but he knew from experience you got nowhere by being apologetic and ingratiating.

Lopez' eyes became ice cold. He opened his mouth, then closed it. He must have had a riposte ready but it died unsaid.

'What do you intend to do?'

The question was superfluous. Terms of reference had been hammered out before Van Ekeren left Melbourne. He momentarily wondered if Lopez was taking a cut on claims settlements, then dismissed it. He knew Lopez was on an excellent salary and expense account, why should he bother? It also came to mind he could have waxed more indignantly if he felt strongly about it, but he seemed to be making a tactical withdrawal.

'I'll pay a visit to the warehouse in question and examine the police report,' Van Ekeren replied. 'Then arrange for a reputable firm of loss adjusters to investigate.'

'You want to see the Police Report?'

'Yes, that is normal procedure is it not?'

'Well...yes...but this is not Australia, things are not quite the same here in Taranga.'

'You mean the Police will not allow a foreigner to examine their report?'

'There could be difficulties. We have two levels of police here, the local police and the National Police who come under the Ministry of Security.'

'You mean there is red tape? I don't follow.'

'It was politic to...well...they didn't want any adverse publicity.'

'Adverse publicity?'

'Matters here are pursued somewhat differently,' said Lopez. 'Some of the stolen equipment had government connotations, they are not anxious for its true nature to be divulged.'

Van Ekeren was way ahead of him by this time. The government or somebody else had been importing something they didn't want anyone else to know about.

'You are telling me the National or Security Police showed no interest?'

'That is so.'

'I don't quite follow,' he did but decided to let Lopez expand on it.

'We informed the central police complex in Taranga City, as this was a warehouse dealing with imported dutiable goods, we assumed it would come under the auspices of the National Police, presumably the equivalent of your Federal Police. They...did not...wish to know.'

Van Ekeren was about to ask why not, then deemed it pointless, no doubt there would be polite platitudes or evasions, perhaps Lopez himself had no answer to it. Yet he was puzzled, why should the police show no interest at a break-in at a warehouse containing dutiable imported goods? That didn't make sense. Could Lopez be a party to something vaguely suspect? But despite his initial dislike and wariness of the man, there was something about him that indicated honesty and professionalism.

Van Ekeren also needed Lopez' co-operation while he was here, otherwise he could spend all his time in the hotel room. He would have to play it by ear and then hit them hard with a scathing report after returning to Melbourne. But he was still curious.

'Why should they say that?'

'I don't know,' replied Lopez. 'I discussed it with Corriea, the warehouse manager and he then reported it to the local police district. By contrast they were very prompt, they attended within half an hour.'

'The local police arrived within half an hour but your National Police displayed a complete lack of interest?'

'That is so.'

'They were busy with other matters?' Van Ekeren asked cynically. Lopez shrugged and Van Ekeren began to feel uneasy, he felt something was going on he knew nothing about. For the present he decided to play along with it.

'Quite possibly so, there have been problems in outlying areas and perhaps they had to devote their time and manpower elsewhere.'

That had an element of truth. There had been reports in the local Taranga City English language newspaper and in the Melbourne papers before he left. Insurrectionary groups were causing trouble. There were religious factions such as Islamic Fundamentalists and Buddhist minorities, together with Maoists plus the power group demanding integration with Indonesia, the last named heavily interlaced with elements of Islamists and Maoists. There had been isolated attacks on outlying police stations and military installations, a close inshore oil rig had been hit by rifle fire, while there had been cases of prominent citizens being kidnapped and held to ransom.

'Nevertheless, you'll have to examine and survey the

burglary location,' Lopez' change of direction startled Van Ekeren. He had been expecting a battle royal before he could inspect the warehouse.

'Yes, that's the main reason I'm here,' he replied. 'Without a survey report they won't adjust the claim in Melbourne, if I don't do it somebody else will.'

That last point was insurance for Harwoods and Van Ekeren himself, pointing out if he was prejudiced in any way or fobbed off, somebody else would be sent, maybe two.

'Yes, I see that,' said Lopez.

'If you could make the necessary arrangements I can go to the warehouse in the next day or so.' Van Ekeren said.

'I see,' said Lopez. 'When will you wish to go?'

'Whenever is convenient,' Van Ekeren replied airily. He felt some empathy for Lopez, he was being squeezed like a nut between other interests in Taranga and Harwoods in Melbourne. It seemed there was some government interference. If corruption was endemic in Taranga, he could hardly be expected to be a paragon of virtue or fight a one-man campaign against it.

'Very well, I'll arrange it,' Lopez picked up the phone and spoke into it, or more accurately he rapped orders into it. There was a knock at the door and a man entered.

'Toro, Mr Van Ekeren has to see the warehouse building where the burglary took place, can you arrange it?'

'Oh yes sir,' Toro sounded obsequious and Van Ekeren took an instant dislike to him. He was running to plumpness, with a receding hair line but with a tuft of hair at the front of his head which was long and brushed back. He was smartly dressed but had an air of servility about him.

'See to it as quickly as possible, either today or tomorrow.'

'It will be done, sir,' he gave a half bow, Van Ekeren half

expected him to tack the word 'Excellency' onto the end of the sentence as he evaporated out of the room. He was the antithesis of the young secretary. Quite apart from her physical attractions, she had personality, made you feel at home, possessed a smile that made a man feel ten feet tall, made damned good coffee and looked physically fit. Toro did not!

'What exactly did occur at the warehouse?'

'The warehouse took a large delivery of electric motors on behalf of a mining company operating at the north end of the island. Also, Taranganese Industries are replacing their computer systems and ordered a large quantity of computer hardware from California sent via Jakarta which arrived about a week ago.'

Van Ekeren perused the claim sheets.

'And all these items were stolen.'

'According to TI... yes,' Van Ekeren looked up as Lopez spoke. There had been a slight emphasis on the word 'according' which caused the upward glance but his face was impassive.

'So, there was forced entry at the rear of the premises, the goods were removed through the hole.'

'We are led to believe that is what occurred.'

'Has any assessment been carried out by local loss adjusters?'

Lopez shook his head.

'No, I deemed it best if this particular assessment be arranged through Australian Head office in Melbourne.'

'Why was that?'

'I had...reasons,' Lopez said, then changed the subject. 'In any case it exceeded the claims limit your office imposed upon us, anything over $AUS 80,000 must be handled from head office in Melbourne. You'll have to see the warehouse manager, Gorge Corriea, you'll find him to be co-operative, most co-operative,' he continued. 'You will need to see Mr

Rijkaard of Taranganese Industries too. He handles details of all their incoming shipments.'

Van Ekeren raised one eyebrow, but again Lopez was impassive.

'Very well, 'Van Ekeren replied and Lopez rose to his feet. Van Ekeren was about to raise the question of the fire claim which exceeded the burglary claim Lopez had handled himself, but decided to let sleeping dogs lie.

'Shall we go to lunch?' Lopez said.

CHAPTER 5

Lopez didn't stint when he entertained, not only was he the perfect host but Van Ekeren found him a stimulating companion. Lopez took him to an exclusive restaurant that rivalled anything at the Paris End of Collins Street in Melbourne, spotless white tablecloths and the seats were of the best leather. The waiters were impeccably dressed in red dinner jackets which instilled a considerable atmosphere.

'You like our Taranganese food?'

'Up to a point,' said Van Ekeren. 'Although I draw the line at snake.'

'A delicacy...for some,' Lopez smiled. 'But...I can only agree with you, if one is not used to the idea it can be disquieting.'

A waiter approached with two plates of soup.

'You've been here before?'

'Here...?' momentarily Van Ekeren thought he meant the restaurant. 'Ah...you mean Taranga? Yes, I have, several years ago when I worked for Watermans, and last year for Harwoods.

I met your Mr Heeremans on both occasions, he was involved with Watermans and now with Harwoods.'

'Ah yes, Heeremans of course...' Lopez sampled the soup. '...you may try this without fear, Mr Van Ekeren,' he smiled '...it is not snake! Let me see, Heeremans...a good man in some ways.'

'But not all?'

'He would have been better off had he not become involved in politics.'

'Politics?'

'He is a member of...how would you say in Australia...the Establishment. He associated himself with Government circles...there is nothing wrong with that of course,' he rolled his eyes as though checking for eavesdroppers, then continued. 'He has every chance of becoming the next Minister of Commerce.'

'How will that affect us...and you?'

'Difficult to say, one can never be sure ...which way the cat will jump...eh?' he waited while the waiter replenished his glass and departed, then continued. 'Too much commitment one way or another can be disastrous if things change ... but, matters are hardly likely to change, are they?'

'Perhaps not,' Van Ekeren had the feeling Lopez was trying to tell him something. He had some idea of Taranganese politics; enough to follow the drift of Lopez' conversation.

In England or Australia, it didn't matter a damn if a director was involved in Parliament, the company would gain prestige whatever side of the House he or she sat, subject to the proviso they didn't take part in political decisions that affected their financial interest. Yet in emerging countries, where democracy was shaky or non-existent, difficulties were prone to arise. Violence could be vented on politicians and anyone associated with them.

They devoted their time to the soup and the wine, both of which were excellent. Lopez finished his and sat back.

'Maybe we are all hypocrites,' he said. 'You'll find many Muslims who only pay lip service to the ban on alcohol, but it can be deadly politically if he is ever accused of it by a rival. Buddhists and Hindus here are divided into so many sects it is almost impossible to walk the streets without offending one or the other. I have been here many years and believe I can now manoeuvre through the average day without offending anyone but it can be difficult at times.'

'You were not born here?'

'No, I was born in Goa,' Lopez inclined his head at the waiter heading in their direction. 'Can we have another bottle?'

'Yes sir, immediately sir.'

'But a half bottle if you please.'

Lopez turned back with an air of resignation and made a gesture, which indicated he was not altogether satisfied with the service.

'You are Portuguese?'

'Mainly yes,' Lopez inclined his head to one side. 'A description that suits on occasions but my ancestry is very mixed, I even have an English great grandfather.'

'Really?' Van Ekeren raised an eyebrow.

'He was a black sheep of the family, a non-commissioned officer in a British regiment in India, one of the Hussars. He was twice broken back to corporal yet won medals for bravery between times. When he left the Army he stayed in India, we know for certain now he had illegitimate children in England and several angry fathers on his track. He moved to Goa, set up in business and married my great grandmother, who was Goanese. He died shortly after the Great War, long before I was born.'

'What was his name?' Van Ekeren was intrigued.

'Croft, he came from the West Country so I'm told.'

'An interesting life. Did the family stay in Goa?'

'Yes. I was born long after the Second World War. My grandfather was Goanese and married late in life — to one of the Croft daughters. My grandfather devoted time to developing and expanding his father's business before starting a family and in time my own father inherited the business. Despite his fondness for the family business, which dealt with imports and exports and some insurance on the side, he realised India wouldn't tolerate the Goa enclave indefinitely. He sold up and got out before any Indian take-over became imminent.'

'He was wise.'

'As it turned out, he was. He obtained a good price; he could have got more but didn't push it as he wanted to get out. The business he offloaded had potential, after we moved here and before India made her move, he often discussed it with me and debated whether he'd made the right decision. Then India moved in and we knew he'd been right.'

'What did he do after that?'

'After selling up in Goa he brought us all here and started a small business, mainly in the drapery line. He did consider Australia, but that was in the days of the White Australia policy. When I went into business, I started a small shop of my own, at his insistence. We had great affection for each other, but he said if we were in business together, we would quarrel and he was probably right. I dealt mainly in copper work for the tourist trade. But for a sequence of events I would probably still be doing that.'

'What events were those?'

'A heavy truck came through the shop frontage and wrecked the building, after colliding with a car which crashed into the shop next door and caught fire... as did the shop together with mine. It also affected the shop next door but one, the fire brigade took an eternity to put the fire out.'

'That was rough.'

'Rougher than you think, I had minor burns and suffered from shock. I was frightened for my life when that truck thrust through the frontage,' Lopez gave a dry chuckle. 'I must have broken the world long jump record into the back room, then the high jump when I vaulted the rear wall.'

'Was it insured?'

'It was. In my brash innocence I wouldn't have bothered, but my father insisted and paid the premium,' Lopez sipped his wine, nodded with satisfaction and inclined his head at the wine waiter. 'I was hasty to condemn the efforts of our wine waiter, you must try this, Mr Van Ekeren; he has done us proud.'

Van Ekeren tried it, Lopez was right.

'It was a blessing in disguise, the accident decided me. What is it you Australians say about an ill wind? I was disenchanted and bored with selling knick-knacks anyway, too much tatting outside the doorway, like they do in Singapore and Hong Kong.'

'You moved into insurance?'

'Yes, I was fascinated, my lawyer showed me the claims papers. Not only did it involve damage to my stock and the landlord's building, but damage to the motor vehicles. My insurers were claiming off the insurers of the truck and the car. The car driver was the proximate cause of the accident so the truck insurers claimed off him and his insurer, but the truck driver was guilty of contributory negligence. There was damage to other shops, to public property...street lamps, pavements and a traffic light...! Truly an intriguing exercise.'

Van Ekeren could relate to that. He had studied papers relating to large industrial claims and appreciated Lopez' fascination.

'I couldn't get into brokers without experience, so I started selling Life assurance, an easy way to enter the insurance profession,' said Lopez. 'I moved into superannuation, then the broking market. My first foray into insurance broking was disastrous, my employer specialised in cheap motor insurance but had a lack of definition.'

'Definition?'

'Defining what belonged to his clients and the insurance companies and what was his,' Lopez said cynically. Van Ekeren could empathise, this type of situation had been known in Australia. He began to appreciate Lopez, humour was well hidden, but when it emerged it was like gold. 'He was abusing the cover note system, regrettably not an unusual occurrence in insurance circles the world over.'

They both smiled ruefully, there had been such cases in Australia and similar rorting had occurred in British insurance circles.

'He was insuring heavy trucks, which commanded high premiums. He would issue a cover note for one month through Insurer 'A'. On expiry, he arranged cover through Insurer 'B' for the next month, then repeated the process with Insurer 'C'. He may then arrange permanent cover, though occasionally he issued cover through Insurer 'D' if he thought he could get away with it. Then when arranging the policy through the last insurer he asked for an initial insurance period of say eight, nine or ten months pro rata, saying his client had a common renewal date for all insurances. Insurance companies, keen for business at the time, usually agreed.'

'So, he pocketed at least a quarter or one third of the premium,' Van Ekeren grimaced. 'What happened with Insurers 'A', 'B' and 'C'?'

'Regrettably cover note systems were poorly administered

and issued cover notes were often lost in the wash! Audits of issued cover notes were notoriously lax and probably still are. He invested the premiums he had collected in either land, interest bearing stocks or shares. Inevitably he made one appropriation too many, companies locked onto what was happening and tightened systems. It wasn't just him, lack of regulation at the time ensured some operators were not quite… well… not quite right, if you understand.'

'I get the picture,' Van Ekeren nodded. 'What happened to him?'

'There were unfortunate experiences with truck drivers, inevitably claims arose whilst one or two of them were between two insurers and they were caught without cover. He went to the wall…and over it…literally! He skipped Taranga and was last seen heading for Malaysia.'

'And you?'

'I saw it coming and left beforehand,' Lopez gave a rueful smile. 'I was naïve; I never suspected anything dishonest was going on. He had visited Indonesia for a week, buying land and shares with premiums he had accumulated and left me in charge. During his absence I received phone calls from Government offices, taxation authorities, lawyers, dissatisfied claimants, the lot! During one call I opened his desk drawer to look for information and found a veritable Pandora's Box, threatening letters from lawyers, police authorities and angry policy holders, writs, final notices…!'

'You got out!"

'Damned quick! I left my resignation on his desk and legged it. I started broking on my own, initially some insurers wouldn't touch me, but I persevered. I merged with another broker, an honest man this time who knew me. We worked together for about seven years, mainly personal insurances and small business. Then Harwood Larbalestier & Luck appeared; a window into larger styles of business. I sold out to my partner, and here I am.'

'Any stigma from your past?'

'Not now. It's water under the bridge, working in a large and reputable combine blurs the image of past history. But I have learnt never to trust people until I know them, never take them at face value, particularly politicians and religious leaders!'

'Do you have any problems here with those?'

'With political leaders...yes. One has to be forever vigilant. Today's friend, in power, can be a liability tomorrow when he isn't...either in power or a friend or both. Religion? In this country, it pays to be reticent, say nothing, never show it on your sleeve or in your home.'

'What...I mean...what religions can be a handicap?'

Lopez caught the confusion and smiled.

'To answer your question, which you tactfully avoided asking, I am a Christian, brought up in the Catholic Faith. Goa being a Portuguese enclave it was, inevitably, the strongest church and many of its population were either born into it or converts.'

He sipped his wine, then glanced at Van Ekeren from the corner of his eye.

'That makes me all right then, does it?'

'What?'

'Being a Christian? A Catholic?'

There was a return of the steely look and a trace of the former hardness in his voice.

'No!' Van Ekeren shook his head and likewise instilled an element of steel in his reply. 'Religion means little to me. I mix with so many different people I just don't see it any more. But

I know in some countries it means a great deal and can cause otherwise good individuals to do very bad things.'

'Very profound, Mr Van Ekeren, you've clearly read the quotation by Stephen Weinberg that good men do good things, evil men do evil things, but it takes religion to make good men do bad things. Regrettably that maxim applies here, which is why I say nothing.'

'Always best in the circumstances, it can cause problems,' said Van Ekeren.

'Tell that to the Jews,' Lopez said cynically.

'History's scapegoat,' agreed Van Ekeren. 'But being a minority group anywhere can be a problem.'

'Like being of Dutch extraction in Australia?'

Van Ekeren shook his head.

'That has no effect at all, except for occasions when I'm asked if my name is one word or two ...and how do I spell it?'

Lopez' face creased and he smiled.

'That is one problem I never have'

His humorous demeanour increased. He was smiling to himself when the waiter arrived with the bill.

CHAPTER 6

Van Ekeren had been back in his hotel room for five minutes when there was a knock at the door. An indignant Westerman was outside.

'I've had my camera nicked,' he snorted angrily. 'So much for their bloody four-star hotels!'

'Five-star,' Van Ekeren corrected him. 'Have you told the manager?'

'At great length. A fat lot of use that was! It was probably him that nicked it.'

'You'd better come in,' Van Ekeren was aware Westerman's voice was raised and guests and staff members may overhear. He indicated his whisky bottle.

'Yes, thanks...I need one,' Westerman accepted the glass, put some water in it and tossed it back.

'Where was it?'

'In my room, I left it on the bed.'

'What did the manager suggest?'

'Nothing! Except to hope for the best as far as I could see.'

'He may or may not do anything, I'm not sure what law they have here regarding liability of hotels for guest's effects. He knows he runs one of the best hotels in the city, also that petty pilfering happens.'

'Well surely that must worry the bastard!'

'He's got competition as he would have in Sydney or Melbourne, but they are like he is, fully booked. Dissatisfied customers can't go elsewhere, unless they want to rough it in your two or three stars. Also remember, it's state owned, they don't have the same outlook as your Sheraton or Hilton. Also, with a full employment policy in Taranga he won't want to offend any staff in case he loses them and would have trouble replacing them.'

'If they go around pilfering, he's better off without them!'

Van Ekeren decided to change the tack.

'It may not have been a member of the staff, people are able to walk into hotels, it can happen in Melbourne and has, we've had several claims like this. Were you insured?'

'I...yes...I think so. There's cover on my household policy in Australia, but I also had travel insurance, the firm cover it for me.'

'Have you got the policy with you?'

'Somewhere, unless they took that as well!'

'Let's have a look. Come on!'

Van Ekeren poured him another whisky before they went to his room, which mollified Westerman a little. He delved into his documents and extracted a travel insurance coupon.

'You have to inform the police, it's a policy condition. Have you done that?'

'Police! What can they do if the hotel doesn't care?'

'Probably nothing but their appearance alone may start

something. If you want the policy to pay out, you must inform the police. It's a condition of all insurances relating to theft or burglary. Whether or not you believe they'll do anything is immaterial. If you don't inform them, you invalidate your claim.'

*

Westerman eventually phoned the police, they asked him to report it to them in person. The next morning, they went to the Central Police Station. Westerman began to entertain second thoughts, but with the insurance man's zeal to prove the reliability of his profession, Van Ekeren insisted. He detested pilfering and petty thieving, anyone's possessions in a hotel should be sacrosanct. Westerman emphasised the camera was just his second string and worth only $120, but Van Ekeren insisted it would cost more than a second-hand estimate to replace. He also pointed out, any police presence at the hotel might bring results if it was an inside job and discourage repetitions.

The police station interior was similar to the average Melbourne or Sydney watch-house, with a counter, stacks of files in racks, and a glass gun case against a far wall behind the counter. Westerman's statement was taken by a young constable reminiscent of his average Victorian counterpart. Westerman had to sign each page. When they emerged half the day was gone, even Van Ekeren began to wonder if it had been entirely worthwhile, but remembered the experience of Bill Flowers nine months before. Flowers' electric razor and dictating machine had been stolen from his hotel room, the visitation of a police sergeant had brought about the sudden reappearance of his property within 24 hours.

As they returned to the hotel Van Ekeren had a sudden prickly feeling, he swung around and noticed among the shoppers and pedestrians, a man staring into a shop window about 20 metres behind them. Now he thought about it, he had a feeling he'd seen this man outside the police station when they left it.

As they walked on the feeling persisted. He caught sight of the suspected follower twice in the angled glass of shop window returns and looked back as they mounted the hotel steps. The man was passing by with other pedestrians, gave them a cursory glance as he did so, dropped his eyes as Van Ekeren looked at him and walked on. He was nondescript, had a leather jacket and a dark hat. He looked a muscular type.

Van Ekeren didn't mention the incident to Westerman, they had a beer at the bar, then returned to their respective rooms. He reached for his papers and began to prepare for his visit to the warehouse the next day.

*

Van Ekeren examined the warehouse, constructed of concrete blocks and situated near the docks.

'A reasonable edifice,' he muttered to himself. He checked with the driver who confirmed it was the right place. Lopez had sent an impressive car, a flower on the floor denoted it was probably used in the wedding business.

The chauffeur indicated he had another job but would be back in about an hour. Van Ekeren wondered if it was a wedding.

He viewed the rear of the building, he wanted to see as much as possible before he entered the front office. The building occupied about 7,000 square feet of floor space, was built of concrete blocks with a corrugated iron roof. The sliding door at the rear was distorted, presumably caused by intending thieves or careless delivery drivers, but still looked solid. There were some broken windows, but behind them were substantial bars. The front roller door was open and men were loading bales from a trolley onto a small tray truck. None of them gave him a second look as he ambled into the building.

He threaded his way through piles of boxes and cartons and headed for the office. The occupant was on the phone and he heard snatches of conversation. Whoever it was, was speaking in Dutch.

'...here now ...he's sorting them out now! He's coming now you say, I thought it was another hour...oh all right, no problem.'

The answer he received appeared to satisfy him and he put down the phone. He shouted something and a man in overalls appeared. They held a short, animated conversation before the man in overalls looked over his companion's shoulder and spotted Van Ekeren standing by the door. He tapped the seated man on the shoulder who looked up.

'Yes ...hallo,' he said. 'Can we help you?'

'Good morning,' Van Ekeren said pleasantly. 'My name is Van Ekeren.'

He moved in and flipped a business card across the desk. 'Mr Lopez will have informed you I was on my way. I seem to have arrived early.'

The office manager dismissed the man in overalls and shook him by the hand.

'Corriea,' he said. 'Gorge Corriea.'

'I understand the break-in was through the wall on the north east corner. Is that correct?'

That had been gleaned from the file Lopez produced the previous day. Corriea nodded and moved to the door.

'The north-east corner is over here,' he said.

Van Ekeren already knew where it was, he had verified the position of the warehouse from a street map and knew which street abutted on the northern side.

'Can you show me where the break-in occurred?' he asked.

'Of course,' Corriea replied. 'Please, this way.'

He was a thin man with a dark brown skin and very vivid eyes. He had slim tapering fingers and tended to place his thumbs together and drum his fingertips against each other. He had switched to English, he spoke it well with an accent that had Latin connotations, maybe his native language was Portuguese, but his pronunciation of Van Ekeren was faultless. It struck Van Ekeren a man who spoke Dutch, English and Portuguese was wasted as a warehouse manager. Corriea strode to the office door and he followed.

Corriea led the way to the north-east corner, they picked their way through piles of goods and various other items stacked on the floor and on shelving. Van Ekeren remembered, from discussions in Melbourne, the maximum sum insured for the warehouse capacity as a whole was estimated at AUS $5,250,000, but the present value of the stored goods would be nowhere near that.

Wooden cases about a metre and a half long were stowed in neat piles against the northern wall, stamped 'Taranga City Sports'. Van Ekeren paused by the crates, he was a keen golfer but Corriea suggested the gear was probably for baseball.

The wall was of concrete blocks, there had certainly been a breach but the hole had been repaired. Van Ekeren turned to Corriea.

'Where were the motors?'

'Motors?'

'Motors!' he explained patiently. 'It was motors that were stolen, was it not?'

'Motors...yes,' Corriea agreed. 'But that wasn't all. They removed a quantity of goods and one computer equipment container, although the motors were the main item. Some tobacco imports were also taken from the bonded area in the north-west corner.'

'What were the motors for?'

'I'm not sure, something to do with mining, I believe they were headed for the northern area of Taranga where there are coal mining operations. Some were for drilling, offshore drilling is also being carried out, but whether they would have been for that I've no idea. Some items were for ventilation of mine workings.'

'I think you're right,' Van Ekeren perused Lopez' file. 'I have a copy of the manifest. It was a burglary, I understand.'

'It was,' agreed Corriea. 'They came through the wall, there's some toilet cubicles on the outside of the building at this point...' he tapped the wall just above the repaired section '...we believe they hid in there during the late afternoon with some equipment, when we all left, they knocked a hole in the wall.'

'Are the toilets in use?' Van Ekeren asked.

'Yes, it's a block of four. They only occupied one cubicle so it didn't cause any problems,' Corriea grinned. 'If they'd occupied all four and anyone was desperate, they'd have had to bottle it.'

'Maybe Taranganese are more polite than Australians, we'd probably have battered the door down,' Van Ekeren commented. 'So, they came through the wall and emerged here. Is there an alarm?'

'They reached the key board over there,' said Corriea. 'We've been intending to have the system updated. It's been in for years.'

'They knew and used the combination?'

'It looks that way,' admitted Corriea. 'They also seemed to know where the dead spots were because they reached the key pad without activating it.'

'An inside job?'

Corriea shook his head.

'Unlikely if we're talking present staff,' he said. 'It's possible former staff could have been involved who knew the code. We've obviously been lax.'

The old story, Van Ekeren thought grimly. It can never happen here; the alarm will be sufficient. But an alarm system is only as good as the people who operate it. If an employee who knew the alarm code left, especially one who departed with a grudge, always change the alarm code. In fact, change it at regular intervals irrespective of whether anyone had left in a huff. However, Australian professional thieves could circumvent many alarm systems and no doubt the same prevailed in Taranga.

'What's happening about the alarm now? You'll be changing the code?'

'We already have,' Corriea answered. 'But next week we're installing a new system, laser beams and infrared ...the lot!'

'What was taken?' Van Ekeren consulted the clip board.

'The bonded store was broken into, tobacco and cigarettes were taken, plus some motors which I mentioned before. A couple of computer equipment crates were also taken.'

'A couple?' Van Ekeren perused his clip board. 'Just a couple?'

'That was all, yes.'

'Where are those that were left?'

'Somebody came and quickly collected them after the event,' said Corriea. 'After I discovered the break-in, I advised management and Mr Lopez what had happened. He said he would advise the insurers and the police.'

'How soon after the event did the police arrive?'

'I'd say about four hours, something like that. Mr Lopez advised the national police station first since it's a Customs warehouse, but they seemed very off-hand so Mr Lopez asked me to contact the local civil police. But the owners of the computer crates arrived first. I wasn't too sure about them moving stuff out before the police arrived, but we had a call from the national security police complex in Taranga City, they said to allow them to remove the crates. After they had gone the local police arrived.'

'So, before the local police arrived, these computer people, presumably on behalf of TI and with the connivance of the national security police authority, removed all their stock?'

'Everything!' Corriea agreed.

'The national police authority sanctioned that?'

'They did. I wasn't too happy about it so I checked with TI who seemed very vague and most surprised their equipment had already arrived. I spoke with the national police authority again, but they said everything was in order. I was put onto someone from the Ministry of Internal Security.'

'The Ministry of...! Good God! What about the remainder of the motors?'

'They've gone,' said Corriea. 'They've been collected by the mining company. They came a few days after the break-in. I have the paperwork in the office.'

'When were those collected?'

'After the police, the local police that is, had done what they had to do. I had no problem with that.'

'Was that the only hole?' Van Ekeren indicated the new concrete blocks in the wall.

'Just the one hole,' said Corriea. 'We had it repaired quickly to prevent another raid. We had it reinforced with steel wiring, and when we have the new alarm system installed, I shall have some of the wiring placed along that wall corresponding with the outside toilet blocks.'

'Very wise,' Van Ekeren nodded approvingly. 'Someone did a good job patching it.'

'The insurance brokers, that is, Mr Lopez, suggested a firm who did an excellent job.'

'When was the hole patched up?'

'Late last week,' said Corriea.

They returned to the office pen, where the overalled foreman sat at a small table checking invoices. Corriea produced the paperwork. After checking, everything appeared in order.

'What are these?' Van Ekeren asked. Photographs were attached to the paperwork.

'The computer items that were stored here, plus others of the stolen motors. I took these shots immediately after the break-in and before the remaining goods were removed. Mr Lopez insisted, he also has copies of these prints.'

Van Ekeren scrutinised the prints. Those crates looked very long to be holding computer equipment. A metre rule had been laid alongside the nearest crate to indicate its length.

'That was Lopez' idea as well, was it?' Van Ekeren indicated the metre rule.

'Yes. Roberto is very meticulous.'

Van Ekeren didn't question that.

'Have you documents for the motors and the rest of the stuff?'

'In the office,' Corriea answered.

'I'll have a look at them.'

The paperwork for the motors appeared in order; they were in the name of Tyler Kaye De Jong Mining Co. There were nine shown on the manifest and on the claim form they were claiming for five of them. Van Ekeren had seen all he wanted

'Who owns the building?' he asked.

'Taranganese Warehousing,' answered Corriea. 'Mr Lopez deals with all the warehousing company's negotiations.'

'Is he a shareholder?'

'I believe he is, but you'll have to ask him that.'

'These seem in order,' he handed the documents back to Corriea. 'But I have to check with Taranganese Industries, who do you deal with there?'

'Mr Rijkaard.'

A truck arrived and the foreman left the office to deal with it. Corriea watched the process for a few seconds, then turned to Van Ekeren.

'You are acquainted with Mr Lopez?' he asked

Van Ekeren nodded.

'He is a good man,' he lowered his voice as the foreman returned to the office. 'He does things right, you understand?'

His eyes met Van Ekeren's as the foreman re-entered. There was a brief conversation, the foreman scribbled his signature on a form and departed. He clambered into the truck which bumped its way out onto the roadway.

'More goods on the way out?' asked Van Ekeren.

'Goods come in and goods go out,' Corriea smiled. 'Just as well those have gone now. A ship docked this morning and we'll be full again tonight. Hello, here's your car'.

The hired limousine drew up outside. The chauffeur entered the building and exchanged a few words in Portuguese with Corriea. Van Ekeren had sufficient knowledge of the language to be able to pick this up.

'Yes, we've finished here,' he said. 'You are just in time I think.'

Van Ekeren turned to Corriea. 'Many thanks for your assistance.'

They shook hands and he departed in style.

*

'Something strange for sure,' Westerman later commented as he sipped a whisky in his room. Van Ekeren had shown him some of the photographs he'd brought back with him of the various crates within the warehouse. 'Those crates holding so called computer equipment, they look far too long. Is your man on the level?'

That had been bugging Van Ekeren. In some ways Lopez had been difficult, but on the other hand didn't present as one who would stoop to dishonesty. He would have little control over what goods came into the warehouse, although as representative of the insurers of the building and/or the contents he would want some idea of what was stored there.

He appeared to be a capable administrator and if any hazardous goods came into the risk location, he would insist on being informed as this could affect the insurance coverage. He also had good taste when it came to ordering wine, was well mannered and competent. As Van Ekeren thought of Lopez' office he found himself wondering if the secretary could type.

CHAPTER 7

The warehouse visit had been satisfactory, yet it did indicate something was offline. For a bonded warehouse, precautions and safeguards appeared lax for storing goods on which duty had not yet been paid. A similar Australian establishment would be well protected and alarmed and the routine would be most rigid. He was also concerned about the computer equipment. On viewing some of the photographs Westerman had commented the crates seemed very lengthy for computer equipment. In addition, Corriea had seemed edgy about some aspects and had stressed Lopez was a good man. Why did he feel that to be necessary?

'He must be,' Van Ekeren shook his head in perplexity. After many years in commerce he was a reasonable judge of character, although one couldn't be right every time. What he couldn't understand was, Lopez appeared to be a good operator, yet was involved with a large burglary claim where something was odd. Why had the National Security Police been involved with the shipment for Taranganese Industries, which were computer items?

The alarm in the storage facility was another aspect, codes should be changed frequently, especially when people left their employ whether in a huff or amicably. This could have been covered up by Lopez, he could have employed a local loss adjuster who could be persuaded to give a glowing account to Melbourne of the warehouse's defences. Yet he hadn't! Further, was it being unreasonable to expect a small, emergent country like Taranga to adhere to best commercial practices prevalent in the Western world?

*

Westerman indicated to the barman they needed refills; it was hard to keep up with him when it came to Scotch. He was four ahead already, as sober as a judge and increasing his lead.

'If he *is* on the level, somebody receiving imported goods via that warehouse is playing games. I'll wager it wasn't computer equipment in those packing cases.'

'I'll be seeing Taranganese Industries tomorrow,' said Van Ekeren. 'I'll see what I can find out.'

*

There was no need to make an appointment with Taranganese Industries, Lopez phoned the following morning at 8 o'clock, he had arranged a meeting with one of the managers, Mr Rijkaard, for 10 o'clock. He had also arranged for a car to deliver Van Ekeren to the door

The arrangements ran strictly to plan, he had breakfast and was stowing papers into his brief case when reception advised the car had arrived. Rain was falling but the car was near the front door.

He was driven to an impressive office building in the city centre and the driver said he would wait in the company car park. Van Ekeren entered the building, asked for Mr Rijkaard and was directed to the sixth floor.

Rijkaard met him at the door of the office and indicated a vacant chair by the window with a good view of the city. He was of mixed race, with a dark complexion but his features were European. He was plainly efficient, his office was reminiscent of that of Lopez, neat, tidy and everything in place. The file on his desk related to the insurance claim.

He ascertained Van Ekeren didn't take sugar with coffee, issued an order for two cups through his secretary, then got down to business.

'I understand we have to discuss the claim for our computer equipment.'

'Yes,' Van Ekeren produced his file. 'I'm not clear on one or two aspects.'

'What are those?'

'Firstly, these crates do not bear any resemblance to containers of computer towers or monitors,' he flipped photographs across the desk. 'Secondly, I was informed by the warehouse management very few of these crates addressed to you were taken in the initial break-in. The others were collected the following morning by people purporting to be from TI, who subsequently turned out to be from the Ministry of Security.'

Rijkaard examined the photographs and pondered.

'What are these?' he asked.

'I thought you could tell me. They are apparently addressed to your company.'

'These containers cannot be ours,' said Rijkaard.

'But this label says they are,' Van Ekeren indicated one of the enlarged photographs, and a clearly legible label in one of them.

'They are certainly addressed to us,' Rijkaard looked puzzled. 'But they couldn't be ours. Our shipment was fully described by the firm who forwarded them from California.'

He handed over documentation, which described the shipment as being 20 crates containing personal computers and monitors with each container's dimensions specified. They certainly didn't correspond with those photographed by Lopez and Corriea.

'These are what your suppliers sent to you?'

'It appears so,' responded Rijkaard. 'These must be what were despatched to the docks for shipment to Taranga. Our shipment arrived in Jakarta from Los Angeles, according to the paperwork. We were later advised there had been a break-in at the Taranga City warehouse and part of our shipment had been stolen. That was the subject of our claim submitted to the insurance brokers and Mr Lopez, and presumably onward to yourselves as the insurers.'

'But according to the warehouse paperwork the shipment that arrived was these containers, with your name on them and the same shipment number.'

Rijkaard checked the photographs again and inclined his head quizzically on one side.

'I've never seen these containers before. What has happened here?' he asked.

'I'd say your shipment was switched for something else en route, that came in under the radar of your customs here. Does your local customs authority closely examine everything that enters Taranga under your name or do they pass anything addressed to TI carte blanche?'

'I believe everything of ours goes straight into the bonded warehouse,' said Rijkaard. 'As long as it's sealed at the other end and the seals are unbroken, they pass it through. Taranganese

Industries is an important part of the Taranganese economy and a vast amount enters under our name. If they persistently held up everything of ours it could have a detrimental effect on the nation economically.'

'Well something fishy has happened here,' Van Ekeren said grimly. 'I'd say your computers are still in Indonesia somewhere, and these items...' he indicated Corriea's photographs '...were substituted somewhere along the line. Someone from the Ministry of Internal Security picked them up, in haste, before the local police investigated the break-in.'

'This is unbelievable,' Rijkaard riffled through his papers. 'This means an entire shipment has vanished into thin air.'

'It also means...' added Van Ekeren '...the claim you submitted to us is null and void. Our cover under this policy was for fire, burglary and various other risks for your goods stored within the warehouse. These computers of yours clearly never reached it.'

'I can see that,' Rijkaard drummed his fingers on the desk. 'We have a problem.'

'Not necessarily,' Van Ekeren said. 'You have another course of action. These goods, the computers and monitors would, or should have been, covered under a 'Goods in Transit' or a marine insurance contract underwritten in Los Angeles where the computers originated. You, or your suppliers, have to recover from the marine insurers of your suppliers. If your suppliers can prove the goods left the ship and went into the warehouse in Jakarta, or were replaced or disappeared somewhere between there and the docks, then cover should still apply. I assume the original marine insurance coverage would be in force until it reached its destination, which for the marine insurers would or should be the warehouse in Taranga City.'

'But what on earth was in those crates?'

'That is what we must try and find out,' Van Ekeren said grimly.

*

The subsequent interview with Lopez was not illuminating.

'I can offer no explanation for it,' Lopez spread out his hands. 'I was advised there had been a break-in and went to investigate. I also received a copy of the shipping documents, the ones you have there and had no reason to question them.'

'Did Mr Corriea take photographs of the crates before they were removed by whoever it was the next morning?'

'He did, at my instigation, since one or two of them were removed by the perpetrators during the raid. We also took photographs of other items that remained where similar items had been taken. We are nothing if not meticulous Mr Van Ekeren.'

'This changes the whole aspect of the claim.'

'It certainly does,' agreed Lopez. 'I would say the computers earmarked for Taranganese Industries could be excluded from the warehouse burglary, it seems they were never there. As you said, they must fall under the Goods in Transit policy or the Marine Insurance of the American shippers. The remainder of the items intended for other organisations would still be part of a valid claim under the warehouse coverage.'

It was left at that. The journey from Melbourne had been made worthwhile economically since the warehouse claim on the Australian insurers had been reduced by 75%.

*

Van Ekeren was prevailed on by Westerman to go out for a drink that night, after previous sessions he should have known better but agreed before he realised he'd committed a tactical error. To spend a night out with a man who could soak up vast quantities of alcohol without noticeable effect and who assumed you could keep pace with him was a mistake of the first magnitude.

When they returned to the hotel Van Ekeren wasn't too sure of his footing as they climbed the stairs. He had drunk so much he didn't trust the effect of the rise and fall of the lift, especially one subject to the hiccups of the Republican Hotel lift shaft. Westerman had been all for taking the lift, then grumbled all the way upstairs, but Van Ekeren insisted. He was entertaining feelings of irritation with Westerman. True, he was a companion but possessed traits that represented the worst in the English or Australian character. He treated foreigners as brainless idiots and anyone not of Anglo-Saxon extraction was a Wog, Boong or Dago. What was worse, his attitude became obvious to all and sundry when he'd had a few drinks which for anyone accompanying him could be profoundly embarrassing. To him the possible involvement of Lopez in a dicey situation seemed more and more logical as the whisky took hold. The man was Asian, wasn't he? ... with a southern European name to boot! Bloody Wog! No... correction, bloody Dago! This persisted despite Lopez being completely innocent of any wrongdoing.

Van Ekeren disagreed with Westerman's manner, but he did agree that initially Lopez' involvement with any chicanery had looked possible. While not too enamoured of Lopez, he had attained respect for him and now thought any complicity with a shonky claim quite unlikely. A group of unprofessional thieves could have robbed that warehouse, although their knowledge of the burglar alarm code was worrying. Another feature was somebody, not Taranganese Industries, had claimed ownership for most of the crates that bore their name and ostensibly carried computer equipment. Corriea had said somebody removed them the following morning at the behest of the Ministry of Internal Security.

'I'll shee...see you in the mornin'...morning,' Van Ekeren became irritable as his speech slurred in an obvious manner to Westerman, who grinned and nodded.

'Yes, all right,' he strutted off to his room whistling, with no deviation from his path nor uttering a false note. Van Ekeren cursed him soundly and entered his room.

It was in darkness, yet his inebriated senses indicated he wasn't alone. He caught a whiff of cigar smoke. He closed the door and reached for the light switch, but as the feeling of not being alone intensified he changed his mind, reached for the door handle to get out again, then nearly passed out with fright as a hand was laid on his shoulder.

CHAPTER 8

'Christ Almighty!' he twisted to one side with nerves screaming and heart racing. He swung his left hand around defensively and struck someone a severe blow with a backhanded Karate chop which brought forth a curse. He dropped to the carpet and heard a thumping sound accompanied by a grunt of pain. He was trying to crawl to Heavens knew where when the light came on and blinded him.

Two men stood by the door within a few feet of him, one spitting like a cat and holding his knuckles. He must have tried to return Van Ekeren's karate chop and hit the door panels after Van Ekeren hit the floor. Both were presumably indigenous Taranganese. The sore knuckled one, the larger of the two, was also nursing his cheek. He was muttering angrily and seemed to be contemplating another attack, this time with his boots. The other man intervened and assisted Van Ekeren to his feet.

'Our apologies,' he flicked some unobtrusive dust from Van

Ekeren's shoulders and tried to brush him down. 'We didn't mean to alarm you.'

'Bloody hell!' Van Ekeren exclaimed angrily. 'I'd hate to be around when you do!'

The other man permitted himself a faint smile and ushered him to the chair. He graciously poured Van Ekeren some of his own whisky, which he handed to him. Such was his state of shock, he accepted it and poured it the same way as the night's previous intake, then gasped as his stomach revolted and began to burn.

'What the hell are you doing...?' he began but the other man raised his hand, which gave Van Ekeren time to examine him. He was dressed casually, so much so that Van Ekeren wondered how the hotel staff had let him in. He was about 5'10", had a moustache, a baseball cap and a check shirt with jeans, which did look clean. He was also smoking a cigar; the hotel room reeked of it and was making Van Ekeren's head reel. His companion was a surly giant of a man, simian features with a pair of eyes that darted all over and around Van Ekeren. His demeanour was of a snake about to strike. He was built like a Rugby League forward, big, muscular and mean with it. Not the sort of man to trifle with.

'We had to take this unorthodox means of contacting you, Mr Van Elderen,' the smaller man said smoothly in slightly accented English. 'We have a hectic routine these days as you can imagine, but are working to further our claim, our demands.'

'Your claim?'

'Of course,' he twirled his moustache; maybe he fancied himself with the girls. 'We have a right to take and claim what is rightfully ours?'

Van Ekeren pursed his lips. The acquisitive attitude of

policy holders in Taranga appeared to be similar to the average Australian, take the insurance company for as big a ride as you could...insurers had large financial backing, it was everybody's right to milk them for what they could, inflate everything! Was he one of those responsible for the removal of that equipment the morning after the burglary? Or did he represent others who had had their shipment stolen.

'Providing you don't try and take too much,' he said pointedly as he recovered his composure. 'That way you destroy it for everybody.'

'What?'

Van Ekeren repeated it with emphasis which appeared to astonish his companion.

'You have an independent mind, Mr Van Elderen,' he said. 'Do you know who I am?'

'No, can't say I do,' Van Ekeren replied irritably. 'Incidentally my name is Van Ek...!'

'I am Julius Lebak, head of the Taranganese Nationalist Council.'

'Oh!' Van Ekeren instinctively proffered his hand but Lebak jumped like a scalded cat. He eyed the outstretched hand suspiciously before he tentatively reached out and shook it. Really, these Taranganese perpetually had their eye to the dramatic. Surely, if the head of Taranganese Industries Group wished to make contact why the hell didn't he get his secretary to ring and arrange an appointment instead of sneaking into bedrooms at night and creeping around in the dark? 'Who's your friend?'

'My...my...friend?' Lebak seemed astonished such a question should be asked. 'You mean...?' he jerked his head at his companion.

'Who else — he *is* with you isn't he?' Van Ekeren asked

coldly. He had been told by friends he could be cutting when he didn't like anyone. It came to the fore now.

'With me...of course...you are a very strange man, Mr Van Elderen,' he looked perplexed. 'We don't usually ask who people are, or for names, Mr Van Elderen.'

'Then how the blazes do you transact your affairs?' Van Ekeren asked testily, equally perplexed. 'And, if you'll excuse my mentioning it, I can think of a better time and place to transact business than in a hotel room in the middle of the night.'

'Ah...regrettably we have to meet when and where we can,' Lebak gave his moustache another twirl. 'But I didn't intend to discuss...business, it was to meet you to see if you were a man who could be...um... trusted.'

'Really!' this put Van Ekeren on his guard, if he was going to offer a bribe for turning a blind eye to discrepancies or irregularities in that burglary claim he had another thought coming. 'Where exactly do you come into this. Have you heard from Mr Rijkaard?'

'Mr Rijkaard?'

'Didn't he send you?'

'No, I'm not familiar with the name.'

Van Ekeren could only accept that, he was aware in large organisations, like Taranganese Industries, it was quite possible heads of various departments could be unknown to each other, particularly if they worked in different buildings. Van Ekeren had a friend who worked for BHP, he was forever meeting people at company conferences he had never met before who, like him, had been with the company for over 20 years.

'We have a complex enterprise which needs you to play your part, to ensure all goes smoothly so we attain all our aims, everything we are entitled to...and more!'

'What? I don't quite follow.'

'We are engaged on a matter of much delicacy, are we not?' Lebak nodded knowingly and again Van Ekeren had to allow for the Taranganese penchant for drama.

'Delicacy is the word,' Van Ekeren replied, emboldened by liquor and exasperation. 'But I don't quite follow you. What are you asking me to do?'

'What we are going to pay you to do, I wanted to meet you to discuss how we could deal with any problems that arise, to ensure all goes smoothly. We haven't met before, I wanted to ensure you were wholly with us when pursuing our aims and fully conversant with what you have to do for us.'

'You...you...what?' Van Ekeren started back in astonishment. 'What are you expecting? Are you suggesting sharp practice or fraud?'

'Have I not said so for years?'

'I...eh? You what?' This was an answer he hadn't expected. 'I don't follow you.'

'Have I not said this all along...eh Madang?' Lebak said triumphantly to his companion, momentarily forgetting previous reluctance to broadcast names. The giant nodded in agreement as he kept a watchful eye on Van Ekeren. He was still rubbing his cheek and looked as if he was contemplating the joys of exacting retribution...slowly.

Van Ekeren reflected Madang didn't look like executive or managerial material, he was more fitted for the front row of a Rugby scrum. Maybe in Taranganese society captains of industry had to have bodyguards, he had read something about the kidnap danger to executives in the English language newspaper.

'If you're aware of the problems surely you can do something about them,' Van Ekeren said testily. 'I shall submit a report and frankly, so far I haven't been impressed.'

'You ...you haven't been...!' Lebak's double take nearly

cricked his neck. 'You haven't been ...impressed? Why not? What is wrong?'

Lebak clearly wasn't used to being addressed in this fashion, breath hissed out of Madang. Van Ekeren's nose picked up the exhalation and wondered what he'd had for supper.

'A child could see there was something odd about computer equipment containers eight feet long,' Van Ekeren snapped. 'What's more, I'm not happy about the alarm system in that warehouse either. It seemed to me as if it came out of the Ark.'

Lebak was so surprised he sat down heavily in the chair.

'You...you know...about the warehouse storage?' he demanded. 'That is not in your sphere of operations. How did you know about that?'

Now it was Van Ekeren's turn to be surprised, surprised a Taranganese Industries executive didn't know a claims investigation would be carried out, or that Van Ekeren had been to the warehouse to do just that. Surely any business head would know it was the first requirement for any insurer in the event of a large claim.

'Of course, I knew about the warehouse,' Van Ekeren said frigidly, really these Taranganese must think all Australian insurers were stupid and fair game for fraudulent claims. 'I saw the report, checked its location and had a look around.'

Lebak burst into a stream of what sounded like Portuguese verbiage, Van Ekeren didn't catch it all, but had sufficient knowledge of the language to pick up the gist. Lebak's mode of speech was liberally spiced with Portuguese and Dutch expletives, but most swear words were in Dutch and he fired off those first. Madang watched Van Ekeren even more carefully as the tirade progressed, but also looked baffled.

Lebak paused to draw breath, then let loose again. He stood and harangued Madang, who relapsed into sullen silence.

'Who told you?'

'I was advised before I came here. It was on a file somewhere, probably a memo written by someone. We *do* keep a check on things. We like to know exactly what's happening so we can deal with matters as and when they arise.'

'A memo ...? In writing? My God!'

Van Ekeren really couldn't see why he was invoking the Almighty nor what all the fuss was about, surely even in Taranganese business circles one didn't send representatives on overseas trips without a briefing. Or maybe they did, which would account for what was, seemingly, the abysmal performance of the Taranganese Industries Group where nobody seemed to know who was who or who was doing what.

The calls of nature from the skinful he had consumed caught up with Van Ekeren, he stood and walked to the toilet. Madang moved across, stood before the toilet door and barred the way.

'What the hell...!'

Lebak motioned to Madang who opened the toilet door and peered cautiously inside, Van Ekeren exploded.

'Do we have to go to these ridiculous lengths,' he snarled furiously, this was reminiscent of a James Bond scenario. 'I merely want a bloody piss, anyone would think the place was bugged the way you're carrying on. If this is how you conduct your affairs then I'd just as soon deal with someone else, or pull out altogether.'

He slammed the door behind him and delivered slap bang in the middle of the pan, it was probably heard two floors down, reminiscent of Niagara Falls. He washed his hands and stalked back into the main bedroom. Lebak eyed him icily.

'You say you are not going to honour any deal you made with us?'

'Any dealings agreed to have already been set in motion. I am now going to bed,' he snapped irritably. 'If you wish to play cops and robbers all over the hotel that's up to you. I'll do the job I have been asked to do but during civilised hours. If you want to see me during the day, call me and I'll come and see you, but I'm not in the habit of gallivanting around, conducting negotiations and settlements in hotel bedrooms in the middle of the night. Now go and let me rest. I'll see you in the morning.'

His manner was offensive and aggressive, fuelled by fear he was going to throw up and he didn't want to do that before an audience. He just wanted to be rid of these people and stop talking because the very act of making conversation was likely to precipitate the said throwing up. He tore off his jacket and flung it to the end of the bed, then re-entered the bathroom and began cleaning his teeth, they clearly got the message because, when he emerged, they had gone.

He resolved the next time any question of appointments and meetings came up he would make it clear he resented being approached in this manner at this time of night, being obviously sounded out to see if he'd make a false report, or at best an inaccurate one, for a bribe. Further he'd appreciate it if they would pronounce his name correctly.

*

'You will be leaving for home very shortly I take it?' Lopez clasped his hands together.

'Very soon,' Van Ekeren agreed. 'I have some loose ends to tie up.'

'Will you be seeing anyone else from the Taranganese Industries Group?' Lopez paused to sip his coffee, as did Van Ekeren. It was beautiful coffee, maybe that was the secretary's *raison d'être*.

'I've no idea,' he said. 'I've already had contact with Mr

Rijkaard as you know. I also had contact from somebody else but his mode of approach was unorthodox to say the least.'

'Would that have been Malik?' asked Lopez. 'He is something of a maverick.'

'No, it wasn't him, though the name was something like it,' Van Ekeren racked his brains to recall the bedroom invader's name, but it had gone. His whisky sodden state at the time hadn't assisted the memory process. 'He had an assistant with him; his name sounded like...Nabang... something like that.'

'Nabang?' Lopez looked puzzled. 'I don't know the name.'

'It's of no consequence,' said Van Ekeren. 'But there are some aspects of this claim I don't follow.'

'Indeed!' Lopez straightened up.

'Those boxes that were removed...by whoever did remove them...the following morning, seemed to me to be strange shaped boxes to contain electrical motors, computer gear or whatever they really did hold.'

'Yes?' said Lopez.

'I'm not altogether happy about it,' Van Ekeren said. 'It doesn't affect us unduly now, we won't be paying a cent for those.'

'You must be the judge of that.'

'There was clearly something strange,' Van Ekeren persisted. 'What were those motors for, the ones that belonged to the mining company?'

'Something to do with pumping equipment, for the coal industry I think they said,' said Lopez. 'I have not seen them, of course.'

Van Ekeren considered it in silence.

'Mr Corriea said they were something to do with air conditioning, maybe air conditioning equipment for the mines.'

'You could be right,' Lopez took another sip of coffee. 'But if you're not satisfied with anything, that must go into your report, anything untoward must be noted, especially those long flat crates.'

Lopez sat back and he gazed out of the window to the harbour scene in the distance. He appeared to Van Ekeren to look relieved.

'I'll be in touch with you this afternoon,' Van Ekeren rose.

'I'll look forward to it,' said Lopez, also rising. 'You'll provide me with a copy of your report?'

'Yes. I'll have to make use of your secretary ...for the word processing of the report,' he added hastily and perceived a glint of amusement in Lopez' eyes. As his thought processes considered the secretary again, he realised Lopez had asked to have a copy of the report, not the draft before he released it. In effect Lopez was asking to see it after the original could have been despatched, he wasn't contemplating suggestions it be amended, or less politely, doctored!

*

'Bill, there's something funny going on here! This claim doesn't seem right.'

'I know!' Flowers shouted. 'This is a lousy line...can you hear *me*?'

'Yes ...what do you mean? You know?'

'We were told there might be something fishy so we were asked to assess it.'

'Asked...who asked us?'

'Why Lopez of course.'

'Lopez asked us?'

'Not in as many words,' Flowers shouted. 'He drafted his memo very cagily, like all these bloody Orientals. Reading between the lines, he wanted someone to come over and look at the claim, he wanted an outsider, perhaps it was difficult for the man on the spot to be the arbiter.'

Lopez had asked Melbourne to look at the claim! As this realisation struck home, a load lifted from his mind. Dislike the man he may, but the idea he could have been involved in the strange disappearance of those long crates was disturbing. He seemed straight, in more ways than one, his office was well appointed, tastefully furnished and well run.

'I wish you'd told me.'

'Thought I had,' said Flowers. 'Sorry Doug. Look, we'll appoint the necessary loss adjusters, then you can forget it. We'll handle it from here.'

'I've finished now have I?'

'Pardon!' bellowed Flowers.

'Nothing,' Van Ekeren said. 'I'll see you in a week.'

'Before then I hope.' Flowers replied.

Had Van Ekeren realised how long it would be from that moment, he would have taken the plane home that night.

CHAPTER 9

The following morning, he received a smile from Lopez' secretary that gave him a feeling of well-being. He obeyed her injunction to be seated as she informed him Lopez was in and would be a few minutes. He handed her the draft of his report, she gave him another smile as it was handed over. She set it up on the small stand before her and commenced hitting keys on her keyboard.

By God! She could type, and fast, her fingers fairly flew over the keys. Then Lopez indicated he was ready and Van Ekeren rose to go, for once his eyes were on her flashing fingers and nowhere else. He walked into Lopez' domain.

'You have completed your report?' Lopez asked.

'I have,' Van Ekeren replied guardedly, still with qualms as to where Lopez stood.

'Have you arrived at any conclusions?'

'Yes,' he answered uneasily. 'Some you may find interesting, I have pushed liability for the original shipment, the computer gear, onto the marine insurers of TI's suppliers. It appears to me what was in those long crates was not computer towers and monitors.'

Lopez permitted himself a smile.

'Good! That is excellent news. I will read it later when Jeanette has finished it,' he said. Van Ekeren eyed him quizzically but again Lopez seemed like a man with a load lifted from his shoulders. 'When do you return?'

'Tomorrow,' Van Ekeren said. 'I'm not sure of flight times yet.'

'I will ask Jeanette to find out for you,' he picked up the phone and gave instructions in Taranganese. 'You will do me the honour of lunching with me?'

*

Lopez was not talkative during lunch, he seemed pre-occupied, although his demeanour could accurately be described as courteous and coldly polite. There was a moment of animation when a police car went past the restaurant with siren blaring, he watched it pass and raised an eyebrow.

'Trouble?' Van Ekeren asked tentatively. 'Or just another road accident?'

Another two vehicles went past with sirens blaring, Lopez shook his head.

'Not a road accident, I'd say trouble. It could be an incident somewhere; perhaps a small disturbance...who knows. We've been having insurgency troubles recently.'

'Serious?'

'Not easy to say,' Lopez replied.

'Anything that could affect you, in a business sense that is?'

'Again, not easy to say. These are difficult times, and in times like this it's best to maintain a low profile and keep quiet, one never knows who will be winners or losers, therefore it's best, unless you are one of the ruling elite, to not commit yourself.'

'Who is fighting who?'

'Everybody,' Lopez replied cynically. 'We have Shi'ite Muslims versus Sunni Muslims and both of these versus Buddhists, Christians against them both and also infighting between Protestants against Catholics. We also have Hindus and Taoists, who keep themselves to themselves, plus a few Jews and we also have some Communists. Really God, or Gods if there's more than one, must at times smile wryly at the outrages perpetrated in their respective names and the protestations of virtue by the perpetrators.'

'Indeed, they must.'

'We have a further complication in that Indonesia is hungrily eyeing our oil reserves and off shore oil fields. We also have an excellent deep-water harbour in Taranga City, suitable for deep sea tankers and large warships. We are geographically too close for comfort, placed as we are in the Timor Sea south of Indonesia. They could take us over just like that.'

'Like East Timor?'

'Easier than East Timor; they have been considering it for years. A large following here is sympathetic to the idea and want us to be part of Indonesia. It is suspected they are receiving assistance in arms and cash.'

'How will it affect you, if they do?'

'It could make things difficult for non-Muslims. Further they wish to develop the oil fields much quicker than is happening now. Taranga is exploiting them slowly as an accumulating asset. Indonesia would bring in foreign capital, probably from the West or more likely China, which will hasten development to satisfy demands for more and cheaper petrol, especially from the Americans and the Chinese. The Chinese economy is now expanding at a very fast rate.'

'Is the unrest a problem for commerce?'

'People who are not strictly for one side or another can be dragged in, not because they have any strong feelings but because somebody has a hold over them,' Lopez looked thoughtful. 'There are often unwilling accomplices, sometimes because of technicalities that leave them vulnerable, or threats against their business, family or person.'

'Oh!' Van Ekeren sensed Lopez was talking personally.

'Yes,' Lopez broke his bread. 'Happily, one can sometimes take evasive action by sticking to well established practices within one's profession. Consequently, if events take a certain course, one can hardly be blamed.'

'Really!' Van Ekeren was becoming intrigued.

'Yes' Lopez' eyes wandered over the restaurant, then he pushed over a neatly written screed. 'I have looked out some flights home for you, do any of these times suit?'

Van Ekeren scanned the list.

'Any one of these will do.'

'Shall we have a liqueur?' Lopez' looked around for the waiter.

Van Ekeren wasn't averse and nodded. Lopez signalled to the wine waiter who came over.

'You have done a good job, Mr Van Ekeren.'

'I am glad you think so.'

'I do indeed,' Lopez' eyes, though still cold and aloof, seemed to lose some of their iciness. The man's body language spoke volumes, as though a weight had been lifted from his mind. 'Have you been contacted by the Targanese Industries Group since we last spoke?'

'Not exactly,' Van Ekeren hadn't heard from his midnight visitors since their eccentric bedroom visit. 'I've heard next to nothing, apart from Mr Rijkaard, who you contacted for me. I did have one contact; you'll recall I mentioned this before.

It was one evening in my hotel but nothing concrete was discussed.'

'In your hotel? That is unusual!' commented Lopez. 'Normally they don't speak to anyone after office hours...the divine right of Government employees! You have similar problems with your Public Service, I think. You've had one meeting; you say?'

'Just one.'

'Who with?'

'A man named ...' Van Ekeren paused, what was that damned man's name? 'There were two of them. I thought one of them was named Nabang or something, a big fellow. The other, who seemed in charge, was called...Rabak...Labank... Labek...or was it Lebak?'

'Lebak!'

'Something like that, do you know him?'

'Lebak ...I know someone of that name, not in Taranganese Industries that's for sure. Lebak...hmm!' Lopez laughed as if at some private joke.

'Why are you laughing?'

'Sorry,' Lopez looked apologetic. 'That was unforgivable. Excuse my bad manners but the Lebak I am thinking of is hardly a captain of industry. You must have been mistaken, perhaps you misheard the name. Was it perhaps Le Bas?'

'It may have been,' Van Ekeren replied, the events that night had been unorthodox and took place while he was three sails to the wind.

'That is quite likely as Le Bas is among their top executives, but I've never known him to go out at night. He has a perpetual fear of being kidnapped.'

*

Van Ekeren was having a farewell drink with Westerman.

He was starting to appreciate and understand Westerman a little better now, after his feelings of aversion the previous night. Westerman's more outrageous racial and political pronouncements were clearly part of an act he was playing, a semi-humorous act so much a part of him that anyone who didn't know him could easily mistake it for the real thing. Many of us are guilty of adopting various alter egos.

Westerman adopted a Victorian England pose, often referred to as a Colonel Blimp outlook; one which Van Ekeren had to admit at times was amusing. Westerman would react to given situations or remarks in the same way present day society tends to assume the Victorian English would. He had much in common with the instigators of 'The Goon Show', whose humour was often ostensibly pompous which mocked the mode of thought prevalent in Victorian England by exaggerating it. Van Ekeren had told Westerman about his night visitation.

'Waiting for you in your room, eh?' Westerman was saying. 'Probably went through your belongings while they were at it, like all bloody wogs.'

'Why should they do that,' part of Van Ekeren rebelled and attempted to dilute the prejudice Westerman embodied, even though he now recognised it as exaggerated humour.

'Looking for anything of value, so they can raffle it off on the Black Market. Never occurs to the bastards to work for it, just bloody steal it.'

Van Ekeren had ruefully reached the conclusion one had to accept Westerman's projection of himself, when the phone rang. He answered it.

'Mr Van Elderen?'

Christ! There was little doubt who *that* was.

'Yes, and incidentally my name is Van Eker...!'

'Can you join us within the hour?'

'Can I do what? Within the...!' his voice went up an octave. '...oh yes, I presume so. You don't give much notice...what for?'

'We have much to discuss,' there was a trace of sarcasm as if to ask why else they would want to call a meeting. Van Ekeren ground his teeth with irritation.

There was another aspect. If they were trying to make him alter the terms of his report, they had another think coming. He was not going to be a party to fraud, not even in a passive sense. He enjoyed his work and wanted to progress within the insurance world, one hint of bribery or corruption and he'd be gone forever.

'I'm not sure that anything you say will make me alter my opinion,' he said stiffly.

There was a silence at the other end, then Lebak cleared his throat.

'You are an unusual man, Mr Van Elderen.'

'I don't really see that,' Van Ekeren replied. 'And while we're at it would you please get my name...!'

'I respect you for it, Mr Van Elderen, but we must meet to discuss detail, whether we agree on the finer points or not. I understand you have to get back to your station.'

'My station...? Oh ...yes...!' it seemed an odd turn of phrase for describing Melbourne office '...well naturally I have to return. I'm catching a flight in five or six hours.'

'Ah yes, very wise, it would tempt Providence to stay here too long until the time is ripe...eh?'

'Until...what?' Not for the first time this wretched man's turn of phrase puzzled him. 'It would what...? Oh, I suppose so. I don't quite see...!'

'We shouldn't take too long,' Lebak didn't seem aware of Van Ekeren's puzzlement. 'If the meeting takes longer than anticipated, which I don't think is likely, we can always arrange to have your flight delayed.'

'Yes, oh well, thank you, that's very kind…! You can do *what*?'

'Delay your flight, of course, all it needs is a phone call from the right quarter. Do you have your report?'

'Yes.' Van Ekeren scratched his head in perplexity; Taranganese Industries must have one hell of a pull if they could delay flights by picking up a phone. Despite his irritation, he was impressed. 'But about my report, I won't change it, Mr Lopez already has a copy.'

'Mr….Lopez! You mean the insurance man, the man from the bonded warehouse?'

'Of course, who else?'

'You gave *him* a copy? Why?' Lebak sounded agitated.

'Why? Because he was involved with the crates and the burglary, he had a right to know what is going on. He said he would be in touch with you this afternoon,' Van Ekeren allowed a harsher note to creep into his voice. 'Look here, Mr Lebak, a man has a right to be informed when he is as involved as Mr Lopez. You gain nothing by going behind people's backs. You'll gain more co-operation from Lopez by keeping him informed.'

There was silence before Lebak cleared his throat.

'You may be right, but you have taken a risk. I will sanction it this time, but next time first consult with me. If there is a leak, we may have to deal with Mr Lopez.'

'Deal with him?' Van Ekeren didn't quite understand the phraseology or the manner in which it was uttered. 'But aren't you dealing with him now, he was involved with the matter, or deal, from the start.'

'Indeed, but you should have consulted me first. He was only concerned on the edges, not with the finer detail. I am in charge of matters here and make any decisions that affect the outcome of anything we set in motion.'

'How the hell could I consult with you first when I've seen little or nothing of you since I've been here,' Van Ekeren's irritation rose to a peak as he objected to the peremptory tone of this man. He recalled the ill-mannered and uninvited incursion into his hotel bedroom. 'I've only seen you once; when you came uninvited into my bedroom and sat around in the dark drinking my Scotch. I'm not sure I altogether like that mode of procedure.'

There was another short silence, then Lebak gave a dry chuckle.

'I think I like you Mr Van Elderen, I prefer a man who is outspoken, even if I must insist my will must always prevail.'

'Look, its Van Ekeren, not...!'

'Madang will pick you up within the hour,' he hung up.

'What was that?' asked Westerman.

Van Ekeren gave him a brief résumé of the conversation with Lebak. Westerman looked puzzled then shrugged.

'These bloody wogs have a penchant for the dramatic and they never did have any manners...except bad!' he snorted. 'I'd keep the bastard waiting when he does get here! Just tell him you're British.'

Van Ekeren grinned at that.

'With a surname like Van Ekeren I could hardly convince him of that!' he said. 'Another thing, the bastard can't even pronounce my name correctly.'

'Then mispronounce his, that'll show the sod!'

'That'll be easy enough, I can't remember for certain what it is.'

'Good, well that makes two of you, doesn't it?'

CHAPTER 10

Madang was surly when he appeared at the door, Van Ekeren deliberately kept him waiting a few minutes, but didn't overdo it as it could jeopardise catching his flight. He didn't have much faith in Lebak's assurance the company had sufficient influence to delay the departure of a commercial flight.

Madang led the way to the ground floor, for some reason he refused to take the lift. If Van Ekeren hadn't known he was just a minion, albeit it an unorthodox one, of the largest industrial group on the island, he would have said Madang's manner was unorthodox and resembled that of a man with something to hide. His demeanour was positively furtive. He slipped around corners and peered in all directions as though expecting booby traps at every juncture. Van Ekeren recalled what Lopez had said about Le Bas, Lebak or whatever his blasted name was, having a fear of being kidnapped and held to ransom. Maybe Madang was dominated by the same thought processes. When they eventually reached the ground floor and crept stealthily out through a side door even Van Ekeren was peering nervously over his shoulder.

They walked, or crept, along the passage at the rear, at which point Van Ekeren was pushed against the wall as Madang's restraining arm caught him across the chest.

'What the blazes...?'

'Shhhh!' Madang hissed and Van Ekeren waited with nerves jangling as two civil police crossed the end of the alley. Really, this was taking the Taranganese penchant for drama too far. One could hardly suspect police of being involved in kidnapping rings.

'Look here, do you mind telling me what the hell is...?'

'Quick! Through here.'

Such was the urgency of his tone Van Ekeren obeyed automatically, they ducked through a gap in the wall and headed for a car parked on a block of waste land. There were many blocks like this near the city centre where older buildings had been demolished to make way for new. This particular block had digging equipment at one corner, a sign he'd seen earlier that day indicated it was a station site for the new Taranga City underground railway.

Fruit stalls had moved into one end of the vacant block to sell their wares and there was unsold stock dumped at the other. There was a nauseous, pungent smell, though it certainly swamped the musty aroma that emanated from Madang.

Van Ekeren was mildly surprised at the car. Despite accepting that in Third World countries they couldn't live exactly like their counterparts in New York or Sydney, he hadn't expected anything quite so frugal. It was a Toyota, which showed signs of age and wear. He clambered into the rear seat and wrinkled his nose at the smells from Madang; the fruit stall dumps and the car's interior. Madang occupied the front passenger seat, his aroma swamped by others in the confined space. As Madang settled himself the driver pointedly lit a cigar, maybe he too had reservations about Madang's toiletry omissions.

He uttered something in the Taranganese dialect and they set off, the suspension was not good and registered every bump and manhole cover. The car twisted and turned through city streets and eventually arrived in a side street off the city centre. Van Ekeren climbed out and looked around in bewilderment, he had been to many business conferences in his time, some in quite modest locations, but this didn't equate with any venue in Sydney, Melbourne or Perth. The street and the buildings were quite unprepossessing, but after recent experiences nothing surprised him.

'Come,' Madang ducked into an alley between two buildings. He evaded some bins as they crossed a yard and reached a door where he knocked three times, paused, then knocked again twice. Van Ekeren looked skywards in exasperation; the sense of drama exuded by these people was beginning to try his patience.

They were admitted after a searching examination through a peephole, an exaggerated procedure that almost raised Van Ekeren to screaming pitch. It was becoming reminiscent of a Hollywood 'B' movie. They entered a room housing a large oblong table in the centre, with chairs around it, mostly occupied. The room's interior did raise expectations somewhat, it had the appearance of an office with what looked like a conference room table. Filing cabinets and a printing press were in the corner.

Lebak or Le Bas sat at the head and Van Ekeren had to admit the man did exude some presence. He rose, greeted him cordially and shook him by the hand which appeared to impress the rest of the gathering, about ten men, all casually dressed and smoking heavily.

They clustered round Van Ekeren and slapped him on the back, which hardened his resolve. He was *not* going to be a party to a fraudulent or exaggerated claim no matter how ingratiating they might be, he would have to live with himself afterwards. He was escorted to a chair, at which point he realised what he had thought was a conference table was not! He hit his knee against a trestle and realised it was several tables all pushed together with a green cloth spread over it. He gritted his teeth as his kneecap hit the woodwork.

'Gentlemen, this is Mr Van Elderen.'

'Van Ek ...!' he began, but his voice was drowned out by applause.

'Proceed Franco, with your report. We have much to get through tonight.'

A small man, wearing horn rimmed glasses, stood up and commenced reading from handwritten sheets. He spoke Dutch with a pronounced accent but Van Ekeren had no trouble in following what he was saying. He listened keenly, but was no wiser to what he was talking about as he ground on. Occasionally there were rumbles of approval, which Van Ekeren could not fully comprehend. The events he was describing appeared to chronicle damage caused to property or equipment with resultant delays in production.

He looked around the assemblage and sadly shook his head as he took in the appalling mode of dress that presumably prevailed in Taranganese business circles. Admittedly, Australians tended to dress less formally than their fellows in London or New York, on a hot day in Sydney they would probably all divest themselves of jackets and ties, but amongst this group he couldn't spot one tie, let alone a loosened one. The dress of most of them at best could be termed unorthodox, at the worst untidy or downright sloppy. There were jeans, check shirts, 'T' shirts and a couple of leather jackets. Lebak himself sported a combat jacket, the camouflaged variety although he seemed smarter than most.

Bill Flowers had once appeared at a Friday afternoon meeting carrying a combat jacket which he had casually draped over a chair before the meeting commenced. After the meeting Flowers was attending one of those 'paint ball' mock warfare groups. Van Ekeren wondered if that form of entertainment was prevalent in Taranga. He came back to reality with a jerk, Franco was still droning on.

'Contacts have been made with our brothers in the northern province who have accepted our demands as theirs, who wish to belong to a wider political and economic sphere. They have offered us assistance with men...' here he paused meaningly '...and materials.' He gave a conspiratorial smile as he mentioned the word 'materials' and there was a rumble of laughter around the table. Lebak permitted himself a smile and hammered the table with his fist.

'Let us proceed,' he turned to a man on his right. 'What have you to report?'

This time Van Ekeren was completely at sea, the next man's report was in Dutch, but it may as well have been in Double Dutch. Van Ekeren struggled to translate the speaker's jargon into business verbiage, he succeeded with some aspects but failed miserably with others.

The pseudo references to the military, military parlance and procedures Van Ekeren accepted. He knew sales executives in Melbourne business circles and elsewhere, whilst haranguing sales staff during aggressive sales campaigns, sometimes used military verbiage, such as eliminating competition, fighting on two fronts or moving into sectors occupied by others.

It all added drama, but in Taranga, presumably with their penchant for dramatic gestures, they seemed to push it to extremes. References to 'our troops', and 'lines of communication' he could stomach, even 'increase our fire power' made some sense in sales parlance. He could recall an insurance sales manager using similar phrases some years back when he had been addressing sales reps under his control. But there was one puzzling reference regarding another organisation, presumably a rival one, where the speaker mentioned, in passing, they were to be eliminated.

This on its own Van Ekeren could have accepted as having a double meaning but he experienced qualms of unease when a brief case with reddish stains on it was produced, purporting to have been removed from a rival salesman. He was all for healthy competition, but this seemed to be taking it to extremes. He began to wonder what commodities they were selling; surely competition couldn't be that vigorous.

The speaker finished and another took his place. Presumably he was the advertising executive, long haired and untidily dressed, Van Ekeren could imagine him directing sleazy commercials for ladies' underwear or advertising diversions for business executives after a hard day at the office. Up to a point his report seemed to make sense as he was working on some plan for approaching the television station and broadcasting their message at regular intervals. He referred to another plan for keeping their rivals out after they had established themselves, which appeared to incorporate an element of brute force, but again Van Ekeren attributed this to excessive drama and enthusiastic use of parallel paramilitary nuances. The speaker sat down to enthusiastic applause.

The next contributor, wearing a loud, cross checked shirt,

advocated an approach to the Police Force. Van Ekeren was disconcerted when he produced an automatic pistol, which he had been fingering throughout the previous addresses, which he freely brandished throughout his own. He spoke in the local Taranganese dialect tinged with Portuguese, although Van Ekeren's Portuguese was somewhat rusty he did catch part of what he was saying, occasionally the speaker relapsed into Dutch where he was able to make more sense of it. He appeared to advocate an aggressive campaign waged on the custodians of the Law in their main barracks and the local City Police Station which could bring about tremendous results and could well win the campaign for the company and cause.

Van Ekeren was inclined to doubt this. If the police in Taranga City were paid on the same scales as their New South Wales and Victoria counterparts, he could think of better sectors of the community to concentrate an aggressive sales campaign. He also doubted that controlling the police barracks, as the speaker put it, would necessarily guarantee sales in all police stations throughout the country. He felt strongly enough on this point to interject and make a comment.

'They obey orders from City Central Base,' the speaker responded coldly, plainly resenting the interruption. 'They have respect for Authority and will obey any directive from their central command.'

'I don't quite follow,' Van Ekeren persisted. 'Some people resent change, if they are used to say...one brand of washing powder, or even breakfast cereal, then they will stick to it regardless of what their superiors or leaders say. I can't see a directive from their Central Base will cause them to change.'

Lebak sat back and broke into laughter, as did many of the others. They initially looked puzzled but took their cue from him, apart from Madang and the speaker who both looked perplexed. Lebak hit the flat of his hand on the table and shook his head.

'Truly you are a man with a strange turn of phrase, Mr Van Elderen,' he said 'Never before have I been compared to packets of soap powder or cornflakes.'

Van Ekeren thought Lebak was perhaps identifying himself with his products too closely, but let it pass, maybe he had said enough. Although his comment appeared to have gone down surprisingly well, to cause roars of laughter had not been his intention.

The next speaker wore a jacket and was smart compared with the rest. He stood in the shadows near the door and appeared to have arrived late accompanied by several minders. He emerged from a group of four men; his companions looked ready for trouble and moved with him when he advanced to the table to deliver. He removed his jacket before he spoke, he was either too warm or had decided to descend to the same level as the others. He had short hair and wore light canvas trousers, a blue shirt and rimless glasses. He had arrived during the previous address.

As a speaker he was completely different from the preceding ones, he was relatively calm, yet when he placed emphasis on certain aspects, he did it well. It was during his expert and well delivered address that Van Ekeren began to suspect he was attending something other than a conference of a business undertaking.

The speaker put his message over in terms that suggested he was planning to start a riot, but as he continued it sounded more like a revolution. As he neared his final close Van Ekeren realised this was precisely what it was. This realisation also cleared any puzzlement regarding previous speeches, there was no question now of double entendre or play on words, the meaning was perfectly clear.

'...after we have eliminated resistance at the police area, and Balou here has captured the television and radio stations and broadcast our message, we shall invade Government offices in Daru Street. All senior members of the present ruling clique, cabinet and regime must be tracked down and eliminated. We cannot risk anyone surviving and becoming a rallying point.'

A rumble of approval, was broken by Lebak tapping his pen on his pad, and a rumbling from Van Ekeren's belly as his bowels turned to water. Lebak called for order.

'Continue, if you please, Alvaro.'

'Much of our plan depends on the power breakdown, timing here is essential, it must occur precisely at the right time so there is no media transmission, and restored when we are ready to transmit our own message,' Alvaro paused and looked around the gathering. 'It will also enable us to blockade the main fuelling point for the Army tanks. They will have just returned from Army exercises in the north and will be low on fuel. But the power black-out is essential, I must be assured this will be carried out and on time. In addition, communications must be faultless, we must be able to talk to each other so we can synchronise the power going off and coming back on.'

There was a buzz of approval, Lebak raised his hand.

'This, I agree, is vital. This will be the responsibility of the esteemed member on my left who has just arrived from over the water. Before we move onto that, do we have the latest consignment of rocket launchers and AK 47s?'

'Yes,' Alvaro referred to his file. 'They were delivered under the cloak of Targanese Industries. They were substituted for merchandise TI had ordered through Indonesia. The original shipment was intercepted and replaced, as far as I know it was all tipped into Jakarta Harbour. We were able to collect our shipment quickly after arrival at the warehouse.'

'I understand there were difficulties.'

'Yes, there were. By a coincidence there was a burglary at the warehouse, thieves broke in and stole merchandise which included one of our crates. We put out feelers amongst police informers and our own security police, but we haven't found out who the thieves were. Strangely there has been no sign of these stolen items and they have not surfaced either in city police circles nor the black market. We understand air conditioning equipment was also stolen plus quantities of electrical appliances.'

'We don't know who the thieves were?' Lebak commented. 'That's very strange.'

'Very strange indeed,' Alvaro commented. 'What is of even more concern is that I was informed by one of our undercover operatives a snooper from Australia was in the warehouse yesterday asking awkward questions.'

'From Australia? Who was he?'

'Said he was a loss adjuster, investigating the burglary on behalf of the insurers,' continued Alvaro. 'But my department had already had him and another man followed as a matter of routine, I believe they could be foreign agents or local police spies, they previously called on the civil police station and I wondered why insurance assessors would do that? We are investigating and hope to identify them both.'

Van Ekeren gritted his teeth and dug his finger nails into his thigh. It was imperative he didn't pass out from sheer fright. So, he and Westerman *had* been followed to and from the police station.

'That swine Lopez promised there would be no investigation

by insurers,' Franco said angrily. 'Perhaps we should call on Lopez again, he was warned members of his family would be under threat if he didn't act as instructed. If he has been in touch with the civil police, then...!' he drew his hand expressively across his throat.

'And as an un-naturalised citizen he could be deported?' added Alvaro.

'I made it clear if he didn't co-operate and ensure the smooth passage of our crates through the import process, there would be severe consequences for his family,' said Franco.

'What sort of consequences?' asked Lebak.

'He has a very attractive wife and an even more attractive daughter.'

'What exactly did you say, or threaten?'

'I intimated that if he wished them to stay...attractive...then we wanted no problems,' added Franco.

'You said *that*?' Lebak looked and sounded disapproving. 'Threats like that do our cause no good, Franco. As for Lopez, I have no liking for the man but this may not be his fault. This man could have been an insurance assessor. With small to medium sized claims, just plain pilferage, the local management is empowered to investigate them, but in cases of theft of large quantities the Australian management always appoint their own assessors and investigators. There have been cases under our present corrupt regime where claims have been known to be fraudulent.'

'We managed to remove our merchandise before he arrived,' said Alvaro. 'Unfortunately, criminal elements, so far unidentified, took advantage of the general lack of security to break in the day after our equipment arrived there.'

'This was not just a spot check?'

'By the insurers you mean?' Alvaro shrugged. 'I'm not sure,

but one of our agents within Lopez' organisation checked the file. It appears Lopez had no choice but to involve his Australian management and representatives of the Australian insurers; he could be telling the truth.'

'You said two men were in touch with the civil police?' growled Franco. 'I think they would be spies.'

'We are making enquiries about that,' said Alvaro coldly.

'Is Lopez to be trusted?' asked Lebak.

'He has to be,' commented Alvaro. He removed his glasses and polished them vigorously. 'He has never taken out naturalisation, under the new legislation passed last year he is now a registered alien...the new rules affect many like him, this will reduce as the years pass.'

'Has he applied for citizenship now the new law has been passed?' Lebak asked.

'I understand from investigations he has, but we have arranged for it to be delayed. He was born in Goa, which gives us a lever. If he steps out of line he could be sent back there, we should use that as a threat.'

'Plus, he has fears for his family,' grunted Franco. 'I made it clear any disfigurements would be permanent.'

Lebak looked irritable and thumped the table with his fist. Whatever Van Ekeren thought of the man and the ethics of his group, he had to concede he was an excellent chairman, he never lost control. Further, from his expression as he eyed Franco, he plainly disapproved of the threats Franco had made to Lopez and his family.

'We agree 'H' hour will have to be 11.00 hours on the 24th, that is, two weeks from now, almost to the hour,' Lebak stated. 'Much of the timing will depend on our noble friend Mr Van Elderen, who as you know has recently been...transferred... from somewhere north of here. He is an expert in his field, having been Chief Electrical Engineer at a main State Power complex. Mr. Van Elderen is new to our ranks, but has been a sympathiser and comrade for many years. He recently arrived from overseas and is currently alternating between his new position here and his old one. He will be returning there shortly, but will be in charge of the Taranga City power complex on the day and will know exactly what has to be done. Is that correct, Mr Van Elderen?'

'True!' Van Ekeren's voice rose two octaves in sheer panic and came out as a frightened squeak. Many pairs of eyes turned to him enquiringly as he repeated it more loudly.

'*True!*' he said again and the windows almost rattled with the vibration. The time to stand up and make a clean breast of it, that there had been an unfortunate mistake and it was a clear case of mistaken identity, was long gone. Matters had gone too far to embark on an innocent explanation and laugh it off. This was no laughing matter. If he came clean now, he would finish up dead.

'Mr Van Elderen was briefed by our good friend Bosuka, who assured us of his reliability. Bosuka cannot be with us, if he were to be seen here it could compromise him and his country's government...but Mr Van Elderen can be said to represent him.'

There was sustained applause at the mention of Bosuka, Van Ekeren was profoundly thankful he wasn't present. He modestly accepted the plaudits on Bosuka's behalf and clenched his teeth to stop them chattering, a facial contortion that in present company could be interpreted as grim determination. He had to maintain the fiction and get out alive, he had no doubt the presence of an innocent stranger would be treated as seriously as that of a police spy or informant. If he didn't convince them of his bona fide, he could be floating in the harbour the next morning. He gulped, swallowed and just stopped himself from fainting.

'Now we'll hear from our good friend.'

There was applause and faces turned to their 'good friend', who was totally unprepared to deliver an inspiring message. His main preoccupation was to stop his teeth chattering, his knees from trembling, and his bowels from making an unauthorised movement. His vocal chords were also quavering like an opera singers'.

He rose shakily to his feet, swallowed several times and flexed his knees. He *had* to look convincing and with *that* realisation small doses of courage actually returned. He thought of Val, which boosted his morale to some degree. He looked around the group and tried not to look at the man in the cross-checked shirt, still fingering his automatic, or at Franco who could consider him another candidate for facial alteration.

He began to speak.

'Brothers!' that was a happy inspiration; he recalled the first message thrust under his hotel bedroom door. 'This is a proud day for us all, I am proud to be here as part of the ...the...' here words failed him, 'plot' didn't seem appropriate, nor 'conspiracy', both indicated something underhand and the more dedicated brethren may take umbrage '...the...grand design for the betterment of our...er...your island.' He had been going to say 'nation', but had a suspicion the plot could involve merging with another larger country and nation could indicate separatism and be deemed inappropriate.

While pondering over the next sentence to ensure it wouldn't be tactless, he paused. They burst into spontaneous applause, which gave some breathing space while he desperately struggled to think something to inspire a bunch of ruthless thugs and revolutionaries.

'There should be no difficulties with my part in the ...the... grand design ...' he was being repetitive but couldn't help it. He had no idea whether the absent Van Elderen was employed by the main power supplier or was going to make an unauthorised entry into the plant accompanied by insurgents. 'I will arrange for the switch to be turned at the right moment ...as yet I have no concrete plans, I prefer to expand on this aspect nearer to the event when I have studied the routine and lay out at the plant.'

'How will you do this? How will you get into the main generating room?'

Inwardly Van Ekeren soundly cursed Franco, he hadn't thought of that yet. This blasted man was a bloody menace!

'I...I...have a contact there who will give me the routine they work, the machinery and switchgear may not... won't... differ much from my previous position.'

'Who is your contact?' Franco persisted. 'Do we know him?'

This fucking man could be the cause of him finishing up in the harbour with a knife in his back. Van Ekeren had a flash of anger but from anger came inspiration.

'I'm not prepared to say,' he said cuttingly. 'I trust him, and he trusts me. I am *not* going to blurt his name out in front of many people I don't know.'

'Very wise,' Lebak commented; Franco flushed and looked put out. This seemed to confirm he and Lebak didn't hit it off too well. Lebak's intervention was more relevant and welcome than he realised, but if anyone were to ask Van Ekeren what plans he had formed already he would be in trouble. Then somebody did.

'What plans do you have so far?' asked the man with the cross-checked shirt.

'I'm ...not prepared to say...' Van Ekeren began shakily but happily Lebak intervened again.

'That question could also involve giving Mr Van Elderen's accomplice away,' Lebak snapped; he plainly didn't like Check Shirt either. 'He has already clarified that aspect. Carry on, Mr Van Elderen.'

Van Ekeren could have embraced him from sheer relief. He swallowed and recommenced. He decided to keep away from anything too specific about the coming coup, and launched into the most rabid radical bullshit he had ever heard or spouted. It sounded like a delivery from a flag waving revolutionary.

He borrowed considerably from rhetoric heard and read in the Press delivered by political leaders from time to time, paid compliments to Lebak in the process and to the aims of the Revolution. He even included references to Robespierre, Che Guevara and Lenin in his confusion. Considering he was shaking with sheer fright he thought he did fairly well and finally sat down trembling like a leaf.

As the applause died down, Lebak eyed him keenly.

'Well done! Are you all right?'

Van Ekeren was about to assure him he was fine but decided against it. If he looked off colour there was no point in denying it, even revolutionaries could catch the flu. Besides, he wanted to get out as quickly as possible before he fainted, threw up or worse. He decided to take advantage of the lifeline.

'No, I feel dreadful,' he whispered. 'I think I might have the 'flu or something, or maybe eaten something. I've been feeling crook...er...off colour all day,' he cut short the Australian colloquialism which could cast doubt on possible East Indian or Dutch origins.

'Will you be able to stay?'

'I...I...think I'd better go. I just need a good night's sleep,' Van Ekeren said and added as a lightener. 'I don't think your colleagues would like it if I threw up during the meeting!'

Lebak laughed heartily and clapped him on the back which nearly precipitated the feared phenomenon. Those within earshot murmured sympathetic condolences. Lebak rose to his feet.

'Mr Van Elderen is leaving us now, he...has another appointment. We are very grateful you were able to join us, Mr Van Elderen.'

'Thank you.' Van Ekeren stuttered. Lebak turned and waved to Madang.

'Go with our blessing, Madang will take care of you.'

Van Ekeren didn't like the sound of that. He hoped Lebak wasn't in the habit of making ironic or double entendre utterances.

CHAPTER 11

Madang left Van Ekeren by the void building site, he wasn't sorry as he'd been having immense difficulty in preventing himself from throwing up from sheer fright during the return journey. Madang probably sensed this as he pointedly sat in the front seat with the driver and opened all the windows.

Van Ekeren picked his way over the brick ends and rubbish, ducked through the gap in the wall and walked to the hotel. Westerman was in the foyer.

'Hallo old son, what's new?' he eyed him with concern. 'My God! You look awful.'

'I feel awful,' said Van Ekeren tersely, for once glad to see Westerman. 'Come up to my room.'

Westerman followed, still concerned. Van Ekeren went into the bathroom and had a drink of water from the tooth glass which made him feel a little better. He took it with him into the sitting room and Westerman, who had armed himself with a glass, offered him some of his own Scotch.

'What's the trouble, what's happened?' he asked.

Van Ekeren told him, Westerman listened attentively, to his credit he didn't interrupt once. He started grinning as Van Ekeren neared the end of his yarn, and broke into laughter when it had finished.

'Is that all,' he guffawed. 'Life wouldn't be the same in some countries without somebody trying to be top dog and unseat somebody else. That's one advantage of constitutional Monarchy, nobody wants the job and when he or she dies the succession is automatic, only the heir apparent qualifies... poor bastard! If they want a new President or Prime Minister, it never occurs to these blighters to resort to the ballot box, they just reach for their guns.'

But Van Ekeren wasn't in the mood for cynicism and utterly failed to see any humour in the situation.

'What the hell do I do?'

Westerman's unhelpful reaction was causing his brain to solidify.

'Nothing, old chap!' Westerman realised levity was not appreciated and became serious. 'What if there is going to be a revolt, what business is it of yours? Do you know who the right party is?'

'Well...no!'

'Which means if you intervene you could easily choose the wrong side. Just let them get on with it.'

Van Ekeren wasn't sure, he felt Westerman's simplistic solution was no answer to his present predicament.

'What do you suggest?'

Westerman scratched his chin as he considered the question, Van Ekeren's serious and frightened expression had at last communicated itself to him. His Colonel Blimp veneer had slipped and the real Westerman beneath the exterior briefly took over.

'Do nothing,' he said. 'It's nothing to do with you, or with me. We have no idea how government is run here, whether it's good for the country and the population or not. What if the revolutionaries are better for the country than the incumbent government? Forget your Left and Right wings, the Left wing would possibly be good for most countries in South America, and a dose of Right wing may be good for countries in Eastern Europe or Cuba. What *is* the situation here?' Westerman drummed his fingers. 'I have no idea, I'd hesitate to intervene on behalf of one side or the other. In any case the current lot seized power by a coup.'

That did make sense. Where two unknowns were involved, who was he to jump in on behalf of one side or the other? How was one coup better than another? How would another coup affect nearby Australia if Lebak and his henchmen took over? Van Ekeren didn't know, he remembered reading the week before that Australia and Taranga were haggling about oil rights. Indonesia was also involved in the discussions as the recently discovered oil field encroached on waters they claimed were under their jurisdiction. But assuming Side 'A' or Side 'B' were either pro or anti-Australia, did that give him the right to intervene either way? What about the rights or welfare of the average citizen of Taranga?

'Well I'm going home tomorrow. I'll be glad to see the back of the blasted place.'

'Then you've hardly time to do anything about it, have you?' retorted Westerman. 'If you go to the police now, you'll be held up here for another week while they make enquiries, you might even be thrown in a cell, they wouldn't want you wandering around broadcasting a message like that. And what information can you give them?'

'Well, I can ...er...hmmm!'

'It's all a bit vague and airy fairy isn't it, it's possible you may be giving them something they know already, except possibly the date and they might even know that. The police might even be in favour of the coup or could even be amongst the instigators. Where would that leave you if you go to them and start blurting it out to them and saying you know everything?'

'Oh Christ!' Van Ekeren covered his face with his hands, he hadn't considered that.

'As for this man Lebak, he isn't unknown, his name was mentioned at the construction meeting I attended yesterday. Not clear exactly who or what he is, nobody seemed anxious to tell me much about him. I gathered he's a radical who favours some tie up with Indonesia.'

Van Ekeren nodded thoughtfully. He recalled how Lopez had reacted when he said he thought Lebak had been a representative of Taranganese Industries, vastly amused.

'You think I'd better forget it?'

'Will you ever forget it?' Westerman gave an ironic grunt. 'You'll remember this for the rest of your life, Doug. Here! Let's have a drink...or two! Whatever happens they'll kill each other off during the squabbles and that will be a few less mouths to feed and a few less hotheads to worry about!'

His Colonel Blimp veneer was returning, but what he had said while the mask had slipped did make some sense. It was no concern of theirs, and it could be presumptuous to intervene on one side or the other. To do so may be supporting the wrong cause as far as the common people were concerned. Hadn't Flowers said De Souza had led an Army coup?

Having settled the matter to their satisfaction he and Westerman set about demolishing the Scotch bottle...then the phone rang. Westerman answered it, said 'Yes, he's here.' He handed it to Van Ekeren. It was Lopez.

'Mr Van Ekeren, I have a proposition to put to you.'

'Yes,' he answered guardedly.

'I would like you to accompany me to a government reception, being held tonight.'

*

Van Ekeren took a taxi to the address Lopez had given him. It was a large house in a fashionable and desirable suburb. He opened the front gate and walked up the driveway. Lopez saw him arrive and was waiting on the front step. He escorted him to the living room and briefly introduced him to a young man who Van Ekeren thought needed a haircut. He had tattoos on his arms and was dressed in jeans that had seen better days and were far too small. Lopez waved him to a chair and excused himself on the grounds that he had to change.

Van Ekeren conversed briefly with the young man, Julio, who responded mostly in clichés. There was a trace of effeminacy about him, which Van Ekeren deduced from his mode of speech and hand gestures. During the perfunctory conversation, he poured himself a drink without bothering to offer one to Van Ekeren.

Lopez re-entered, he was dressed impeccably in dinner jacket and black tie while his shoes gleamed like beacons. After Lopez' phone call and the import of it, Van Ekeren had hastily changed into suit and tie, he was certainly outshone.

'We are nearly ready,' he said. 'Have you offered Mr Van Ekeren a drink, Julio?'

'Er ...no,' Julio uncrossed his legs and looked petulant. 'No...I didn't.'

'I'll attend to it,' a female voice broke in and a young woman entered the room from behind Lopez. She was dark haired, about 5'8", slim, well-proportioned and fashionably dressed in a black skirt, white blouse and wore a red neckerchief that supplied a splash of colour. Lopez irritably waved her to the drink cabinet in the corner.

'Scotch and dry...er...ginger ale that is.' Van Ekeren said as the young woman raised one eyebrow. He was wondering where she fitted into the scheme of things, she must be Lopez' daughter. 'Thank you.'

She certainly knew how to prepare a Scotch and dry, the proportions were just right. He sipped it appreciatively as she sat down opposite Julio and joined in the conversation. Lopez excused himself and left the room.

As the conversation progressed it registered with Van Ekeren that they didn't like each other. Twice Julio asked Van Ekeren a question, which was interrupted by the girl who asked him another. She also contradicted Julio in the middle of a statement he was making that had political/social undertones. They became involved in an argument that indicated their political stances were not in accord. There was a brief flurry of argument before they both remembered there was a guest present and turned their attention to Van Ekeren again, the girl gave him a smile he would have killed for, similar to those fired in his direction by Lopez' secretary. For a moment, he thought the sun shone more brightly, even in the evening.

Lopez re-entered the room and nodded, he was now ready. Van Ekeren finished his Scotch and moved over to join him, said his farewells to Julio and the girl which she acknowledged, then she made some sharp comment to Julio. As they entered the hall a slim grey-haired woman was in the hall-way, as she moved towards Van Ekeren, he became aware of her carriage and bearing, not unlike the young woman he had just left. She was plain featured, yet there was something about her that overcame any physical shortcoming or facial irregularities. Women who had a magnetic personality, a sincere smile, good carriage and who spoke well could knock a shapely, big busted blonde with a cheesy smile for six. This woman was probably late forties to early fifties, and though no ravishing beauty her features had an aura of personality. See her face in a crowd and you wouldn't look twice, yet be acquainted with her for about ten minutes, talk with her and watch her move and you would be aware you were with a presence.

'You haven't introduced me, Roberto,' she said pointedly.

'Ah...you are correct...my apologies,' Lopez took her hand. 'This is Amanda, my wife...Mr Douglas Van Ekeren, from Australia.'

'Your wife! I am very pleased indeed to meet you, Mrs Lopez,' Van Ekeren, to his surprise, found he was shuffling his feet, such was the presence of this woman.

'A great pleasure,' she responded in kind and it was indeed. Her magnetism raised his estimation of Lopez, they obviously complemented each other.

They made their way to Lopez' car and Lopez backed down the driveway.

'Who answered the phone?' asked Lopez as they passed through the gates.

'Westerman,' Van Ekeren replied. 'He's also going to be at the reception tonight.'

'Why is that? Who or what is he?'

'A civil engineer, he is attending a Civil Engineers conference somewhere in the city,' Van Ekeren replied. 'He's something to do with the underground railway construction. I don't know him all that well. I'd never met him before I arrived here. He's not a bad chap.'

As he completed the brief character synopsis of Westerman, he thought of Westerman's alter ego, and wondered whether Lopez would share that opinion.

'I am sorry for the short notice, Mr Van Ekeren,' Lopez said as he drove up the street, 'I was invited some time ago and was taking an insurance colleague but he has gone down with the flu. I was asked if I could suggest anyone else who would be suitable and naturally, I thought of you. It will be an experience to attend a Government function, even...' here he paused, smiled and added ironically '...a nation as small as this one, though I imagine these functions are much the same the world over.'

Van Ekeren grunted, not able to comment as his experience of governmental functions was limited. Yet he appreciated being asked by Lopez, even as a last-minute substitute, to think that he came within the ambit of Lopez' estimation of a 'suitable person' was oddly gratifying.

'Who was that young man at your house?'

'Julio? He is my wife's nephew. He is from Sri Lanka. He has been staying with us for some months and ...' with a slight hardening of tone' ...it looks as though he'll be with us a few months longer.'

'Hmmph!' Van Ekeren left it at that, it seemed Lopez didn't like him either. 'Who was the young lady?'

It was no surprise when Lopez turned his head, there was a proud smile on his face.

'That was Maria, our daughter.'

'She is a credit to you,' said Van Ekeren. 'A most personable young woman'.

Lopez positively beamed. Yet it had been not been flattery by Van Ekeren. He really meant it, having been most impressed with her intelligence and bearing. Then a jarring thought struck him, that bastard Franco had been talking of disfiguring Lopez' daughter. For the first time, he began to entertain doubts, was he was doing the right thing by doing and saying nothing? Then his thoughts were distracted as Lopez spoke again.

'Have you ever met a Head of State?'

'Not intimately,' Van Ekeren said. 'I have met two Victorian Premiers at functions they attended, I also met John Howard and Paul Keating briefly when they attended functions in Melbourne.'

'Two formidable people.'

'Yes, they are.'

'Voters prefer someone they can look up to.'

'Yes,' Van Ekeren replied. 'In the military, an ordinary soldier wouldn't respect an officer who was ineffectual. What is your ideal for a political leader?'

'That's a difficult question. The first requisite is a stable constitution where the Head of State respects election results.'

'In many countries they don't,' grunted Van Ekeren.

'Quite so,' Lopez gave a rueful smile. 'In America, the presidency seems to be the province of millionaires or somebody backed by them. In France the President appoints Prime Ministers and can sack them on a whim, the President being responsible for overall policy.'

'Or his mistress!' Van Ekeren uttered cynically.

'How true of the French,' Lopez broke into laughter. 'When you see the calibre of some elected incumbents and their mistresses one perceives the advantages of the system whereby the party leader becomes the Country's leader, not the reverse.'

'What do you have here?'

'We have a constitution to which we pay lip service but the military rules. We are not sufficiently mature for Heads of State to move aside when their time is done. There is no umpire or neutral incumbent to watch over the constitution.

The Military is never far away. With Indonesia breathing down our necks perhaps total democracy is impracticable.'

'Does America hold any power and influence here?'

'Not a great deal, yet probably still too much,' Lopez swung the car into a large gateway with a gatehouse manned by police. 'Americans think only in terms of what is good for America, I sometimes wonder if those in the Middle West realise a whole world exists outside the USA.'

He wound down the window.

'Lopez ...this is my invitation. My companion is Mr Douglas Van Ekeren.'

The policeman eyed Lopez' identification papers then waved them through.

'What do the Taranganese people think of Australia?'

'Australia? Hmm!' Lopez parked the car and switched off the engine. 'They see Australia as a country with European origins with links to colonialism. As for our Government... they have a more mature view. To them Australia is a market and a source of goods. Your population and armed forces are not large; therefore, you are not a threat.'

'So, just neighbours, nothing more. Are we seen as racist?'

'Yes, but in many respects this view is exaggerated by our own prejudices. Our rhetoric reverts to the White Australia line whenever we have a dispute with Australia.'

Van Ekeren didn't have time to press further, they had been talking in the car for some minutes and two soldiers were making their way over, possibly thinking they were lost or else to check on them. They hastily left the vehicle and Lopez waved his pass at the oncoming soldiers who checked it and waved them forward. They walked towards the white building, which resembled a last refuge of the old British Raj. It looked impressive in the gathering darkness surrounded by coloured lights.

Lopez waved to an officer who raised a hand in salute, he obviously knew Lopez. As they reached the door an impressively uniformed doorman opened the door with a flourish and waved them in. Van Ekeren looked appreciatively at the concrete steps and ornately tiled floor within.

'Most impressive,' he said to Lopez. 'What a magnificent floor.'

'Well-polished, with beeswax polish; the steps are scrubbed every day with detergent ...both products of Taranganese Industries of course,' commented Lopez dryly. 'But watch how you place your feet, at times they overdo the polish.'

CHAPTER 12

The first person Van Ekeren saw was Westerman.

'Hello, old man,' Westerman had already had a few and as usual seemed unaffected except for a flush around his cheeks. 'Seen the PM yet?'

Van Ekeren shook his head and introduced Lopez. They both sized each other up as they shook hands.

'A pleasure to meet a friend of Mr Van Ekeren,' said Lopez, courtly as ever, while Westerman muttered: 'Likewise.'

They engaged in small talk until one of Westerman's colleagues arrived and took him off to introduce him to one of De Souza's Cabinet.

'What did you say he is?' Lopez selected a savoury offered by a passing waiter.

'An engineer,' Van Ekeren answered. 'Something to do with bridges.'

'Bridges indeed,' Lopez selected another savoury.' Hmmm! These are good, too good. I must not have too many or I shall start putting on weight. There are many bridge engineers in the city, many firms have been offering tenders. The government has commenced work on a suburban rail system, you've already seen how congested our roads are, but the nature of the soil and the terrain dictates that much of the system will be above ground.'

'It may well be,' he thought Westerman had said something about a road bridge but his mind was still in a state of panic about Lebak and his group, he couldn't recall exactly what Westerman was. Besides, he was not anxious to pursue the subject nor the acquaintance of Westerman right now. If Westerman's Blimpish facade was in vogue he would condemn Lopez both as a Catholic and a Dago!

'An interesting fellow, not very sure of himself yet an expert in his field,' Lopez pushed a savoury plate out of reach. 'Very unsure of himself, yet tries to hide it by being over forceful, even to the extent of jutting out his jaw. Have you noticed that?'

Van Ekeren glanced at Westerman as he conversed with a Government official, now Lopez mentioned it, he had been aware of that! Similar to a boxer trying to prove he hadn't got a glass jaw. 'You may be right!'

'I *am* right, look at him now,' Van Ekeren turned to see Westerman holding forth aggressively to another, possibly junior, Minister who had joined his group. Yet there was something in his aggressive stance, Van Ekeren couldn't quite define it, which suggested deference.

'He tries to hide his deficiencies under a facade of aggression. Up to a point it works, few would cross swords with him and risk a confrontation. Yet I think he would crumple if they did.'

'Perhaps,' Van Ekeren wasn't keen to pursue the subject.

'He tries to assume a stance of superiority, but if you study him well his facade becomes clear. Not like you, eh? Mr Van Ekeren?'

'You what ...! What do you mean?'

'Forgive me, I am being presumptuous.'

'You are, but since you've got this far, I'm curious to know what you mean.'

Lopez hesitated, aware he was guilty of a transgression. Van Ekeren looked at him levelly, with more curiosity than aggression.

'You are not too sure of yourself either, Mr Van Ekeren, in situations new to you...a not uncommon phenomenon with many of us. But you react differently from your friend over there. You defer and endeavour to remain inconspicuous until you are more certain of your surroundings. Where our friend resorts to aggression, you resort to questions and flashes of humour. There is little aggression in you, it would take a lot to rouse you ...but I wouldn't care to be around when it happens. You dislike confrontations, and many people, I think, underestimate you.'

He paused, nearly helped himself to another savoury, but refrained and pushed the plate away. Van Ekeren said nothing so he continued.

'Yet I prefer somebody like you, in business or as a friend. You think long and hard before you move, though often you may overdo matters and reach a decision too late. To me you present as an honest man, yet you hesitate to say what you think, not from cowardice, but consideration for people's feelings.'

He eyed Van Ekeren quizzically.

'You're not sure of me either, are you, Mr Van Ekeren?'

'I don't follow,' Van Ekeren didn't take kindly to being psychoanalysed, especially as the analysis was near enough to be uncomfortable.

'You have a reserve about dealing with Asians, or Orientals, do you not? You don't altogether trust us, being Australian doesn't help the process I know, maybe we're guilty of not entirely trusting Australians.'

Van Ekeren looked at him in silence, feeling he had been stripped to the bone.

'Try one of these,' Lopez indicated another plate.

'I'm not hungry, I'll see you later,' Van Ekeren said curtly and headed for the toilets. Damn and blast the man! May he rot in hell!

*

When he emerged from the washrooms, he had no immediate desire to re-join Lopez, although he did feel lost without him since he had come as Lopez' guest and Westerman was the only other person he knew. However, Westerman caught sight of him, called him over and introduced him to a grey-haired man who, Van Ekeren gathered, was someone big in the construction and engineering business. He was also big in girth; he must have been about 17 stone. Van Ekeren missed his name, but his hand felt like a piece of blubber.

Westerman was talking in his usual aggressive manner to a Government official, a thin, gaunt looking man whose eyes were alive and intelligent. Van Ekeren smiled as he thought of Westerman's likely comment if he was later asked to describe the man.

Van Ekeren looked up. Lopez was at the other end of the room conversing with a blonde haired European, he seemed engrossed although his eyes did flicker round and engage Van Ekeren's for a second.

'You bastard!' Van Ekeren muttered and commenced a desultory conversation with an official from the Targanese Ministry of Agriculture. He felt angry with Lopez, mainly because what he had inferred had been accurate. Like many Westerners, Van Ekeren knew he did experience some discomfort with Asians or Orientals, especially when conducting business negotiations when differing mind sets of people from other continents tended to be highlighted. Maybe Lopez was resentful of this and had vented his spleen. Whatever the reason he had delivered a rapier thrust through the ribs and Van Ekeren didn't like it, maybe because Lopez had pricked his sense of guilt.

'You like our country?'

'Pardon...oh yes!' Van Ekeren replied absently. 'You have done much work here.'

This polite riposte always went down well, though one had to be careful in case it sounded patronising. This time it went all right, the minor official beamed. He was a spare man, olive skinned and, surprisingly, with blue eyes. They had a few minutes of conversation before there was activity by the door.

'The Prime Minister is here,' the official headed towards the crush near the door and disappeared in the crowd. Van Ekeren found himself with Westerman's weighty friend again who offered him a piece of cake. He politely declined and concentrated on the man who currently led Taranga.

He was a spare, grey haired man, his hair was brushed straight back to, as Van Ekeren discovered later, conceal a small bald patch on his crown. Faces can be divided into cruel, decisive and indifferent. This one fitted into the middle category, there was firmness about the jaw line that suggested De Souza was capable of making hard decisions and sticking to them no matter how unpalatable they may be. He was about 2 inches off six feet, of slim build with a slight hunch to his shoulders.

Van Ekeren eyed him with interest; it wasn't every day he came face to face with a reigning Prime Minister. He was about to turn again to Westerman's engineering friend when a face in De Souza's entourage caught his eye. Van Ekeren turned away, then looked back again as recognition struck him like a blow from a baseball bat. It was one of those who had been present at that nightmarish meeting of Lebak's Revolutionary Council, the little man with rimless glasses whose speech had made clear the real purpose of that meeting to Van Ekeren, the man named Alvaro. He blinked and looked again. It was him, no doubt about that. There was even that little mole on the left cheek and the small pimple on the forehead. A thrill of alarm ran through him as he looked at him ...what the hell was going on?

Lopez caught his eye. He was leaning against the wall looking moodily into his glass. There was a circle of space around him bounded by talking groups. His eyes fastened on Van Ekeren, who felt that Lopez' isolation was self-inflicted so that he could attract his attention. Impulsively he crossed the room; Lopez saw Van Ekeren approaching and turned to fill his glass. He must have known Van Ekeren had been irritated by him and realised he had overstepped the mark. Having calculated all this Van Ekeren approached warily.

'Have a drink, Mr Van Ekeren.'

'No thank you, I prefer to keep my wits about me if I am going to meet a ruling Prime Minister,' his tone was level, but not offensive.

Lopez raised one eyebrow.

'You get used to it,' he said pointedly.

'In a country this size, with such a chequered history it must be difficult to avoid them.'

Lopez nearly choked over his drink and Van Ekeren almost felt the hot retort that was forming. Lopez visibly checked himself and smiled icily.

'Let us not fight, Mr Van Ekeren.'

'Well...' Van Ekeren was about to say something on the lines of '...you started it by being so bloody analytical!' but thought better of it and cooled it. The man was offering an olive branch and it was unfair to berate him after the shock of perceiving one of Lebak's men in the Prime Ministerial entourage.

'I'm sorry,' he said in a conciliatory manner. 'It was my fault, what I said was offensive.'

'Any fault was mine, Mr Van Elderen ...I'm sorry...Van Ekeren,' Lopez sipped his drink.

'Who's that man with De Souza?' asked Van Ekeren.

'Which one?'

'The one he's talking to now, with the rimless glasses.'

'Oh him ...he is Minister of something or other,' Lopez scratched his cheek pensively. 'Something to do with the Security Police Department. His name is...hmm! ... Delgado, something like that...yes that's right, Alvaro Delgado. He is Minister for Internal Security.'

'Internal Secur...?' Van Ekeren paused as another memory came home to roost. '...wait a minute! You mispronounced my name a moment ago, what did you call me?'

'I don't follow you.'

'You called me Van Elderen,' he recalled Lebak's meeting again, a shudder enveloped him together with a cloak of foreboding.

'Did I? Oh yes so I did,' Lopez considered, then nodded. 'I was talking to someone before you came over...that gentleman over there.'

He indicated the blonde man he had previously been talking to.

'Who is he?'

'An electrical engineer. I believe he used to be Superintendent of an Electrical authority in Indonesia and left them some weeks ago; I'm not sure of his present status. Truly a man of power, he once held the electrical grid of Jakarta city in the palm of his hand.'

'He held command of a city power complex...' Van Ekeren's mind began to race. His voice trailed away as everything fitted into place. 'What... what was his name?'

'Van Elderen ...Johannes Van Elderen.'

CHAPTER 13

'Roberto, good to see you.'

'I called you last week, Juan, you are a very busy man. I couldn't get past your outer office.'

De Souza and Lopez clasped hands warmly; they seemed to know each other well and like each other.

'Juan, this is a good friend and colleague of mine, Mr Douglas Van Ekeren. He is from Melbourne in Australia.'

'A pleasure, Mr Van Ekeren,' De Souza's handshake was warm and firm. 'You are indeed fortunate to have a friend like Roberto.'

Van Ekeren, still shell-shocked from recent revelations, murmured something he considered appropriate and was introduced to Mrs De Souza. She was a grey-haired woman of about 50, but she seemed to be very aware of the proximity of any men nearby and knew how to carry herself. She had her hair swept back into a large bun, her face was remarkably free of any lines and her eyes were very alive and questing. She was also very slim and youthful looking. She was aware he was appraising her and raised one eyebrow, which indicated she wasn't averse to receiving appreciative glances, yet also giving the message she was not open to offers. She reminded him forcibly of Mrs Lopez, they were very similar.

'Welcome to our country, Mr Van Ekeren,' she offered her hand. then her eyes slid to one side. 'Good evening, Roberto.'

Lopez raised her hand to his lips and inclined his head gravely. The man certainly had his share of airs and graces.

'Are you here for very long, Mr Van Ekeren?' asked De Souza.

'No sir. Regrettably I leave in the morning.'

'A pity, there are many beautiful spots to visit in our country, have you seen anything of the countryside? Have you seen the Neparto Falls?'

'Neparto Falls?' the description was vaguely familiar, he remembered it was a well- advertised waterfall in the centre of a large natural park, there was a brochure about them in his room. 'No, regrettably I have not. I must return one day to see them.'

He was doing well in the small talk, but conceded he was being well led.

'I wish you could, since you are a friend of Roberto's you have my personal invitation to visit here any time you may wish. Are you married, Mr Van Ekeren?'

'No,' he replied. 'I hope to marry soon.'

If I can get a damned divorce...he thought.

'Excellent, you must both come very soon.'

'You are very hospitable, sir.'

'When you are a leader of a country, however small, it is refreshing to meet people of our own type, who are not making requests or have an ulterior motive. I feel I know you very well, Mr Van Ekeren.'

'Thank you, sir,' he couldn't think of what else to say then inspiration came. 'Being President must be onerous.'

'It is, you never feel you have done enough,' sighed De Souza. 'Sometimes people make their dissatisfaction very clear, possibly they are right.'

'Er ...yes...perhaps,' Van Ekeren thought of Lebak.

'No doubt you meet the same kind of thing within your insurance profession, people are never satisfied. Whatever you do they suspect your motives.'

'Indeed, they do, sir,' he replied, De Souza laughed and Van Ekeren followed suit.

'I wish you well, Mr Van Ekeren,' De Souza smiled and extended his hand. 'I must leave you now; as you will appreciate there are others who expect me to speak with them. It has been a pleasure Mr Van Ekeren...you will return to our country soon, I trust.'

'Indeed, I will, sir.'

The leader and his entourage passed onto the next group. Van Ekeren's eyes followed them as they moved on and grudgingly admitted to himself, he was impressed.

'He seems a good man,' he commented to Lopez as De Souza moved onto the next group.

'He is,' said Lopez. 'It will be disastrous for us all if he ever falls.'

'Is that likely?'

Lopez shrugged then helped himself to a sherry. He became caught up in conversation with another man. Van Ekeren was about to follow suit when a voice said in his ear.

'Good to meet you, who are you?'

He turned, it was the man with the rimless glasses. He nearly dropped his glass as the ends of his fingers went numb.

'You are...?'

'Van...Van Ek...eren,' he began to feel sick.

'Welcome to our country.'

'Th...thank you.'

'I understand you are in the insurance industry?'

'I ...I am, yes,' his hands begin to shake. He felt with every answer he uttered he was digging his own grave a little deeper.

'The Life assurance industry, perhaps?'

'Er ...n...no!'

'Very interesting, insuring one's life, don't you think?' the rimless glasses glinted. 'Life today is full of hazards, is it not?'

'Ye-e-s... yes,' Van Ekeren quavered. He was feeling queasy and his legs were shaking.

'Sometimes we have to take great care to avoid accidents, do we not?' the rimless glasses glinted ominously. 'We decide to avoid them by taking precautions and not doing anything stupid...eh? You understand me?'

'Indeed ...indeeee ...' Van Ekeren's voice died away into a whisper as Delgado moved on. He clenched his teeth as his jaw begin to tremble with fear.

His complexion must have undergone a severe change, for Lopez eyed him with great concern as Delgado departed. Van Ekeren doubted whether Lopez could have heard the exchange as he had been briefly involved in conversation elsewhere.

'Are you feeling all right?'

'Yes' he snapped.

'I'm sorry. I did not mean to be rude.'

He looked contrite, Van Ekeren recovered himself slightly then shook his head.

'No, I'm sorry. I didn't mean it to sound like that. I'm OK! Who did you say that man was?'

'Which man?' Lopez looked puzzled, then his face cleared. 'Oh, you mean Alvaro Delgado, the man you were speaking to just now?'

'Yes.'

'He is the Minister in charge of the Security Division of the National Security Police Force,' Lopez didn't seem keen to pursue the subject. He turned and indicated a man by the door. 'There is somebody you should meet. He is the General Manager of the National Insurance Company.'

'National Insurance Company?'

The resultant introduction and chat were, initially, something of a light relief, he missed half of the conversation as his head was still buzzing after the thinly veiled threat from Delgado. He registered the name of the insurance man, but soon forgot it. The other was a boring individual who spent most of the conversation assuring him the National Insurance Company was financially stable and that Van Ekeren wasn't to believe any wild stories or malicious rumours to the contrary. He repeatedly plugged this so vehemently that Van Ekeren made a mental reservation to check their balance sheet on his return to Melbourne and investigate the possibilities of removing them from any large risk portfolios.

'The Russians and Chinese have great confidence in us,' he said enthusiastically. 'They have invested much in our venture, while the West generally has let us down.'

Probably by insisting on proper underwriting procedures, Van Ekeren thought viciously.

'What is the position of your motor insurance account?' he asked out loud. 'Are you able to run it profitably?'

'What?'

Van Ekeren repeated it; the other man didn't seem to like it and ignored it. He began extolling the virtues of the Russian and Chinese re-insurance underwriters again and Van Ekeren began to lose interest. Lopez stood eyeing the two of them with a cynical smile on his face, then turned on his heel and left.

'You bastard!' Van Ekeren thought furiously and turned again to his tormentor. He was a bald-headed man with a wizened face and an accent difficult to understand, English with a heavy Dutch accent and yet with a Portuguese inflexion. It was impossible to get a word in edgeways as he warmed to his theme and equally impossible to break away.

Van Ekeren backed slowly away but the other followed, they passed through a group of five men in animated conversation, Van Ekeren actually managed to greet one or two of them as they passed through like one galaxy passing through another, but his tormentor was relentless.

They emerged through the other side with their own one-sided conversation and that of the other group continuing unabated. They were heading for Delgado, in the next small group, so he halted abruptly but still the insurance man persisted.

Van Ekeren was fascinated by a small fleck of saliva on the other man's lower lip that stuck to his upper teeth, it stretched and reduced in size as his mouth opened and closed. When his mouth was shut, a rarity, it contracted into a small bubble before stretching out full length again. With his stomach already churning with sheer fright Van Ekeren felt queasy.

He looked around desperately for Lopez, but he was on a phone at the far end of the room. He was eyeing Van Ekeren with an expression difficult to analyse, either sympathy or indifference.

He nearly caught Delgado up, he eyed Van Ekeren stonily as he passed him, but not even Delgado held terrors for Van Ekeren just then, his only aim was to get away from this obnoxious man.

A waiter headed towards them, Van Ekeren tried to gate crash the next group but the waiter gripped his arm.

'No drink for me, thank you.'

That was the last thing he wanted, he would probably bring it straight back up again.

'You are Mr Van Ekeren?'

'Er...yes,' not for the first time that night he wished he wasn't! Damn this wretched insurance man and damn and blast Delgado, as for that bastard Lopez...!

'There is a phone call for you, sir.'

'A phone ...what? For me?' Van Ekeren was incredulous, who on Earth would be phoning him now? But he couldn't care less; this was manna from Heaven and not to be scorned. He excused himself, followed the waiter and was directed to a phone in an alcove.

'Hello!'

'Mr Van Ekeren?' It was Lopez.

'Yes.'

'Meet me by the large flower pot, near where the Prime Minister is now. Do you see it?'

'Yes, I see it. You mean now?'

'As soon as you like.'

He joined Lopez by the flower pot, Lopez smiled as he approached.

'My apologies, it was necessary for you to meet the man, his ability to talk the hind leg off a donkey has not diminished over the years. I gave him ten minutes with you. I trust it did not seem too long.'

'Ten minutes!' Van Ekeren was bitter. 'I thought it was three hours.'

'It was, in fact, fifteen minutes and a few seconds, but I concede it must have felt like hours. But better a brief encounter here than meeting in his office where you couldn't escape.'

'Amen to that!' Van Ekeren broke into a rueful smile.

'You smile — you are relieved?'

'My oath! You're a devious bastard.'

'Am I?' Lopez looked puzzled, then smiled. 'Why yes, I suppose I am.'

'Why did you use the phone?'

'Because if I had come over to rescue you, I would have been caught as well and he would still be battering both our eardrums. People always give precedence to a phone call, even in the middle of a business conference. I extricated you without causing offence to anyone, except perhaps to his next victim, who he has now isolated. See!' Lopez pointed. 'Poor devil!'

Lopez steered him to the centre of the room.

'There are many interesting people here, the Deputy Prime Minister is over there, and also the coach of the national soccer team. I often wonder who is the most important.'

As he led the way over to the two men, he again looked at Van Ekeren with concern.

'You are all right, are you?'

He was about to hotly deny any feelings of ill health, but on reflection decided to admit it.

'No, I'm feeling terrible.'

'Then we shall have quick words with them and depart,' Lopez looked at his watch. 'Tonight, you will be my guest.'

'No really I...'

'My wife insisted, before we left,' Lopez smiled. 'What she says is law.'

He steered Van Ekeren towards the soccer coach. 'A quick word here and then we'll go. At home, we have an abundance of aspirins and stomach pills. You will be far better off staying with us.'

CHAPTER 14

As they left the reception Van Ekeren was feeling decidedly nauseous, a mixture of indigestion, cowardice and panic. The scare inflicted by Delgado and the real Van Elderen had a delayed action, then went to his stomach with a vengeance. Lopez indicated a room allocated for him by Mrs Lopez. He barely had time to ask where the bathroom was, it was an en suite, but reached it before he disgraced himself.

Lopez left him to it, when he finally returned Van Ekeren was sitting on the bed feeling very chastened. He opened the window.

'You are feeling better?'

'A little!'

'Something you ate...or drank perhaps?'

'Perhaps!' It was neither, it had been someone he met but he had qualms about telling Lopez that. He recalled what Westerman had said, if you do have advance warning of a possible coup, who are you to decide who's right? That had resolved him on his course of action, or inaction, although he now experienced misgivings. What side would Lopez be on? For all his sarcasm, his ability to read character and his propensity for rubbing Van Ekeren up the wrong way, he was beginning to like and respect the man.

'I'll see you in the morning, Mr Van Ekeren,' Lopez moved to the door. 'Incidentally I took the liberty of re-booking your flight.'

'You did what?' past resentment initially rose to the fore, but subsided as he realised Lopez had done him a favour, he was in no shape for an early flight. 'Oh...yes...thank you.' Then he had a thought. 'But what about my baggage, I must collect it from the hotel.'

'Have no fears about that, I will organise everything.' Lopez paused by the door. 'HLL Insurances will pay the bill, Melbourne office can settle up with us later.'

Van Ekeren felt the room take a slight spin and then right itself. 'Yes, I'm still feeling a little queasy...' he thought to himself '...I could do with a good night's sleep.'

'Thank you, Mr Lopez,' he said.

'Goodnight Mr Van Ekeren.'

*

He had a rude awakening the next morning. Lopez entered in an agitated fashion with a cup of coffee and said he had heard from the hotel that Van Ekeren's room had been broken into. Van Ekeren still had a slight headache from the night before, due either to fright or alcohol.

He completed a hasty toilet, hastily swallowed a cup of coffee and a couple of Panadols before they departed for the Republican Hotel where they were greeted by the manager. He was in an advanced state of agitation as he led the way to the lift.

'I must apologise on behalf of my country, and my

countrymen,' Lopez had looked furious but was now under control. 'It is unthinkable, you a guest in our country.'

'Don't worry too much,' replied Van Ekeren. 'I had little of real value, no cameras or anything like that. I'll miss my electric razor, if they've taken it, but it was insured.'

'Was it indeed?' Lopez' mouth quirked upwards. 'How fortunate you thought of that.'

'Wasn't it?' Van Ekeren replied. 'I think my insurer is financially stable.'

Lopez smiled and gestured for him to leave the lift first as they arrived on the 5th floor. They strode down the narrow corridor, a uniformed policeman was standing outside the room, suspiciously eyeing anyone who approached. Westerman was outside trying to engage him with small talk... not very successfully. Then he spotted Van Ekeren.

'My God! Doug, old son! Am I glad to see you!' Westerman impulsively shook his hand and then that of Lopez. The barriers were down, the chauvinist facade temporarily disconnected. 'Nobody would tell me anything, I wasn't sure if anything had happened to you, old chap.'

Van Ekeren clapped him on the shoulder, Westerman's genuine concern was moving and he clearly had Van Ekeren's adventure with Lebak and his revolutionaries on his mind.

'I spent the night with Mr Lopez.'

'My God! Lucky for you that you did,' Westerman jerked his head at the guardian constable and the open door of Van Ekeren's room.

'This is a serious matter,' Lopez' tones were icy as the hotel manager quailed before him. 'You say the maid discovered it?'

Van Ekeren had never before seen a man wringing his hands, he had read about it in books, but for the first time he saw somebody actually doing it. The manager was a bald-headed little man with a toothbrush moustache and rimless glasses that reminded Van Ekeren of Delgado, which momentarily caused a flood of adrenalin.

'When she called at the room next door, the maid noticed marks on the door of Mr Van Ekeren's room. She tried the door, it was open. She looked in and saw everything scattered around the room,' he wrung his hands again. 'She is a good girl, honest and has a mother and family to support, she has been here for many years...!'

Lopez cut him short, his objective was to discover what had happened, he wasn't interested in character references for the staff.

'Have you checked Mr Van Ekeren's belongings?'

'We could not ...the Police...!'

'Ah, of course, the Police,' Lopez' tone was still on the cold side but he thawed a little. 'Yes of course. They are here, obviously!'

'They are in there now.'

'Yes, we can see that; then we must see them. Come, Mr Van Ekeren.'

There were three police in the room, a police photographer, a constable and a senior officer. The photographer was packing his equipment away and was on the verge of leaving.

'This is Mr Van Ekeren,' Lopez and the senior policeman shook hands warmly, 'This is Divisional Inspector Hamad.'

Van Ekeren shook hands with Hamad as the photographer left. Hamad was a man of about 5'10", with a large nose and ears and a pointed chin. He had piercing brown eyes which indicated he didn't miss much.

'I want those prints this morning, not next week,' Hamad snapped as he shook Van Ekeren's hand. 'Got that?'

'Yes sir,' the photographer grimaced at the constable as he left.
'Your case and effects are on the bed, Mr Van Eken ...er ...!'
'Ekeren,' interposed Lopez.
'Van Ekeren — I beg your pardon. Would you be good enough to check your belongings, please?'

Van Ekeren did so, to his astonishment little seemed to have been taken. His electric razor was still there, which was a surprise. He looked around and noted the drawers of the small dressing table were open and had been rifled. One of his travelling cases was still standing by the wall, of the other there was no trace.

'Can you say at this stage what's missing?'
He shook his head.
'No, not yet,' he looked at Lopez. 'My razor is still here.'
'No doubt you will claim for it,' Lopez said with an ironic smile and Van Ekeren gave a snort of amusement. Despite the seriousness of the situation that comment struck his funny bone, to two insurance men that was an in joke.

'Of course!' he said emphatically. Lopez permitted himself another smile and turned to Westerman.

'What time is it?'
Westerman told him and Lopez frowned. In the panic, he had left his watch at the house.

'Your plane leaves at 11 am, Mr Van Ekeren,' he said. 'Do you wish to lay a formal complaint against the hotel?'

'A formal complaint? Against the hotel? Good Heavens no!'
'They have a Hoteliers Act here, similar to Australian and British legislation. The hotel is held responsible for the first $209 of each guest's luggage in these circumstances.'

'Why $209?' Westerman asked in a puzzled fashion.
'It is enacted at 1,000 Taranganese guilders, which is what it works out to on the current rate of exchange.'

'What do I have to do?' Van Ekeren asked Lopez.

'Leave it with me. I will deal with the matter, who are your insurers?'

'Sun Alliance Group.'

'A good office,' remarked Lopez. 'I will handle the legal details at this end, I suggest you re-pack your suitcase and be quick about it. I will also deal with the police aspect. Normally they would require a statement and that could take several hours, if not days. Hamad is a friend of mine, I'll fix it.'

'Thank you.'

'I will probably charge you an extortionate handling fee ... say 25%...!' again Lopez gave that rare smile.

'That seems most reasonable,' Van Ekeren replied and they both broke into smiles.

*

Van Ekeren spent time checking his possessions and was puzzled after he had done so. One of his travelling cases was missing, he had brought two with him originally, one being carried in the hold of the aircraft and the smaller one being cabin baggage. Further, some of his clothing had likewise disappeared, yet his electric razor remained as did some other oddments, such as spare cuff links, which he thought a petty thief would snap up.

It could have been worse; clothing items could easily be replaced. He still had some casual clothes in his remaining case which he could wear on the flight back to Australia. Since some of his clothing had been stolen, what he had left could easily fit into his remaining bag, which he could take aboard as cabin baggage. He completed packing, the bag took everything and Van Ekeren had a last look around before he left the room.

Westerman shook hands with him warmly as Van Ekeren

left the hotel; the chauvinistic Blimp façade was still switched off.

'Good to have met you, Doug,' he said. 'I'll look you up in Melbourne sometime.'

'That'll be good,' Van Ekeren replied and meant it. 'How long have you got here?'

'Another five days, then back to Melbourne and the footy.'

Westerman shook hands with Lopez, that handshake also seemed warm and friendly. Deep down Westerman seemed to have taken a liking to Lopez, though no doubt if he subsequently met and conversed with Van Ekeren in Melbourne, Lopez would once more be categorised as an arrogant dago.

The journey to the airport was uneventful; he had a drink with Lopez at the airport bar. The flight was on time and they had 20 minutes before boarding.

'It's been good to meet you, Mr Van Ekeren,' Lopez said. 'I mean that. I trust we may meet again some time.'

'I hope so too,' Van Ekeren replied and also meant it. He thought back to his initial dislike of the man and marvelled at how outlooks could change. As they stood to head for the departure lounge a thought struck him and he caught Lopez' sleeve.

'By the way, who is Julius Lebak?'

'Lebak?' Lopez was startled. 'What a strange question, Mr Van Ekeren. Why do you ask?'

'I...um...heard the name mentioned at the reception last night. Who is he?'

'Lebak?' Lopez pursed his lips as he considered. 'He leads a revolutionary group. He claims to be Left Wing but his actions at times show an utter disregard for those he claims to represent. He is ruthless and completely lacking in finer feelings. He is a rebel leader, an insurgent if you like. If, Heaven forbid, he ever gained control of this country he would be a strong leader...but I suspect he would dispose of all and any opposition, then sell us out.'

'Sell you out?'

'There is a strong movement for us to be incorporated in a larger...country...no names, no pack drill. He is thought to be, no, known to be, receiving cash and arms from them. He is also rumoured to have strong links with China, which is casting covetous eyes at our oil reserves.' Lopez inclined his head on one side and looked around as he delivered this general statement.

'Are you saying his coming would be a disaster?'

'You ask some strange questions, Mr Van Ekeren.'

'I'd like to know...I'm curious.'

'You choose a strange time, too. But we have about 15 minutes so I can fill you in on our chequered politics. Our present ruler, Juan De Souza, is leading us slowly out of the morass of ex-colonialism and the inefficiency and corruption of an oppressive communistic regime. He is humane, but a realist. You have met De Souza, an enlightened man, but he can be tough and there have been occasions when he has *had* to be,' he paused and looked around as if checking whether anyone was in earshot. Nobody was.

'We possess vast oil reserves under the ocean floor near our shores. De Souza is slowly developing it for our own use and for export purposes. Another nation, near to hand, is eyeing these reserves with great interest, or should I say avarice, they want them for themselves, but the oil field does not extend to their current territorial waters. The only way they can gain access is by extending their territorial waters and that can only be by annexing our island nation.'

'Lebak would surrender to this...large neighbour?'

'He would, although surrender is the wrong word for him. He is believed to be part of the scheme of things. If he and his ilk come to power, there is no doubt he would sign a Treaty giving them access, he would sign the oil fields away altogether, he may ...hmmm ...even sign away Taranga as an independent nation. This has happened before in this part of the world, though one takeover has since been reversed, I am referring to East Timor.'

Van Ekeren nodded.

'It is suspected he is beholden to paymasters who will want their reward should he gain control,' continued Lopez. 'Outside paymasters who are paying him for what he is doing and others, within our country now, who also want power.'

'I see,' Van Ekeren turned towards the boarding gate. 'Thank you for telling me.'

'Why do you ask...have you heard something?'

'Taranganese Airways Flight TG 47 is now boarding,' the announcement came over the tannoy system. Van Ekeren hesitated, but time had caught up with him.

'Yes I...!' He hesitated but realised he had to board the aircraft. 'No, nothing, I was just interested, I overheard the name in conversation last night that's all.'

They shook hands again, Lopez gave Van Ekeren a salute and they parted. If that infernal announcement had not come when it had, he would have told Lopez about Lebak, Delgado and Van Elderen and then left Lopez to report it to whoever he felt appropriate. But punctuality, and the strict airline timetable, superseded everything.

As Van Ekeren went towards the entry gate, he looked back. Lopez was walking towards the Airport entrance when he too looked back. They both stood immobile for a few seconds, then Lopez raised one arm. Van Ekeren responded, before Lopez vanished through the revolving doors. With a heavy heart Van Ekeren showed his boarding pass at the loading ramp. The implication of what Lopez had told him was slowly sinking in and he began to perceive by saying nothing he had taken sides.

His thoughts were of Delgado, the despicable Franco and the latter's intentions regarding Lopez' wife Amanda, and his very attractive and vivacious daughter Maria, intentions that Franco would clearly enjoy putting into practice. Van Ekeren experienced the sickening realisation by doing nothing he had chosen the wrong side!

CHAPTER 15

It was a Taranganese Airways aircraft, which operated the route in conjunction with Qantas. He could find little fault with the aircraft or the Flight Attendants. Air Lines are the means by which nations, especially newly emergent ones, demonstrate their status and equality with all other nations. The airlines are made to work, even if nothing else does.

It was noticeable when the British and French were pulling out of Africa, every newly independent nation first of all purchased tanks, military aircraft and warships if they had a coastline. Their next step was to purchase prestigious passenger aircraft for their domestic airline to impress all foreigners, then, if there was any money left after the new rulers had lined their pockets; that would be spent on the welfare of the general population, if they were lucky!

Van Ekeren sat next to a grey-haired gentleman who had a refined English accent.

'McDermott,' the other man extended his hand as Van Ekeren sat down.

'Van Ekeren,' he replied. 'Douglas Van Ekeren.'

'Nice to meet you Doug,' said McDermott. 'Where are you heading? Are you Dutch?'

'Second generation Australian,' Van Ekeren answered. 'I'm from Melbourne.'

It was no surprise to discover during conversation that McDermott was an Australian diplomat on his way home for a session of leave prior to taking up a new appointment. He had just completed a posting to New Delhi where he had been for three years, he mentioned he was hoping for cooler climes.

They chatted in desultory fashion prior to take-off during which time McDermott gave a brief history of himself and his calling. His age was difficult to place, he could have been anything from 45 to 65, his hair was grey flecked with white, his face was lined, presumably from exposure to the sun, but his voice and manner was of a much younger man. He was hoping for a new appointment in Washington DC... seemingly his ambition...which indicated he must have some years yet in the service.

'How was Taranga for you?'

'I wasn't sorry to get away,' Van Ekeren said with perfect truth, glad the subject had come up. He had an urge, after his talk with Lopez, to confide in someone about Taranga and their internal problems. McDermott, with his diplomatic background, seemed as good a sounding board as any. He gave McDermott a general picture of events and the position as Lopez had described it in Taranga, but didn't mention Lebak nor his own inadvertent participation in events.

'A not unusual position,' McDermott sighed. 'So many of these countries fling out the Colonial powers and obtain independence but have no idea where they are going nor what sort of nation they want to be. Often a strong man will take over, but invariably they become infected with delusions of grandeur and assume the trappings of dictatorship. In many cases there are tribal rivalries, with little in hastily written constitutions to stop ambitious men assuming supreme power.'

'Like Nrkumah in Ghana.'

'Exactly like Nrkumah, but there were many far worse than him. Idi Amin springs to mind, and Dr Banda in later years. In Zimbabwe, the British left a democratic constitution but with people like Mugabe who are not democratically inclined and refuse to heed election results it is doomed to failure. When the dictator goes, either by death or revolution, democracy takes over briefly but as the so-called Arab Spring showed, it can be nullified after the first election when the elected government ensures there won't be any more and another dictatorship is born.'

'Who are the combatants in Taranga?'

'From what you say De Souza is typical of those who emerge after a dictatorship is swept away. His type actually emerged initially in Revolutionary France in 1789 and Soviet Russia in 1917. Mirabeau and Kerensky led the way but they were swept away by extremists, which could happen here.'

'Would you say De Souza is the best man for Taranga?'

'I would say yes. In many respects, he reminds me of Cromwell, though certainly not as cruel. There is a Left Winger named Lebak trying to depose the regime, that man would be an utter disaster. He is a fanatical opportunist and Australia strongly believes another nation or piper is calling the tune.'

Van Ekeren sank back deep in thought, the words of the experienced diplomat confirmed what Lopez had said. He was still pondering when he fell asleep.

*

He was woken by a jolt and clutched the seat in alarm. McDermott grinned and pointed through the window.

'We are making an unscheduled stop, I'm not clear why, we haven't been in the air longer than about twenty minutes, we left Taranga behind and then turned back. A garbled message came over the intercom in erratic English. I couldn't make it out.'

The aircraft was circling an airfield on a peninsula; the sun was gleaming off the water, while wisps of cloud drifted into view temporarily blotting out the landing area.

'It seems to be a fertile region,' commented McDermott.' But if we are over the southern coast of Taranga, I have heard this is where they've had trouble with guerrillas.'

'My God!' Van Ekeren felt cold fingers of fear clutch his heart.

'Have no fears, I doubt whether Lebak or any other guerrilla organisation would be able to penetrate the defences if they are prepared to allow an airliner to land,' said McDermott, as he peered through the port. 'Besides, it would hardly suit his image as an alternative government candidate if he destroyed national airline property.'

'Why are we landing?'

A passing steward answered his question.

'We have a minor mechanical defect but it's something easily fixed. It is nothing to be alarmed about.'

Van Ekeren settled deeper into his seat. Didn't they always say that? He hoped the steward was right.

After the aircraft landed the passengers were disembarked and accommodated in the airport building. It was obviously not a main airline establishment, it had a military look with several fighters parked. Inside was a coffee bar which dispensed acceptable coffee. Van Ekeren ordered coffees for himself and McDermott, which they drank slowly while other passengers milled around or sat grumbling. There was some activity around the aircraft, five men were examining the port wing with affected interest, but apart from standing around they didn't seem to be doing much. As he put down his cup he looked keenly at McDermott.

'Are you all right?'

'Somewhat under the weather, I must admit,' McDermott mopped his brow. 'The heat is overpowering; the air conditioning isn't very effective.'

Van Ekeren looked at the ceiling, two large fans were slowly turning, but apart from disturbing the flight patterns of squadrons of flies they had little effect. There were no signs of any other air conditioning equipment.

He looked around the lounge. The passengers were sitting or standing in small groups, the men seemed to be trying to ascertain what the trouble was, or working out the complaints they were going to make when they reached Sydney. The women in the main were either resigned or trying to curb recalcitrant children.

A man who had purchased coffee from the coffee bar was walking through the various groups looking for a place to sit. He made his way towards them. Van Ekeren assumed he was Australian as he wore a loud coloured shirt, shorts and knee socks.

'G'day,' he said cheerily, confirming Van Ekeren's analysis of his nationality as he put down his cup. 'Mind if I join you?'

He didn't wait for acquiescence; but plonked himself down and nodded cheerfully to the two of them.

'Bloody nuisance this, any idea what it's all about?' he asked

'They seem to be doing something to the port wing; the

flight attendant told us it was a small defect,' Van Ekeren inclined his head towards the window through which they could see the aircraft.

'I don't give a shit what they say, they're doing bugger all,' announced their new companion.

'They must be doing something,' said McDermott mildly, still looking a bit green.

'Pigs arse they are,' grunted their new friend. 'All they've done is remove one of the plates, peer inside and then chat amongst themselves. I ought to know, I'm an aircraft mechanic at Sydney Airport.'

'Surely, they must be correcting something,' McDermott said in mild protest.

'Really?' Van Ekeren experienced a sudden tremor in his stomach as he looked at their new companion. 'Are you sure about that?'

'Quite sure,' he said. 'If you're looking for something you don't take an inspection hatch off three times and then put it back again and do bugger all except chat amongst yourselves while it's off. If a part had to be replaced, we'd have seen something arrive, and from my observations, nothing has.'

'Maybe the pilot has his own drink cabinet there,' suggested McDermott.

'Maybe,' the air mechanic grinned and sipped his coffee. 'My name is Driscoll, by the way, Bill Driscoll.' He extended his hand to both of them.

'My name is Doug,' said Van Ekeren. 'This is Mr McDermott.'

'Alistair...Alistair McDermott.'

'Hallo Doug, hallo Al,' Driscoll said cheerily as McDermott winced at the abbreviation. 'Where you heading?'

'Sydney.'

Driscoll was irrepressible; he asked all sorts of innocuous

questions and gave them a potted life history. They had a slight respite when he rose to fetch more coffee.

'How much longer do you think?' asked McDermott.

'God knows!' Van Ekeren answered. 'Here...are you OK?'

'No!' McDermott clutched the table with both hands. 'This heat is getting to me and I feel crook...bloody crook!'

The use of an expletive, so foreign to him, emphasised how bad he must be feeling.

'Do you feel like a walk outside?' Van Ekeren asked. 'It might be cooler out there, or at least the air will be fresher.'

'Good idea.'

Van Ekeren took his arm; he seemed to have gone grey. Driscoll came back from the coffee dispenser, put down the coffee cups and gave him a hand. They assisted him to the door where there was an armed guard. He eyed them quizzically, but Driscoll spoke to him in his own language and he seemed to accept it.

'What did you tell him?'

'I said we were part of the inspection team and that Al here was the Departmental head,' said Driscoll. 'If we'd said Al was crook, we might have run into transit problems, quarantine and all that. They can be a bit sensitive about anything to do with illness on flights.'

'Oh!' Van Ekeren felt uneasy about lying to Authority, even, as in this case, junior members of the military.

'That gun looked loaded,' McDermott remarked as they paused briefly for him to get his breath.

'It was!' commented Driscoll. They had walked some distance from the building and were approaching the aircraft. He started pointing to the underside of the wing, turned to McDermott and began making exaggerated gestures.

'Just ignore me, I'm trying to build up some atmosphere

to look official, an alibi to justify us being outside the air terminal building,' he grinned broadly. 'They've had guerrilla troubles here. Some of us came here a few months back, there was trouble with a Qantas jet. We were sent over as we didn't want those blokes buggering it up. I remember we heard rifle fire in the hills while we were working.'

'I can hear rifle fire now,' said McDermott.

'So can I.'

They stopped and listened, something was going on in the distant hills.

'Probably shooting crows,' retorted Driscoll. 'They do a lot of that. They pay a bounty for every ten they shoot.'

'Bloody hell, it's getting hotter by the minute,' said Van Ekeren.

'To hell with this, Al isn't looking too good. Let's get him back on the plane,' snapped Driscoll. 'Leave this to me.'

'But they may not allow it,' protested McDermott.

'They will if you look the part, but who said we were going to ask?' Driscoll retorted with a broad grin. 'Just straighten up and look like aircraft inspectors.'

'But I can't ...' Van Ekeren protested. 'What if they stop us?'

'I'll do the talking, if we fail, then we've tried!' grinned Driscoll. 'Are we bloody Australians or are we not?'

'We are indeed!' McDermott perked up a little.

'Then rules are made to be broken, just look interested when I point at the underside of the aircraft, maybe do a bit of pointing yourself! Look as if you've noticed something and I'll jot down a few squiggles in my notebook. OK? Now...follow me.'

Such was his air of authority they did just that without question. They walked around the group who were examining the wing, Driscoll paused and exchanged words with a couple of them and pointed up into the open patch on the wing. There was chatter and laughter, some backslapping, then Driscoll came back to them.

'Bloody odd,' he said. 'They said they'd just been told to remove the plate and hang about, seems screwy to me. Anyway, that's not our worry. Our job is to get Al back on the plane where it's cooler.'

They walked around the aircraft away from the group, Driscoll occasionally indicated the underside of the fuselage, and obviously expected Van Ekeren and McDermott to look interested, while he fastidiously jotted down notes with his ball point pen. A ramp led out from the rear door near the tail, Driscoll calmly mounted the steps, climbed aboard and the other two followed. No flight attendants were in evidence, they made their way to their seats and sat down. Driscoll sat with them, Van Ekeren was glad of that as they needed him to explain what they were doing there if anyone challenged them.

'Feeling better now?' Driscoll asked McDermott.

'Yes, much better, it's certainly cooler here even though the air conditioning isn't fully operational.' McDermott turned to Van Ekeren and smiled. 'I think the illegality of Mr Driscoll's approach released enough adrenalin to eliminate my nausea.'

They had been chatting for about 15 minutes when Driscoll peered through the port.

'What *is* going on over there? They seem to be vetting the passengers.'

The other two had a look, he was right. They could see guards checking papers. From what Van Ekeren could see of them they were not regular Army, nor the ordinary police force members as the uniforms looked different.

'Who are they?' asked Van Ekeren.

'I've seen those uniforms before,' said Driscoll. 'Blokes dressed like that vetted us when we were here fixing that

Qantas aircraft some months back. They're something to do with internal security, security police if you like.'

'Maybe we should go down,' Van Ekeren's respect for authority taking precedence.

'Bollocks to that!' Driscoll said heatedly. 'Here I am and here I stay. If they want to look at my papers they can come here and do it.'

'I tend to agree,' McDermott settled deeper into his seat. 'I'm comfortable and cool and mean to stay that way.'

'You can go if you like,' Driscoll said dismissively.

'No thanks!' Van Ekeren replied. 'I've got to stay here and check on you two.'

So, they stayed and eventually all the other passengers, looking hot and bothered, clambered aboard again. They did not look pleased. The presence of the trio didn't appear to be noticed by the airline staff, passengers came aboard and sat down in their seats before any flight attendants came near, when they had done that nobody could have said whether anyone had already been on board or not.

*

The aircraft had been flying for about two hours when McDermott awoke with a start, stretched and yawned.

'Where are we?'

Van Ekeren peered through the port but all he could see was sea, with a smudge on the horizon that could have been land or a cloud bank. Below he saw a white feather on the water denoting a ship's wake, the size of the ship wasn't easy to judge.

'Somewhere over the Timor Sea, I'd say,' he replied. 'Maybe they can see Australia from the other side of the aircraft.'

'Good, I'll be glad to be home again,' said McDermott. 'I wonder what we stopped for.'

'Your guess is as good as mine,' Van Ekeren peered through

the port but could see nothing of interest. 'It was very strange, though.'

'Another strange thing is we seem to have accumulated another passenger.'

'Have we?'

'That man in the front row of the seats on the right,' McDermott jabbed his index finger in that general direction. 'That seat wasn't occupied when we left Taranga City. He's probably Taranganese, perhaps from the East Indies area, could even be southern European at a guess. He's walked up and down the aisle a couple of times, seemed very inquisitive.'

'He probably went to the toilet.'

'Well he appeared to be looking closely at every passenger when he went in both directions as though he was checking everybody,' said McDermott. 'He certainly boarded the aircraft when we made that unscheduled stop. That seat, two rows up, was definitely empty when we originally took off.'

'Maybe he missed it at Taranga City.'

'Which again raises the question, was the stop really for a defect, was it scheduled, or was it official? If it was official, could it have been for that fellow?'

'Maybe he's an engineer or mechanic,' suggested Van Ekeren.

'But Driscoll said there was no defect and though in normal circumstances he's the type of man I'd avoid like the plague, I'm inclined to believe there wouldn't be much about aircraft maintenance he wouldn't know,' McDermott looked puzzled and ran his hand through his hair. 'It appears there was no damage or work carried out worth speaking of, yet we make an unscheduled stop ostensibly because of a defect and pick up another passenger. Very odd'

'Which makes it contrived . . . yes I agree. It is very odd.'

'Well, it'll all be the same in 100 years.'

'Quite so,' Van Ekeren dismissed the matter from his mind and fell asleep.

*

On arrival at Sydney Airport he shook hands with McDermott and had a short conversation with Bill Driscoll before passing through Customs. The Taranganese man headed for Customs and since Van Ekeren had no baggage in the hold he headed straight for Customs as well.

McDermott's luggage received no more than a cursory look and after they made their farewells, he made his way through the door and disappeared. Van Ekeren turned his case so the 'Regular Flier' plastic tabs showed, the Customs man fingered it, then nodded and waved him through. He passed into the crowded lobby where it seemed half the population of Southern Europe was awaiting a sight of their relatives. He saw Driscoll's back as he headed purposefully for the upper level and the bar, but McDermott had vanished. The Taranganese was leaning against a pillar, he was speaking into a mobile phone with a single bag at his feet.

'Cab sir?'

'Cab? Oh yes, I'm catching a flight to Melbourne early tomorrow morning. I'm staying at the Grand Hotel overnight.'

Another man materialised at his elbow, he looked like a hotel porter, like the cabby he was presumably another of the many Indians or Fijians who were moving into the Australian melting pot.

'Carry your bag, sir?'

'Yes.'

'Leave it to me, sir,' he seized the case and made his way through the crowd.

'Wait a minute!' the transaction had been so abrupt Van Ekeren wondered if he was a bag snatcher.

'Sir?'

'Where are you taking that?'

'The taxi rank, sir, there's a cab waiting.'

He had never before had so many offers of a cab when arriving at the airport. Normally it was a case of waiting in a long queue or joining a scrum.

'I want the Grand Hotel.'

'Good as done, sir!'

Van Ekeren was ushered out by the porter and another man who waved to a cruising cab that passed by the queue of taxies and drew up before them.

'Wait a minute, shouldn't we have used that one over there...?' the expression of the driver in the first cab on the rank expressed similar emotions. He leant out of his window and shouted something, Van Ekeren didn't catch it all but it seemed to be an enquiry as to what was happening, expressed in forceful terms.

The moving cab drew up and Van Ekeren was ushered across to it, the door opened and he found himself inside it.

'Grand Hotel in Pitt Street,' he said.

The driver, an Asian, revved up and the cab took off, then suddenly ground to a halt.

'What the blazes have you stopped for?'

'Sorry sir, a dog'

'What? A dog...here?'

The offside door opened and the Taranganese climbed in, followed by the porter and the first man who had offered him the cab.

'What the hell? This cab is taken.'

'So are you, Mr Van Ekeren,' said the Taranganese and something hard jabbed into his ribs. 'Say nothing, and don't move. We don't want any accidents, do we?'

'Who the hell are you?'

'My name would mean nothing to you, just keep still and keep quiet. I become very nervous when there is noise or sudden movements.'

The cab turned into the mainstream of traffic. Van Ekeren became grimly aware he'd been kidnapped in broad daylight.

CHAPTER 16

'What the bloody hell is going on?' Van Ekeren was reduced to spluttering indignation, 'You can't hi-jack people in the middle of Sydney.'

'We can, and we have,' was the quiet reply from the Taranganese. 'I think you have a very good idea of what's going on, Mr Van Elderen.'

The Taranganese was looking at him pointedly as he uttered the name 'Van Elderen', which caused his resistance to collapse completely.

'What do you want?'

'A chat, Mr Van Ekeren,' he looked out of the window. They were on the main highway to Sydney. 'Plus...the pleasure of your company for a spell, shall we say for a few weeks?'

'Few weeks...!' Van Ekeren began to splutter again. 'I shall be missed; people will know I arrived at Sydney Airport...I'm being met at Tullamarine.'

'You were, all that has been taken care of,' the Taranganese responded. 'So...let us hear no more about it...eh? And please don't make any sudden movements; they may be your last.'

Silence fell as the car gathered momentum. Van Ekeren saw a police car in the mirror and had the wild hope they may stop the car for some infringement, but the driver thought so too and throttled back within the speed limit. Van Ekeren wondered if it would be possible to leap out of the car when they reached the Sydney streets, but that hope was dashed when the vehicle turned away from the main conurbation. They were on a freeway and were heading in a southerly direction, which in the long run could mean Melbourne.

'Where are you taking me?'

As a conversational gambit, it was not a success. His captor brought his hand across his face in a blow that almost stunned him and knocked him across the man sitting on his other side, who had posed as a porter.

'You'll find out, Mr Van Ekeren,' his voice was soft and menacing. 'No more questions!'

Van Ekeren sat with his hands over his face, the blow had been vicious and his eyes were watering with pain and anger. What were they intending to do, kill him? His entrails curled at the thought and he started to pass out from sheer panic. With a supreme effort of will he countermanded it and the symptoms slowly dissipated. What had the man said? It had been something about having the pleasure of his company for some weeks. Why weeks? What was that date mentioned at that meeting he had gate crashed? The 24th? That was...yes...that was three weeks from now, that was the date of the coup d'état.

There was nothing he could do, the other occupants of the car seemed to be types used to violence who would not hesitate to resort to it. He cast a sidelong glance at the Taranganese, he could also briefly see his features in the driving mirror when the vehicle negotiated righthand bends. His face was expressionless but there was an element of cruelty.

Van Ekeren thought of Lopez when he had given his views on the opposition to De Souza, it slowly dawned that by keeping silent he had assisted the insurgents. He had few doubts now who was the wrong side. Anyone who kidnapped Australian nationals when they got in the way and then struck a helpless man could not be considered the 'right' side.

What could he do? Escape for now was out of the question. He was wedged solidly between two characters who were clearly what could be termed...enforcers. Did they intend to merely restrain him for the prescribed necessary weeks, or would he be ...? Van Ekeren shuddered as a mental picture of the despicable Franco came to mind. His solution appeared to be to maim or kill people, would his present captors be any different?

There was logic in keeping him incommunicado until the coup. When it was over, why bother to keep him or even kill him? They would then be the regime, the masters and presumably the Australian government would be negotiating with them.

As he wrestled with the problem, he caught a glimpse of his tormentor again as the vehicle swung round another bend. He was slightly tanned, or maybe of olive complexion, had brown eyes and a small moustache, with a small scar on his cheek. When Van Ekeren thought about it, something about him suggested the European more than the Asian, while his accented English sounded something other than the accent produced by Taranganese nationals when they spoke English. The man on the left was pale skinned, but he had the look of an Islander. The driver he could not place for sure, he could only see the back of his head, but he seemed Asian and could be Indonesian or Sri Lankan.

His mind ran riot as the road stretched out before them, he alternated between three weeks in captivity that may not be so bad, and summary execution that was. He wasn't sure what happened after that, subsequently he liked to think he fell asleep from fatigue, but on sober reflection was inclined to believe he fainted from sheer fright.

*

He came to with a start, the road was lined with tall trees and they were parked behind a van on one of those wayside halts plentiful in Australia. When people travelled up to 600 kilometres a day, they needed stopping places off the road for refreshment and bodily relief. In many cases barbecue facilities were provided which, surprisingly in these days of vandalism, usually remained unscathed. Vandals probably didn't feel the necessity to venture far out into the country areas to smash things up when there was so much to defile and denigrate in the cities and suburbs, like bus stop shelters and phone booths.

The Taranganese was outside arguing with another man who must be the van driver. The Islander was still sitting next to him, any ideas he may have had of leaping out and making a dash for it were negated by a hard object jammed into his ribs. The Taranganese, if indeed that was what he was, was smoking a small cigar and smoke was trailing thinly through his nostrils. They settled their differences and the other man opened the rear door of the van.

'Out!' Van Ekeren did not feel disposed to argue. But as soon as he hit the ground he became completely disorientated, the earth rocked beneath his feet and his stomach did what it had threatened since he had woken up. He threw up and spattered the shoes of the Taranganese and the lower part of his trousers.

'Mierda!' he snarled furiously and hastily backed off while the van driver roared with laughter.

'You can travel alone in the car, Juan!' he said.

Van Ekeren threw up again, but Juan was out of range. Vomiting made him feel better, even more so since by puking over Juan's shoes he could not help feeling he had scored. The mess his vomit had made of them went a long way to repaying Juan for that backhander.

'We'll see you at the house,' Juan snapped angrily. He didn't look pleased, probably because the other had uttered his name. But that was immaterial now. His exclamation had identified his nationality to Van Ekeren who had some knowledge of European languages and nomenclature. He was a Spaniard.

'I'll take the northern route,' said the van driver.

Van Ekeren was shepherded into the back of the van; the door was slammed shut and something was flung in after him that looked like his suitcase. It was pitch black in the back of the van so he was unable to ascertain what it was. There was a sudden jolt as they set off again.

*

Van Ekeren had read many books on World history, he was well aware of the millions spent in ages past and the present day on instruments of torture. After his experience, moving from that wayside halt to his eventual destination, he could categorically state that all money spent for time immemorial on torture had been largely wasted. All that was needed to reduce prisoners or victims to a state of acquiescence was a fast driver, an Australian road in need of maintenance and a windowless van with suspension in need of servicing.

Having reached a regular pace, the driver set out to hit every bump and ridge between Sydney and Perth. Van Ekeren was flung from side to side of the van, once he hit the roof when the van went over what felt like a hump backed bridge. He bounced from one side of the van to the other and from front to back.

He developed a splitting headache with the incessant drumming, his stomach revolted and threw up its contents, mercifully lacking in quantity since he had previously deposited most of it onto Juan's shoes. He bounced and rolled through his puke, slid forwards and backwards, with no warning of turns to right or left. When the van eventually came to a halt he had never ever felt as ill and miserable as he did then. If he'd any secrets to divulge, he would have cheerfully blabbed out everything he knew and anything he didn't, anything to avoid further exposure to the driver, the van and the road.

The driver and the Sri Lankan ushered him out into some trees, he thought his last moment had come but they were actually being considerate, they had stopped for him to empty his bladder which unlike his stomach was full to capacity. It was a great relief, he walked up and down revelling in the fresh air before they shut him up in the van and started off again. This time the ride was smoother; the driver must have seen his condition and took pity on him. In addition, progress was not so unpleasant in that the Sri Lankan had looked into the back of the van and had swilled down the interior with a bucket of water. Like many wayside stops, this one had a tap and running water. True, he now had a wet floor to contend with, but better water than vomit.

As they journeyed on, he thought about his predicament. It seemed with the knowledge he possessed he had to be held incommunicado for at least three weeks. But where were they taking him? It seemed to be a long trip from the Sydney area, they could be anywhere in the centre of New South Wales, maybe heading south for Victoria or south west for South Australia. He tried placing his eye against the crack between the two rear doors to ascertain his whereabouts, but with the bumps in the road it was a hazardous undertaking. All he could make out was the majority of overtaking vehicles had New South Wales number plates. But it was becoming darker outside, soon the restricted view of number plates would not be possible, maybe the next morning he could try again.

There was another stop in the dark, the van drew up a long way from the road and the Sri Lankan took the precaution of securing Van Ekeren to him by means of a rope around his wrists that prohibited any thoughts he may have had of making a run for it. Again, he had a very full bladder; the length of time he stood there in full stream caused the van driver to make some comment which made the Sri Lankan grin in acknowledgement. At the time Van Ekeren totally failed to see the joke, but in later days was able to smile about it. It was one of the stock jokes frequently exchanged in gents' urinals.

The van set off again and Van Ekeren settled himself in the front corner of the van, wedged into the corner by his travelling case, for that was what it was. He was so weary and fuzzy headed by this time that he fell asleep.

*

His demeanour on waking was not good, in fact if he had ever felt worse in his life he could not recall when! His stomach was empty, probably a blessing, his head ached and he felt dizzy. He rolled over and peered through the crack between the rear doors. It was still dim outside, the road stretched out behind as the van continued on.

A car was coming up in the distance, he strained to see the number plate and register its colour. He caught a glimpse of the plate on another car that flashed past in the opposite direction, it looked green and white. That could indicate either Victoria or Queensland. The car coming up from the rear had a yellow and black plate which indicated New South Wales. Difficult to say where they were, possibly still in New South Wales, perhaps near either the Queensland or Victorian border.

He tried to estimate how far they would have travelled, at a rough guess about 160 kilometres from Sydney, maybe more. He drew a deep breath, he was ravenously hungry, but thankfully didn't feel any nausea. The human body will eventually accept adverse conditions, a few days at sea and most stomachs become acclimatised to the heaviest motion and seasickness recedes, similarly with a bumpy road and a van.

They stopped for lunch, of sorts, in a woody clearing just off the road. He did entertain thoughts of making a break for it, but they were ahead of him and roped him to a tree. He was furious at the indignity but they took no notice, he actually felt his pride was salved when the van driver fingered a pistol throughout the meal and occasionally aimed it at him to reinforce the point. He vastly preferred to have his movements restricted by the threat of a loaded gun than being tethered like a goat.

They performed their toilet, again he was rendered immobile by having his feet hobbled, but this time a request for a sojourn behind a hedge was genuine, he could not have run for it to save his life.

He was locked up in the van again and it set off. Despite the rough motion and the inability to focus his eyes on anything, his stomach retained its contents and completed the process of digestion. He kept his eyes glued to the crack in the van's rear but still the passing number plates denoted New South Wales.

*

He awoke to a rumbling and vibrating noise, the van shook

and rattled and his teeth jarred in his head. He made his way
to his vantage point and peered through the crack. They were
traversing a narrow bridge, behind the van a single line railway
track stretched out. He was still trying to work it out when the
van left the bridge and hit the road again. The railway line
curved off and ran to the left where it ran parallel to the road.
He caught sight of a board bearing the caption 'New South
Wales' which indicated they had just left it and were in another
state. Which one? Van Ekeren's guess was Victoria, the bridge
indicated a river that must be, surely could only be, the River
Murray. He knew of various crossings where road and railway
shared the bridge. The bridge connecting Moama and Echuca
was one river crossing where this phenomenon prevailed but
where were the others? Was there a railway crossing at Mildura?
What about Swan Hill? But this certainly wasn't Swan Hill.

There were thus four possibilities as far as he could see,
Echuca was one and others were Mulwala and Yarrawonga,
with Tocumwal being another choice. He racked his brains
to work out which was nearest to Sydney, he had a feeling it
was Mulwala but there couldn't be much in it. The town was
unidentifiable since most Australian country towns looked
much the same with wide streets lined by shops with canopies
over the pavements.

As they ambled through the main street, he caught sight
of a sign post over the intersection they had just crossed, the
arrow pointed to the left and said 'Cohuna'. Then they were
through the town and he found he was contemplating the
green and white, and white on black number plates of Victoria.
He sat cross-legged and thought, and thrust his back against
the side of the van for support. That confirmed it. He knew
which state he was in now, and roughly where he was. They
had just passed through Echuca.

The information was currently of little help, though it may be later on. As the van bumped through the suburban areas of Echuca on the highway and then onwards into the countryside beyond, Van Ekeren again pondered on the possibility of escape.

*

After an eternity, during which he alternately slept, felt sick, dizzy, hungry and suffered bladder discomfort, they left the road and headed up a track. It was not well used, though there were wheel marks on the gravel. There were bushes on each side of the track, they finally swung in a semi-circle with the road still in view in the distance, and halted with a scream of brakes. Van Ekeren skidded up to the driver's cab end and fell flat on his back. The door of the cab slammed, there were footsteps outside followed by scraping noises as the rear door opened and he was blinded by sunlight.

They were at their destination. He had time to see it was an older style house standing in its own grounds, there was the inevitable corrugated iron roof and a large veranda and porch. At a guess, the house was about 25 squares on the ground floor, with an upper storey.

He was hustled into the house and upstairs, he caught sight of three other people as he was pushed and shoved upwards and was directed forcibly along the landing towards a room at the end. The Sri Lankan gave him a shove and he was precipitated onto a bed. He was left to contemplate the luxury of lying on a bed that was stationary and not bumping about, in a room that had a window and a view, but with bars on the outside. In the corner of the room was another door, he tested it and it gave easily. He found a small room containing a diminutive wash-hand basin.

He moved over to it, unzipped his flies and with an 'Aaaah!'

of satisfaction relieved the pressure on his bladder. The fact that he may later have to wash his face in that basin was of no consequence at the time. He ran the taps and swilled the bowl. Then he lay back on the bed, revelling in the fact it was standing still, before he fell into a deep sleep.

CHAPTER 17

He awoke with the sun streaming through the barred window, despite his predicament it was comforting to know the sun still shone in his direction. He made his way to the wash-hand basin and rubbed soap and water over his face, with no qualms when he remembered what he had used the basin for the previous evening. He also cleaned the toe cap of one of his shoes that bore evidence of his queasy stomach on one side. He returned to the bedroom and was startled to see his travelling case standing by the door. He lifted it onto the bed and opened it to check, sure enough, it *was* his.

'Surprising,' he muttered. 'I thought they'd steal the bloody thing!'

He rummaged through it, everything was there, even the quarter bottle of whisky he had packed. He debated whether or not to put on a clean shirt, in the present circumstances was there any point in sullying a fresh one? Then he considered that lolling around in a puke stained and smelling shirt was hardly conducive to good morale. He made a complete change and felt better for it. He returned to the washroom and sluiced his old shirt several times under the tap, then hung it over the shower recess.

A key grated in the lock and a man entered bearing a tray. He looked Anglo-Saxon; there was nothing of the Latin or Oriental about him. He set the tray down and departed without a word, maybe that confirmed his Anglo-Saxon status more than anything else. Van Ekeren had no time to feel upset about lack of conversation, he fell onto the tray and consumed everything on it, he even found himself eyeing the serviette and wondering if that was edible. As he ate, it occurred to him the food could be drugged, but he was so ravenous he couldn't care less. The surly Anglo-Saxon entered the room an hour later and collected the tray.

'Where am I?' Van Ekeren demanded; the food had bolstered his courage. His captor didn't answer; he merely removed the tray, stalked to the door, and re-locked it after him.

'Bastard!' Van Ekeren ground out furiously, if the other heard he gave no sign.

His bladder was full again, he re-entered the wash-room and afterwards had a look around. There were no outlets, though the walls and ceiling had possibilities as they sounded like plasterboard. He had a look through the bedroom window, which was not encouraging, the bars and a thick wire mesh looked substantial, he wondered if it had been used as a prison before.

In the distance he could see passing traffic on the road they had arrived by and beyond it a railway track, both about a kilometre distant. There was also the sheen of a watercourse.

He also wondered whether he would ever be let out of the room, without proper toilet facilities this could be awkward.

He tried to calculate how many people were in the house, the food carrier was one he hadn't seen before. There was the van driver, the Sri Lankan and Juan, wherever he was from, at a guess either Spain or South America. He hadn't been seen since the van and the car parted company, but from their parting comments Van Ekeren gathered Juan may re-appear soon. He hoped, maliciously, the puke was still on his shoes.

Two hours later he had meticulously examined every part of the room, apart from the window the door was the only exit. There was a small fanlight in the wash-room, only big enough for a cat. He opened the window and tested the mesh, but the thick wire was solid, it was all he could do to budge it. He gave up and examined the garden below. There was a rockery and a freshly mown lawn. The drive curved around the lawn and headed for the distant road.

As he looked out, a small cloud of dust appeared on the track. As it approached, he saw it was the car in which he had initially been confined, the presumed taxi outside Sydney Airport. Juan was at the wheel; he cornered with a flourish which flung gravel against the wall of the house with his rear tyres. He stalked into the house accompanied by three others, one was a man built like a gorilla.

He heard a buzz of voices down below; it was not easy to gauge where they were coming from but it seemed to be from directly below. He pressed one ear to the floorboards and listened hard, he caught the odd word occasionally but couldn't make any sense of it.

Footsteps sounded on the stairs, he lay on the bed and shut his eyes. He didn't want to be seen taking too close an interest in his surroundings. He heard the door open, opened his eyes and saw Juan standing there, holding a pistol.

'Come, Mr Van Ekeren...or should I say Van Elderen...eh?'

he laughed but there wasn't much humour. 'I'll show you where the toilet is.'

'Look, I've had enough of...!' but this time he saw it coming and ducked, with the lack of contact Juan lost his balance and his shoulder hit the wall. He cursed angrily; Van Ekeren decided silence was the better option.

'The toilet is in this direction. We shall allow you to use it twice a day...no doubt the wash-hand basin in the room will serve you most of the time.'

They walked along a landing, it turned at right angles and had four doors and a window overlooking a hillock at the side of the house. The last door was the toilet, any hopes he had of it being a possible escape route were dashed as the window was the same size as the fanlight in the wash-room.

He examined the landing on the return journey but all the other doors were shut. The stairs led downwards against the wall into a large hall below and he could make out the front door through which he had entered the house. The floor below was tiled, the property looked as though it was the original house of a grazier; the house could have been erected originally in the 1870s, with additional rooms built on over the years. He was escorted back to the room that served as his prison cell and was left to contemplate his fate.

The routine was the same for the next three days, breakfast every day at 7 am, brought in by the surly Anglo-Saxon, whom he mentally christened 'Smiling Morn'. His face never altered from a grim set with the corners of his mouth turned down at the ends, he reminded Van Ekeren of a preacher he used to know who preached hell fire and damnation to his flock, frightening all the old ladies and giving the children nightmares.

Smiling Morn was dressed each morning in old brown trousers and a check shirt, which he changed on the fourth morning. Mid-morning Van Ekeren was escorted to the toilet, an inflexible routine to which, fortunately, his bodily rhythm was able to adjust without too many problems. At midday he had a meagre lunch, again brought by his unsmiling jailer and the plates were removed at about 3 pm. Tea was at 6 pm, after consuming that and after the plates were removed, he was again escorted to the toilet. Then he was left to his own devices until he turned in for the night.

There was a bedroom next door, he heard footsteps climbing the stairs at night, the opening of a door and then the creaking of bed springs. He heard a higher pitched voice and the rumbling low tones of Smiling Morn so it appeared it was his marital bed next door.

On the third day he realised the toilet chain was terminated by a piece of wire that acted as a handle, obviously the original had broken off and was never replaced. On an impulse, he detached the thick piece of wire and tucked it inside his shirt. As a young boy he had attained some notoriety in the local school-yard and neighbourhood for opening doors that were locked, with the primitive and unsophisticated locks usually affixed on house doors this had never been difficult.

On his return to the bedroom he examined his find. He worked on the piece of wire for a spell, inserted the end of it into the bed springs and managed to make a kink or bend at the one end. Then he knelt by the door and inserted the wire into the keyhole.

He found the tumblers immediately, but after ten minutes of probing nothing happened. He was about to give up in despair when he felt the end of the wire grate against something within and felt, more than heard, a click. With rising excitement, he tried the door but it was still locked. His heart sank into his boots but he tried again and felt empty space where previously there had been a tumbler. He inserted the wire again and fished around. This time he found the second tumbler, heard another click and this time the door gave when he turned the handle. His heart beat so loudly he feared they may hear it downstairs.

He peered around the doorpost and saw the empty landing extend before him. He crept out onto the landing, but heard footsteps below. He panicked and scuttled back into his prison cell, but nobody came upstairs. He shut the door and considered his course of action, should he make a run for it or lie doggo? He decided now, with everyone wide awake, was not the ideal time for making a break. But could he lock the door again?

He could not! The realisation nearly made him pass out in his panic. They would find the door unlocked, jump to the conclusion he had made illicit use of the lavatory chain handle and take it from him, rendering him helpless again.

'Bugger it!' he said feelingly after another ineffectual twiddle with the wire. He finally gave up and hid the wire under the wash-hand basin. He discounted hiding it under the mattress, that would be the first place they would look.

Smiling Morn brought his evening meal up at 6 pm, there was a rattle at the door followed by another rattle as he rattled the key in the key hole, the handle turned and the door opened. He looked perplexed, put down the tray and tested the key in the lock. The bolt flashed in and out, he seemed satisfied, shrugged his shoulders, went out and locked the door behind him. Van Ekeren could hardly believe his luck; he was so relieved it must have been two minutes before he attacked the food.

On the fourth day Juan the Spaniard brought up the breakfast tray and leant against the wall while Van Ekeren consumed the tray's contents. He did so cautiously, wondering if it were drugged but it didn't taste any different. Juan watched with a malicious smile, Van Ekeren found time to surreptitiously look down at his toe caps and was afforded some satisfaction, they looked stained and dull. The vomit had done its work.

'You know why you are here, Mr Van Ekeren?'

It seemed pointless to deny it so he briefly nodded before returning his attention to the toast and marmalade. Whatever his criticisms about the prison, he certainly had no complaints about the toast. This seemed to confirm a woman was on the premises.

'You became involved with matters that did not concern you.'

'Yes,' he answered shortly. He felt it inadvisable to be too conversational.

'Which means until we have done what we have to do, you stay here, you understand?'

'Where are we?'

'Australia,' Juan smiled grimly. He did not look too bad when he smiled, but there was a hard turn to his mouth. Perhaps snakes smiled before they bit their victims, Van Ekeren decided he preferred Smiling Morn.

'When will you let me go?'

'I've told you, when the task we have to do is complete.'

He was not a tall man, he was of medium height with what is best described as a long back and sides haircut and a moustache. He was wearing sports slacks, a leather jacket and shoes with crepe soles, often termed brothel creepers. The lines on his face denoted both cruelty and humour; perhaps he laughed when old ladies slipped and fell over or when he was torturing someone. His age was not easy to place, middle thirties seemed a safe bet. He looked lithe, like a cat. He would be a difficult man to catch off guard. There was a bulge in his pocket, Van Ekeren had little doubt what that was and, from past experience, his ability to use it.

'Then you will let me go?'

'Of course.'

'What is your interest, you are not Taranganese?'

Juan tensed, Van Ekeren feared he had gone too far and would be on the receiving end of another backhander. Then Juan shrugged, clearly knowledge of his origins was not important. He certainly had an accent, though his English was good it was discernible, his 'I' sounds tended to come out sometimes sounding like 'ee', his pronunciation when he said '...when the task we have to do is done...' the word 'is' sounded like 'ees'. This seemed to confirm Van Ekeren's diagnosis on the journey in, that Juan was a Spaniard.

'You have feenished?'

There it was again. Van Ekeren nodded and he came over to pick up the tray. There was a mild smell of garlic and of cigars. He walked out, whereupon Smiling Morn appeared briefly and locked the door. He wondered why Juan had brought the meal. Juan? What was a Spaniard doing here? Not much doubt of it now, the furious shout of 'Mierda!' when Van Ekeren had puked over him stamped him as a Spanish speaker. Yet what would a Spaniard be doing in Australia working on behalf of Taranganese dissidents? Van Ekeren shrugged and walked to the window, what difference did it make? He was a bastard!

He heard a car moving down below and the engine note sounded different from those heard so far. A van drew up, parked near the house and two men entered the front door.

He sat on the bed and thought. So far, he had seen four men, presumably in the house on a regular basis. There was Juan, Smiling Morn, together with the Sri Lankan and the van driver. Possibly there was a woman somewhere, judging by the higher voice tones from the room next door and he had sensed a woman's touch on the tray, not only was the toast acceptable but the tray was neatly laid out.

They intended to keep him, so Juan had said, then release him. He thought hard about the possibilities and the more he thought about it the less he liked it.

Taking the two possibilities, firstly the coup succeeded and secondly, the coup failed. With the first scenario, if it succeeded, would he then be released? Despite his hopes it seemed unlikely. Would the new Government want to leave itself open to charges they had forcibly kidnapped and detained an Australian national in his own country? It would cause an uproar that would cause them extreme embarrassment for a considerable time. No Australian Government of any political colour would allow a matter like that to rest, they wouldn't be allowed to as the Press would make a meal of it.

Taking the alternative scenario, what if it failed? Would he then be released? He stood up and paced the floor with thoughts occurring to him that were even less palatable. He could identify certain Government figures who were implicated in the coup, Delgado for one. Possibly there had been others around the table that evening who were, if not government ministers, possibly top Public Servants, military or police. That they were casually and/or untidily dressed he discounted, if Van Ekeren himself had been a government minister or top public servant involved in a proposed coup d'état, he certainly wouldn't roll up to clandestine meetings dressed in a suit and carrying a ministerial brief case.

Then there was Van Elderen, his 'double Dutchman', deeply involved in his capacity as a power expert. If the coup failed, if it didn't get off the ground there was a chance many of the rats wouldn't have fully emerged from their holes when it was snuffed out. Some members would therefore be able to carry on as before without their secret ever coming out. No other coup member would be likely to betray them, by doing so they would either betray themselves as well or, if they were in custody, would prefer to have friends in high places on the outside with influence. That left Douglas Van Ekeren, a foreigner, with possible knowledge of identities of highly placed participants in an abortive coup.

What would a successful or unsuccessful coup leader do in those circumstances with an insignificant foreigner who could identify some of the coup participants? Van Ekeren considered; if he were a member of the conspiracy what he would do. He thought about it and came up with an answer, which he didn't like!

There would be obvious advantages in his permanent disappearance, if he were never seen again there would be nothing to tie him in with subsequent events in Taranga. It would be known that he had reached Sydney Airport, if he vanished after arrival it wouldn't necessarily be traced back to Taranga; he could even be the victim of a mugging that went wrong. His arrival at Sydney Airport would have been recorded, not only by the airline computer system but could also be confirmed by Driscoll and Alastair McDermott. Yet how would they hide...his body ...he felt his toes begin to tingle at the thought of it and his nerves screamed when there was a creak from the ceiling as the beams contracted. They could hide it ...him...in here, yet was there anything in this house to connect it to Taranga?

Who owned the house? Did it belong to Taranga, had they rented it, or did it belong to a Taranganese coup sympathiser, a naturalised ex-citizen over whom they had some hold? Yet who was Smiling Morn? That man was an obvious European and probably British or Australian in origin. Was he the owner of the house? Was he a bankrupt farmer who had leapt at the chance of receiving easy money to pay his rent and rates?

What should he do now, make a break for it? He had the means of opening the door and making his own exit, assuming he could get out of the house. He didn't want to open the door too many times, if Smiling Morn came on his regular visits and found the door unlocked more than once, even he would start to put two and two together. Van Ekeren decided he would have to make his escape that night.

CHAPTER 18

Alan Kelsey, of ASIO Counter Espionage and Anti-Terrorism, looked up as Mike Duval, a younger member of the organisation, entered his room accompanied by a middle aged, grey-haired gentleman. Kelsey proffered his hand which the newcomer shook warmly.

'Thanks Mike,' Kelsey indicated a vacant chair as Duval left the room. 'I'm Alan Kelsey. Please take a seat, Mr McDermott.'

'The name is Alistair,' McDermott sat down. 'It's good of you to see me at short notice.'

'I understand from the Department of Foreign Affairs you had concerns regarding events on a flight from Taranga.'

'That is so,' replied McDermott. 'There was a peculiar occurrence before we left Taranga airspace and another strange event when we arrived in Sydney Airport. Have you seen this morning's newspapers?'

'I have. What particular news item should I be looking at?'

'Let me start at the beginning,' said McDermott. 'I was

until recently Australian High Commissioner at New Delhi. I was returning home and stopped off in Taranga. I spent a couple of nights there with an old friend currently posted to the Australian Embassy in Taranga City.'

'Who is that?'

'Charles Richards, we spent time together in Europe, but that is by the way,' said McDermott. He went on to explain about the flight from Taranga City airport which was followed by the unscheduled stop in Taranga, that the aircraft had left Taranganese airspace but did a U-turn and returned to a military airbase on the island.

'That's unusual. You say there was something even more odd about it?'

'Yes, I accepted the initial explanation that there was a minor defect with the aircraft, like everyone else I had no reason to question it. While we were in the airport buildings, a fellow passenger named Driscoll, insisted nothing was being done to the aircraft.'

'Why should he say that?'

'He said he was an aircraft technician stationed at Sydney Airport. I had already started to feel under the weather with the heat, but I took a turn for the worse, so Driscoll and another passenger named Douglas Van Ekeren decided to take the law into their own hands. They got me back on board the aircraft unofficially as they thought it would be cooler.'

'Nice of them?'

'Yes, we sneaked through a side door and got back on board without being seen by security guards. Driscoll chatted with some of the mechanics en passant, he spoke Dutch and a smattering of the local language and so did this other man Van Ekeren. From what the mechanics told Driscoll, who pretended to be one of the airport technical staff during our unauthorised re-entry, it seemed to confirm there was nothing wrong with the aircraft.'

'So why did they land there?' Kelsey sat up with a jerk. 'Wait a minute...Van Ekeren! That name rings a bell.'

'Yes, it will. Let me continue, I'll come to that.'

'Sorry, go ahead.'

'I spoke with other passengers during the flight and afterwards, they said while they were in the airport building at this temporary stop, they were all vetted closely by security police, passports were examined minutely as were their airline tickets.'

'Strange. Why should they do that?'

'During my stay with Charles Richards at the embassy he gave me some background to the present situation in Taranga. From the description the other passengers gave of these officials who did the vetting, they would definitely have been security police, the political variety, not the ordinary civil constabulary or customs.'

'They were looking for somebody?'

'On reflection that seems a distinct possibility,' McDermott nodded. 'Eventually the passengers were returned to the aircraft and we took off again. The three of us were already on the aircraft all this time and were in our seats when the rest of the passengers returned.'

'Did the authorities find who they were looking for?'

'It didn't appear so, no, from what I was told by other passengers,' McDermott shook his head. 'Everyone came back on board as far as I could see, but there was one additional passenger.'

'What about him?'

'I don't know, he looked olive skinned, possibly Taranganese, possibly southern European, I really don't know. I noticed him because he sat in a previously empty seat two rows ahead of me.'

'This other passenger, his name was Van Ekeren you say?'

'Yes, that was my other point. I got to know Douglas Van Ekeren during the flight, we talked a lot and he asked me many searching questions about the internal politics of Taranga and various other countries, he seemed an interesting fellow. We parted at Sydney Airport and went our separate ways, but I later heard, via newspapers and news bulletins, that Van Ekeren was wanted by the police because he was a suspected drug runner. His case was found on the luggage carousel, it was never collected and contained narcotics.'

'That was what I heard, from newspapers and television.'

'Douglas vanished according to the press, but I must say from my brief acquaintance with him that...well...' McDermott shook his head in perplexity '...he didn't seem ...!'

'They never do,' said Kelsey. 'But this raises another point. Do you think he was the one the security police were looking for?'

'Again, with hindsight, that seems a distinct possibility.'

'Did you see Van Ekeren after disembarking?'

'I saw him board a cab, there was an altercation because the cab in question jumped the queue and the other cabbies were furious. But there was one thing, which didn't register until later when I saw the newspaper reports. Van Ekeren's travelling case was stowed into the taxi by a porter; I saw this clearly as I was also waiting by the cab rank for a government vehicle. It was the one he was carrying as cabin baggage. He never went to the carousel.'

'He had two suitcases?'

'I only ever saw the one and I saw it stowed into the cab before it left. Another thing, that cab didn't look like a cab, it might have been a private hire vehicle.'

'Have you told this to the police?'

'Not yet, I came here first.'

'Why?'

'I don't know,' McDermott shrugged. 'Just a feeling I had, coupled with the presence of security or political police at the unscheduled stop.'

'All right, leave this with us, Alastair. We'll follow it up.'

After McDermott left, Kelsey sat deep in thought, then picked up his phone.

'Can you come in a minute, Bob?'

When Robert Bramble, his deputy, arrived Kelsey motioned him to be seated. He went through the story McDermott had told him.

'What do you reckon, Bob?'

Bramble, a thick set, dark-haired man, rubbed his chin.

'Could be bugger all,' he said. 'But I agree with you and McDermott. It's worth a look.'

'See if you can trace this fellow Driscoll, apparently he's attached to Sydney Airport in the Qantas maintenance area,' said Kelsey. 'We'll see where we go from there.'

*

The rest of the day was uneventful. Lunch came and went and Van Ekeren had his usual walk to the toilet. While there he heard a phone ring nearby, it cut off quickly as it was answered but from the lack of voice reverberations it clearly wasn't answered on the instrument he'd heard ringing. That meant there was an extension in the bedroom next door.

If the exchange name and number was written on the dial, that would supply a clue to the location. On the way back to his prison cell the other door along the corridor was slightly open, inside was a double bed and a bedside table with a phone on it, one of the older style instruments with a dial.

There was a departure from the usual routine for his evening meal which was brought by the Sri Lankan. Whether or not he was from Sri Lanka Van Ekeren never established, but that was how he identified him.

'Hurry up, Tara,' he heard a terse comment from someone, his food bearer had delayed while going over to the window to peer out.

'Get knotted,' Tara replied with spirit as he left. 'I don't take orders from you, De Ryk'.

Tara's response had been addressed to one of the new arrivals. Van Ekeren finished the meal in silence, listened to the buzz of conversation below, then the door opened and Smiling Morn appeared. He took the tray with his usual woebegone expression and stalked out, not missing the knife Van Ekeren had appropriated. There was a muttered confabulation outside, he was talking to somebody but their voices receded as they went downstairs.

Van Ekeren considered his next course of action. To escape he first had to ensure the landing outside stayed in darkness. This meant either removing the light globe or making sure it was a dud. If he removed it altogether his gaolers would know for sure there was some monkey business going on, if it fused then it was just one of those things. Van Ekeren decided to fuse the one in his own room and then swap them over, it may assist any escape bid should the landing be in darkness.

He reached and took out the electric light bulb and shook it hard but the filament in the bulb seemed to be distressingly stable. He raised his eyes skywards, at home one only had to look askance at a light for the filament to come adrift. When you wanted the damned thing to go out of order it seemed to have a constitution of cast iron. He hammered it against the dresser, still the filament didn't dislodge.

'Bugger you, you bastard!' he mouthed furiously and banged it again, but he had to take care not to hit it too hard in case it exploded. He raised it in his hand and shook it hard, finally the filament came adrift.

'About bloody time!' he breathed with satisfaction and stuck it back in its socket while he considered the best time to switch the globes. Maybe now was as good a time as any.

As he picked the lock again his mind wandered. If they were going to dispose of him why hadn't they done it on the road during the long journey from Sydney? Maybe that was too risky; if his body had been discovered too soon and he was identified questions could be asked that linked him with Taranga. They must have made arrangements in a hurry at Sydney, since their original plan had been to pluck him off the plane at the unscheduled stop in Taranga, they hadn't had time to finesse their arrangements. Their plan had been thwarted by the initiative of Driscoll who got the three of them back aboard the aircraft. They probably hadn't had time, or even thought, to include a spade in the van as essential equipment, the hurried change of plan meant they hadn't had time to consider details. He shuddered as he reasoned it out.

Westerman could supply interesting information if he heard of Van Ekeren's fate. Westerman? Would the coup members know that he had confided in Westerman? On the other hand, since plans had obviously been hastily made to kidnap him at Sydney airport, what to do with him next had likely not entered their calculations. If a drastic decision had to be made, involving even more drastic action... he shuddered ...maybe it had to come from higher up.

Why were they keeping him incarcerated? Either to release him when all was over...a contingency he no longer considered likely ...or were they preparing for his permanent disposal to ensure he'd never be found? Sheer panic arose which he quelled with an effort. He needed his wits about him, to surrender to hysteria or pass out from sheer fright would condemn him to death.

Yet his conclusion seemed near the mark. To kill him at the house was hardly advisable if preparations were incomplete. Corpses had a habit of befouling the atmosphere, nothing could be worse than a casual caller, such as a meter reader, stumbling across a murder which might mean the meter reader had to be disposed of as well. A missing meter reader would be followed up, his employers and the police would soon pinpoint the area where he had disappeared. Van Ekeren's stomach started to erupt and he angrily quelled it. The last thing he wanted was to throw up now. He needed his last meal for energy if he was going to make the break.

The lock clicked, he turned the handle, had a hasty look from side to side and made his way onto the landing. He reached up and removed the globe, replaced it with the broken one and re-entered his room. He put the landing one into the room's light socket. He crept to the edge of the balustrade and peered over, three doors opened off the hallway downstairs, two to the left of the stairs and one to the right. The door to the right was open and he could hear voices.

One of the new arrivals left the room below, Van Ekeren gathered he was the man named De Ryk, a vicious looking brute, a big man with his hair line drawn back onto the top of his skull. What hair he had was frizzy indicating he could have native or possibly African ancestry. He tried a door under the stair well and cursed loudly.

'Use the one upstairs, Abbott takes hours when he gets in there.'

Van Ekeren gasped with panic as De Ryk turned and headed

for the foot of the stairs. He was going to use the upstairs toilet. Van Ekeren turned, scampered back and dived into his room. But he had made a mistake, he was in the wrong room! In his haste he had landed in the room with the double bed and the telephone.

He thought he'd try again for his own room, but it was too late. De Ryk was near the top of the stairs. He eased the door shut and tried to get under the bed. It was not high enough.

'Oh! My God! My God!' he rushed across the room to the door and stood behind it hoping he would be hidden if De Ryk entered. He heard him hit the landing and make his way to the toilet with measured tread. The door opened and closed, then there was silence, punctuated a few minutes later by De Ryk breaking wind down the pan with such violence it must have fractured every pipe in the house.

Now was his chance to get back, he was about to open the door when he remembered the telephone, an opportunity to see where the house was located. He checked over the dial, the small label read 'DUM 23'. That meant precisely nothing.

Then it rang! He nearly jumped out of his skin and adrenalin ran through his system from head to toe. It rang twice then stopped. On an impulse he picked up the instrument and placed one hand over the mouthpiece.

'Hello!' it sounded like Juan.

'Hello, this is Claudio. Is that Rivera?'

Juan gave an affirmative grunt.

'Is all well?' he asked.

'Very well at present,' replied Claudio. 'Has De Ryk reached you?'

This elicited another affirmative grunt from Juan.

'Put him on, will you.'

Van Ekeren felt his nerves start to scream again, they

could send somebody up to fetch him, he could take it in the bedroom and there was nowhere to hide. He listened with his other ear and heard yet another violent discharge down the pan that denoted De Ryk was still busy and had probably blasted the Doulton insignia off the earthenware.

'He's not here right now; he should be down in a few minutes.'

'How is Van Ekeren?'

'Quiet and scared,' replied Juan. 'He'll be no trouble'

Van Ekeren found time to experience indignation at that, the nerve of the bastards! His demeanour had been one of lofty disdain since his arrival.

'Well you should be rid of him soon, De Ryk has the box in the van,' there was another affirmative grunt from Juan. 'Make sure it's a long way from the house, and make it deep.'

'Are you teaching me my job?'

'No, no no!' Claudio said hastily. 'But we must be rid of him. He's a danger whatever happens. We shall probably have to dispose of any people with whom he had contact, one of them is on the list anyway.'

'Who is that?'

'That damned Goan Lopez. He is unreliable and well disposed towards the present government. We're sure he put the Australians onto that claim before we could move those rockets and repeating rifles out of the warehouse. That burglary brought those Australian loss adjusters into the picture. A damned coincidence we could have done without.'

'Lopez brought the Australians in to expose us?'

'It's possible. It seems Lopez did have discretion in the matter whether to involve the Australians or not, according to our man on his pay roll. Our man tried to prevent it without success.'

'Hmmm!' was Juan's contribution.

'There's another man Van Ekeren was friendly with, we're not sure who he is but they were seen going to the civil police station together. We don't know why but that damned Inspector Hamad is certainly not one of us, they may have been meeting with him'

'Who was this other man?'

'His name is Weston, or Westman or something like that, he may be a spy and have connections with Inspector Hamad, we must make sure he doesn't survive our takeover. It will not be unusual for foreigners to be shot by accident during a coup...eh Juan?'

They both chuckled heartily, Van Ekeren began to feel sick.

'When will you do the job?'

Van Ekeren felt his hair prickle. Were they back to discussing his execution?

'Tomorrow, we'll take him out in the van.'

'In my position I'd sooner not know the details. I'll be with you tonight anyway. Give me an hour or so. But Van Ekeren, won't he resist?'

'He'll be out like a light, after a hearty breakfast.'

Van Ekeren gently put down the phone and ran for his room, in his haste he forgot De Ryk could easily materialise on the landing outside the toilet door. Luckily, he didn't, he was still busy and emitted audible proof as Van Ekeren scuttled back to his room, closed the door behind him and collapsed on the bed. He nearly passed out and had to thrust his head between his knees to ward it off. Still the light headedness persisted, the back of his neck sweated and his stomach began to join the act, but persistent pushing of his head between his knees brought slow relief. He gritted his teeth furiously, now was not the time to pass out, he needed every moment of consciousness he could muster.

There was no doubt he had to break out tonight, they had just pronounced his death sentence, and similar sentences on Lopez and Westerman.

CHAPTER 19

It was pitch dark outside and Van Ekeren trembled with impatience and anticipation and viewed the stars in the sky with mixed feelings. If he was going to reach the outside and make a successful escape, he wanted it pitch black out there. He could hear movement below, twice footsteps came upstairs, the second time he heard a muttered curse from below as the light failed to come on.

Heavy footfalls paused outside the door, he froze with horror at the thought that someone may enter his room. Whoever it was stood there for some seconds, then broke wind on a low key which slowly rose as he ran out of pressure, it must be De Ryk. There was a click and the thin line of light under the door indicated they had replaced the light globe. He sat back in exasperation, all his effort in changing over the light globes had been a waste of time. Or had it? The exercise had enabled him to accumulate useful information which could have saved his life. De Ryk entered the next room; he was only a few minutes then left and went downstairs again.

'Bastard!' he muttered but after reflection concluded it didn't affect matters overmuch. He could ensure the landing remained in darkness when he made his break by simply removing the globe again, if he got away it wouldn't matter whether they noticed its absence or not.

The noise downstairs recurred, the buzz of conversation became more distinct, followed by more footsteps on the stairs. Somebody said something and didn't sound too happy so he assumed it was Smiling Morn. He also heard a woman's voice, a harsh nagging voice which explained why he looked so miserable. It seemed they were going to bed in the bedroom next door. Van Ekeren had usually been asleep by this time, trying to drown out horrific thoughts in his mind by slumber, so although he'd made an educated guess, he hadn't been absolutely sure whose room it was...with De Ryk's propensity for flatulence he was glad it wasn't his.

'...never told me it would come to this sort of thing, I'm just not happy ...!' Smiling Morn said mournfully, then it died away to a confused mumble.

'You should have thought of that,' the shriller female voice carried further and reached Van Ekeren clear as a bell. 'You were tempted by the money, you and your damned gambling!'

It seemed Abbott (Smiling Morn) and his wife were not enthused about the way things were going. Maybe they had some inkling matters were going beyond the question of merely receiving rent from foreign nationals and now realised there was a possibility of misdemeanours or even murder being committed. Van Ekeren wondered how they had become involved but clearly money was the key.

He waited impatiently for them to settle, the bed creaked

noisily as though an elephant was jumping on it, he wondered how big Mrs Abbott was. He had never been so aware of their next-door presence before, although this was the first time he'd had his ear pressed against the wash-room wall. Usually he would have been lying on the bed on the other side of his prison.

Abbott did much pacing up and down the room, maybe he had to steel himself before committing the irrevocable act of climbing into bed with her. A shrill command brought about an answering complaining rumble from him, which brought an angry squawk from his spouse. Maybe he had landed on top of her. As they sorted themselves out Van Ekeren walked to the door, applied his eye to the crack between door and jamb and prised it open a fraction. The landing was in darkness apart from a glimmer from downstairs.

It was darker outside, the stars showed as pinpoints, he had no idea of time but it must be about 10.00 pm or later. He returned to his vigil within the wash-room, the creaking in the next room was continuing. They were either still jockeying for position or else she was pursuing Abbott around the bed, with a voice like that he couldn't imagine any man forcing his attentions on her. She seemed to have caught him, judging by her crisp commands, he feared they may come through the wall, bed and all.

The creaking ceased and there was a rumble of conversation. Mrs Abbott's shrill tones were prevalent and she didn't sound pleased, perhaps his performance had been below par. Van Ekeren realised why he looked so woebegone, a man could do without a woman who nagged him in the middle of the sex act, an accompanying orgasm, if any, was unlikely to be inspiring.

The shrill tones subsided into an equally shrill mumble and then subsided. She had either fallen asleep or Abbott had strangled her. Van Ekeren tiptoed to the door and peered through the gap again, the glimmer of light below persisted. Time to go. He looked quickly round the room, saw the table knife he had appropriated from the food tray the other day and decided to take it with him. As an offensive weapon it was useless, but it may be handy as a screwdriver or lever.

He slipped through the door, reached up, removed the light globe and placed it on the floor a short distance away to give the impression it had fallen out and bounced. He crept to the top of the stairs and looked down. The glimmer came from an outside porch light, plus there was a thin band of light showing under one of the doors.

He had the choice of creeping silently inch by inch, or tiptoeing fast to get out of the place quickly. He was still debating the question when he hit a stair that creaked. He hadn't heard any creaking boards since he had been incarcerated, why the hell did it have to creak now? To Van Ekeren it sounded deafening, but the reverberations died away and nothing happened.

He crept down the stairs, stumbled and angrily cursed himself. He peered around at the foot of the stairs and was about to make a run for the front door when he heard the sound of an approaching vehicle. He nearly had kittens on the spot as headlights flashed into the hallway and lit everything up like a beacon. He just stopped himself from running through the door with the ribbon of light underneath it and tried the next door to the right.

The room was in darkness, with a musty smell that was familiar, then he banged his knee against some obstruction. The hall light came on as someone hammered on the front door and there was an exodus from the room next door. The light filtered in through the half open door of the room he was in, he dared not close it. In the half-light, he ascertained he was in a sitting room, with a couch, easy chairs, a table with chairs around it, a radio and a television set. There was also a cabinet with a glass front. He rushed across and dived behind the couch, he hit the back of his head against the wall and landed heavily on his left shoulder. He regained his breath as the light flashed on and several pairs of feet trooped in. His heart sank, undiscovered he may be, but he was trapped.

The musty smell increased in intensity and he realised what it was, someone was smoking a cigar, he assumed it was Juan. De Ryk was also present, he signalled his presence in his usual manner, this one took the form of a short, staccato blast. There were others present whose voices Van Ekeren did not recognise. Conversation was initially limited to enquiries about the journey of those who had just arrived and requests for drinks.

'How is our prisoner?'

'Sleeping, I imagine, Claudio,' he heard Juan say. 'The sleep of the innocent!'

Sleep of the damned more like, Van Ekeren thought savagely from his hiding place behind the couch.

'Innocent or not, we must dispose of him. Bad luck on him but we can't run the risk of him talking afterwards, whether we win or lose,' said Claudio. 'I discussed this at length with comrades back home, if we succeed, we'll be in trouble with Canberra for kidnapping one of their citizens, it could affect future oil negotiations. If we fail...well...we'll all be compromised, he couldn't be trusted to keep his mouth shut if we then let him go, he knows too much.'

'Who is he?'

'A nobody!' replied Claudio, obviously one of the recent arrivals. 'I was told he accidentally penetrated a meeting of our coup committee without being discovered until they'd all said too much. He was mistaken for Van Elderen, who none of us had met at that stage.'

Behind the couch Van Ekeren bridled indignantly...a nobody?

'How was he mistaken for him?'

'The names were similar and he was in the hotel where Van Elderen told us he would be staying, but the damned fool booked into another hotel a few doors down the street without informing us.'

'So, this man knows Van Elderen is one of us?'

'That is so, if our coup fails and we dispose of him, Van Elderen will be in the clear. His associates will not be compromised either. This will leave the door open for us to use his services again if we fail and have an opportunity to strike again. Electricity failures or power cuts are not uncommon; one occurring coincidentally at the time of an attempted coup could be explained away, even if some may have suspicions. But let us not talk of failure. We've waited too long. We must dispose of this man. He was in any case too friendly with that swine Lopez ... if he hears of Lopez' death he would talk if we let him go.'

'Why must we dispose of Lopez?'

'Unreliable and too friendly with De Souza. When that Customs warehouse took delivery of our arms, he somehow discovered what was in the shipment and tried to betray us to the police authorities. Luckily the man he informed was Commissioner de Boer!'

There was a rumble of laughter.

'Lucky for us!' said somebody and there was more laughter.

'So, we paid Lopez a visit,' said another voice. 'He has a very attractive daughter, I've seen her. He was told to keep his mouth shut if he wanted her to stay that way.'

'How can we be sure he'll say nothing?'

'We have a spy in his household, his nephew, who did his task well. But Lopez is no fool ...damn the man. We now know he was responsible for Van Ekeren's arrival, we don't know what he told him.'

'Van Ekeren investigated that warehouse burglary. Isn't that why he came to Taranga?'

'Yes, according to our man on Lopez' staff, what's his name?'

'Toro!'

'Toro. That damned creep. He said having an Australian investigator for a claim that size was normal procedure, but the loss was close to the limit they could have handled themselves.'

'Why didn't they?'

'Because Lopez found a way of not assisting us directly.'

'There was another man at the hotel, an associate of this Australian.'

'Toro discovered his name was Westerman, we don't know much about him but he could be a police spy, he and this man Van Ekeren paid a visit to the city police station earlier on, they must have reported to somebody. He could be Australian intelligence'

'Then he will have to be eliminated too., he may know too much. What does Lopez know?'

'Not much, but enough. He probably knows where the guns went and who collected them from the warehouse. So...he must go before or soon after the coup on the 24th ...the sooner the better.'

'What about us here?'

'Abbott is getting cold feet. He says he's a Communist but I don't trust him. It seems to me he just resents authority. If he had lived in the Soviet Union, he would have been a Tsarist.'

'Doesn't he know the Soviet Union is history now?'

'Once a diehard, always a diehard. He still has North Korea and Cuba to look up to.'

There was a chorus of laughter.

'When do we leave here?'

'Juan, after you dispose of Van Ekeren you will return to Sydney and catch a flight back to Taranga. You will be needed there when the coup breaks.'

'What about my money?'

'You will get that in Taranga City, or Jakarta.'

'I want some payment before then, how do I know you'll pay me...in cash! My payment could just as easily be in bullets.'

'Listen Rivera, this is stupid talk ...!'

'Is it?' Juan sounded cutting. 'No. You listen! I am not stupid, nor am I one of your nationals or damned underlings. I am in this for money, who pays me if you fail? Another point, perhaps in time someone will think I'm another one who knows too much, so I'll take my money and make my own way out. And ...incidentally...I can take care of myself. You understand?'

There was silence. It appeared they did.

'And if you ever want me in future, you call me...all right?'

This time the silence appeared to indicate that everything was not quite all right, yet it was encouraging to know villains fell out or didn't fully trust each other. Nevertheless, Rivera's point of view was not unreasonable.

'Where will you go, back to Madrid?'

'Where and when I go is my business and I'll go with my money, if that is OK with you,' Rivera responded with a trace of sarcasm. 'If you don't like it then get De Ryk or Tara to dispose of Van Ekeren. Maybe they can take the shot at De Souza on the 24th instead!'

The ensuing silence was broken by the door opening, and the clink of glasses. From the lack of comment Van Ekeren gathered neither De Ryk nor Tara were over enthusiastic about his suggestions of grave digging or marksmanship and his offer wasn't taken up.

'We'll check the television late news, to see all is well...on the surface.'

There was a click as the TV was switched on and an announcer gave a preview of a program due to be run the following day. Van Ekeren shuddered as he wondered if he would still be around when it was broadcast, then the news began. Much was of little interest; the Prime Minister had left on an overseas trip, leaving his deputy to answer questions in Parliament. There had been riots in a republic in central Africa; an oil slick found in Bass Strait was washing ashore near Wilsons Promontory, an earth tremor in Turkey, and two large oil tankers had collided in the English Channel and polluted beaches in England and France.

'That's not news!' Rivera snorted and the mutual animosity temporarily abated as there was laughter around the room. Even Van Ekeren smiled at that one, there had been a near miss in the Channel the previous week and another tanker had run aground three weeks previously scattering oil over beaches on the French Mediterranean seaboard. The next item aroused his attention.

'There have been several reported sightings of the missing businessman Douglas Van Ekeren who vanished after landing at Sydney Airport. He has not been seen since leaving a case containing a quantity of narcotics on the luggage carousel. Police opened the case yesterday after a tip off and have removed it for further examination, while questions are being asked how Mr Van Ekeren

passed through Customs in Taranga while apparently carrying these narcotics. Anyone sighting Mr Van Ekeren is to report to the police immediately, it is not wise for members of the public to challenge him, it is believed he could be dangerous.'

What? Van Ekeren was aghast. What on earth...!

There was a buzz of conversation and laughter from within the room. He missed the rest, but on straining his ears he heard the news broadcaster make references to overseas Test cricket so it seemed his own news item had concluded.

'You did well, Fino. A pity, that stuff cost money.'

'All in a good cause, it was poor quality and the quantity was small, whatever they said on the news. But we've given logic to Van Ekeren's disappearance. Was that news item on earlier today?'

It was, according to De Ryk, he also mentioned a phone call had been made to the police in the small hours to enable them to lock onto the uncollected bag on the carousel.

'We wanted the police to make their discovery that morning,' he concluded.

'The most wanted man this year,' there was another roar of laughter. 'Was this carried out by your people, Claudio?'

'We had his travelling case, stolen from his hotel in Taranga.' Claudio responded. 'We couldn't arrest him at Taranga City, too many questions would have been asked and it could have drawn attention to us. To compromise him we laced his bag with drugs and had it slipped into the hold when we forced it to land.'

'Surely the forced landing would have attracted more attention than arresting him at Taranga City?'

'The reason given was safety, a mechanical defect. The airline Chairman is one of us.'

"Whose idea was that?'

"Lebak, his idea was to have Van Ekeren snatched from the aircraft at the military air base and produce his travelling case as proof of drug running.'

'Surely, he would still have been a threat, he could still talk.'

'We planned to have him shot trying to escape,' said Claudio. 'But we couldn't find him. Somehow, he evaded us and flew on to Sydney, so we inserted the bag onto the flight.'

'Who supplied the narcotics?'

'Lebak.'

'Coming from that cretin they would have been piss poor quality!' snorted Rivera which caused more laughter.

'Very likely,' responded Claudio. 'We had to pay the bastard, but it wasn't a huge quantity, nothing to excite any drug baron? But despite improvising at short notice we got hold of Van Ekeren and here he is!'

They moved onto general topics, which related to Taranga and their imminent coup which was hoped could lead to a 'merger'. It seemed this latter option was not certain as it was not official Indonesian government policy but merely that of a faction. Van Ekeren gathered one of the recent arrivals, Claudio, was someone of importance since most of them, apart from Rivera, presumably still resentful about his delayed payment, appeared to defer to him. Van Ekeren started to analyse their conversation and the content of the TV newscast.

Westerman? What had he done? Westerman was included in their assassination plans as a person of suspicion because they had both visited the police station where they had been for a large part of the day to report Westerman's damned missing camera, which had never turned up. Their visit to the local police had been misconstrued as informing on the coup or colluding with the authorities. Now Westerman was in the firing line.

As for his own plight, the travelling case stolen from his Taranganese hotel had been used to compromise him by finishing on the carousel at Sydney Airport after being unloaded from the aircraft in the normal way. Either somebody had noticed it going around and round or there was a tip-off. With suspicions an abandoned bag could contain an explosive device it would have been examined, possibly by sniffer dogs, who would have detected narcotics.

Police and Customs would be anxious to interview him. Some luckless Taranganese Customs official had probably been given an unjust rocket for enabling Van Ekeren to get through with a case containing drugs. It had clearly been shipped to the air base after the hotel burglary to justify removing him from the flight at the air base, but when Driscoll's initiative foiled that, it had been placed on board at the unauthorised stop to nobble him at Sydney.

Despite their comments on the poor quality of the drugs, when the media got hold of the story it would reach the proportions of a suitcase packed with high grade stuff worth millions. If, subsequently, he was ever discovered in a shallow grave it would be assumed he had fallen foul of a crime syndicate over a drug dispute.

'Bloody bastards!'

He cringed as he realised he'd muttered it audibly ...could they have heard? But they were laughing at some comment of De Ryk's, probably an anecdote about inflicting pain on some luckless victim.

What he had overheard indicated severe problems. Assuming he made the break and was successful, to whom could he turn for help? Presenting himself at the nearest Police Station now seemed less attractive. He could imagine the incredulity of a country policeman if he tried to inform him of an impending coup d'état in a neighbouring Asian nation.

As soon as he identified himself, he'd find himself at the bottom of a Rugby scrum of excited country policemen, who'd drag him to a cell and lock him up before triumphantly informing Melbourne they had arrested the criminal of the year, without listening to what he had to say. By the time interrogating officers questioned him it could be too late, the coup could have taken place and Lopez and De Souza could have been assassinated, and probably poor Westerman as well. Allegations of having been forcibly detained by persons unknown in country Victoria would seem like a concocted story by a desperate, apprehended drug runner.

What now? Who to contact? The Taranganese Embassy? Where was that? Canberra very likely, maybe he could locate it if he reached the Federal Capital. But how could he get there...could he phone them? Would they believe him? He could visualise the face of their Military Attaché as he tried to tell his story ...incredulity...we've got a lunatic here...ring the Australian Federal police and trace the call! In his mind's eye all he could foresee was incredulity and disbelief.

The gathering began to break up, he heard them rising, the clink of glasses as some of them replenished their supply. He pressed his face to the floor and could see feet heading for the door. The carpet tickled his nostrils and he brought his hand up to kill the sneeze. Three pairs of feet were left.

'Have you heard from Lebak?'

'Indirectly, there was a message over the radio a few hours ago. He was bitching because Van Ekeren got out of Taranga, but I'm not clear how we could have prevented it without causing suspicion.'

'Yes, too risky, that damned man McDermott was too close to him in the airport building, and that other man. Then they vanished; Delgado's Security Police were searching all over the air base for him. I couldn't believe it when I saw them in the aircraft when the passengers re-embarked. We were stuck, we could hardly go through the whole procedure all over again; questions would have been asked and there could have been a riot. The Minister of Transport and Taranga City Airport were already asking awkward questions and the pilot was becoming difficult.'

'Lebak reckoned we should have done more.'

'Lebak can say what he fucking well likes, the man's a bloody fool,' snapped Claudio. 'If it comes to that, Lebak should have killed Van Ekeren in that mock burglary on his hotel room.'

'He wasn't there.'

'Then he was out of reach when Delgado arranged for the aircraft to make that stop,' Claudio retorted. 'Lebak is a bloody idiot!'

'What does Lebak think we were supposed to do? Arrest and dispose of McDermott and the other man as well? Think of the trouble *that* would have caused!' Rivera was becoming exasperated. Van Ekeren could see his point of view. It was infuriating to be on the receiving end of criticism in the field from some damned fool sitting 1,000 kilometres away.

'There should be no mistakes this time,' said De Ryk. 'I'd like to do the job myself and make him squirm first.'

Van Ekeren went cold with horror. He wondered what De Ryk had in mind. Perhaps breaking wind three feet to windward would be his idea of torturing a man to death.

How much longer were they going to stay in there chewing the cud? Then somebody yawned noisily, the feet moved towards the door.

'I'm turning in, who's on duty tonight?'

'Tara, if the silly bastard stays awake.'

Tara on duty! That would make things difficult. Damnation! If he met Tara outside, he may have difficulty spotting him against the black backdrop. The light clicked off and they left Van Ekeren to his thoughts. He almost wished they hadn't, what he had heard was disturbing.

Footsteps clumped to the other end of the house, presumably there were sleeping billets on the ground floor. This meant they weren't going upstairs, which reduced the possibility of anyone having a sudden inspiration to check their prisoner. It would also enable the long-suffering Abbott to concentrate on the task in hand and receive some approbation.

Van Ekeren remained behind the couch for another 15 minutes, it seemed like a comfort zone and he was reluctant to leave its security. But saner counsel prevailed, he realised if he stayed there indefinitely, he'd be recaptured for sure, his bladder would soon demand movement. He went to the window, it was stuck fast and refused to open. He could not believe his bad luck. He strained at it so hard he was in danger of slipping a disc...it remained stubbornly shut.

He swore loud and long, the amount of invective he put into it gave some relief. He crept to the door and peered out, the hallway was in darkness. He tiptoed to the front door and tried the handle, it was locked.

Never had he been so near to breaking down completely, he was frustrated at every turn. He cautiously tried another door; that too was locked. Seething with rage at the injustice of Fate he tried the next door which opened. He listened intently before he entered, the stars were visible through the window and he headed towards it. He sensed a table, or dressing table, against the righthand wall, he rested his hands on it for support and his fingers came into contact with something hard and cold. He traced over it with his fingers, it was a handgun.

He picked it up gingerly and advanced to the window. The room next door must have housed a generator, it hummed and bumped and the noise came through the wall almost without restriction. The window was open but had a flywire screen. He pressed it but it refused to give, then he remembered the table knife. He pushed the blade against the fly wire, and it gave with a tearing noise loud enough to be heard in Sydney. He sawed down one side and it peeled away. He was about to thrust one leg over the sill when the generator cut out and he heard a sound that turned his blood to ice. Footsteps outside the door. There were more footsteps and the rumble of voices, then the door handle clicked as though a hand was resting on it. The conversation continued, he had to get out of the room quick before anyone entered. As his eyes became used to the half-light, he made out a bed, clearly someone slept in here. The conversation outside continued, he heard the sound of breaking wind and then silence. It must be De Ryk's room! He nearly panicked there and then.

The flywire tore and caught on his clothing as he levered himself through the window. He fell onto the, fortunately soft, flower bed below. He was free...for now! He looked back into the room he had left and ruminated. For the first time since he had left Sydney the Gods had looked in his direction, and briefly nodded.

CHAPTER 20

The first thing he did when outside was panic! He rushed across the yard heading for the open countryside or where he guessed it might be and must have tripped over every bucket, tree root and length of wire in a 25metre radius, as a finale he walked straight into a five-bar gate. These collisions and the resultant noise must have roused every indigenous animal within a five-kilometre radius as he blundered around during those terror-stricken minutes.

He was still clutching the pistol appropriated from De Ryk's room, miraculously during his blunderings he didn't discharge it. He also contrived to lose one shoe in a bog, which took about four hours to retrieve, while replacing it he mislaid the pistol, which he had placed on the ground without marking the spot.

He located it and took a grip on himself. He fixed his eye on the distant road and set off towards it at a regular pace.

He wondered where Tara was while he was making all this commotion, Rivera's comments regarding his inability to stay awake seemed well founded.

He wasn't sure of the time, not having a watch, but assumed it was just past midnight. As he headed for the road, he could see occasional vehicle headlights on it and pondered on the chances of being picked up in the middle of the night. He had to accept, if the average motorist encountered a wild-eyed hitch hiker at midnight, he would give him a wide berth. He had nearly reached the road and, while extricating himself from a muddy ditch into which he fell headlong, looked back at the house and nearly had a fit.

It was all lit up, he could see shadowy figures rushing about in front of it, headlights came on and began to move across the yard. What had caused anyone to check on him he could not guess. Rivera, blast him, one of those perfectionist bastards who took his work seriously, could have decided to carry out a last-minute inspection! Or maybe Mrs Abbott had been propelled head first through the wall.

Where did that leave him now? In trouble! He discounted his plan of heading for the road, it would be pointless anyway as he calculated the chances of hitching a lift were nil. That left the possibility of trekking across country flitting from bush to bush. But which direction should he go? On reflection, did it matter? Surely his first priority was to get the hell out of the vicinity, no matter in what direction. Where was the nearest village or town, where was the nearest telephone?

The headlights of the vehicle heading from the house were nearly onto him, he realised he was in an exposed position and dived into the ditch again, squirmed around a bend in it and surfaced in the middle of a wattle bush. The car skidded to a halt, he dimly made out the driver as he got out, then the van pulled up behind with a squeal of brakes.

'How do we know he headed this way?' That was De Ryk.

'In the middle of the night he'd head for civilisation, the road,' Rivera said coldly.

'But wouldn't he assume we'd think that?'

'I doubt it,' Rivera was cutting.' He would be in a wild panic. I doubt he would even think that way.'

Damn and blast the man, he was right first time.

'What now?' another voice which could have been Fino. It didn't sound like Tara.

'De Ryk, head up the road towards Melbourne, we'll go for Ouyen. I think he'll try to hitch a lift, we'll do him a favour and pick him up.'

Van Ekeren heard De Ryk give a dry rasping chuckle, and shuddered.

'In the meantime, Tara and Fino, search back along the track, maybe he hasn't made much distance yet.'

Van Ekeren felt his mouth go dry, Rivera would have made a good general; the bastard missed nothing. He froze within his wattle bush and waited, he could see shadowy figures milling around the two vehicles before two of them detached themselves and headed down the track flashing torches.

'No use heading down the middle of the track, you bloody fools,' Van Ekeren heard Rivera shout. 'Get off it. You'll find him in the ditch or in a bush somewhere just off it. Look for him in the ditches, like this one here.'

Christ! That could only mean the ditch he had just left for the wattle bush. He saw the beam of the torch flash up and down it and flicker through the foliage of the bush in which he was hidden. He prayed he had nothing on his person that reflected light. He held the handgun low down and ensured the table knife was under his foot. He saw a dark shape drop into the ditch and the torch described a wide arc.

'Shit!'

'For fucks sake what is it now?'

'I'm up to my bloody knees.'

Fino helped him out, Van Ekeren could sympathise with Tara, he'd fallen in that ditch already. There was another brief Council of War during which Rivera did most of the talking while Tara sulkily cleaned himself down. Most of it was what could loosely be called encouragement, the type of encouragement the coach of an Aussie Rules side would give his men at quarter time when they were 60 points down after a spineless performance. He told them at length what he thought of them, their performance so far, his expectations for the future with asides on their parentage. His verbiage was so extreme Van Ekeren was surprised his bush didn't catch fire. They listened in abashed silence.

It ended when Rivera and De Ryk entered their respective vehicles and roared off in opposite directions. Rivera flashed past Van Ekeren's bush and receded into the distance. He had indicated he was going to head for Ouyen so Van Ekeren decided to head elsewhere. His plan was to cross over the track and head for Melbourne, but he had to do it without being spotted by Fino or Tara, no doubt desperate to redeem themselves after their recent dressing down.

The torches flashed up and down, they peered into bushes without much enthusiasm, now that Rivera wasn't around their performance could, at best, be termed sloppy. They hung around far too long near the road, he didn't dare move his position. A glow appeared in the distance and became brighter and brighter, he decided against movement as he could be silhouetted. He sat in his bush and considered. He still had to cross the track to head for Melbourne, but if he were to head at right angles to the road — would that be east? This was possibly a direction he may be expected *not* to head; he wouldn't need to cross the track but he would have to cross the road.

The torches were now heading back to the house, with occasional forays into bushes, ditches or paddocks to check anything suspicious. Van Ekeren began squirming across the wet grass, still clutching the pistol. Less than three days ago the thought of guns was anathema to him, he had never held one before let alone fired one in anger. Now he was grimly clutching a loaded pistol and was prepared to use it if apprehended by Rivera or any of his henchmen. After what he had heard while behind the couch during their drinking session, he would not hesitate to pull the trigger and shoot to kill.

He lay flat as a heavy truck thundered past. It had been approaching for some time and bathed the whole immediate area in light. He clearly made out Fino and Tara, who had promptly dived into nearby bushes. Anything more calculated to arouse suspicion was difficult to imagine, guilt maketh cowards of us all.

They had a perfect right to be on that track any hour of the day or night, yet such was their guilt they had scurried into bush and ditch. Van Ekeren hoped the truck driver had some nous and would report it to the nearest Police Station but it was a forlorn hope.

'Some bloody hope!' he muttered as he squirmed toward the road. The road was slightly higher than the surrounding terrain at this point and he had to crawl up a slight bank about three feet high. The main problem would arise when he reached the road and had to dash across. He had reached the edge now and the tarmac was about a metre away. There was some long grass in front of his nose, he looked back at Fino and Tara, they were over 50 metres away and slightly below his level.

More headlights were approaching in the distance; he resolved to take the plunge. He squirmed over the rough gravel, reached the tarmac and began to crawl across on his stomach, using knees and elbows to propel himself forwards. He covered the last few metres in a rush, lost his balance and started rolling. What a brilliant idea ...he rolled and rolled until he hit the grass on the other side of the road and rolled down the bank on the other side.

He found a ti tree bush, crawled under that, found another beyond it and crawled towards that, then another. He flitted from bush to bush, always keeping his previous haven between him and his pursuers.

He lay low as the approaching vehicle came closer, it screeched to a halt at the head of the track. For one delirious moment he thought it may be the police, then subsided into despondency when he realised Rivera had returned. He angrily tooted the horn and the other two came running up the track towards him.

'Have you looked in there?' he shouted, pointing to Van Ekeren's previous haven, the wattle bush on the side of the road.

'Er...yes...er...no!' Tara's desire to lie crumbled in the face of Rivera's anger.

'No?'

'No!'

'Then do it...I'll do the other side of the road. He may go parallel to it.'

As Rivera strode off in the Melbourne direction Van Ekeren had the wild idea of stealing the car, but if Rivera had the keys with him, he would be lost, knowing the man it was doubtful he would make such an elementary mistake.

Van Ekeren tried to put himself in Rivera's shoes. A panic-stricken man would head for the road (which he had done). He would then very likely run north or south alongside it, more likely south towards Melbourne. No fault there with his reasoning, Van Ekeren would have done precisely that if Fino and Tara had not been in the way. Panic having receded Van Ekeren was now climbing the bank, he flitted to and from two more bushes and reached the summit which was the top of a gentle slope about four metres above road level. He crawled on his belly over the crest and peered back at the torches.

Rivera had been right so far, being diverted by circumstances had resulted in Van Ekeren selecting a different direction. But knowing Rivera, he too may calculate the sequence of events and come to the right conclusion. Van Ekeren wasn't going to wait to find out. He struck off down the bank away from the road and made off at right angles, heading for open country.

He regulated his progress to a steady walk, there was no point in rushing around the countryside in a panic and running around in circles. There was also the danger of putting a foot in a rabbit hole, the last thing wanted right now was a broken ankle.

He still held the pistol and the table knife reposed in his back pocket. He had not had cause to use either of them, but he did have a problem. With his ignorance of firearms, he wasn't sure if the safety catch was on or off, or how to adjust it, or which *was* the safety catch.

He handled it gingerly, he had recently read a book about the real Wild West. Main street shoots outs had been rare; most shots were fired in wild exuberance either into the air or into the lettering of saloon facades in fits of drunkenness.

One statistic he had registered was that a considerable number of shooting deaths had been caused by guns going off accidentally, in many cases while still in their holsters.

Yarns of marksmen shooting six holes into the 'O' of a saloon sign were entirely without foundation, every gunslinger worth his salt only had five shots in his handgun, with the hammer resting on an empty chamber. Butch Cassidy, the notorious Western outlaw, had been buried eventually between a Swedish prospector who had shot himself whilst dismounting from his mule, and a prospector who had been drying out his sweating dynamite over a fire, and blown himself up.

Despite these possibilities, he was loath to be rid of the firearm or the table knife, but was aware his two worst hazards would be either shooting or stabbing himself.

The terrain was flat, but there were no signs of life, apart from the occasional glare of headlights reflected in the night sky. He crossed a railway track, the temptation to follow it had been wellnigh irresistible, but he calculated Rivera would check on that when daylight came, he would assess what an ordinary citizen in a blind funk would do. It was also very cold, he was tempted to break into a brisk trot to keep the blood circulating, but this he overruled because of the fear of tripping over an obstruction or a rabbit hole. He didn't relish the idea of being discovered with a broken ankle by De Ryk, who clearly enjoyed his work and would exploit such a situation to the full.

He kept his eyes on the moon as he progressed, the ground was soft, objects were rolling and squashing under his feet and he wondered what they were. They seemed to come every few yards or so. Frequently he looked back; he could still see occasional headlights as they travelled the road he had crossed. He reasoned it wouldn't take them too long to calculate he had crossed the road and was travelling at right angles through paddocks.

As he headed in what he assumed was an easterly direction, he considered his long-term strategy. Previously the thought had crossed his mind of lying low until after the coup, but that was impracticable. It was imperative somebody was informed about what was planned in Taranga, the lives of two, possibly three, of his friends were at stake, Lopez, Westerman and ... if he could consider him a friend ...De Souza.

With De Souza and Lopez on one side, and Rivera, Delgado and Lebak on the other there was now no doubt who were the good guys and who were not. Another point was the comments overheard regarding the travelling case found at Sydney Airport, about being a wanted man and his case containing narcotics. His cabin baggage case had been brought to the house; they had clearly inserted his other case, the one stolen from the hotel, into the aircraft's hold at the unscheduled stop which had finished up on the carousel in the normal way. The lines between Taranga City and Melbourne must have been humming. The case never reached Customs since it landed on the carousel direct from the aircraft's hold and stayed there. The television broadcast had indicated Douglas Van Ekeren was 'dangerous and not to be approached.'

He was still working that one out when he became entangled in a barbed wire fence, he scrambled through and over it as best he could, scratched the back of his hand and tore a small hole in his sleeve. The wire also scored a mark down the side of his shoe as he wriggled through the last strands and regained his feet. He glanced behind and his blood froze. Two lights were dancing along behind like will o' the wisps: they were heading in his direction.

'Hells Bells' he said loudly and promptly cringed as he

remembered how sound carried at night. He gauged how far behind they were and soundly cursed Rivera. He had little doubt it had been his inspiration to search in this direction. He would have to speed up and maybe vary his direction. Rivera would likely assume that a panic-stricken escapee on the run would attempt to reach a point as far away as possible, which would mean a straight line.

The torches were right behind and heading for him. He struck off to the right, nearly twisting his ankle in a rut and stumbling a considerable distance before falling on his knees.

He wondered whether to throw the gun away, he couldn't see himself using it in anger, although had he met anyone by the house, he probably wouldn't have hesitated to use it. He covered about 100 metres while he thought about it and decided to retain it.

He landed on the road before he realised it was there, his first emotion was one of relief almost as though he had gained sanctuary. He ran along it for about 100 metres with sheer exuberance and, it must be admitted, some panic before saner counsels prevailed and he struck off across the paddocks again.

He reached the top of a slight rise, looked back and received a nasty shock. The torches had turned right where he had turned right, and had just reached the roadway.

'How the hell...?'

He stopped and had a good look; sure enough, they were still coming, though his sprint down the roadway had gained some ground. Yet how could they have known he had turned off at an angle? They couldn't have seen him despite the bright moonlight, not at that distance...could bloody Rivera read his thoughts?

But how could they have known? He puzzled over that, but came back to reality with a jerk as he realised he had to keep moving, apart from keeping his distance he had also begun to shiver with cold.

He continued near the ridge of the rise, he wanted to see where the torches went when they hit the road. That was the first cheering sight all night, they were indecisive and the torches waggled around in all directions. The road was having the same effect that a watercourse would have on bloodhounds.

'They seem to have lost the scent,' he muttered as he ducked below the rise and headed for what he assumed was due south. He trotted along for about 100 metres and then peered over the ridge again.

'Shit!'

He could not believe it. He could see the three segments of torchlight converge into one. One had followed the direction he had taken, the other two had headed off in the opposite direction. Now all three were following the route he'd taken.

How could they know which way he had taken? He dropped to a fast walk as he negotiated a small creek and headed for the frost laden grass on the other bank. He could see footmarks in the grass on the far bank which warned that there must be sheep or cattle around, just in time as he blundered into a small flock of sheep and they scattered before him. Without that prior warning, he would have wandered straight into them and most likely have uttered a yell of alarm that could have been heard in Ouyen.

The presence of sheep indicated a farmhouse in the vicinity, but it could be miles away, in any direction. Could he reach a phone? A phone was all he needed to baulk the pursuers. There were no lights in sight anywhere, apart from headlights that flashed across the sky. Some of the sheep were running in front of him, he followed their footprints that could be seen in the frost covered grass, reasoning that if there were any obstructions, they would run around them. He followed them for some distance, they were so frightened of him that they kept well ahead.

He was also a little confused as to which direction they were heading, he had lost his sense of direction and realised he could be heading back towards Rivera. He was relieved to see the torches were still well behind so he headed away from them, fell into a hole, scrambled up, lost his bearings, fixed the Southern Cross in the sky and headed for that.

Again, he wondered how they were tracking him, was Rivera reading his mind so accurately he could forecast his thought processes? When he had struck off at right angles before reaching the roadway they had followed unerringly. Damn and blast them! Damn and blast Rivera!

He stumbled across another paddock, scattered yet more sheep, trod on more of those small cylindrical objects again and again puzzled over what they were. He tripped and fell, buried his face in a small cluster of them, then realised what they were.

'Shit!' he ground out, accurately! They were sheep turds.

He scrambled to his feet and looked behind, the torches still persisted. He found himself in another roadway and remembering his success last time he started along it at a brisk trot.

He had covered three hundred metres, congratulating himself upon a good move, when he was suddenly bathed in light from car headlights. He had the sickening realisation his enemies had outthought him, never had his morale been at such a low ebb, he was absolutely desolate.

'Hold still, Van Ekeren and don't move!'

He shielded his eyes with his left hand, turning half away

to stop the pain to his eyeballs caused by the intense glare. He dimly made out a figure standing by the car and another climbing out of the driver's seat. The car was about thirty metres away.

'Come over here!' they commanded. Van Ekeren obeyed, turned face on and for the first time they caught sight of his right side as he swung around. He was too sick with disappointment for any thought of resistance or escape.

'Christ! He's got a gun!'

The implications of the gun in his hand hit them long before it hit Van Ekeren. From two over-confident, somewhat cocky and sloppy would be captors, presumably with confident smirks on their faces, they degenerated into something resembling two panic-stricken schoolboys. The nearer one stepped back and onto the toes of his companion, who stumbled sideways. The front man continued his backward progress and fell against the front of the car, temporarily blocking one of the headlights. Awoken to the possibilities, Van Ekeren raised his hand and pressed the trigger, with startled squawks they scuttled around the side of the vehicle. The gun failed to fire. He hadn't released the safety catch. While he struggled to find it, still bathed in light, one of them started fumbling under his armpit for his own gun. There were shouts from down the road, but as the first man's hand emerged holding his pistol Van Ekeren found the safety catch, clicked it over and pulled the trigger.

As an opening salvo, its effect was worth far more than its accuracy. It must have cleared the car by about three feet, but the explosion of the gun and the screaming ricochet of the bullet as it bounced off a nearby tree trunk must have been unnerving.

Van Ekeren dived off the road, he believed he was moving out of that accursed light before he realised he was moving ahead of it and was thus still within the lit-up area. In a fit of temper, he took careful aim at the headlight and squeezed the trigger. It stayed on, but there was a deafening crash as the bullet hit the windscreen at an angle, smashed a hole in it and presumably made its mark in the interior. He changed position and eased his way behind the car as two oncoming men with torches opened fire at roughly the point he had been before. They must have fired off half a dozen shots as Van Ekeren floundered away into the welcoming darkness. The torches were all over the road as he heard an angry shout from Rivera to cease fire, the Spaniard realised the risk of them hitting each other.

As Van Ekeren ducked and ran through various items of undergrowth and scattered white stones, he could see figures behind him in the headlights. Rivera was in the van of the torch-bearers; Van Ekeren could hear him remonstrating and cursing and could understand his irritation. How they had isolated the point where he'd be, Van Ekeren could not fathom. With maps and vehicles, they had an advantage, plus they had radio contact. Van Ekeren's only strategy was to be unpredictable, which seemingly up to now he had *not* been, apart from turning up with a firearm. Yet having out-manoeuvred Van Ekeren and taken him completely by surprise, Rivera was not being unreasonable in expecting they should have caught him. They had been overconfident, thinking it too simple; the unpredictable factor being Van Ekeren's possession of a gun and his willingness to use it.

There were more sheep ahead; Van Ekeren could see their foot marks in the frosty grass ahead of him. Then it hit him with tremendous force, his utter stupidity in not working it out before.

'You idiot!' he snarled at himself, probably far too loudly and he angrily bit it back. So *that* was how they'd been tracking him. His black footprints had shown up clearly in the frosty grass like beacons. He cursed and raved at himself as he ran, with them being armed with torches and radios it must have been child's play to follow his tracks. Only sheer luck and their utter carelessness born of over-confidence had saved him.

There was a bevy of black animal footprints ahead of him, he ploughed into the centre of them and struck off at an angle as he reached the far side of the black morass. That would gain a little time before they picked up his track again. Yet they would be wary about approaching too close now they knew he had a gun and wasn't averse to using it.

He smiled as he thought of the effect of his erratic shooting. It would take them a little time before they could use the car, they'd have to scrape out broken glass first as the seats must be covered in it. He hoped Rivera would cut his backside on it.

CHAPTER 21

Streaks of light were in the sky when he hit the next road, he paused and debated whether to use it. It was straight and clear, so he warmed himself with a brisk jog trot for about two hundred metres with a watchful eye on both front and rear. But he began to feel the hair prickle on his scalp eventually so he decided to return to the paddocks and strike across country again. True, one of their vehicles was probably immobilised, but they had plenty more.

Somewhere in this God forsaken country area there had to be a phone. With the number of sheep that persistently got in his way and found their way between his legs there must be a farmhouse somewhere nearby. He kept his eyes open for lights and observed one in the distance.

He landed on another road, this was running east to west as far as he could judge by the lightening sky, he used it for another warming three hundred metre dash before again taking to the paddocks. The sun wasn't far below the horizon now. He stumbled over some more sheep and had a shock when he ran into a cow, which was probably more frightened than he was. She retreated with a startled grunt while Van Ekeren lay on the ground panting. He rose to his feet and then fell flat again as headlights cut a swathe across the paddock. He crawled to a small bush and peered through the foliage.

A Holden station wagon had stopped about fifty metres away. It started and stopped again roughly the same distance further on. He wondered if it was one of Rivera's men, its occupant alighted each time but merely walked to the roadside and then climbed back into the vehicle. It finally rounded a bend in the road and vanished behind a clump of trees, the sound of its engine receded in the distance.

Daylight was closer. He stepped onto the road again and found a large oil drum, painted white and lying on its side on top of two large white painted stones. There was lettering on its side, difficult to decipher in the half light, but it looked like 'McAllister', clearly the name of the farmer or homesteader at the end of the driveway. Mail boxes in the country tended to be large as everything was deposited in them ranging from mails to supplies. They had to be waterproof too, at busy times a farmer could fail to collect his mail for several days.

He wondered what had been delivered, his stomach was demanding sustenance and the thought crossed his mind there could be food in it. He reached inside and found a newspaper. He opened it out but it was impossible to read in the half-light. His reading was cut short as more headlights appeared in the distance. He tossed the paper back and dived behind the nearest bush. It was another station wagon, which behaved much like its predecessor, but this time Van Ekeren could make out what was being delivered.

Milk! As the wagon disappeared, he emerged and advanced

to the mailbox, perceiving the irony that country dwellers should produce the stuff and have it delivered back to them like everyone else in the towns.

He reached in, grabbed a carton, opened it and drained it; he was half way through the second one when more lights flashed in the distance which caused him again to take cover. This one flashed past and again he emerged from the bush. He finished off the second carton, relieved himself into the ditch and went on his way with the newspaper tucked under his arm. He felt pangs of conscience about the farmer, but quelled his qualms with the determination that one day, if he survived, he would seek out that mailbox and leave a bottle of Scotch.

The sky was lighter in the east and he deemed it wise to be well away across the paddocks before the countryside was bathed with sunshine. The sky was clear, he didn't know whether to be pleased or sorry, a sunny day would make life more bearable but would also increase the visibility range of his pursuers. He felt a slight temperature rise, the frost, nearly the cause of his undoing, was still on the ground but there was less of a nip in the air.

*

It was daylight but still misty as he peered through the trees on the small hill and viewed the small settlement below. Initially he had thought it was a large farm, but among the buildings was the inevitable milk bar, a small church and what could only be the local hotel. As he viewed it, he saw other shops and a service station materialise out of the rising mist. It was one of those small settlements that proliferate in country areas to service nearby farms and homesteads. This could be his chance to use a phone, but there were complications in that he had no money. He wasn't sure of the reaction if he were to march into the local milk bar in a dishevelled state and ask to make a free phone call.

The foliage in the small clump of trees was quite dense, he cast his eye around and could see over a wide area but saw nothing to cause alarm. There was some activity below, a car came up the street with its sidelights on and sounded its horn outside the petrol station. As it was filled up Van Ekeren sat and considered his position.

With no money he was in trouble, not only was the prospect of making a phone call difficult, but short of stealing he was unable to obtain any food. He tapped the rolled-up newspaper against his forehead, but it brought no inspiration.

He was still feeling the cold, although as the sun rose higher in the sky that would be less of a problem. He unfurled the newspaper.

The story on the front page about the Prime Minister on a Government flight occupied more space than it merited, presumably there was currently a dearth of news. There was also a picture of the damaged oil tanker in the centre of a large oil slick plus a rough map showing where it was. He turned to the second page, the overseas news, then the third. He turned to the fourth page, there was a photograph with his name underneath. He scanned the article.

MISSING BUSINESSMAN
Police are still searching for missing insurance broker Douglas Van Ekeren, who vanished after his flight landed at Sydney International Airport. As a result of a tip-off Mr Van Ekeren's travelling case was discovered abandoned on the airport carousel and was examined by Police. It's believed a large quantity of narcotics was found.

Mr Van Ekeren is requested to contact Police, but anyone seeing him is asked to contact the police immediately, not to approach him.

Mr Van Ekeren has not been in contact with his employers nor members of his family since landing in Sydney. His company refuses to comment on his disappearance.

Of Dutch extraction, Mr Van Ekeren has been resident in Australia for over 20 years. He makes frequent overseas trips for his firm, mainly to Asian locations.

His eyes almost popped out of his head. He read and re-read the article before the salient points percolated through. It was a classic case of innuendo and bad English, possibly the reporter had been excited at being allocated space to write about such a hardened criminal, maybe his first expedition into the recesses of the Underworld.

Van Ekeren was now classified as of 'Dutch extraction', Australian readers would feel better if the miscreant was a foreigner except for, in this case, any Dutch Australians. That he had been living in Australia for 20 years was true enough but misleading, they had omitted the relevant point that he was an Australian citizen born in Australia. No doubt Al Capone had been identified as a Neapolitan when arrested.

They had condemned Van Ekeren out of hand, insinuating darkly that previous frequent trips to the hot spots of Asia could include all sorts of illegalities and pernicious, unnatural practices. The worst was the sting in the tail, the insinuation he was dangerous!

He was now presented with even more severe problems, which re-emphasised he could hardly surrender to the police with a wild story of an impending coup in Taranga and protestations of being kidnapped.

Drug runners were not popular with the guardians of the law, there was always the possibility the denizens of the local station may ...accidentally...propel him or cause him to stumble, down the steps leading to the cells for good measure. Whatever the outcome, Van Ekeren could spend valuable time trying to convince them of his bona fides and the coup, even if successful it could then be too late and Lopez and De Souza, and probably Westerman, would be dead.

He sat among the trees for some time, numbed with shock. Previously he had considered ringing the office, but that photograph had come from his staff file, the firm insisted all staff members submit a photograph for file purposes. The police would very likely have a trace on the office line to track incoming calls. Damnation... who the hell could he ring?

The office was out; the police were out. Even if he firmly convinced the police he was not a drug runner it could take so long there would be time for three coups d'état. Another difficulty was lack of cash that negated a phone call anyway. One idea that occurred to him was to waylay some child on his way to the milk bar and relieve him of his pocket money. That was a good idea. If the Press were calling him a bastard, he may as well be one.

Who else could he contact if not the police, his local MP? That course of action was promptly rejected. Leon Irving was full of enthusiasm to assist asylum seekers on the high seas in leaky boats, or members of the working classes being exploited by bloated capitalists, anything outside those lines he demonstrated a complete lack of interest. He also had strong views on drug runners and dealers, if Van Ekeren were tainted in that sphere, he wouldn't touch him with a barge pole, he'd lose too many votes. That left him at Square One — if not the police...then who?

He must have been puzzling over it for half an hour before a possible solution occurred to him. The Australian Federal Police he dismissed out of hand, they would probably have the same view and reaction as the Victorian police. But there was an alternative, or two alternatives. Why not ASIO or ASIS?

This was their *raison d'être*, to deal with internal affairs of the nation or the internal affairs of other nations. They dealt with intelligence, which was what he had in his possession, whether it related to Australia itself or elsewhere. Surely, they would be a better prospect than the police.

Van Ekeren ruminated that his many years as a law-abiding citizen were a positive disadvantage. A hardened criminal would have strutted down the main street, explained he had just changed his trousers, left his money behind and would coolly ask if he could use the phone. As it was, he sidled furtively down the slope, crept between two fences separating two properties and finally slunk into the main street.

A pedestrian and a cyclist passed by as he hit the main street, he peered so long and hard into the shop window of a second-hand shop, that housed the worst array of junk he had ever seen, that he attracted the attention of the proprietor. He must have looked a likely prospect as the proprietor advanced to the door and greeted him like a brother. Van Ekeren gave a sickly grin and sidled away. The shop-keeper shrugged his shoulders and retreated into the shop.

There was a public phone inside the milk bar, which doubled as a post office, dry cleaners and greengrocers. He hung around indecisively for ten minutes, the proprietor eyed him suspiciously. Again, he utilised his sickly grin and departed down the street while wondering what to do. If only there was a public call-box he could be all right, with the phone inside the post office cum milk bar people would hear every word he uttered.

A small boy approached on his way to the milk bar. Van Ekeren decided to accost him and moved across.

'G'day, my boy...er...laddie!' he said ingratiatingly.

The small boy eyed Van Ekeren with suspicion and didn't return the greeting. He put his hands behind his back, could he read his thoughts?

'Going for some lollies?' he asked conversationally.

'Yes,' the boy's demeanour made it clear he wouldn't be diverted from his course of action, and when he achieved his objective, he wasn't going to share them either. He was aged about 6 or 7 with a shock of blonde hair and blue eyes that would have turned old ladies' heads, but to Van Ekeren he appeared to be a greedy selfish little brute with a mean look.

'How would you...how ...are you?' Van Ekeren floundered as he tried to steer the conversation into a charitable mode.

'Johnnie,' he answered, obviously not hearing right.

Van Ekeren decided small talk was a waste of time and decided to come straight to the point, a tactical error as it turned out.

'How would you like to give twenty cents to an...old man... down on his luck?'

'No!' Johnnie leapt back and thrust his hands behind his back.

'What?' Van Ekeren was nonplussed and resisted the urge to box his ears. 'Now look here sonny, all I want ...!'

'*Mum!*'

Van Ekeren didn't wait to see whether he was bluffing, he beat a hasty retreat and made his way out of the settlement fast. He didn't have the gall to ask the milk bar proprietor for the use of his phone after that. He couldn't have aroused more attention or acrimony if he had fired off a cannon in the middle of the street. He bitterly ruminated he had probably added yet another item, attempted child molestation, to his eventual charge sheet.

CHAPTER 22

'**M**r Driscoll?'

'That's me,' Bill Driscoll turned from the motor he was servicing, in the workshop near Sydney Airport, and eyed the two men quizzically. 'Who wants to know?'

'Could we have a few words?'

'What about?' Driscoll placed his screwdriver on the bench as he realised they possessed an aura that denoted authority, possibly police. 'Who the hell are you? Police?'

One of them produced an identification badge which Driscoll examined.

'Security and Intelligence!' Driscoll was stupefied. 'What the hell have I ...?'

'Nothing sir. Is there a place where we can talk?'

Driscoll jerked his thumb at the door leading to the yard.

'Out there, I guess, what *is* this?' he asked. 'How can I assist ASIO for God's sake?'

'You were on a Taranganese Airline flight from Taranga

City to Sydney Airport last week. Is that correct?' asked the tall fair-haired man.

'Yes, I was. Bloody rum flight it was, too.'

'Why do you say that?'

'Because we made an unauthorised stop at a military base called Aleasino and hung about in two bloody hundred-degree heat while several mechanics played silly buggers and did fuck all with the port wing,' snapped Driscoll. 'We'd have been hanging around in that bloody heat for another four hours if we hadn't done something about it.'

'How did you know the name of the base?'

'Because I've been there before on the job for Qantas. I'm writing to Taranganese Airways to ask for part of my fare back.'

'You'll be lucky,' the other security man said with a smile and Driscoll grinned.

'Yeah...guess you're right,' he said ruefully. 'But it'll tell the buggers I took a dim view.'

'You said you did something about it. What did you do?'

'Have I done something wrong? Am I in trouble? Is the Air Line saying we...?'

'No, no, no!' the fair-haired man shook his head. 'You've done nothing wrong, we're after information. Just tell us what happened.'

Driscoll hesitated then shrugged. After all, he and the other two, Al and Doug, had done nothing wrong, just displayed initiative. He embarked on the story of the flight from when it left Taranga City Airport, the unauthorised stop at the military airfield, McDermott's illness or heatstroke, and the surreptitious re-entry of the aircraft by the three of them.

'I remember the other two, McDermott was an older bloke, something to do with Foreign Affairs I think, the other was a businessman, Van Ederen or something. Nice fellow.'

'Tell us about the reason for the diversion. You mentioned to McDermott you thought the stop was unnecessary, that they did nothing to the aircraft.'

'Ah...you've spoken to Al, have you? Yes, I did tell him that and I meant it. Naturally I was interested, being in the game, but I could see no reason for the hold up. When we were by the aircraft just before we snuck back on board, I spoke to some of the aircraft mechanics; they were as mystified as I was.'

'What mechanics?'

'The fellows standing under the wings, mechanics and technicians. I knew a couple of them, when Qantas have problems close at hand in Indonesia or Taranga, they prefer us to fix them, they don't trust the locals so I've met a few Taranganese on the job. When I asked what was wrong and why we had to land they just shrugged their shoulders, one of them said it was because of an order from some high up in government.'

'Did he say why, or who ordered it?'

'No, I did ask but a supervisor arrived then so he just gave a head shake and clammed up,' Driscoll looked curious. 'What's this all about?'

'The other man, Van Ekeren, had you ever seen him before?'

'No,' Driscoll shook his head. 'We only got involved because he was with Al and that was because they sat together on the plane. When Al got crook we were both worried about him and decided to get him back on board where it would be cooler.'

'Did anything occur while the plane and passengers were grounded?'

'Like what?'

'When we interviewed Alastair McDermott, he said all the passengers were vetted, all documentation and passports were checked.'

'Yeah, that'd be right,' Driscoll agreed. 'I spoke with some of the passengers afterwards; those sitting near me. They said everyone was vetted, a few of them said the blokes questioning them gave them the creeps.'

'You've no idea who or what they were looking for?'

'No,' Driscoll shook his head. 'They weren't looking for me, that's for sure.'

'What about Van Ekeren, could they have been looking for him?'

'Doug?' Driscoll looked pensive. 'Well, I dunno. Possible, he looked a bit edgy I thought, but nothing I could put my finger on.'

'OK. Did you see him at all when you eventually landed at Sydney Airport?'

'No, I was one of the first off, I never looked back.'

*

It was early morning, Van Ekeren had slept rough in a haystack and busily plucked pieces of hay from his person. He reached the road again, looked in each direction to check there was no sign of Rivera or De Ryk, and spotted a heavy vehicle lumbering towards him.

The truck faltered, accelerated, hesitated, then reluctantly ground to a halt. There were two men in the cab and they looked down at Van Ekeren with some distaste. He gave a cheery grin and wave, which mollified them to some degree.

'Where yer heading?' asked the man in the passenger seat.

'Charlton or Wedderburn.'

He had accomplished something during that fiasco the previous day at the last settlement. He had discovered its name, which meant nothing and which he had since forgotten, something East he thought it was, but had emerged onto a road with two road signs, pointing in opposing directions. He selected Charlton in preference to Wycheproof, as the latter could take him in what he assumed was the direction of Rivera and his hoods. Logically that might have been a good way to go, plough straight through and beyond them, but his fear of them was such he dismissed the idea.

There was a brief delay while they considered. The odds of two tough looking truckies versus a dishevelled hitch hiker finally decided them, if there was any trouble, they could handle it. The man in the passenger seat moved into the middle and Van Ekeren clambered up.

This suited him, he wanted to be in a position where he could get out in a hurry, after seeing that picture in the newspaper he was wary of exposing his features to anyone without leaving an avenue of escape. As he settled into the enclosed space, he realised he carried a slight odour, he had been running, trotting and sweating the perspiration of fear all night without any chance of having a wash.

The driver put his foot down, as though trying to reach Charlton or Wedderburn as quickly as possible to be rid of the aroma.

'Nice day,' Van Ekeren remarked brightly.

'Too right,' answered the man in the middle. 'Where you from?'

Van Ekeren wasn't sure if the enquirer meant his place of abode or where he had just been. He wasn't sure where he was and what places were behind him, but said 'Ouyen', which seemed to pass muster.

The pistol was in his trouser pocket, with the safety catch on, he made sure of that to avoid shooting his balls off when he sat down. The bulge could be noticeable if anyone was looking for it. It started to rain, drops spattered on the windscreen and the driver set the wipers going.

'Bloody weather,' he commented. 'What's your name?'

'Doug,' Van Ekeren answered without thinking, then could have kicked himself, a false name would have been vastly preferable.

'John!' said the driver. 'This is Fred'

Introductions thus complete, he thought, as the guest, it was up to him to keep the conversational ball rolling.

'What are you carrying?' he asked and could have bitten his tongue off. That was the sort of question a member of a hi-jacking gang would have asked for the edification of colleagues waiting further up the road.

But they didn't take umbrage at that, they chatted on for some time about their load, a complete kitchen being delivered from manufacturers in Adelaide to Albury. Somehow this led onto racing, Van Ekeren wasn't sure how, but talk to the average Australian truckie and eventually all conversation leads to football or the racetrack.

'Who do you fancy for the 3.30?'

Fred picked up a newspaper and Van Ekeren's blood froze in his veins. Fred merely gave the small Van Ekeren picture on the exposed page of the 'Sun' a passing glance, turned to the back pages and flicked over until he reached the racing news.

'Stormy Weather,' he commented.

'That'd be right,' John said darkly as the rain intensity increased.

'Not bad odds,' Van Ekeren added brightly, determined to keep their attention on the racing news.

'OK. We'll have a go on Stormy Weather — $5 each way — big spenders...eh?' John cackled with laughter and Van Ekeren joined in, anything to distract attention from the front page.

Fred perused the paper and selected three or four more runners. The main meeting of the day was at Randwick. Van Ekeren knew a little about horseracing and made occasional intelligent comments. Finally, they settled on what they were going to back.

'Where's the next TAB?' he asked. He hoped they were not expecting him to chip in with some cash, he wasn't sure he could satisfactorily explain how he came to have no money whatsoever. He didn't want to mention it either, if he did it could be interpreted as an attempt to touch them for a few dollars and he didn't want that.

'No need, we'll ring it in,' Fred made the call on his mobile phone to his bookie then turned to another page and started to read. To Van Ekeren's jaundiced eye, although his picture was at the foot of the page, it seemed to fill the cab. Thankfully the picture bore only a remote resemblance as he had been smartly dressed when it was taken, clean shaven with a short haircut, whereas now he had three days' beard and looked as if he had been dragged through a hedge backwards.

'Bastards!' Fred said with feeling. 'Scrounging off the rate payers, these bastards just get away with it, be different if we did it.'

So far, so good. He was referring to a tax evasion case in Toorak, although his sentiments were awry because the tax evader, being in court, clearly hadn't got away with it. Van Ekeren had an inspiration and produced his own newspaper stolen from the post-box.

'They mention it here,' he thrust it across Fred's newspaper. 'They don't think much of Stormy Weather either, look they don't tip him at all.'

'Don't they?' said Fred, which necessitated further reference to the racing pages. Several kilometres were covered discussing the merits of the Randwick field, which diverted attention from the drug runner article.

Van Ekeren decided to alight at Charlton. He couldn't

stand the tension of having his picture staring at him in short flashes and wondering if Fred would spot it too. He was also having palpitations every time a car overtook them, he seemed to see Rivera in every one and once he was sure he saw De Ryk coming the other way.

'Wonder if they've caught this bastard yet?'

Van Ekeren's blood turned to ice. Fred had discarded the racing page and was checking the middle pages again.

'He needs bloody shooting!' John negotiated a sharp bend. 'Dutch, isn't he?'

A hot denial rose to Van Ekeren's lips which he quelled, he could feel his hair standing on end, his mouth went dry and his temples began to sweat. He decided silence may be more noticeable than a comment.

'Indonesian I thought,' he said eventually. 'That's what the newspaper said.'

The Sun had said nothing of the sort, but if he threw in a red herring to hint the hunted man was brown skinned and possibly slant eyed so much the better.

'These bloody wogs ought to be kept out,' Fred said pointedly, a sentiment with which Van Ekeren wholly concurred when he thought of Rivera, Tara, De Ryk and Fino.

'My Oath!' he responded, anxious to establish his Australianness for as many generations as possible, and added 'Bastards!' for good measure.

'He needs stringing up by his heels.'

'Too right' Van Ekeren just avoided adding the word 'Cobber'. That form of address wasn't used much these days, using it could be overdoing it.

They finally reached Charlton, a small town with a population somewhere around 1,300 according to the road sign. He was edgy as they entered the main street and passed the inevitable milk bar and phone box. He was anxious to be out of the cab before the similarity of the picture and his own features should forcibly strike them.

'Thanks for the lift, fellahs,' he said as the truck's pace slackened. 'Thanks very much...just here will do fine.'

'You're welcome...er...what did you say your name was?'

'Doug...Drug ...er...*Duff*,' Van Ekeren floundered miserably. 'Duff Cooper.'

If anything sounded false that did, but once he had uttered 'Doug' he had to change it to something similar and 'Duff' was all that came to mind. Cooper seemed to follow it like 'Whitlam' would follow 'Gough' and 'Churchill' would follow 'Winston'! He remembered the name, a British politician in the 1930s, because his maternal grandfather had disliked him intensely, Van Ekeren couldn't remember why.

'Nice to have met you ...er... Duff!' said Fred. 'All the best.'

'Thanks lads. I hope Stormy Weather comes in OK.'

As he opened the door the pistol slipped out of his pocket, he made a grab at it to stop it falling and lost his grip on the door. He fell out, and just managed to drop feet first onto the tarmac, nearly wrenching his left arm out of its socket as he hung onto the driving mirror stanchion. The gun evaded his grasp and fell onto the roadway, followed by Van Ekeren.

'You all right, mate?' Fred asked anxiously, still seated in the middle.

'Fine...and thanks for the lift.'

The truck moved off and ambled down the main street. Van Ekeren was confronted by a small boy who gazed wide-eyed at the gun, which he had just retrieved. He tucked it nonchalantly back into his pocket and walked away with as much dignity as he could muster.

'Mum...he's got a gun!'

'Hush Billie, stop shouting!'

'But he had a gun, I saw it. He put it in his…!'

'That's enough Billie, come on and stop being silly!'

Thank God for the superior wisdom of the adult, Billie was led away still protesting he had seen an item of artillery in the main street. Van Ekeren walked towards a nearby call-box and reflected if he could get away with that, he could get away with anything.

CHAPTER 23

Alan Kelsey paused as Denis Shackleton and Phil Jackson, two ASIO operatives attached to his department, waylaid him in the corridor.

'What did you get from Driscoll?' he asked.

'Not a great deal,' answered Shackleton. 'He told us much the same as McDermott, but as an aircraft mechanic he was adamant there was no reason for that stop over. He also confirmed what McDermott said about the vetting of passengers while they were at Aleasino military airfield, he reckoned they were looking for somebody.'

'Could they have been looking for Van Ekeren?'

'I asked him that but he had no idea. We asked him whose idea it was to re-board the aircraft unofficially, was it Van Ekeren's. He said not, it was purely Driscoll's own initiative. He said McDermott was plainly distressed by the heat so Driscoll took it on himself. Being an aircraft mechanic employed on airport rosters he knew the drill, how to make himself inconspicuous in airports and avoid authority.'

'Any comments on Van Ekeren?'

'Just an ordinary bloke, he thought, said he seemed a nice fellow.'

'That means bugger all,' replied Kelsey. 'Photographs of some of the nicest blokes I've seen have been KGB assassins. But I've just had words with Colin Minton of ASIS. Colin's recently had a report from Gary Phillips in our Taranga City embassy, Gary reckons something's brewing. He says he's heard from an informant over there that there could be a coup in the wind. We've passed it onto Francis Burton. He'll contact the Foreign Minister about it.'

'Are we suggesting Van Ekeren's disappearance could be connected with that?'

'God knows!' Kelsey shrugged. 'But there's something bloody peculiar here, he's had no history of anything to do with drugs, and no police record. He's a previously upright citizen and he's just vanished. We've now got two other people, one a respected member of the diplomatic corps, who vouch for him disembarking at Sydney Airport.'

'What was he doing in Taranga?'

'That's my next task.'

*

About ten o'clock in the morning, after being dropped off by the truck and much thought, Van Ekeren decided to contact ASIO. His first attempt to contact the guardians of the Australian nation ended with an irate member of that same nation hammering on the door of the telephone kiosk with her umbrella. He emerged and was treated to a dose of vitriol by that same citizen, who spent the next half hour in the box, presumably telling her luckless victim on the other end of the line how long some unkempt man had kept her waiting.

As for ASIO his confidence in the ability of the Commonwealth to withstand the attentions of Russians, Chinese, Indonesians, fanatical Muslims, or any other foreigners who wished to impose their will on Australia, was badly shaken. Had Melbourne been in the throes of a dive bomber attack he had no doubt the telephonist, and the secretary who succeeded her on the line, would still have been asking the same damn silly questions.

Admittedly there had been two obstacles which wouldn't have endeared him to anyone representing a security organisation. They probably received many calls from nut cases who thought it funny to leave bizarre messages and farting noises or else block the line by leaving the phone off its hook. Persuading them to take a reverse charge call had resulted in a spirited debate between the Telstra operator and the switchboard operator of ASIO. Finally, the latter had reluctantly acquiesced, but having established contact Van Ekeren had been wary about identifying himself.

He couldn't predict the reaction of a junior switchboard operator when she realised she had a dangerous fugitive on the line whose identity was plastered all over the media. He, probably unjustly, considered a junior switchboard operator could be overcome by excitement, hold him on the line and call the police before passing him onto an intelligence operative.

'Hello...could I speak to...to...ah...!' and it was at this point he began to realise how difficult it was, who the hell did he ask for? Someone in authority?

Maybe he expected too much, having accepted a reverse charge call from the wilds of a Victorian Country District, very likely against regulations, the operator was justified in expecting more than a vague request.

She asked what it was about, he said it was confidential. She persisted, he repeated it was confidential. Did he want the National Crime Centre? No, he didn't want the National bloody Crime Centre! He unbent and said it was about Taranga. She advised him to contact the Foreign Affairs Ministry in Canberra, he demurred whereupon she suggested the Taranganese Embassy.

He realised he was phrasing it badly so asked to speak to somebody in the Intelligence Section, he had important information. What about? Taranga! Could I suggest the Foreign Ministry in Canberra or the Taranganese Embassy, the Taranganese Tourist Centre was open at 2.00 pm. But he persuaded her it was Intelligence he wanted and she passed him over to some secretary. Any visions of James Bond, or characters from a John Le Carré novel dissipated, the voice at the other end sounded middle aged, irritable...and disbelieving. Mr Shackleton would be in at eleven.

Bang! Bang! Bang! ...went the umbrella on the window of the booth and 'How much longer was he going to be in there?'

He would ring again at eleven.

Bang! Bang! Bang! 'You've been in there for half an hour!'

'Bloody Hell! What's the flaming use?'

He retired to a picket fence by the side of the road and sulkily sat on a short stone pillar near a gateway. He hadn't been expecting to galvanise ASIO into top gear, with Red Alerts sealing off Canberra and a helicopter squadron descending on Charlton to ferry him to the national capital, but he had expected a more enthusiastic reaction. Instead of Australia's top security organisation, he seemed to have contacted the equivalent of the Control organisation of the television series 'Get Smart'.

Bitterly he watched the senior female citizen of Australia regale her unfortunate friend on the other end of the line with every subject under the sun. He picked up a small stone and tossed it from hand to hand while he contemplated whether or not to throw it at the phone box. It would be satisfying, but it may also bring the police into the equation. He tossed the stone aside but had been sorely tempted.

He had about an hour to wait until eleven. He was even more bitter when he thought of Mr Shackleton taking his time to get to the office, he should be in at nine like everyone else. He moved off the main street into a paddock the other side of a water course, he felt he was attracting attention where he was. He was also ravenous, if he didn't get results soon the police would pick him up anyway for shoplifting, petty pilferage or collapsing from malnutrition.

He did entertain the idea of asking the nearby greengrocer for a free apple, but he looked an unsympathetic bastard. He displayed a belligerent interest as Van Ekeren paused by his shop with an ingratiating grin, so he hastily continued on his way, trying not to look at the succulent fruit on display.

Van Ekeren felt quite weak at the knees when he headed up the street again, he hesitated for so long by the phone box that he was pipped by another elderly lady who took root in it. As he waited, he wondered what to do if they refused to reverse the charges.

Eventually the demand for the box tailed off and he managed to dial the operator again, ask for the number and said he wished to reverse the charges. At ASIO it was the same switchboard operator and his heart sank. He feared she would refuse, but eventually he was told to go ahead.

'Mr Shackleton, please.'

'Which Mr Shackleton?' was the reply. 'William Shackleton or Denis?'

'Great God in Heaven!' he didn't think it possible! By this time an invading army could have swept south from Darwin and occupied Alice Springs. He opted for William.

'I was speaking to his secretary about two hours ago.'

He wasn't sure if this was a wise move, they hadn't got on too well last time. The secretary came on the line again, sounded irritable and asked what he wanted.

'For Mr Shackleton's ear only,' Van Ekeren managed to sound mysterious.

'In what sphere?'

'To do with Taranga'

'You'd better ring Foreign Affairs...!'

'To blazes with Foreign Affairs,' he shouted angrily. 'Is Mr Shackleton there or not?'

Apparently, he was. There was a whispered consultation with a hand placed over a mouthpiece. This was beginning to infuriate him, what the Hell was he paying taxes for?

'William Shackleton!'

'Good afternoon,' he fought the urge to resort to sarcasm. He needed this man as an ally. 'I have vital information.'

'What about?'

'Taranga!'

'What about Taranga?' but at that point Van Ekeren clammed up. He wasn't going to play his trump card too soon. He wanted transport from his present predicament. He was persistently watching the street. He had no desire to renew acquaintance with De Ryk or Rivera.

'What about Taranga?' Mr William Shackleton persisted

'I have important information that...that...!' he had an inspiration '...that could severely affect Australia's oil supplies.'

William Shackleton digested that one.

'Who are you?'

'My name is unimportant at this stage...' he said pointedly, if he told him the damned fool may alert police and get him arrested '... but something is going to affect the Taranganese oil supplies in the near future.'

'Yes. What is that?'

'I want to speak to someone about it. It's vital!'

'Well, you'd better write in and make an appointment, as you can appreciate, we are very busy here. I suggest you submit a report in writing at the same time as fixing an appointment and we can evaluate it in due course.'

'Jesus Ch...!' Van Ekeren regained control with an effort. 'How long will that take?'

'About three weeks.'

'Three weeks!'

'That's the best I can do for you, Mr . . .er . .'

'This is bloody ridiculous!'

'I beg your pardon.'

He tried another tack.

'You deal with intelligence, from overseas, that is?'

'That is another department.'

'What! I thought I was speaking...! What department am I speaking to?'

'This is the Accounts and Assessments Department.'

'It's what! I don't bloody believe it!' words failed him. He decided to become polite again and asked who dealt with Overseas Intelligence. Apparently it was Mr Denis Shackleton or Mr Kelsey, the former was presently out of the office but the latter was probably the best to speak to. He asked for Kelsey but he was in conference. He was put through to a Mr Tremlett and went through the merry-go-round again with suggestions to contact the Taranganese Embassy, the Foreign Ministry or the Tourist Bureau.

'And you are...?'

'Van Ekeren!' he answered sullenly. He hadn't intended to break cover and use his name but by this time he was so exasperated it slipped out before he could bite it back. In any case, by now he was way past caring whether he was arrested by police, died of starvation or shot up the backside by Rivera. It seemed he could do or say nothing right and was having serious doubts, with the lunatics in charge of Security, whether his country deserved to be saved from foreign invaders.

'Van Ekeren...you mean the man who is missing ...from Sydney Airport?'

'Yes,' he answered bitterly, surprised the other knew anything that occurred beyond the confines of his desk. 'The drug runner...so called!'

'I'll just put you on hold a moment, Mr Van Ekeren ...!'

'No you don't, just fucking listen to me will you!' This man Tremlett plainly meant him to hold on while he called the police, before he did that Van Ekeren wanted to have his say and hang up quick before they traced the call, assuming they hadn't done that already.

'I found out about an impending coup d'état while I was in Taranga. I was kidnapped from Sydney Airport and held at a country house near here ...*for God's Sake believe me!*'

'What's this about a coup?'

'Come and get me and you'll find out,' he said coldly. 'It affects De Souza, Delgado and others.'

There was another silence then he asked Van Ekeren to hold on a minute.

'Why?' Was he going to ring the police?

'I'll pass you to someone else. He will assist you.'

'Who?' Please not William Shackleton again.

'Alan Kelsey, he's handling this.'

'I was told he was in conference.'

'He'll be out of there damn quick when I tell him who's on the line,' Tremlett said not without humour. 'Just hang on, it should be only a few minutes, I'm putting you through to the conference room where he is.'

There were a few seconds of music, some clicks... then a voice said: 'Kelsey.'

'Look,' he began. 'My name is Van Ekeren...!'

'I know who you are. Mr Tremlett has just filled me in. I've been trying to track you down for days. Where are you?'

He told him and mentioned he was being pursued by his late captors who had guns and were not averse to using them. Kelsey asked who they were.

'How the hell should I know?' he became angry and impatient again, afraid any minute Rivera might appear in the street. 'One is named Rivera and another is De Ryk.'

'What? Who did you say?'

'One of them is named Rivera and another is De Ryk.'

'Rivera? Did you say Rivera?'

'Yes, I did.'

That seemed to be the magic word. Kelsey spoke at length to Van Ekeren for five minutes, then rang off.

As Van Ekeren put the phone down a car drove up the main street and stopped outside the milk bar. The driver climbed out, it was Rivera. Van Ekeren remained in the box, turned his back and pretended he was on the phone. As Rivera entered the milk bar Van Ekeren replaced the phone and dodged behind the box. Rivera exited the milk bar with a packet of cigars and lit one as he peered up and down the street, then climbed back into the car and drove off.

CHAPTER 24

The conversation with Alan Kelsey had been crisp and to the point, the complete antithesis of anything hitherto experienced at the Australian Intelligence organisation. Kelsey had clearly been receiving advice from a subsidiary team as he spoke to Van Ekeren, being given background information on the town of Charlton as they spoke.

'One of our operatives will contact you where you are,' he said. 'There are hotels in the town probably on the main street...' here he broke off and was clearly consulting, '...the Cricket Club Hotel, can you see it?'

'I think I passed it a few moments ago ...wait...yes I see it, it's on the corner where another street joins the main street.'

'Good, that will be your rendezvous,' said Kelsey. 'Your contact will be David McKay, fair haired, six foot or thereabouts, blue eyes. He's currently at Ballarat, he'll drop what he's doing but it may take a few hours. I suggest you lie low somewhere either in the town or just outside it, keep well off the road in case the people chasing you pass through. Got that?'

'They already have.'

'What? Bloody hell, then stay under cover. Go into the saloon bar of the pub, I suggest about 1 o'clock to 1.30. David McKay will travel fast and should be there roughly at that time. Any signs of your pursuers now?'

'Not right now, he seems to have passed through. I hitched a lift to Charlton in a truck, but there haven't been many trucks travelling through. They could come back here if they lock onto the one that picked me up.'

'Then stay off the street and be in that pub at one o'clock.'

*

The art of the secret agent is to be inconspicuous and unobtrusive. But Van Ekeren found to his cost there is no quicker way to draw attention to oneself than to sit in an Australian hotel in a country town and not have a drink. He couldn't help it, he had no money. Nor could he just get up and leave, if he did, he may miss the ASIO contact.

The landlord asked him several times if he was all right, enquiries not so much kindly as bordering on the pointed and sarcastic. Van Ekeren had no knowledge of licensing laws provisions, was a weary traveller allowed to come in and merely rest or, when entering licensed premises, was he obliged to purchase solid or liquid refreshment? He was also given a wide berth by other patrons, when anyone came within nostril range, they hastily withdrew.

His previous opinion of the intelligence services returned and sank to a new low. It was possible the longer he hung about the quicker the patience of the landlord would run out, he could be asked to leave or alternatively he could deem him suspicious or undesirable and send for the police.

Further, if De Ryk or Rivera decided to search local taverns he could be a sitting duck and they would find some excuse for frogmarching him out. He couldn't see the landlord objecting, with the aroma accompanying him he had already cleared a three-metre radius where he sat. Not only that, he was ravenously hungry and the smell of ale, coffee, toasted snacks and pies was becoming unbearable.

There was a half-eaten pie on a plate on the next table, it had been there when he entered and was obviously abandoned. He had taken a few surreptitious moves towards it, trying not to attract the landlord's attention. He had nearly made it when a young girl entered the bar-room from a kitchen doorway and began clearing tables. With a sense akin to panic Van Ekeren increased his rate of creep to two inches every ten seconds, he had nearly made it when she changed direction and scooped the pie into a slop bucket. He couldn't recall ever experiencing such sickening disappointment while his stomach gave a disapproving rumble that must have been heard north of the River Murray.

He cast a jaundiced eye around the bar room, there was nobody who remotely resembled an ASIO contact. True, he didn't quite know what to look for, though in his present cynical state of mind it wouldn't have surprised him to see someone wearing a steel helmet labelled 'Secret Agent' or a 'T' shirt with ASIO on the back.

There were five men in the bar, one in a corner holding a newspaper which blanketed him entirely, and two men fronting the bar chatting to the landlord, they looked like farmers. A man with a brief case was also at the bar, he looked like a traveller, while a young lad in a blue sweater was chatting up the barmaid, with some success. Van Ekeren eyed the man with the newspaper and thought him a possible; he caught the man's eye but he merely raised an eyebrow and continued reading.

Three more men arrived before the newspaper reader made a move, a driver who had parked his car across the street, an elderly man who ordered a whisky and beer and a younger man who entered later and joined him. These two looked keenly around the bar-room and chatted to each other; Van Ekeren considered them possibles as well.

The newspaper reader rose and came over, hesitated and then entered the toilet to his right. A man and woman entered from the street and occupied a corner. The toilet door opened, the newspaper reader emerged, took no notice of Van Ekeren and vanished through the street door without a backward glance. Did he have to follow him? Was the plan to meet in the car park? Was the room too crowded for secret assignations between an undercover agent and a fugitive? After some thought he decided against it, his somewhat scanty instructions had said nothing about soliciting secret meetings outside.

'Got a light mate?' Van Ekeren jumped as the presumed traveller paused by him; he too was on his way to the toilet and had a cigarette in his mouth.

'I don't smoke' Van Ekeren replied and waited for a secret signal.

'All right, thanks mate,' he wrinkled his nose as Van Ekeren's general atmosphere hit his nostrils. He entered the toilet, reappeared moments later and exited through the street door.

Had something gone wrong? The two farmers said their farewells and left, as did the young man in the blue sweater. The car driver emptied his glass and wiped his mouth. He turned around and said 'Nice day out there,' to no-one in particular, it could have been to the barmaid now the opposition had vanished.

'Not bad,' said the landlord and turned his piercing eyes onto Van Ekeren. 'You all right mate?'

'Yes, thank you,' he ground out, flushing with embarrassment, where the hell was this bloody man McKay? Rivera or no Rivera, he would have to leave soon and wondered if a bullet in the gut was preferable to the acute embarrassment he was presently suffering, to say nothing of the pangs of hunger. The car driver then approached Van Ekeren.

'Nice day.'

'Is it?' his tones must have had icicles as he looked desperately around for his ASIO contact.

'Where are you heading?'

Damn and blast the man, why didn't he go away. The last thing Van Ekeren wanted was to look as if he was part of a twosome when his contact, if he ever damned well appeared, would be looking for a man sitting on his own. If this bloody man was going to offer him a lift, refusing it was going to be difficult.

'Bendigo,' he uttered ungraciously, it was the first place that came to mind.

'Goodo! I'll give you a lift.'

'No, I can't, I'm waiting for a fr...!'

The car driver grinned and rubbed his nose.

'My name's McKay, Dave McKay. My car's over the road.'

'Christ! You kept me waiting long enough!' Van Ekeren's temper broke as he entered the car and slammed the door.

'I'd have been a bloody sight earlier if it hadn't been for your Taranganese friends'

'What! Where are they?'

'All over bloody Charlton, there's so many of the bastards

242

they've probably caused a traffic jam in the main street,' McKay sounded bitter.

'How would they know I was here?'

'I don't know. How did you get here?'

'I thumbed a lift in a truck, I think it was heading for Albury.'

'Well, that may be the answer.'

'How come?'

'Truckies talk to each other, they have their own brand of Citizens Radio, they chatter to each other across the air waves...useful if you're warning other truckies about speed traps or accidents blocking highways.'

'Well they'd hardly talk about hitch hikers, would they?'

'Don't be so damned naïve,' McKay peered left and right before he crossed an intersection. 'They talk about any and everything. If your friends have access to radio that would be the first thing they'd do, allocate someone to listen to the truckies band.'

'But would they tell everyone about a hitch hiker?'

'They talk about football, racing, hitch hikers, speed traps, girls on the road who want a lift or something else,' snapped McKay. 'I've done the same thing myself...for speed traps that is...' he added hastily. '...if they get a hint you're in this neck of the woods that's where they'll be...and they are. I've spotted two already.'

'How do you know it's them?'

'I just do! How do crims spot a copper a mile off...just bloody instinct!'

'How could they isolate the car we're in.'

'They could blockade every road and see who's going in or out, there aren't that many roads in or out of this one-horse town. The railway is out; with the number of trains a day we get here we'd be hanging around until tomorrow morning. We were going to use a chopper but the damned thing developed a hydraulic problem and spattered oil everywhere.'

'When did you get here?'

'About half an hour ago.'

'What do we do now?'

McKay cursed and ignored the question.

'You said a man named Rivera was involved?'

'Yes.'

'Well he's no bloody fool.'

'Who the hell is he?' Van Ekeren said angrily. 'When I mentioned his name to Kelsey, he seemed to have a fit!'

'He's a professional assassin or hit man. If anyone needs anything done that involves taking a shot at anyone, Rivera is their man.'

'Well if you know that, why is he wandering about unmolested?' Van Ekeren was scandalised. 'What the hell are you people doing? Why hasn't he been arrested?'

'We have to find him first. Secondly, when or if we catch him, every do-gooder in town will rally round saying how misunderstood he is, that he had a bullying father and a wayward mother who took him off the tit too soon, and the wicked Americans forced him to do it,' McKay said bitterly. 'Does that answer your question?'

'Surely you have the resources of the law!'

'Pigs arse! Look at the fuss if we arrest any suspected terrorists. We have to provide a damned good case to hold them for 28 days, if we make any mistakes or omissions we're accused of racism, brutality or both, by the compassionista and then some smart arsed lawyer and do-gooder magistrate says they are mentally ill and gets them off to go and kill somebody else.'

'What do we do then?'

'Use our heads and run like hell! Rivera will probably lock onto us before we're four miles out and we've nowhere to hide.'

'Why not? Can't we just drive to Canberra?'

'It's not that easy!'

'But can't we ask for reinforcements? Rivera seems to have enough resources.'

'Rivera has some cabal in Taranga behind him, he has unlimited resources on call.'

'Well you represent the Australian government! What about our resources?'

'We haven't got any sodding resources. My job is to get you to Canberra to see if you've got anything useful! All I have is this blasted car out of our car pool, courtesy of the ratepayers of Australia, many of whom are ashamed we exist. This damn car will stand out like a sore thumb.'

Van Ekeren's euphoria at being rescued by the country's top security and intelligence department had evaporated. From the efficient organisation he had envisaged it seemed it was operated by a crowd of parsimonious and whingeing hacks.

'Why?' he resorted to sarcasm. 'Has it got 'Secret Agent' written on the boot lid?'

He shouldn't have said that, but was exasperated, hungry, and disillusioned. When he thought of ASIO he had in mind something on the lines of James Bond, fast cars and being hoisted out of moving vehicles by helicopter and rushed to the centre of government where grateful intelligence heads, faces working with emotion, would shake him by the hand and clap him on the back. All he had had so far was frustrating conversations with Messrs William Shackleton and Tremlett of Canberra…and now this cynical bastard.

Yet, Van Ekeren knew in his heart McKay's angry tirade against the hearts and flowers brigade who justified actions of terrorists had substance. These were arguments with which Van Ekeren had sometimes sympathised, but after this week's events he was having second thoughts.

'No, we had "Drug Runners Incorporated" stencilled on the back window,' was McKay's cutting answer. 'Somehow it seemed more appropriate!'

'Get stuffed!' Van Ekeren snarled, furious because he'd asked for that. They travelled for a couple of kilometres in silence before Van Ekeren eventually had to ask the question. Why would their vehicle stand out?

'Because we have ACT number plates,' responded McKay. 'The thought may occur to Rivera that the man he's chasing could enlist the help of one of the intelligence organisations. An ACT registration might indicate that. All he has to do is put two and two together, and chase after it.'

They roared out of Charlton heading for Bendigo, a few miles out a car was parked under a tree with Tara leaning nonchalantly against the bonnet. Van Ekeren gave a startled squawk and ducked down.

'What the hell...?'

'That was one of them.'

'Jesus! Doing that you may as well have pulled your jumper up over your head or maybe leant out of the window and shouted 'Here I am'.'

'What was I supposed to do, stare at him?'

'No, just keep your bloody eyes open! You should have seen him and ducked down long before we reached him, not just as we were passing him!'

'Well perhaps you should tell me what to do in an emergency, you're the bloody expert.'

McKay ignored that one, looked in the mirror and grunted.

'He hasn't registered anything yet, but don't bank on it being indefinite. I'd say he spotted the ACT number plates. Hold on!'

He accelerated and the countryside raced past. Van Ekeren looked back. Tara was still in the same position, looking in their direction although he looked bored and totally at ease. He was holding what could be a mobile phone. Van Ekeren reflected his relaxed demeanour would abruptly change if Rivera or De Ryk appeared on the scene.

'How do you know of Rivera?' Van Ekeren asked.

McKay asked an oblique question.

'What business are you in?'

'Insurance broking.'

'Do you know people from other firms of brokers?'

'Yes...but that's different.'

'What's different about it?'

'Well if you know each other so well, why wasn't he arrested when he came in?'

'A good question...' McKay gave a hollow laugh '...he has the ability to change his appearance, apart from his other accomplishments he's an expert at disguise and he has several genuine passports. I've no doubt he's now using a Taranganese passport. There are many like him, sometimes you pick them up when they pass through airport security, many times you don't. Let's face it. If anyone wants to land in Australia how *do* we prevent them? For years we had these bloody leaky boats streaming across the Timor and Arafura Seas full of so-called asylum seekers, when we stopped them, we were accused of brutality. We have a coast line so vast we can't police the lot, there's no limit to remote places light planes can land.'

Van Ekeren could see the point. He peered through the rear window. The road was clear for three kilometres or so, with small blobs indicating vehicles a long way behind.

McKay reached into his pocket and produced a mobile phone. He held it in one hand with the other on the steering wheel, pressed one button and held the phone to his ear.

'Shit!' he said.

'What?'

'We're in a dead spot.'

McKay rummaged with one hand under the dash and produced a small radio transmitter. He handed it to Van Ekeren.

'Switch that on and adjust the aerial until you hear something.'

'What am I listening for?'

'What do you think? Anyone calling us.'

'Do you know where people like Rivera are likely to head when they reach here?'

'Sometimes, not always,' McKay eased the car around a wide righthand bend. 'If they have a base near here that's news to us. You'd better fill me in on what happened to you.'

Van Ekeren studied McKay as he related what had happened since he left Sydney Airport. He had previously noted McKay was about 6 feet, with piercing blue eyes and fair, wiry hair that curled naturally. His accent was slight, he had the occasional Australian twang, otherwise he could have come from anywhere in the English-speaking world. His general demeanour, as Van Ekeren had discovered, was heavily weighted to cynicism and sarcasm, maybe an outlook attained by members of all security organisations after years in the game.

McKay listened without interruption, except when Van Ekeren mentioned the attempt to wheedle money out of the small boy, he thought that amusing. After laughing he leant over and produced some sandwiches out of the glove box.

'Left over from this morning. I was going to ditch them so dig in.'

Van Ekeren continued the story as he munched, the bread was hard and stale but it ranked as the most delicious meal he'd ever tasted. He even licked the crumbs off his fingers and the paper before attacking a half-melted chocolate bar.

'Thanks,' he said and meant it.

'All part of the service.'

That brought Van Ekeren to another subject. He told McKay of his initial contact with ASIO and the problems he encountered.

'I heard about that from Alan Kelsey,' McKay replied. 'A case where someone didn't use her loaf. A new girl was on reception when you rang in. Your type of call wasn't in the Public Service training manual!'

'What do you mean?'

'A man on the run asking for assistance, plus asking us to reverse charges, threw her completely. First off she thought it was a hoax.'

'I wouldn't blame her for that,' mused Van Ekeren. 'Do you get many hoax calls?'

'Too many, we received one recently that related to nuclear pigeons shitting atomic crap over Sydney.'

'Inventive!'

'Yes, and a waste of our bloody time. After cackling with laughter, they left the phone box receiver just dangling which blocked the line. You were put onto Bill Shackleton who tends to think in straight lines like a public servant. Alan gave them both a rocket while the girl was temporarily taken off the switch for retraining.'

'Seems to me she isn't the only one,' Van Ekeren said pointedly, bitterness over his experiences during the last week coming to the fore. 'It's appalling when people like Rivera can kidnap ordinary citizens from airports and rampage all over the countryside.'

'Really?' McKay responded coldly. 'With our penny-pinching budget, we can't be everywhere. Nor can we take steps to apprehend people or forestall coups d'état if those who find out about them keep their bloody mouths shut.'

'What's that supposed to mean?'

'You say you found out about this coup while you were in Taranga City?'

'Yes.'

'Did you inform anybody?'

'I...I...no I didn't.'

'Why not?'

'Because...!' Van Ekeren hesitated. It was because Westerman had persuaded him it was nothing to do with him.

'Come on! Enlighten me, I'm all ears.'

'Well...because I didn't know what it was...!'

'Don't give me that crap. Didn't it occur to you to see or call our man at the Australian Embassy and put him in the picture?'

'What would he have done?'

'A damned sight more than you did,' snorted McKay. 'Maybe you were too busy stashing your drugs away to bother about bloody terrorists.'

It took a moment for that one to sink in, then Van Ekeren hit the roof.

'Look here, those bastards planted ...!'

'That's what they all say,' McKay said flatly. 'Spare me the sordid details. I thought it was icing sugar they asked me to bring in, or washing powder.'

'Oh, pig's arse!' Van Ekeren seethed with fury as they drove on, but while raging at McKay's verbal foray, which he knew was deliberately provocative, he was furiously angry with himself. He had had some justification for being reticent directly after that scary meeting, he didn't know one side from the other, whether it was Lebak and his cohorts or the De Souza government who were the good guys. But his inaction subsequent to that had been a desire not to become involved, a lack of initiative and cowardice. He knew McKay was right; he should have contacted the Australian embassy.

In addition, after he had met De Souza and had heard the views of Lopez on the subject of Lebak and the on-going insurgency, there was no doubt what course of action he should have taken, a viewpoint confirmed by the spinechilling conversation with Delgado at the reception. He should have told Lopez at the airport but had funked it.

'What happened in Taranga, what were the details?'

'Get stuffed'

'That will get us nowhere,' McKay reached for his mobile phone and went through the same procedure as before, uttered an exclamation and tossed it onto the dash.

'Are we still in a dead spot?' Van Ekeren offered an olive branch.

'Yes,' McKay reached into his pocket and produced a small dictating machine. 'If you won't tell me, tell your country and anyone you respect in Taranga who may get killed. Put it on tape, you've got 30 minutes on each side of the tape.'

Van Ekeren nearly threw it back at him but realised by doing so because of antipathy towards McKay he would compound the error he'd already committed. Delgado, Rivera, De Ryk and their associates had meant to kill him to prevent him talking, so where was the justification for refusing to talk now? If he kept quiet, they were going to kill people, De Souza and Lopez included. He thought of Lopez' wife and daughter, also under threat of mutilation and this hardened his resolve. He turned on the recorder and began to dictate.

After about five sentences he turned to McKay.

'I gather you have two colleagues named Shackleton.'

'Yes, as unlike as chalk and cheese, uncle and nephew.'

'Well I hope I meet the other one sometime.'

'You will,' said McKay. 'He's already been to see your friend Driscoll.'

'Driscoll?' Van Ekeren looked puzzled before light dawned. 'Oh... Driscoll! He's the airline engineer.' He thought for a moment and then added. 'He's the bloke who saved my skin.'

'Now you can save others,' retorted McKay, whereupon Van Ekeren recommenced dictating.

CHAPTER 25

'**C**alling AY 72'

'AY 72,' McKay seized the radio and responded.

'Marcus Templeton, Dave, we've tapped into the Signals Directorate and Telstra towers in your immediate area. We're picking up transmissions, reception is patchy but we're making sense of them. They are on to you. They tracked you from the hotel, they toured all the pubs and described your passenger. From what we've overheard they claimed to be Federal Police. They left on the Bendigo road ten minutes ago.'

'Shit!' replied McKay. 'Thanks, Marcus. AY 72 out!'

He turned to Van Ekeren.

'That's all we need. I knew Rivera was no bloody fool but he locked onto us quicker than expected.'

'Who was that?'

'Marcus Templeton, he's a wizard with computers and anything electronic. He's tapped into the Telstra local mobile phone towers.'

'You can listen in to peoples' private conversations?'

'Yes, any objections?'

'Er...no,' Van Ekeren was startled by the revelation but deemed it best to say nothing. 'But how did they lock onto the relevant conversations?'

'Rest assured they can, I'm not sure either, that's Marcus' province. I understand it's by locking onto key words.'

'Key words?'

'It's a refined art. For instance, if the word 'assassination', or 'suicide bomb' is uttered over the phone lines it triggers alarm bells and by an electronic process locks onto the call.'

'I've read about that, the CIA do it,' said Van Ekeren. 'But terrorists would be aware of it too, they'd avoid using them, wouldn't they?'

'Yes, but we're aware of euphemisms they use, something like "taking out" or "Allah's will" or some such, I've no idea what they'd be.'

'Bloody hell!'

'Hold on ...!' the next bend nearly took McKay by surprise. 'That's not our problem anyway, our immediate problem is this ACT registration number which could act like a beacon for them.'

'Surely it's not the only ACT number plate around here.'

'Agreed, but as far as they're concerned any ACT plate will be worth a second look!'

'What do we do now?'

'Go as fast as we can,' his tone verged on the sarcastic. 'They'll probably catch us in the end, by sheer weight of numbers and by communicating with each other.'

'So, we're not out of the wood yet?'

'Are we buggery! You'd better tell me what happened in Taranga,' said McKay. 'Have you completed dictating into that machine?'

'As much as I can remember, it's a bit sketchy but the main detail is there.'

'Well fill me in as well, the way things are these bastards may yet bail us up. If they do, we need this information spread over as many sources as possible, you, me and this recorder.'

Van Ekeren gave him the gist of the sequence of events in Taranga City, McKay gave more than one wry smile as he detailed the meeting chaired by Lebak when Van Ekeren was totally unaware what people were talking about, the true nature of the meeting and what he had got himself into. Despite the seriousness of the current situation even Van Ekeren found himself smiling at some hapless misinterpretations he had made during that meeting before realisation dawned.

'A classic double entendre.'

'Double Dutch more like,' growled Van Ekeren. 'It was caused by two bloody Dutch names that sounded similar.'

'How did you feel when you got back to your hotel?'

'Like a prize prat!' Van Ekeren said bitterly. 'No...more than that, a shit scared prize prat! I was even more of a bloody prat when I was persuaded by Westerman to do nothing.'

'You weren't to know who was who.'

'Don't make excuses for me, you made that point a short time ago,' retorted Van Ekeren. 'From what was said at that meeting, in hindsight it's bloody obvious who the bad guys were, especially that nasty little shit Franco and what he said he'd do to Lopez' daughter. It was even more bloody obvious when I met De Souza in person and after a conversation I had with Lopez.'

At this point the radio began to crackle.

'Calling AY 72!'

'AY 72,' McKay responded.

'According to a recent conversation they have just passed through Wedderburn.'

'How the hell have they reached Wedderburn already? They've only just left Charlton.'

'They must be travelling fast. Reception still patchy but I'm keeping up, Dave.'

'You've done well, Marcus, keep in touch,' McKay clicked off and turned to Van Ekeren.

'Bugger it! I'd say they're heading in our direction.'

He peered at the surrounding countryside.

'There are no roads turning off anywhere and if there were, we'd still stand out because the countryside is absolutely flat.'

'What's the good news?'

'There isn't any! I reckon they'll catch up with us within 15 kilometres at the most, that will give us about 12 kilometres or so to turn off.'

'Turn off?'

McKay swung around another bend with screeching tyres and Van Ekeren feared they would spin off the road. 'We'll have to turn off somewhere.'

'If you say so, but can't you summon up help?'

'Help!' McKay plunged deeply into sarcasm. 'You mean contact all our local ASIO agents in Wedderburn, Inglewood and Bridgewater? They'll all come to the party driving their Armed Personnel Carriers. We'll call up the police as well if you like! My cover will be blown and when they find out who you are, they won't believe either of us. They'll throw you into the coldest police cell this side of Bairnsdale.'

'There must be somebody who knows where we are.'

'They do. Marcus will have briefed them on roughly where we are. But they won't have an accurate fix.'

'Why don't you ring them on your mobile?'

'Because the bastard won't bloody work, we might as well be in the middle of the Sahara.'

'Where the hell do our taxes go?'

'Not to the telephone company obviously and certainly not to the security services, I can assure you of that!' McKay was vitriolic. 'All we ever get is brickbats from do-gooder politicians and religious extremists who enjoy privileges here that don't exist in the regimes they support or excuse and want us to emulate.'

Van Ekeren said nothing. As a teenager he had identified with people who tilted at authority and protested against the existence of security organisations like ASIO and ASIS. McKay swerved to avoid a stray dog and continued his tirade, Van Ekeren wondered if he'd read his thoughts.

'Sometimes I wonder why the hell we bother. Some of my senior colleagues have seen people risk bullets and land mines to flee to the type of regime and society we have here, they've also seen those who failed get shot, or strung up on barbed wire. Some of them saw it in Berlin and I've seen it in East Timor. But when we act to protect our society from regimes like that, we become the villains!'

Van Ekeren deemed it best to say nothing.

At Bridgewater, they turned left onto the Loddon Highway, McKay abandoned any pretensions of beating them to Bendigo. The reports from Marcus Templeton became more frequent, it was obvious De Ryk and Rivera were travelling fast and homing in other units.

McKay too was travelling so fast that Van Ekeren's fear was of being picked up by the police, with three or four vehicles in the same vicinity burning up the road surface it was incredible none of them had been apprehended. He mentioned this to McKay who told him to shut up, he had enough worries trying to avoid being shot full of holes without worrying about speeding tickets.

McKay's ruse worked, but for how long was open to conjecture. Templeton reported that Rivera's military mind had arrived at a logical conclusion when they reached Derby as he reckoned they should have overtaken their quarry by that time. Of the three pursuing cars Rivera ordered one to continue to Bendigo, and the others to reverse course.

'You'll like this one, Dave,' said Templeton. 'Rivera said he approached three small boys sitting on the roadside at the junction of Loddon and Calder Highways. They were collecting registration numbers. They picked up your registration and said which way you went, he said he slipped them $20.'

McKay cursed angrily.

'I've a good mind to head back and snatch that $20 off them. When was this?'

'Just!' replied Templeton. 'They just left Bridgewater.'

'There should be a law against small boys collecting rego numbers,' McKay snapped. 'I should have stopped and boxed their ears!'

'That would have done a lot of good,' Van Ekeren said mildly.

'It bloody would, I'd have felt better!' Van Ekeren had some sympathy with his sentiments.

'Where are we?' McKay asked as Van Ekeren consulted a Shell map on his knee.

'Approaching Serpentine,' Van Ekeren answered.

'If we take the road for Bendigo from there, we'll run into the other car that carried on to there, we'll have to go north to Kerang.'

'We'll never beat them to Kerang.'

'We'll think of something!'

CHAPTER 26

Alan Kelsey entered Bramble's office and sat down heavily in the chair opposite him.

'Have we heard from McKay?'

'Marcus Templeton is on listening watch,' grunted Bramble. 'But there are complications. Van Ekeren wasn't exaggerating when he said he was being chased all over the countryside.'

'We'd better contact the police to see if they have become involved,' said Kelsey. 'How are things with McKay?'

'His phone is either out of range or not working. Marcus Templeton is picking up conversations via the radio network.'

'Good. Do we know the names of those chasing him?'

'Rivera, we knew that, also a man named De Ryk.'

'De Ryk? Do we know him?'

'Yes, he's turned up before,' said Bramble. 'He's a Taranganese of Dutch extraction who's been living here for years, he has a police record for minor offences and has connections to people smugglers. The police have had an eye on him for some time.'

'Well if he's rampaging around the countryside shooting at Australian citizens there's a good case for deporting the bastard,' retorted Kelsey. 'What about Rivera?'

'We know he's one of those in pursuit of McKay and Van Ekeren. They're heading for New South Wales but it looks as though they're going to be hemmed in.'

'Then we'll have to do something and be damned quick about it,' said Kelsey. 'Get hold of Captain Bartlett of the SAS for me, Bob. This calls for intervention. Check with Marcus and see whether the police are directly involved now, with guns popping all over the countryside and speed limits being trashed I'd be surprised if they're not.'

*

The police were now involved, maybe some of the cyclists or other road users had reported that something reminiscent of the Wild West was occurring on various country roads. Had the police done their job properly Van Ekeren and McKay wouldn't have lasted fifteen minutes. True, when dealing with country roads over a large area the long, and thin, arm of the law can't patrol every one. But to park a police car in the middle of a straight stretch of road with a visibility of about four kilometres in each direction, with blue lights flashing, was hardly calculated to catch anyone.

Two rather bored constables were chatting up two blondes in a sports car less than a kilometre ahead, McKay turned off to the side of the road.

'Bugger it!'

They waited while a heavy truck thundered passed before they did a U-turn and went back the way they had come. They watched the two police in the mirror as they receded behind them, they never deviated from their conversation with the blondes and the truck was cursorily waved through. They had no idea they were so close to the cream of the Australian Intelligence service and a hardened and cunning drug runner. Their demeanour suggested resentment at being called to man country road blocks miles from anywhere, where all they would catch would be unregistered farm tractors and blondes. McKay swung the car around a bend and came to a halt.

'What's that ahead?' Van Ekeren indicated a gate festooned with flags and bunting.

'Search me,' said McKay. 'Could be a fair or Country show.'

'We'd best keep away from it then.'

'Hell no! We'll head for it, we stick out like a sore thumb parked here wondering what to do and those bastards will travel up this road eventually. We'll go and join in. Come on … have you got any money?'

McKay grinned as he asked the question, Van Ekeren's answer was abrupt and to the point. They drove to the show entrance and joined a queue of vehicles.

'It's an agricultural show,' remarked McKay.

'Thank you. I can read,' Van Ekeren replied coldly.

McKay paid at the gate and parked in a paddock allocated for car parking. He parked it so they wouldn't be blocked in and could make a quick getaway if necessary. Before he left the car, he twiddled with the radio and listened carefully to the police bands. When he joined Van Ekeren his expression was grim.

'The police are looking for us, it seems someone who narrowly missed getting run over or shot phoned the police and gave them our registration.'

'Surely that's good news?'

'Of a sort, yes,' McKay smiled ruefully. 'But if you want

this information of yours to reach Canberra it will cause complications. They won't listen to anything you say about a coup d'état in an island nation between here and Indonesia, they'll merely lock you up and phone Sydney to tell them how they've arrested the drug runner of the century.'

'Oh, bloody hell!'

'Bloody hell indeed,' replied McKay. 'Let's have a look around, we'll see if there's a back way out of this show.'

There were many tents, stalls and stands, they passed a small paddock with several tractors on show and walked amongst tents and stalls such as coconut shies, hoopla, shooting galleries and stalls selling cakes, stirrups, saddles and dog paraphernalia. As Van Ekeren looked at the cakes the pangs of hunger became almost irresistible.

The sun had passed its best, but was still warm and there was considerable activity. They wandered into an area which contained a plethora of poultry and pigeons, with various awards pinned on the cages. McKay was fascinated by a pigeon with large feather flippers on its feet.

'How the hell does it fly with those things on its feet?'

'Maybe ASIO could use them for carrying messages, you could clip them to their feathered feet,' Van Ekeren said nastily. His temper had not been improved by those appetising cakes but his pride wouldn't allow him to ask McKay to buy one for him.

'Or small packets of drugs,' McKay plucked at his chin. 'How much could one pigeon carry, eh? What do you think — four thousand dollars' worth?'

Van Ekeren saw he was going to get the worst of any exchange of pleasantries, so he wandered off to look at some assorted cocks and hens in the poultry section, who looked them up and down disapprovingly. Van Ekeren was again conscious of an aroma he carried around with him, the pungent smells that arose from the poultry and pigeons were such that he welcomed the competition. He would willingly have stayed there longer to drown out his own odour.

'What now?' he asked McKay.

'We need help,' McKay sounded thoughtful. 'The police are on the lookout for our vehicle and will be onto us soon, there's a police presence in here already from the normal security angle. Our friends will soon track us down as there aren't many places we could have run to earth.'

'How could they track us here?'

'They would have been listening to police bands and calculated roughly where the police think we are,' McKay said ruefully. 'They should be nearing Kerang if they're not already here.'

'You said help?' Van Ekeren queried. 'Help from whom?'

'ASIO!' snapped McKay, and added sarcastically. 'Or would you prefer me to enlist the local Boy Scouts?'

'They'd probably be a bloody sight more use.'

'To people like you looking for customers...yes!'

'What the hell do you mean by that?'

McKay gave a meaning smile and walked out of the poultry barn. Despite Van Ekeren's fury he was scared of being left alone and followed him like a lamb, muttering angrily.

'Where's the car park from here?'

'Over there,' Van Ekeren pointed.

'That track behind those tents leads to it, look, there's a car going towards it. Where did it come from?'

Van Ekeren craned his neck and peered in the direction from which the car had come.

'There's a gateway in that direction,' he said. 'Cars are entering through it.'

'Then that's our way out,' said McKay. 'Let's get back to the car, we'll go out that way and evade those two sex starved constables. Then we'll head for New South Wales.'.

They retraced their steps to the car park, there was an alternative exit they hadn't noticed before. They drove down the other track, which led to another gate opening onto another road. McKay handed over their ticket and they landed on the roadway outside.

'Which way now?' asked Van Ekeren.

'Who cares,' answered McKay. 'We'll head for the first sign post.'

*

They crossed the river into New South Wales where McKay had phone reception and was able to make a call.

'What was that all about?' Van Ekeren asked when he returned.

'They know where we are, before that they hadn't a clue apart from reports from Marcus Templeton, he was guessing at some stages.'

'What will they do, send reinforcements?'

'That may take too long with those bastards on our tail. The way bloody Rivera's mind works it won't take him long to realise where we're heading and where we are now.'

'So now what?' Van Ekeren persisted. He could feel a tingling in his back as if Rivera was taking aim between his shoulder blades.

'I'm waiting for instructions,' McKay said acidly. 'Either we head for Canberra by road, or they send an SAS team to pluck us out.'

'What do we do in the mean-time?'

'We have to stay overnight, find ourselves a motel. You could do with a wash for a start. I'm tired of making excuses when people wrinkle their noses at you.'

'Look I've had enough...!'

'Oh, shove it,' McKay said wearily. 'Just thank your lucky stars we're still alive and somebody knows where we are and are working on it. We've also got reception on this bloody phone at last. OK! The first priority is to get out of sight before Rivera and that bloody gorilla come rampaging up the main street.'

'So...we look for a motel?'

'Preferably one with a shower.'

Van Ekeren ignored that one; he had a feeling McKay had a riposte loaded and ready for firing so decided to say nothing.

'That one has a vacancy,' Van Ekeren indicated a motel ahead.

'Let's hope it has a shower and a laundry!' McKay said pointedly. Again, Van Ekeren thought McKay may have a pointed riposte ready, but had to ask the question.

'I hope you've got enough money,' he said coldly.

'Enough for one. You can sleep outside and stink to your heart's content.'

'Pigs arse!' Van Ekeren snarled furiously.

'Good idea! You stink like one,' McKay said viciously as they turned a corner. 'I'll hire a separate room for you where you can stink away.'

'Can't you charge it to the Government?' retorted Van Ekeren.

'Aye...maybe,' McKay's good humour slowly returned. 'I've got a department credit card so no worries there. You'd better stay out of range...' he hastily amended it as Van Ekeren stiffened '...er...sight...in the car while I book in.'

'Another bill for the taxpayer, I suppose,' Van Ekeren realised immediately he shouldn't have said that, he didn't even know why he did but it was too late to bite it back.

'You should worry,' snapped McKay. 'Without it you *would*

be sleeping in the open — or maybe you'd prefer the house you left the other night. Rivera would be only too pleased to tuck you up.'

Again, Van Ekeren shuddered but held his peace. Now that he thought about it the Government and the taxpayer probably owed him something anyway.

*

They stayed the night in an Echuca motel, Van Ekeren hovered modestly in the car while McKay registered and booked a room. Despite his angry tirade McKay clearly had reservations about hiring two rooms; maybe he sensed Mr William Shackleton of the Accounts Department peering over his shoulder or, more than likely, if Rivera and possibly the police were searching for two men it would be wiser for motel management to register only one.

The first thing Van Ekeren did was have a shower, never had he known such bliss as warm water ran all over him and, for a spell, the aroma that had been following him around was dispelled. He had no change of clothes; he sat wrapped in a towel while McKay soaked all his garments under the shower. Van Ekeren rinsed them out and placed them over the radiator in the main room, it filled the room with steam but they had to be dry for the next day. McKay went out to get food from a local take-away shop.

They watched some appalling tripe on television, neither of them said much, they were subdued and their relationship was still not the best. The drying shirt filled the room with a damp odour, that the washing had not been 100% successful was clear from continuing traces of the aroma, but it was an improvement. Van Ekeren asked McKay if he thought Rivera would trace them, he retorted snappily he thought it more than bloody likely if he had a reasonable sense of smell. After that rebuff Van Ekeren gave up and went to bed. He slept like a log, despite McKay having a Western on TV with a cacophony of gunshots.

They didn't have a good start in the morning either, a police car was outside the driveway that nearly caused McKay to cuff the brick pillar outside reception. They had travelled barely fifty metres when a white Holden van locked onto them and followed them down the street.

Van Ekeren didn't need to verify who it was, McKay peered through the mirror to check, it was De Ryk. He was scowling furiously; maybe he was suffering from his usual physical affliction and had failed to relieve the pressure.

'How the hell did they lock onto us?'

'I'd say they didn't, not specifically,' commented McKay. 'They probably locked onto Echuca as one likely spot, amongst others, and spread out. By now he's rousted up a few more to head in this direction. They must have most of the Riverina staked out.'

'Where are your colleagues?'

'How many bloody men do you think we've got?' snapped McKay. 'Do you think we've got a man in every town and in every Sydney and Melbourne suburb?'

'Surely there must be somebody...!'

'Somebody my arse!' McKay snapped angrily. 'Tell that to the silly prats who cut our budget and never seem to have heard of the KGB, the Mafia, Al Qaeda, the bloody Indonesians... or the sodding Taranganese! We haven't enough bloody money to station people all over the place! It cost a sodding fortune to repair the punctures after bloody leftie idiots strewed tintacks all over our carpark. Don't talk to *me* about fucking reinforcements, those that we do have are all tied up elsewhere...there aren't any spare bods to help us!'

'What the hell do we do then?'

'Run like hell, or turn and fight. Have you got your gun?'

'My g...! Er...yes!'

'Well, check it out. You may need it before the day is out.'

Van Ekeren extracted it from his waistband and fingered it gingerly. He had no idea how many shots were left in it, nor how to check, he feared if he touched or altered anything he risked putting a shot through the windscreen. McKay accelerated and the gun fell from his grasp. His finger had been on the trigger and he profoundly thanked the makers for safety catches, he could easily have put a shot through his foot. In that contingency he would receive no sympathy from De Ryk or Rivera. Further, that would have been a wasted bullet, he was anxious to put as many bullets in their direction as he could...especially at De Ryk.

They took the Newell Highway for Jerilderie, the speedometer reached 160 kph. De Ryk slowly receded, but as he was probably homing his colleagues onto them from various directions, any lead gained on him was valueless although it stopped him taking pot shots. Australian country roads being what they are, there was virtually no opportunity for taking alternative routes, which would probably finish as dead ends in small settlements.

'Bastard!'

Van Ekeren wasn't sure whether McKay was referring to him or De Ryk, McKay swore as he accelerated. Van Ekeren looked back and saw De Ryk had moved up, roughly three hundred metres behind.

'Can't we lose him?' he asked.

'Not a hope, the cunning sod is hanging around just far enough to see what deviations we might make. My guess is he has somebody in front waiting for us.'

'Bloody hell!'

'So ...' McKay said thoughtfully. 'We may have to abandon the car and go on foot for a spell, in some respects we'll be better off as we have our own artillery.'

'Artillery?'

'The two guns,' McKay said. 'It looks as though they may come in handy.'

'You mean start a shoot-out in the countryside?' Van Ekeren felt an adrenalin rush. Until a few days ago he had never held a gun in anger. 'Are you serious?'

'Serious! Of bloody course I'm serious,' McKay rasped. 'Ye Gods! I've never met anybody with such cockeyed, starry eyed scruples! Yes, we'll have to start sodding shooting. If you don't like it you can surrender now, but if any of these bastards come at us with guns blazing, I've every intention of shooting back. You can suit yourself what you do.'

McKay held the steering wheel grimly as the car teetered on two wheels on the next bend.

'I only hope the information you're carrying around is worth it,' McKay continued acidly. 'Frankly, on reflection I should have left you with Rivera, he wouldn't have stood your sanctimonious platitudes either. I suppose you're one of those who believe if we're confronted by people like that we try and reason with them!'

That exchange prevented further conversation for the next half hour. De Ryk remained on their tail while McKay watched the petrol gauge. After he had nearly run off the road twice, he brusquely told Van Ekeren to move the radio dial around to see if they could pick up any communications by De Ryk. They picked up various transmissions, police and ambulance, until near the end of the band Van Ekeren picked up a husky voice that sounded like De Ryk. Another voice answered, unmistakably Rivera. The exchange was brief, but they heard enough to indicate they were being hemmed in by four vehicles.

If they stayed on the highway they could be caught like rats in a trap. McKay told Van Ekeren to get an RACV map out of the glove box to check possible turn offs. Were there any settlements, forests, open spaces? Van Ekeren puzzled over the map.

'Our petrol won't last for ever,' pondered McKay. 'We'll reach Narrandera but unless we fill up we can't travel indefinitely, not at this speed.'

'How are we that low?'

'We've done a hell of a lot of travelling and we haven't filled up,' McKay replied tersely. 'I meant to fill up at Echuca but the buggers were onto us before we had a chance.'

Two forests were coming up, one straight ahead before Narrandera and another if they took a right turn at Morundah, but there was a snag, the radio indicated one of Rivera's men was on that road.

'Where's the Urana man, according to the last message?'

'Approaching Boonoke North.'

'Then we'll have to act now, first we'll deal with De Ryk, then the others, one by one.'

'Deal with De Ryk?'

The idea was so alien and preposterous to Van Ekeren he had difficulty grasping it. The very thought of De Ryk was enough to set his entire system trembling. Where De Ryk was concerned his first thought was to put as much distance between him and De Ryk as possible.

McKay swerved into a wayside halt and stopped. He clambered out and fished his hand gun from his belt which he proceeded to check. By the time they heard De Ryk's engine approaching McKay was ready.

'You'd better count the shots, they cost $1 per bullet,' McKay said sarcastically. 'We don't want to cost the taxpayer too much do we? Have you paid your Union dues?'

Van Ekeren told him to shove it, and more besides. McKay grinned and gripped his gun with both hands. When De Ryk flashed around the bend McKay was looking straight down the road and taking aim. De Ryk registered the sight; screamed to a halt, did a complete circle, revved up and headed in the opposite direction almost in one movement. McKay fired off two shots, Van Ekeren saw sparks fly off the roof as De Ryk vanished around the bend.

'Why didn't you shoot his tyres?' he asked.

'Why don't you stop making snide comments?' snarled McKay. 'If you can do any better, Mr Bloody Perfect, you're welcome to try. Now get back in the car and hold onto this unless it offends your morality.'

He flung the gun at Van Ekeren who managed to catch it but not before the end of the barrel caught him a glancing blow on his forehead. McKay ran around to the driving seat. Van Ekeren refrained with difficulty from throwing it back at him, had he been a fraction angrier he could easily have shot him.

'Now listen on that radio, and listen good!'

Van Ekeren did listen good! He heard De Ryk talking to someone, it was not his usual low-key measured tones; he was gabbling his words and sounded panicky. Although it gave Van Ekeren some satisfaction, it also raised anticipatory fears. What would De Ryk do to Van Ekeren now if he got his hands on him? Rivera wouldn't exactly be pleased either, but at least he'd just shoot and get it over.

McKay swung right, took the road for Widgiewa and headed for the road running north from Urana on which another of Rivera's men was approaching, which Van Ekeren pointed out.

'I'm aware of that, but there's another heading south from Narrandera. There's a forest along here somewhere. We might be lucky and avoid De Ryk, and if there *is* another man along here, we might surprise him.'

They almost succeeded. De Ryk flashed past the road to Widgiewa and continued on the Newell Highway heading north. Any ideas they had of doubling back and heading south along the Newell were discounted as Van Ekeren intercepted a message indicating Fino and Tara were coming up from Jerilderie. They reached the road from Urana and headed north for Morundah, in the wake of their pursuers who were also heading for Morundah. They had reached the turn off for Boree Creek and the State Forest when De Ryk cottoned on. Proceeding at a break-neck speed he and the Narrandera man had met without the fugitives being sandwiched in the middle. He must have examined the map and calculated where they turned off.

'How many cars have they got?' Van Ekeren cried in anguish.

'Enough!' McKay was bitter. 'Surprising how Communists, Fundamentalists and Islamic terrorists can afford all sorts of equipment and refinements, if we ask for funds we only get a fraction of what we ask for...if that!'

Van Ekeren refused to be drawn as McKay remounted his hobby horse, he judged it would be dangerous to comment. He saw McKay look at him out of the corner of his eye, then shrug and concentrate on the road.

They headed for Boree Creek, according to the map there was a State Forest there and McKay had decided to leave the car and take off on foot. Fuel was low and there wasn't enough in the tank for Boree Creek.

'What are we going to do?'

'Try and merge into the landscape, if they catch sight of us, then we start shooting!'

A line of trees on the horizon steadily came nearer and nearer, a large collection of conifers on both sides of the road.

McKay increased speed, Van Ekeren turned up the radio. They heard a confused mumble as their pursuers conferred, De Ryk was just entering the Boree Creek road.

'This'll do,' McKay steered into the side of the road. 'Open that gate and I'll drive through.'

'But it's locked,' Van Ekeren protested.

'Oh dear, it's locked,' McKay gave a passable imitation of Van Ekeren's voice. 'It also says 'No Entry', doesn't it? Dear me! We'd better wait here until the owner arrives and ask his bloody permission, or wait here until they come and mow us down! Get in the car, you useless prick, and I'll deal with it, drive through when I say'.

He got out, armed himself with a tyre lever, and levered off the padlock. He opened the gate and waved the car through. Van Ekeren was so angry he was tempted to drive over his foot, but on reflection decided he needed him as an ally with De Ryk and Rivera in the vicinity.

CHAPTER 27

'**M**y God! Can't you do anything right?'
'Well you walked through it when you went to the gate,' Van Ekeren snapped back with spirit. 'You should have warned me.'

Arguing about it wasn't calculated to get them anywhere, but with their niggling relationship it did let off some steam. It certainly did nothing for the car with its rear wheel in a muddy rut and stuck fast. It wouldn't go forward or back. McKay cursed and raved, cursed the car, swore at the track and reached his zenith when he swore at Van Ekeren. In different circumstances Van Ekeren may have been impressed with his range of profanity and the ability not to repeat himself.

'Get some bracken.'

Van Ekeren resisted the urge to tell him to get it himself, sprinted into the forest edge and gathered some foliage. McKay sat himself in the driver's seat and listened to the radio.

'Shove it under the wheels.'

He did so and McKay revved the engine in short spurts, the car rocked forward and backwards. They couldn't have been in a worse position, being half way through the gate into the forest, sticking out like a beacon for anyone passing along the roadway approaching Boree Creek. Van Ekeren thrust up and down on the car boot as McKay revved up, it suddenly shot out of the rut, skidded along the track and settled across it sideways. McKay gunned the engine but it was stuck again. Van Ekeren collected more bracken, McKay freed it with quick bursts and set off slowly up the track with forceful instructions to Van Ekeren to close the gate. He did so but the car was still in plain view just before it turned the corner in the track which would have hidden it as De Ryk roared up and flashed past. He must have torn up half the road surface and his car nearly did a hand stand in the middle of the road. Van Ekeren turned and ran after McKay who opened the passenger door.

'He's seen us!'

'Shit!' McKay gunned the car along the track. 'Check your gun; we're going to need it.'

*

As cover the forest was not good, the trees were in rows like guardsmen which meant if they crossed the line between two rows of trees, they could be visible for some distance. On the credit side, bracken had grown between some rows which supplied cover, the foresters hadn't cleared it for some time. They abandoned the car in a clearing and took the map with them.

They took to the bracken and were 100 metres into the trees when De Ryk and another car screamed into the clearing. They wasted valuable time stalking the car suspiciously as though expecting an ambush, which gave their quarry another fifty metres or so head start. Another vehicle roared up before De Ryk & Co plunged into the trees, which if nothing else confirmed to McKay and Van Ekeren they wouldn't have lasted much longer had they stayed on the road.

'Bugger it!' was McKay's comment. 'That means there's at least three of them, and possibly more. We'll assume there are five, your friend Dr Ryk was on his own, wasn't he?'

Van Ekeren grunted an affirmative. He was all for rushing north in a wild panic to get as far away from them as possible. McKay favoured slow progress so they wouldn't be seen, in a north-westerly direction and at an angle to the tree lines so their pursuers wouldn't be able to see them by looking straight up the rows. The forest seemed endless to the left, they scrambled that way. Van Ekeren glanced over his shoulder but saw no signs of their pursuers.

'Will we lose them?'

'Don't ask bloody silly questions,' snapped McKay. 'If there are more than four of them, they'll lock onto us quick enough, they can spread out in all directions...it only needs one of the bastards to catch sight of us!'

His words were prophetic; they had travelled barely another 20 metres when Van Ekeren heard a shout from behind. His blood froze as he spotted one of them waving his arms and heard him shouting as he directed the rest. He started to pursue them, despite the distance Van Ekeren recognised Fino. He sprinted after them confidently, clearly De Ryk hadn't had time to brief him on what to expect, it was almost comical to see his change in demeanour when McKay fired off a long-range and accurate shot. Fino stopped abruptly and flung himself flat.

'Come on,' mouthed McKay. 'Run like the clappers, and don't look back, if you stick your foot in a rabbit hole we're finished.'

Run like the clappers they did. They were spurred on by shots from behind as they ran, Van Ekeren was panic stricken as he heard them. The chances of being hit with a hand gun at that range were remote, but it didn't register at the time. He heard a shout from De Ryk and the shooting stopped.

'Run at a regular pace and don't look back,' panted McKay. 'They won't get too close now I've shot back.'

He ran at an easy lope, Van Ekeren fell in behind him and matched his pace. They headed in a straight line between two rows of trees and Van Ekeren's panic subsided, but the temptation to look over his shoulder became irresistible. He did once, tripped over a tree root for his pains and stumbled for about 5 metres. McKay cursed him soundly as they briefly touched shoulders, he didn't catch what he said but it wasn't complimentary.

McKay cantered along easily, again Van Ekeren fell in behind him. He longed to ask what he had in mind, but feared a sarcastic response. The trees stretched ahead but as yet there was no sign of daylight ahead. He wasn't sure whether that was good or not. Were they better off dodging the enemy in the woods or sprinting away in open country?

His mind clicked over his predicament and the information he carried. There was to be a coup on the 24th. He wasn't sure what the date was now but it must be about the 20th. The signal for the coup was to be a power cut brought about by Van Elderen, presumably the coup wouldn't begin without it.

He recalled certain individuals were allotted specific tasks. Balou was to capture the Television station while simultaneously the Government Offices in Daru Street were to be invaded. The power blackout was essential to prevent transmissions by television and radio stations, freeze the Army refuelling centres and generally cause confusion.

While this was going on the man in the denim shirt would be starting a riot somewhere in the back streets, with steps being taken to silence people like Lopez and, it seemed, poor Westerman if he was still in Taranga. Van Ekeren winced as he thought of it, he had to prevent anything happening to these two people he now considered friends, and also De Souza and his family.

He was probably the only outsider who knew of the coup plans, he didn't know much but what he did know could nip it in the bud. If the power failure was forestalled most of the rest would collapse, plus he knew some of the participants, namely Delgado who stood to lose everything if Van Ekeren spilled the beans. He could understand their predicament when he left Taranga and was almost beyond recall. The attack on his hotel room when he was staying with Lopez was either an attempt to kidnap and silence him by scaring him witless, or to kill him to ensure he said nothing. In view of recent events he thought the latter the most likely.

The overnight sojourn at Lopez' house had been a stroke of luck, ironically they had brought that on themselves, since Delgado's presence and threats had provoked such a scare his stomach had done the rest.

There was no doubt if they caught him now, he was a dead man, whatever plans they may have entertained during his house 'arrest' they wouldn't waste time on niceties now, it wouldn't reflect well on a new regime if Van Ekeren divulged he had been kidnapped and incarcerated by them on Australian soil. McKay too could expect short shrift after they had pursued him over most of Victoria and New South Wales. They would have no idea who he was, but his involvement was proven, while his skill with a hand gun made him a bad risk to them. They were probably puzzling how an ordinary citizen who had been kidnapped and intimidated could have found a friend who not only had access to firearms but was extremely proficient with them. Would they think of ASIO?

'We're near the edge of the forest,' panted McKay. 'You run on and I'll go off at a tangent. Head up that slope, run up there and watch for me from the top...and *don't* be afraid to use *that* if I'm in trouble ...if they get me, they get *you*. Got it?'

Van Ekeren got it all right, being left alone with De Ryk and without McKay in the offing was not an attractive proposition, despite their uneasy relationship.

They burst from the trees and puffed and panted up the slight slope, it was roughly 300 metres to the top. McKay ran off to the left and flung himself behind a fallen tree half way up the slope. Van Ekeren panted on and risked a quick backward glance, their pursuers emerged from the trees and promptly opened fire.

He heard gunshots and fell down in a panic; he scrambled up and raced on as they came on after him, two of them with guns popping. Van Ekeren struggled over the crest and then the air was rent by the sound of another handgun. Van Ekeren heard a cry and turned to see one of his pursuers crumple, then sit up holding his leg. The other dropped flat, Van Ekeren scrambled over the summit, lay down and poked his head over the top.

He could see McKay firing shots into the trees from where De Ryk and two others were returning fire. Van Ekeren's first pursuer was still holding his leg and cursing, the other squirmed to a small hummock. Van Ekeren watched him dispassionately, as he was moving away from him he lost interest, until he realised with horror he was reaching a position to fire at McKay, marginally below and only 50 metres away.

As Van Ekeren watched the enemy gunman fired off two shots which landed close enough to cause McKay considerable concern, then Van Ekeren remembered his pistol. He extracted it from his belt, aimed at McKay's adversary and pulled the trigger. Nothing happened! He had forgotten to release the safety catch.

The other gunman fired off two more rounds at McKay, exposed as he was lying with the fallen tree pointing end on to him. While McKay was protected from those in front of him, he was not protected against anyone shooting from the side. The gunman effectively silenced McKay, who had to lie flat as the bullets hummed over his head or gouged pieces from the trunk. This was before Van Ekeren re-entered the fray, this time he released the safety catch before he took aim and gently squeezed the trigger. His safety catch omission had been a blessing in disguise, when he had tried to take a shot initially, he had been over excited and hadn't taken proper aim. This time he had calmed down, gripped the gun with both hands, as he had seen law enforcement officers do on television and took careful aim before he squeezed, not tugged, at the trigger. McKay had already responded to this latest attack, but was firing blind over the still existing roots of the tree. McKay was again peppered by the other's response at which point Van Ekeren opened fire.

Tara, for it was he, looked around in astonishment and nearly jumped in the air. He looked upward at Van Ekeren who fired again after taking careful aim. Tara hastily moved around the hummock for protection and promptly came under fire from McKay. He jumped up and ran down the slope for the trees, leaping and jigging from side to side as McKay gave him another salvo.

McKay abandoned his perch and ran in zig zag fashion up

the slope, there was a fusillade in his direction but he adopted Tara's tactics of diving and dodging. He was probably safe enough from hand guns, but there was always the chance of a lucky hit. He somersaulted over the summit and sat down, clicked the catch of the gun and reloaded from a small ammunition box in his pocket. His piercing eyes bored into Van Ekeren for a second, then he nodded.

'Good 'on yer!' he said and smiled.

Van Ekeren looked down the slope at the injured man, still clutching his leg and cursing.

'What about him?'

'Leave the bastard, they'll look after him. I aimed for what I hit...his leg,' McKay rose to his feet. 'Now come on...or we're dead ducks.'

They ran down the reverse slope, Van Ekeren could feel his heart thumping as they leapt over tufts, hummocks and small tree shoots and roots. Occasional mud patches were additional hazards, he trod on the edge of one of them and repeated his stumbling trick, which brought about another curse from McKay. There was another forest some distance ahead, it could take about twenty minutes to reach it.

There was a sputter of shots from behind as they negotiated a creek bed, which added wings to their feet. McKay turned and fired a shot, the effect was more psychological than accurate, it certainly caused alarm amongst the enemy who promptly backed off and two of them ran into each other. The nearby sound of McKay's pistol was encouraging to Van Ekeren as its sharp reports seemed more menacing than the distant popping of their pursuers' handguns.

'Don't stand staring at 'em unless you want to shake them by the hand,' snapped McKay. 'We've got to reach those trees before they do, or before they hit us. Run, you silly sod!'

Van Ekeren found time for a wry smile as they headed for the distant forest. Their truce and mutual admiration society hadn't lasted long, but strangely he felt more at ease with their customary antagonism.

The forest ahead was called Buckingong, according to a name board set up in front of the outer line, which brought forth an apt comment from McKay. De Ryk and company were about quarter of a mile back, as they neared the (relative) safety of the trees there was a crackle of optimistic gunfire which gave Van Ekeren palpitations.

They entered the outer fringe of trees at a gallop and Van Ekeren promptly fell flat on his face, ramming a fair quantity of dirt into the barrel of his pistol. This brought forth a furious tirade from McKay. Flushing an angry red, Van Ekeren followed him into the deeper shadow of the trees where they paused to take stock.

'Give me that, you clumsy sod!' McKay ground out furiously and snatched the gun. 'Hold onto that and for Christ's Sake don't drop it.'

He handed over his gun, which slipped from Van Ekeren's grasp but he successfully fielded it before it hit the ground. McKay uttered another curse and cracked open the pistol, rammed a thin twig down the barrel and cleared out the offending earth by pushing his handkerchief through it. He seemed satisfied with the result and passed it back.

'Next time shoot with it, it's not for digging the sodding garden,' he snarled. Van Ekeren's rejoinder was equally blistering and to the point. He indicated there was one particular orifice it would give him great pleasure to block with the safety catch off. Despite his anger and exasperation, McKay found time to grin.

'Come on, the bastards will be on us,' he started to flit

through the trees. There was a shout from behind and a few shots, a bullet clipped a tree 20 metres away with a loud crack followed by a screaming ricochet. Van Ekeren felt himself freeze all over and slackened pace, but he took off again as another bullet hit nearby and screamed off into the ether.

They dashed across a track that ran through the trees. Van Ekeren glanced to the left and gave a shout of dismay. A car was roaring up the track with three men in it.

'Oh bugger it...look!' he cried. 'Look!'

McKay turned; the car in question was about 70 metres away and bumping up fast. He stood and took careful aim from the middle of the track, which caused the car to swerve from the track into the grass before he fired a shot. He fired and smashed the windscreen with as pretty a shot as Van Ekeren had ever seen.

'Good shot...bloody goodo!' he shouted involuntarily.

A bullet hit the track before them, flung up some dirt and emitted a dull thudding noise.

'Where the hell did that come from?'

It was De Ryk, ahead of the pack and not far away. Van Ekeren raised his pistol and fired, for once the safety catch was off. De Ryk twisted and fell over a tree root, his gun bouncing from his hand. They turned and sprinted into trees on the other side of the track.

They ran and jumped over tree roots for ten minutes before McKay called a halt with their chests heaving and hearts thumping. There was no sign of their pursuers, with a smashed windscreen and an injured or dead De Ryk they had more pressing matters on their hands. Had Van Ekeren killed him? To his astonishment, he didn't care, no...he hoped he had! Maybe if he had this would reduce the future volume of methane gas polluting the atmosphere.

With a few moments respite McKay reached for his mobile phone. He spoke into it quickly; Van Ekeren didn't catch it but gathered he was speaking to Canberra colleagues.

'What?' he asked.

'They're on their way,' said McKay. 'They were halfway to Echuca but I've told them where we are, or where I think we are. They'll be tracking my mobile phone. Keep your bloody ears open, they're in a helicopter.'

They came across another track and ran down it heading north east, McKay thought they were heading for the Sturt Highway. Van Ekeren didn't argue, he hadn't a clue where they were. They plunged into more trees, he risked a glance over his shoulder but of their pursuers there was no sign. They emerged from the trees and ran across a paddock. The area was bare of cover so they trotted over it fast.

The Sturt Highway, if that was what it was, was visible far ahead and Van Ekeren could see traffic on it. They must have put nearly a kilometre between them and the trees before figures emerged from the forest edge. One of them was clearly De Ryk, Van Ekeren found time to regret his aim hadn't been accurate. They started in pursuit.

*

In the ASIO building in Canberra, Alan Kelsey entered the computer area and paused before Mike Duval's work unit.

'What is it, Mike?'

'I've pinpointed where McKay is, boss,' replied Duval. 'He's at a point north of Echuca, it's near a forest area called Buckingong. He says they're in trouble, they have five people after them and they're getting hemmed in.'

'Where's Captain Bartlett's helicopter?'

'At the last contact they were 40 kilometres west of Wagga and heading west.'

'How long ago was that?'

'About fifteen minutes.'

'So...they'll be much further west now assuming they retained the same heading,' Kelsey ran his finger down the map on Duval's monitor screen. 'Check with Bartlett now, Mike, I'd say he's in the vicinity of Boree Creek or Lockhart, depending on their direction.'

Duval raised the SAS control centre and asked the question, there was a brief delay. After a few minutes he got a reply and turned to Kelsey.

'According to Bartlett they were approaching Cullivel, they've noted the new co-ordinates and are now heading due north for Buckingong State Forest.'

'What's their ETA?'

'Fifteen to twenty minutes.'

'Well tell 'em to pull their finger out. McKay is in trouble and outnumbered, call him and tell him where Bartlett is, when to expect them and where they're coming from.'

*

McKay and Van Ekeren ran for some distance, the road was closer when McKay pulled up and checked his pistol.

'Now we'll give the bastards something to think about,' he lay flat at the top of a rise and took aim. 'You spot the fall of shot.'

The others advanced warily but were obviously nervous of McKay's marksmanship, even with a handgun, and were not anxious to come too close. McKay fired a couple of shots and they dropped flat. As soon as a head was raised, he fired again. His mobile phone rang and he tossed it to Van Ekeren.

'Answer that, it'll be Canberra, I hope it's good news.'

Van Ekeren picked up the phone and pressed it to his ear.

'Van Ekeren,' he announced, then decided more identification was necessary. 'McKay.'

'SAS Canberra,' a voice said. 'You are at Buckingong Forest, right?'

'Yes, we've just left the trees behind. I'd say we're east of the forest.'

'A helicopter is less than ten minutes away,' said the voice. 'Approaching from the south. We are tracking your mobile phone, don't switch it off!'

'No chance of that!' Van Ekeren retorted, which caused amusement from the other end.

'Their altitude will be about 40 metres, they should see you, attract their attention if you can but don't get your head shot off. OK?'

'OK.'

'What was that about?' McKay kept a watchful eye down the slope.

'Helicopter about ten minutes away, altitude 40 metres, from the south,' said Van Ekeren, desperate to give McKay all the facts he could to stave off acid criticisms.

'If we last that long, they're fanning out,' McKay said grimly. He fired again and had the satisfaction of seeing heads duck.

'Keep your eyes peeled to the south...' he ordered. '...I'll watch these bastards.'

He fired off another shot and turned to Van Ekeren.

'Give me your gun, go down the slope where you're out of sight and when you see that chopper jump up and down and wave your arms, take your shirt off if you must and wave that. Got it?'

'Got it,' Van Ekeren tossed his gun over. 'There's only three shots left in this.'

'You found that out without shooting your balls off, did you?' said McKay. 'We'll make an ASIO man of you yet. Now go and start waving.'

*

Captain Bartlett, commanding the SAS unit aboard the helicopter, held one hand to his earphones as the message came through from ASIO Canberra. He referred to his map, then nudged the pilot.

'They're at a point east of Buckingong Forest,' he said. 'Where are we in relation to that?'

'We're currently almost due south and heading north,' responded the pilot. 'That large patch of green ahead is the forest. If they're east of it we'll have to keep it on our left as we go towards it so keep your eyes peeled.'

Bartlett swung around to the three troopers in the rear.

'Did you hear that, Aston?' he said. 'They'll be east of the forest, just outside it now, and that's the forest up there on the left. If you see any movement just shout...right!'

'Right sir,' Aston responded and the other two nodded. Aston adjusted his position and peered through the left-hand port as the forest filled their line of vision.

Down below a desperate Van Ekeren had distanced himself from the rise where McKay was holding off their pursuers, he strained eyes and ears as he tried to pick up signs of an approaching helicopter. He was distracted by occasional gunfire, but was re-assured by hearing it at all which indicated McKay was still in action. He had removed his shirt and the cool breeze made him shiver as it passed over the perspiration of fear, over activity and panic coating his torso, which coupled with the shakes caused him to tremble uncontrollably.

He adjusted his gaze to the side of the rise where McKay was holding court and alarm ran through him as he saw a man come around the side of it and head straight for him. Initially he didn't see Van Ekeren, but as he clambered up the side of the slope to catch McKay on his flank, he turned his head and caught sight of Van Ekeren behind the rise about 100 metres away.

He paused, obviously considering whether to head for McKay or deviate to deal with Van Ekeren. It didn't take him long to calculate which was the easier option. He started to head towards Van Ekeren.

'Shit!' Van Ekeren headed away from him at high speed and the other, it looked like Fino, followed. He fired a shot, more in hope than anticipation, to cause panic, which it did. Van Ekeren sprinted away from Fino who fired another shot and loped in pursuit. The enforced activity certainly eased Van Ekeren's trembling and shakes, although his feet and legs began to feel as if they didn't belong to him as he tried to increase pace.

He risked a glance behind him which was his undoing. A slight dip in the ground caused him to stumble, as he tried to regain balance he fell forward and pitched on his face. With a cry of frustration, he scrambled to his feet and broke into a run, but had lost about 20 metres. There was another shot, but Fino was shooting on the run so the bullet missed by a mile. He stumbled again, nearly fell and gritted his teeth with fury as he ran on.

'Watch where you're going!' he snarled to himself. 'Just bloody run!'

A hedgerow loomed ahead and Van Ekeren desperately searched for a way through, he saw a gap but had to deviate to his left, Fino was able to change direction sooner and took a short cut. This gained him a valuable 20 metres or so which brought him within pistol shooting range. His next bullet was sufficiently close for Van Ekeren to track the fall of shot, it struck a small branch of the hedge about five metres from his nose as he ran for the gap in the hedge. Then he tripped over another tree root and fell headlong, when he scrambled to his feet again there was no doubt Fino would be on him.

As he gave up hope and waited for the inevitable, he became aware of a throbbing noise. He looked around and espied Fino's back as he sped away in a westerly direction. A blast of air struck Van Ekeren, which nearly bowled him over while the sun was temporarily blocked as a helicopter landed less than twenty metres away.

Two men emerged, one headed for Van Ekeren while the other moved after the fleeing Fino. The helicopter took off again and headed for McKay's citadel, about a mile distant.

Van Ekeren stood stock still as a trooper in battle fatigues approached him. He was taking no chances; his weapon was at the ready so Van Ekeren raised his hands in the air.

'McKay?' asked the trooper.

'Van Ekeren,' he responded and the trooper lowered his weapon.

'You all right, sir?'

'I am now.'

CHAPTER 28

Alan Kelsey encountered Francis Burton outside the latter's room. Burton held the door open for him to enter.

'What news of McKay?' asked Burton.

'He's safe, so is the fellow he was bringing in,' replied Kelsey. 'Dave twisted his ankle while clambering to high ground but it's not serious. They'll be in Canberra within the hour.'

'This fellow Van Ekeren says he has news of an impending coup in Taranga City which is imminent, is that it?'

'I understand so,' Kelsey nodded. 'A group of dissidents is scheming to unseat De Souza and his government, as far as can be ascertained at present the plan is to replace them with a group that favours integration with Indonesia.'

'Who's leading this proposed coup?'

'We don't know, we have the usual suspects who are most likely to be involved.'

'Well ensure this man is thoroughly debriefed when he

arrives,' Burton pulled his diary towards him. 'I'll arrange a meeting with Foreign Affairs.'

Van Ekeren's debriefing didn't take place immediately, on McKay's insistence he was escorted to a facility on the sixth floor where he could have a shower. McKay also arranged for two junior male staff to journey downtown with Van Ekeren's measurements to purchase a couple of shirts and casual trousers. When a cleanshaven Van Ekeren finally fronted into a conference room to be faced by Kelsey, Burton and Bramble the brush up and change of clothes made him feel like a new man.

Francis Burton cleared his throat and leant forward.

'Mr Van Ekeren, I understand you have information for us. I suggest you first give us the information you discovered during your visit to Taranga City so we can pass this on to Foreign Affairs. Secondly, we'll require as much detail as you can give us of the premises in which you were incarcerated so we can locate them and send an army detachment to deal with it.'

Van Ekeren indicated he understood and commenced the story of events in Taranga City. They listened intently, Kelsey briefly interrupted when Van Ekeren reached the point, during the meeting he had gate crashed, where finer details of the coup had been mentioned.

'What names can you remember from what you heard?'

'Balou was one, I don't know who he was, while Lebak chaired the meeting. Delgado was one of the leaders who made a short address, I know now he's Minister of Internal Security. He approached me at a function at their Government House, he knew who I really was by that time and the conversation wasn't a pleasant one.'

'I can imagine that!' commented Burton. 'I am acquainted with Delgado, he's a nasty piece of work.'

'What happened after that?' asked Kelsey.

'After the conversation with Delgado, I didn't feel disposed to stick around. I thought I might throw up. Lopez saw I was off colour and took me back to his house where I spent the night. Just as well I did, that night they invaded my hotel room and ransacked it, in hindsight I'd say it was me personally they were after.'

'Very likely,' commented Kelsey. 'Not returning to your room probably saved your life. I'd say the plan was for you to be disposed of, just disappear, they would have concocted some story or accident to explain it.'

Van Ekeren felt a cold shiver pass through him.

'It seems when they found the room was unoccupied, they had a hasty change of plan, or maybe it was Plan B,' Kelsey continued. 'This was to drag you off the plane at the enforced stop at Aleasino and arrest you as a suspected drug runner. The travelling case they stole from the hotel was probably going to be tampered with and produced as evidence of drug running.'

'Somebody arranged for that flight to divert to Aleasino air base,' said Burton. 'They meant to hi-jack you from there. McDermott's illness and Driscoll's initiative saved you. I doubt you would have survived had they picked you up there, they'd have concocted some convincing yarn to satisfy our government, most likely shot whilst evading arrest.'

'Your fellow passenger Driscoll scuppered everything by sneaking you and McDermott onto the aircraft which meant they had to do something at Sydney,' said Bramble. 'They planted Rivera on that aircraft and stowed your case in the hold so it landed on the carousel.'

'Rivera is often employed to fix loose ends; we've come across him before. When things went wrong at the unscheduled stop at Aleasino they put him on the flight,' said Kelsey. 'They probably tipped off Customs at Sydney about narcotics in your bag after they'd kidnapped you, which provided a reason for an otherwise unexplained disappearance.'

'When they hi-jacked you in Sydney it was done hastily without too much forethought about what to do next,' commented Bramble. 'It wasn't even Plan 'C.' Killing you in Sydney was hardly practicable, they had to get you out of the airport initially.'

'Improvising as they did, I'd say they locked you up not quite knowing what to do next. But after they'd held you for a few days it seems they realised you were a problem,' Burton commented.

'The decision was made, either locally or in Taranga, to dispose of you,' said Bramble. 'Luckily you forestalled that by doing a runner.'

'Which has alleviated a problem we had,' said Burton. 'Up to now our government has been falling over backwards to appease Taranga, negotiations regarding the off-shore oil agreement were not going well. When drugs were found in your baggage as evidence our case could have been weakened and the Taranganese could have played even harder to get.'

'As it is now, we hold a few cards ourselves,' said Kelsey. 'An Australian citizen has been kidnapped and incarcerated by Taranganese nationals, on our own soil.'

'That's the understatement of the year,' snorted Burton. 'The talks have been going badly for us. Our masters are desperate to reach an agreement to give us a measure of control in the oil negotiations but De Souza has been playing hard ball. This will help us, Taranganese kidnappers are Taranganese kidnappers, no matter what political colour they are.'

'Plus, the aspect of foreign gunmen starting small wars in our countryside,' Kelsey turned to Van Ekeren. 'Which brings us to the house where they held you. Any idea where?'

Van Ekeren sat back, then had an inspiration.

'Possibly,' he said. 'When I was out of the room, I strayed into a bedroom with a phone extension on the bedside table. The notation on the dial was D — U — M 23.'

'DUM?' Kelsey pursed his lips. 'Any ideas on that one, Bob?'

Bramble fingered his chin.

'Not off hand,' he replied. 'But we should be able to track it. I'll get onto Telstra.'

'Go through events in Australia starting from your arrival at Sydney Airport,' said Burton. 'We should be able to track that house from the phone number, it could be somewhere in the Charlton area.'

Van Ekeren went through it again and wracked his brain for any possible useful details. He indicated if he could revisit the area, he may be able to find his way to the house but couldn't guarantee it. Finally, the debriefing was complete and Van Ekeren was escorted to the door by Bramble.

'We have a unit on the top floor, Mr Van Ekeren,' Burton said. 'We'll be pleased to accommodate you for the next few days, it's the least we can do after all you've been through. You'll want to contact your employers?'

'Yes, thank you. When can I leave and go home?'

'Not yet, Rivera may still be looking for you, a slim chance, but we can't take chances. Also, the police are still looking for you in relation to this drug cache at the airport and we've got to square them first, we don't want you being jumped by Federal Police when you leave the building.'

Van Ekeren had little to complain about with the room, it was comfortably furnished and outshone many motel and hotel rooms he had frequented in recent years. There were a few similar rooms on the top deck, he assumed visiting spies were housed there from time to time...maybe they occasionally had spies' conventions!

'See you in the morning, Mr Van Ekeren,' said Bramble.

CHAPTER 29

The following day Kelsey received a summons from Francis Burton. As he reached Burton's sanctum, he noticed Burton looked chastened with his lips tightly compressed.

'What's wrong?' was his first reaction.

Burton didn't reply; from a lower drawer he produced a bottle of Scotch and two glasses. He looked at Kelsey and raised his eyebrows.

'Too early in the day?' he asked.

'Not if it's free,' said Kelsey.

'Free or freedom is relative,' Burton said heavily and poured out two measures. 'This is early in the day for me and I guess for you, but I've just come from a meeting with the Minister.'

'Which one? You mean ours, Internal Security?'

'No, the Foreign Minister,' said Burton. 'I was handballed across to him by the Ministry for Internal Security.'

'So? What's happened?'

'They have given me their decision and a course of action. I'll give you that first, and try to give the explanation later.'

'What is it, Francis?' Kelsey began to experience unease.

'We have been asked, no...ordered...to say and do nothing regarding the impending coup d'état in Taranga. The government have noted the information and will keep a watching brief on developments.'

'What? Good God! Are you saying the government wants the coup to take place?'

'That's precisely what I am saying. They didn't spell it out in as many words, but the words used were those usually employed when indicating inaction. I still can't believe it.'

'For Heaven's Sake! Why?'

'A variety of reasons, tossed obliquely into the conversation, none of which for the life of me do I find convincing. The first argument that came my way was being a small entity, Taranga is an unviable state.'

'No disputing it's small, but I can call to mind many much larger entities a damned sight less viable.'

'In addition, they indicated the present regime is a military dictatorship; which, bearing in mind the colour of our present government, tends to place them in the persona non-grata category, hinting they are a potential threat to the stability of the region. At least that's how it was outlined to me although I strongly differ from the definition and that opinion.'

'Bullshit!' snapped Kelsey. 'Is this a manifestation of leftish thinking in the government?'

'I'm not too sure what to make of it,' Burton shook his head in bewilderment. 'Leftist — Rightist; if anything, I would say De Souza and his fellow rulers were oriented to the left themselves, so from the political dogma aspect, I'm stumped.'

'That makes two of us!'

'What does make sense to me, which wasn't mentioned at the meeting, is that De Souza is bargaining very hard regarding the oil drilling rights, he's proving a very adept negotiator and is striking a hard bargain. He has also stated his government's intention of controlling and restricting the flow of oil when it is in production whereas we are anxious to exploit and extract as much as we can as fast as possible. This will assist in boosting our revenue accounts.'

'And presumably the government's electoral support,' Kelsey said pointedly. 'They calculate if the coup comes off the new rulers may be more amenable to our point of view and give us what we want?'

'That, to me, appears to be the general idea, irrespective whether the decision makers are in Taranga City or in the long run, Jakarta. There is, however, another angle, Alan.'

'Another? I'd have thought this one was enough!'

'In 1972 an agreement, or treaty, was negotiated whereby the maritime boundary between Australia and Indonesia was drawn along the edge of Australia's continental shelf, which made much sense since it's all part of our land mass.'

'Sounds reasonable, is Indonesia having second thoughts?'

'Not yet, but if De Souza persists with what he wants they could do that. De Souza wants the maritime boundary between Taranga and Australia to be half way between us and them, and despite prolonged haggling he won't budge.'

'Well in the long run I suppose with a country that size it won't affect us that much...Ah!' Kelsey straightened up. 'I see what's coming.'

'What is sauce for the goose is sauce for the gander,' commented Burton. 'If De Souza gets what he wants, then Indonesia will justifiably want the same and demand their boundary with us be re-negotiated. Therefore, our masters are of the opinion if the current Taranganese administration ceases to exist and is swallowed by Indonesia...'

'The Indonesian status quo remains.'

'And the half way maritime boundary demand between us and Taranga will just evaporate, that's their thinking which makes some sense.'

'So, we sit on our hands and throw De Souza to the wolves.'

'That's how it's been presented to me.'

'What about Van Ekeren? What the hell do we say to him?'

'I haven't started thinking about that,' Burton shook his head in a resigned fashion. 'It'll be bad enough telling David McKay.'

'But De Souza is the best thing that's happened to Taranga since the Second World War.'

'I know that and you know that,' Burton spread out his hands. 'But it appears in the short term our masters are more interested in depressing the price of petrol products in Australia, which in the longer term breaks down into votes, than showing any concern for the average Taranganese.'

'So now we do...what?'

'We do as our masters, the government, tell us. We take it on board and say it is in hand and await developments.'

'This is immoral.'

'You're preaching to the converted, Alan,' Burton said sourly.

*

Kelsey returned to his office in a furious temper. He sat and stared at the phone, then made up his mind and dialled a number.

'Gary, this is Alan Kelsey.'

'G'day Alan, good to hear from you, how are things in Canberra?'

'Depends on how you look at it,' Kelsey commented sourly. 'Gary, I have a specific question. From what you've seen and heard since you've been in Taranga City; what's the general view of De Souza and his government?'

There was a brief silence as Gary Phillips, the ASIS head of station in the Australian Taranga City embassy, considered the question.

'I take it we're on a secure line?'

'Yes, we're scrambled.'

'If you want my personal opinion; based on being around the traps for twelve months, I'd say the government is viewed favourably. They're not perfect, there are many things they haven't done and others they've probably done wrong but that charge could just as easily be levelled at Canberra and Westminster.'

'What would be the effect, in your opinion, if De Souza was usurped or overthrown?'

'What! You've heard something?' Phillips was all attention.

'I asked my question first.'

'Yes, all right! To answer yours, in my view, for what it's worth, it would be a disaster for Taranga,' said Phillips. 'For the first time since the island has been independent there is stability. They have a relatively honest and strong government that doesn't resort to dragging dissidents out of their beds in the small hours.'

'Are there any dissidents?'

'You'll always get those, even in Australia! There's a fellow named Lebak running an insurgency in the hills and I've heard rumours of an anti-government plot. These rumours of plot and counter plot have been common currency for some time, usually they come to nothing. I've heard further rumblings of late but can't nail them down.'

'What are the aims of this man Lebak?'

'Nominally he's socialist, for that read communist, and if you're a realist, read Fascist. He professes to be a great admirer of North Korea and Che Guevara. He is also an advocate of being taken over lock stock and barrel by Jakarta.'

'What would he gain from that?'

'Power in a larger fish pond, which would mean increased personal power and kudos, his socialism in my opinion is only skin deep,' Phillips replied. 'He terms himself as a progressive, and we all know what that means in the long run. Introduce any altruistic or crackpot policy and to hell with any question of how it's going to be paid for.'

'We have people like that here.'

'Lebak is the daddy of them all. He is all for complete social security from the cradle to the grave, which has been tried since World War II in many countries and merely caused bankruptcy and a reluctance by many to work. He also believes in absolute control by the state apparatus, I believe he has the idea that if he achieves his aims, in the long run he would be able to convert Indonesia into another dictatorship. Some hopes of that, I think the man is politically naïve and a prat, but he's still dangerous. He is also ruthless, people who cross him have been known to vanish and never reappear.'

'Has he any allies?'

'Probably in Jakarta and he must have the backing of some in government circles here, these types always have,' Phillips came back with a rush. 'You've heard something?'

'We have,' Kelsey replied. 'We're in the process of following up leads and I can't be specific at present, Gary. But can you follow up something for me? See what you can find out about a Dutchman named Van Elderen. He either is or has been a senior electrical engineer with a government utility and we have reason to believe he's in Taranga City. He was recently at a function at Government House so you could commence enquiries there, you may have come across him. We believe he has connections to Lebak.'

'How do you spell it?' asked Phillips and Kelsey obliged.

'Leave it with me,' said Phillips, and added. 'You'll keep me posted, Alan?'

'Francis Burton is taking a great interest in this and is most concerned.'

'That makes me fear the worst,' Phillips gave a short laugh. 'I'll make enquiries, Alan.'

'Wait a minute, Gary, one more question...!'

'I'm still here.'

'From your knowledge of Taranganese government circles and who does what, who would have the power to stop a commercial Taranganese air liner in mid-flight and divert it to a military airfield?'

'Ah! I heard about that; we were discussing it the other day. Their Defence Ministry, Air Safety Control, the Police Minister or the Ministry of Internal Security, plus De Souza himself I imagine. This also came up yesterday when I was at the US embassy with Charles Richards. I'll see if I can find out more about that.'

'OK, I'll wait to hear from you.'

*

Despite the pleasant surroundings, Van Ekeren had a disturbed night, he awoke several times, and twice took turns around the room to stop his mind buzzing.

He was now out of immediate danger, but it struck him he didn't know what the date was, wasn't the coup scheduled for the 24th? He decided to get dressed and make his way out of the room to see if he could lay his hands on a newspaper. He was shaving in the en suite bathroom when there was a brief knock at the door and someone entered. It was a woman, she was dressed in a white coat, since she was carrying a breakfast tray, he assumed she was from the kitchen area. A man accompanied her, he stood by the door as she deposited the tray on the table and they both departed.

Van Ekeren was ravenous and tucked into the scrambled eggs, toast and marmalade with relish, it surpassed anything he'd received during his incarceration. He decided life was definitely on the up and gave them both a cheerful greeting when they returned for the tray.

There was a jarring note when they left, as the door closed there was a clicking noise. He remembered he'd heard it the last time they had exited, but it hadn't registered at the time as he had been concentrating on the scrambled eggs.

He went to the door and tried the handle, it was locked.

*

Kelsey compressed his lips as he eyed David McKay who was opposite him.

'You wanted to see me, Alan?'

'Yes,' Kelsey replied heavily. 'I have some news, or more correctly I should say I have some information for you.'

'So?'

'You're not going to like it.'

'For Heavens' Sake, what is it?'

'Francis Burton had a meeting with Foreign Affairs at Parliament House yesterday, which related to your escapade with Van Ekeren and the information regarding the impending coup possibly brewing in Taranga.'

'I don't know about possibly, after what we went through. I'd say there's no doubt. Those buggers were definitely not playing games. Their aim was to silence us both...permanently.'

'Yes, I phrased that badly. What I have to tell you is that... that...in their wisdom the government...!' Kelsey tailed off, he found it difficult to continue but McKay was ahead of him.

'Are you saying the government wants this coup to succeed?'

'That is the gist of what Francis was told, yes.'

'Christ! Why?' McKay was scandalised.

'It seems it's partly because De Souza is being difficult regarding the oil agreement.'

'And for that we're prepared to allow these bastards to take over? These people were behaving like gangsters. Does Canberra know who they're dealing with?'

'I very much fear that they don't.'

'And we're going to allow it to happen?' McKay said furiously. 'This is East Timor all over again!'

'We have received our instructions from on high,' Kelsey said bitterly. 'I've been in touch with Gary Phillips in Taranga and dropped a few hints as to what we believe is going to happen. I'm hoping he will read between the lines and drop some unofficial hints in the right ears which may nip it in the bud.'

'Christ! I can't bloody believe it!' McKay said angrily. 'Van Ekeren said he overheard a conversation while he was being held prisoner, they were going to kill and bury him in one of the paddocks, an Australian national they kidnapped in his own country.'

'Which brings me to another point,' Kelsey said heavily. 'Somebody has got to tell him.'

'Oh God! You want me to do it?'

'You know him better than anyone else.'

After McKay had departed, Gary Phillips called from Taranga City.

'Yes Gary.'

'I've done some spade work, the order to ground that airliner came from the office of Delgado, he is the Minister for Internal Security.'

'Yes, I know who and what he is. Any reason given?'

'A matter of state security, nothing more specific than that.'

'Have you heard anything regarding a proposed coup d'état?'

'I've been warned off,' said Phillips. 'I mentioned this to the ambassador in passing and a few hours later I was summoned back into the presence and told to leave it alone. He told me I was not to mention it to anyone, either inside or outside the embassy.'

'He's told you to say nothing to anyone?'

'Too bloody right! This is one of those occasions when I can see the advantages of the old Soviet system,' commented Phillips. 'In Soviet embassies, the KGB man was tops, they even told the ambassadors what to do.'

'They probably still do,' commented Kelsey drily. 'So, you've been gagged?'

'Yes, my hands, and lips, are tied,' said Phillips. 'I'm sorry Alan. It's more than my job is worth to do anything that contravenes the ambassador's instructions.'

*

The next morning when breakfast appeared Van Ekeren had polished off the toast and marmalade when there was a knock at the door. McKay entered the room.

'You smell better' McKay appropriated a chair. Van Ekeren offered him a coffee. 'Yes thanks...I will.'

Van Ekeren offered him the coffee cup, and fetched the tooth glass to pour another for himself. McKay nodded appreciatively as he sipped it. He seemed ill at ease and Van Ekeren felt cold fingers go up and down his spine. Was something wrong?

'How's your ankle?' Van Ekeren asked.

'I'll survive,' McKay took a sip of coffee. 'Nothing much to it, I stepped on a stone with the side of my foot when I was climbing that rise. It's a bit sore and I still can't put my full weight on it. Probably give me a couple of weeks off...on Workers Compensation of course. I'm on Bedroom Window Patrol until I'm fully fit.'

Van Ekeren grinned and uttered an apt riposte. Although McKay's remark was similar to others uttered during their uneasy alliance as they rampaged over the countryside, this time there was no rancour, if anything now it was all over there was a strong rapport between them.

On reflection Van Ekeren understood much of McKay's irritation, when being pursued and shot at by the likes of Rivera and De Ryk the last thing he would have wanted would be a 'do gooder' politically correct moraliser for company, especially one who didn't know one end of a gun from the other. McKay cleared his throat, he had something on his mind.

He finished his coffee and eyed the door, which was closed.

'One small point before I say what I've come here to say, we've traced the house where you were held. Remember that phone number you gave us, we tracked it to a small place called Dumosa, just north of Charlton.'

'Good!' Van Ekeren said fervently. 'Did they catch anyone?'

'Nothing to speak of, a married couple named Abbott have been arrested.'

'What did Mrs Abbott look like?' Van Ekeren asked.

'Mrs Abbott? I've no idea, why?'

'Just wondered if she was a big woman,' said Van Ekeren.

'What? Why do you ask?'

'Never mind, just a thought,' said Van Ekeren. 'What else have you come to say?'

'I have something to tell you, officially that is, the idea was to tell you later today,' he said. 'I'm not supposed to be here, now.'

'Why not?' Van Ekeren asked and momentarily some of the former antagonism re-surfaced. 'Am I politically unreliable?'

McKay eyed Van Ekeren, his face was straight and Van Ekeren's heart nearly missed a beat. McKay's eyes darted around the room and back at the door. Then he nodded.

'Yes!'

'What?'

'Shut up you bloody fool, if you shout like that, they'll know you're not alone,' McKay hissed. 'Just listen and don't shout your mouth off.'

He rose to his feet, opened the door a fraction, peered through the crack between door and doorpost before shutting it again. He turned to Van Ekeren again and spoke softly. 'Tell me your opinion of De Souza. What did you think of him?'

'De Souza?' that was one question Van Ekeren wasn't expecting. 'He appeared to be a good man, he seemed sincere, though I didn't have long with him.'

Van Ekeren examined his feelings as McKay eyed him fixedly and wondered whether he was quoting what Lopez had said about the man? Yet Van Ekeren now had considerable respect for Lopez. He had taken an instant liking to De Souza, and an instant dislike to Delgado! As for Julius Lebak, he had no strong feelings, he represented the type of popular leader who would lead the masses in a blaze of misguided altruism and then be disposed of by those who eventually attained power. Such a fate had befallen Neguib, in Egypt and Trotsky in Soviet Russia, and many others of like ilk. He could almost feel sorry for Lebak.

'You know a vast oilfield has been found in Taranganese waters?'

'Yes, I knew that,' Van Ekeren replied.

'Taranga has limited funds to exploit it, but under De Souza they intend to, and do it slowly. They are putting out feelers into financial markets to find funds to do the job.'

'Yes ...?' Van Ekeren wasn't sure where this was leading.

'This oilfield could be of immense benefit to the people of Taranga, and possibly East Timor as well. It would be used for finance to nurture industry, for use in education and technology for the country, and raising general living standards.'

'For sure,' Van Ekeren said. 'This would be of great benefit to everyone. I consider De Souza would spend the money wisely, find export markets and leave a little for his home market, that's how I see it.'

'You've said enough,' McKay walked to the window. 'You believe it should be developed slowly, with an eye to the long term, for the benefit of all in Taranga?'

'Yes, I believe that's how it will be done.'

'It is how it should be done, but reality could be very different ...' McKay turned to face him.'...unless something is done to prevent the alternative.'

'What alternative?'

'That a coup d'état will be organised by personnel from a very powerful neighbour just across the water. This is the coup you stumbled across. Troops could occupy Taranga in the short term, invited to come in to restore order, a tactic often employed by the Soviets when people revolted against them, but once in they will never leave. The country and its infant oil industry will be then usurped and plundered by that very powerful neighbour and a vast industry will be set up. The extraction of the oil will be expedited and it will be ploughed into overseas coffers. Much will then be sold internationally and to us to bolster our own oil reserves.'

'Are you suggesting Australia is involved...?'

'No, not directly, but I have reason to believe we've entered into an agreement. Perhaps that's too strong a word, let's say we have a tacit understanding that if we turn a blind eye and recognise the takeover, as we did initially with East Timor, we shall be granted preferential rates or terms for the exploitation and importation of much of that oil.'

'What...you mean...we're supporting the coup?'

'Not exactly, let's say we don't intend to do anything to warn De Souza or to stop it, for financial or other benefits we hope to obtain.'

'But that's outrageous, it's immoral!'

'International politics and manoeuvrings are full of immoralities, for once I agree with you,' McKay's lips tightened as he looked at the door again.

'What can we do?'

'I can do nothing,' McKay looked grim. 'I am a servant of the state. I could finish up in the ranks of the unemployed and probably be unemployable if I breached security. I love my job and I'm no good at anything else. Besides, you know who to contact in Taranga better than I do. I can't pick up a phone and ask to speak to De Souza; the first question they'd ask is 'Who the hell are you?' The second point is that any phone call would be traced to me ...then goodbye ASIO, Mr David bloody McKay and hello dole queue and possibly hello prison!'

'What are you saying?'

McKay walked to the window again.

'There are various alternatives, there is a fire escape outside for one,' he remarked conversationally. 'There is also a service lift on all floors that leads to the basement plus the usual stairwell. Another point is, we are basically Public Service, walk around the building looking as if you have a right to be here, carrying a file perhaps, and you'll never be challenged, providing you are unrecognised.'

'I don't quite see what ...!'

'Shut up,' McKay snapped irritably. 'Have you heard a word I've said?'

'Yes.'

'Do you want De Souza to be toppled by Lebak and Delgado, with him and his family conveniently shot while their usurpers are putting down riots that Lebak and his thugs started?'

'Well, no...!'

'Do you believe the status quo in Taranga should be maintained?'

'Yes, I do,' Van Ekeren thought of De Souza, and Roberto Lopez. Then he thought of Delgado, De Ryk, Rivera and that despicable little man Franco who would relish disfiguring Lopez' attractive young daughter Maria. That settled any doubts.

'Good!' McKay headed for the door. 'You'll be sent for shortly, don't say too much, just act dumb...which for you shouldn't be too difficult. Just remember what I've said. It will be up to you, if you can evade them long enough to get a warning out somehow...then it is Vive De Souza...eh?'

Van Ekeren was still sitting on the bed after McKay left, he had not moved when McKay poked his head around the door again.

'What?'

'The dialling code for Taranga is 621.'

Then he disappeared again, leaving Van Ekeren feeling perplexed and worried. He had much to think about.

CHAPTER 30

Van Ekeren sat opposite Francis Burton. Robert Bramble was also in attendance. Burton cleared his throat.

'Mr Van Ekeren, we have reason to believe the information you supplied yesterday could be correct, we have been making discreet enquiries.'

'Oh!' Van Ekeren inclined his head gravely. 'That's good!'

'Mr Van Ekeren, you are an Australian and loyal to your country, are you not?'

Even if he hadn't known what was coming, this platitude would have promptly aroused suspicion. An appeal to finer feelings and patriotism presaged that something was about to be suggested that possessed an element of duplicity. McKay's words came home with redoubled force. The adage that patriotism was the last resort of the scoundrel also came to mind.

'Er...yes,' he replied uneasily.

'It is essential our country's position should not be

prejudiced and her interests and standard of living shouldn't be jeopardised. You are aware, of course, of the world position regarding oil?'

He wasn't entirely, although he'd recently registered McKay's brief synopsis on the local international scene. But this wasn't the time to request a geography or economics lesson so he nodded.

'We have every reason to believe...' Burton continued smoothly '...that some of our oil supplies could be affected by the position in Taranga, and that a change of climate could very well be in our interests.'

'You what? A change of clim...!' he raised his eyebrows. Although he had known what was coming this oblique reference still took him by surprise. 'Are you saying you want this coup to succeed?'

'I didn't say that, I said ...!'

'I heard what you said; it sounded crystal clear to me. I think you did.'

'There is a mode of thought in Canberra that a change of regime...that is, a change in circumstances could affect us, financially and economically, for the better. Our government has to consider how a change could affect the interests of Australians generally. Further, Australia does not wish to be seen as interfering in the region to the detriment of our northern neighbours.'

'It seems to me by doing nothing we're doing just that.'

'What? Um...yes,' Burton didn't look pleased at the interruption nor the inference; he plainly preferred it to remain unsaid. 'We have to consider how we deal with powerful nations that are juxtaposed geographically with regard to our own financial and economic imbroglio.'

He drummed his fingers on the desk and added, 'Do you agree?'

Van Ekeren was not quite with him. Burton's last sentence had been composed of words of several syllables of whose meaning he was unsure, he certainly wasn't sure what juxtaposed or imbroglio meant. Nevertheless, he had an inkling where Burton was heading despite him talking like Sir Humphrey Appleby out of the television series 'Yes Minister'. The use of long and involved words could mean anything and probably did. Van Ekeren fingered his chin and tried to look non-committal.

'Therefore, we are not anxious that the information you have brought should...let us say...leak out until the appropriate time, you understand?'

After McKay's recent explanation of the way the wind was blowing, Van Ekeren was way ahead of him, there was no doubt what the Australian government's interests would dictate, Burton had confirmed what they intended to do or not do. They wanted the coup to take place, Taranga would be swallowed up, and Australia would presumably gain oil drilling rights off the coast of a subjugated Taranga from a grateful major nation on more advantageous terms than those proposed by a previous independent Taranganese administration.

'I see!' Van Ekeren felt nauseous as he thought of Lopez and his wife and daughter.

'You'll find we are very self-contained in this building, Mr Van Ekeren, you won't be lacking for entertainment for the next week or so. That is all.'

Van Ekeren rose to his feet, his legs felt weak and he sat down again. Even after being warned by McKay's verbal portrayal of Australia's intent, he still couldn't believe his ears. He rose a second time; Bramble was already standing and ready to accompany...or escort... him out!

Van Ekeren turned to Burton when he reached the door.

'What happened to the men chasing me and McKay?'

'The police have two of them in custody, both have gunshot wounds. We are still searching for the others.'

His phone rang and he gave a gesture of dismissal. As Van Ekeren passed through the doorway Burton answered the call.

'Oh yes, who? Oh Claudio, how are you? Hold on a moment.'

He was clearly waiting for Van Ekeren and Bramble to be out of earshot. They passed through Burton's personal reception area and into the corridor outside. Bramble pressed the lift button, it arrived and they stepped in. It was full, people wearing jackets and carrying brief cases, presumably office workers arriving for their normal nine to five jobs, which indicated to Van Ekeren that ASIO employed clerks, office girls and cleaners just like any other large undertaking.

They stood at the front of the lift, it went up two floors at which point there was a general exodus and Van Ekeren was obliged to step out of the lift as its occupants flooded into the corridor. As he waited to re-enter, it hit him with redoubled force what was going to happen.

If he went along with government policy as outlined by Burton, he was condemning De Souza, Lopez and possibly Westerman to death. Having been acquainted with those organising the coup, Van Ekeren thought it likely Lopez' wife and daughter would also be eliminated. No coup leader, especially Delgado, could afford to keep them alive, especially De Souza's family who could act as a rallying point for loyalists. The viper in the nest, that young man Julio, would receive his reward and consider he'd done a good job.

The coup would affect the daily life and economy of Taranga for years to come, destroy that independent atmosphere and they would be under the heel of the military as the country was subjugated, while Australia formulated an agreement favouring their own economy. Van Ekeren made up his mind, he had to do something, the image of Lopez' wife and daughter, especially the latter who was under the threat of disfigurement, steeled his resolve.

The lift was still emptying, he backed off to one side away from the lift door, Bramble was still inside standing back as the exodus tailed off. Then those waiting on the fourth floor began to pile in. Van Ekeren inched away then backed off and vanished around the corner. There was a door marked 'Stair' which he entered and closed behind him.

He had evaded Bramble, for the present, but what now?

*

As he ran up the stairs he ruminated on the irony of the situation. After all his efforts to reach a haven, namely ASIO, he had jumped from the frying pan into the fire. To discover Canberra, and Rivera and his men, were of like mind was shattering, although his own plight was slightly improved. ASIO didn't intend to quietly dispose of him and bury his remains in a paddock. When they said detention, that was what they meant.

Van Ekeren went upwards, he calculated Bramble would assume he was in a wild panic and would scurry downstairs to find a way out. After being pursued through the countryside by Rivera, Van Ekeren knew the best thing to do was the unexpected. He decided to head for a fire escape, if there was one. He reached the next floor, emerged into the corridor and after a quick look around, began to walk.

His immediate aim was to get out of the building. After that, what next? Get to the Taranganese Embassy? That was not a bad idea, if he could find it.

The entrance to the toilets were alongside the lift shaft and next to the stairway. He paid the urinal a visit which was a great relief, if he was going to be chased all over the building, he preferred not to have a full bladder. He examined the windows; they were of the non-opening variety and being a long way up they wouldn't have been much help if they had.

After a cursory glance through a window, he could see a fire escape, along the wall of a wing that was facing him. There appeared to be an exit leading to it along each floor. He made his way out of the toilet, then froze. He heard running feet and hid behind a pillar as a group of men raced past.

'Ye Gods!' he re-entered the stairway and headed upwards again. The next floor was deserted, nobody was in sight. He entered the first doorway he came to. He could see through the glass front before he entered, there were two offices, both were unoccupied and one was clearly a reception area. In the inner office, there was a wardrobe against the far wall, he had a look inside. There were clothes hanging in there, a jacket, a raincoat, a hat and an umbrella.

He dared not delay too long, it only needed one of Bramble's men to pass down the corridor and catch sight of him through the glass, plus there was always the chance of the occupants returning. He donned the raincoat, seized the umbrella, put the hat on, marched out of the door and headed for the lift, where he pressed the button. It arrived quickly; he stepped in and joined three girls and a pimply youth carrying a box of files.

The girls ignored him and carried on giggling between themselves, the youth appeared to be the butt of their attentions and was clearly embarrassed and self-conscious. They got out when the lift stopped and others entered, one floor lower down the pimply youth got out. The silence was deafening, all the others seemed to be mature Public Servants. Presumably nobody talked in ASIO buildings in case they gave away secrets.

When the lift reached the ground floor Van Ekeren entered the foyer. There were three exits, two into adjoining streets and the other led into a ground floor general office. A group of men stood in the middle and others guarded both street doors. Bramble was directing operations, so Van Ekeren quickly made up his mind, donned the hat and entered the foyer. He tried to appear casual, as if he had every right to be there. He reasoned a hasty retreat into the lift would have attracted immediate attention. He decided not to go for the exit doors leading outside the building, a searching examination could cut straight through his thin disguise, so he headed for the general office accessed from the foyer.

The door to this office opened as he approached and Francis Burton emerged. Van Ekeren uttered an involuntary gasp, hastily changed into a clearing of the throat. There were seats along the wall of the foyer so he deviated, selected one and sat down. There were magazines on a table, he picked one up and started to read, furiously berating himself when he realised he was holding it upside down.

Burton advanced into the centre of the foyer; a man had just entered the building from a limousine that had drawn up outside. They advanced towards each other and cordially shook hands.

'How are you, Claudio?'

'Very well, thank you Francis,' Claudio had a round bald head with black hair around its circumference, although his baldness was alleviated by a central tuft above his forehead that was brushed back. He was dark skinned with bushy eyebrows. Van Ekeren straightened up as he heard him reply to Francis Burton; surely, he had heard that voice before. They walked to the lifts, still conversing. Van Ekeren heard snatches of conversation that sounded like '...had a little trouble ...' and '...

heard you were at the Chinese Embassy reception last night...'
Claudio had a snickering laugh that was also familiar. Before
they entered the lift, a dark suited man exited from it. Francis
greeted him and shook him warmly by the hand.

'Ah, Edward, I think you know Claudio Pécurto, Third
Secretary from the Taranganese Embassy.'

'Yes, we have met before,' the dark suited Edward shook
hands with the Taranganese. 'Claudio...how are you, and how
are things in Taranga?'

'Well, thank you. How are you, Edward?'

Edward then walked across the foyer, had a brief chat with
the gorilla on the door and walked out into the street. Claudio
and Francis entered the lift. Van Ekeren remained on the
seat with sweat pouring from him and a sinking sensation
in his stomach.

His last card had been trumped. It now seemed pointless to
escape from the building. His plan after leaving it had been
to contact the Taranganese Embassy, but he had just seen
their Third Secretary. Not only did Van Ekeren now recall the
man's name, he also recalled his voice and laugh when they
had all been chortling about tanker collisions in the English
Channel. He knew now where he had heard the name Claudio
before, and where he had heard that voice.

He had been one of the men in the room in Van Ekeren's
prison when he had been hiding behind the couch. This man
had been closeted with the conspirators and was a party to
the coup. With the Taranganese embassy closed to him how
could Van Ekeren now warn anyone about the impending
coup? Every hand was against him. He may as well give
himself up and consign Lopez, De Souza and their families
to the firing squad.

CHAPTER 31

He couldn't sit indefinitely in the foyer, someone would eventually query his presence, or the owner of the coat could pass through the foyer and recognise his property. In addition, he was hatless, he wasn't sure whether to put it on again or not, would he stand out wearing a hat indoors? Further, would anyone with a magazine held to his face for a long period without moving attract attention? Admittedly Van Ekeren was where they wouldn't expect him to be, but there was no point pushing his luck.

He had two alternatives, or three if he countenanced giving himself up. He could enter the general office or re-enter the lift. He discounted trying the two exits, they were watching them closely. If he used the lift, he could search on another floor for a fire escape, or perhaps find a service lift, which must have an exit point on each floor.

He decided to try the general office, but wasn't sure of his next course of action if he did. What type of customer would the national security organisation attract? Did people register complaints or information, '...I have seen something strange... or '...I've seen someone carrying a back pack that looks suspicious...!'

Van Ekeren considered being a job applicant but dismissed it. He might find himself before Francis Burton for an interview, who would no doubt greet him with open arms and send for the heavy squad. But he had to do something quick, the group in the foyer had held a short conference and was beginning to break up with members departing in all directions, it was only a matter of time before someone looked more closely at the heavily garbed man sitting in the foyer. Van Ekeren made his decision, stood up, walked to the general office and entered it.

As offices went, it was fairly standard. There was a counter, an interview room to one side, there were many desks, work stations, filing cabinets and desk top computers, with keyboard operators who looked like the average types you'd find in any bank or insurance office. Van Ekeren had quite a shock, it looked so mundane and ordinary. In his imagination he had expected an array of television screens showing scenes and trouble spots around the world, and possibly a firing range. There were computers situated within work stations throughout the floor, similar to any commercial organisation. Presumably intelligence organisations had the same needs as ordinary commercial undertakings and their general office and internal administration areas would look the same.

The receptionist looked up and greeted him, she was an attractive young girl and Van Ekeren idly wondered what qualifications a receptionist would need for an intelligence organisation. Would they need knowledge of languages? Karate? Behind her was a board with names on it with 'In' and 'Out' slots which had little sliding panels. These covered names or left them exposed. He noted Mr Hargreaves was out, so he asked for him.

'I'm sorry, he's out all day. Can anyone else help you?'

He looked at the board again.

'Marcus Templeton?'

'Sorry, he's at our Sydney office today.'

'Michael Duval?'

'He's in Melbourne office all this week.'

'Mr Johannsen.'

'Certainly, I'll see if he's free.'

'What? I thought he was...I mean ...wait a minute, I don't really want to...!'

The board said he was out but the girl seemed to think he was in. He was.

'He'll see you in a few minutes, who shall I say is calling?'

Van Ekeren stared at her helplessly while his eyes flickered over the board again vainly searching for someone else who was Out. His mouth opened and closed; he was about to protest again that Mr Johannsen couldn't possibly be in but bit it back.

'Sir...who is calling? Are you all right?'

'Yes...yes, thank you,' Van Ekeren muttered but he wasn't. He leant heavily for support on the umbrella. He started to feel faint, and shook his head from side to side to combat it.

'Sir?'

'I...my name is ...' he was tempted to make a run for it, but if he did that he'd be apprehended immediately. Three of them were still in the foyer, he could see them through the fluted glass.

'I'm Doug...er...Paul Westerman, Paul Westerman from ... um...Hall & Douglas, Insurance Brokers.'

He considered Westerman would forgive him, wherever he was, for the use of his name, in his panic it was the first name that occurred to him. Instinctive use of the insurance market as an alibi gave him confidence; he had been a salesman in Life Insurance for some years and could easily play the part. If he found himself confronting Johannsen, he'd sell him life assurance, a rebuff would enable him to make a hasty exit and live another day...or hour!

'Go through to his office, it's over there, the last but one. He has someone with him, but he won't be long. Is he expecting you?'

'Yes...No...Yes!' Van Ekeren ground out; she accepted his contradictory answer without question, which was totally at odds with him having asked for a string of other people before settling on Johannsen. Bramble's image in the fluted glass was moving towards the general office so he had to move away from the counter.

She waved him around the side of the counter: he moved quickly and headed for Johannsen's office. Nobody took any interest in him as he walked past. He turned at one point, determined to change direction and vanish through a handy door, but the girl on the counter, with misplaced efficiency, was checking to see if he needed directional help. She waved cheerfully at him and pointed at the waiting area outside Johannsen's office. He gave her a sickly grin and carried on. He passed three empty desks en route, as he did so he looked around, the girl was talking to Bramble. Nobody appeared to take any notice of him, on an impulse he snatched up a pair of glasses lying unattended on one of the desks and pocketed them. As he did so he caught sight of the name plate on the desk, Mr William Shackleton of Accounts. That gave him satisfaction, he considered William Shackleton owed him one! On the last unoccupied desk before Johannsen's office there was a large vanilla file in the 'IN' tray. Van Ekeren picked that up as well and sat down outside Johannsen's domain. There were magazines on the table and he hid the file between two copies of Rydges Magazine. The file had the name Peter Lewkonowicz on the top righthand corner, Van Ekeren wondered if this was a Russian agent they were tracking.

He pondered on his disguise, a glance through the window indicated it was a bright sunny day, a heavy raincoat and an umbrella looked a little out of place. Underneath he still wore shirt and trousers

Should he stay and see Johannsen? Shirt sleeves, even in Australia, wouldn't look much like salesman's garb in a city situation, nor on a day like this would raincoat and umbrella. After consideration, he decided to move on.

The receptionist now had her back to him, he stood and opened the nearest door, through the glass it looked like another general office. He realised he was still carrying the magazines under his arm, they looked out of place so he laid them on top of a filing cabinet. Nobody seemed interested, there were seven work stations in the office with four people sitting in them and two answering phones. Van Ekeren removed the coat and hung it on a coat stand inside the door. One man eyed him quizzically.

'I'll leave this here if I may,' Van Ekeren said with an aplomb that astonished him. 'I've just come from Melbourne. It was raining like hell when I left.'

'That's Melbourne,' the other man commented and seemed partly satisfied. 'What department are you looking for?'

Van Ekeren affected not to hear, but the other repeated it.

'I've been seconded to Mr Hargreaves for a couple of days,' Van Ekeren replied desperately. 'I'm doing a job for him. I come all the way from Melbourne, and guess what? He's not here!'

The other man nodded.

'That sounds like him! He's like that, thoughtless bastard!'

'One of the worst!' Van Ekeren agreed sadly.

'Your coat will be OK there. I'm Fred Albert by the way, who are you?'

'Doug Van Ek...er...Duggan...,' Van Ekeren stuttered.' Bill Duggan.'

'OK Bill, leave your coat there, it'll be OK. I'll see you later.'

'Thanks,' he replied. 'Tell me, where's the gents?'

'Through that door there, just along the corridor.'

Van Ekeren appropriated the stolen glasses from the raincoat pocket: he picked up Peter Lewkonowicz's file and walked slowly to the far door. He closed it behind him and found himself in a corridor; the foyer was at the far end.

He paused to put on the glasses, everything was promptly magnified. He put out his hand to fend off a pillar that loomed up before him, his hand met thin air, he overbalanced and fell onto his knees. He peered over the top of them but the pillar was about five feet away. William Shackleton of Accounts clearly had eyesight problems.

'Bugger it!' he muttered and pushed the glasses onto his forehead so he could easily slip them down if approached by anyone. His eyes were still fuzzy and out of focus as he stepped forward, he felt dizzy, teetered over again and stumbled against a potted plant.

'Hell!' as a disguise they may be effective in one respect but deadly in another, he'd be black and blue if he wore them for long. Reeling around in a corridor looking drunk would also attract attention. He decided to head upwards again; maybe he could find a service lift.

With the Lewkonowicz file under his arm he went up the corridor and the next flight of stairs. On the next floor, two very young men came towards him wheeling a trolley. One of them gave him a hail and he nearly took to his heels with fright, but in the nick of time realised the young man was asking the destination of his file. They were clearly the file transporters, moving files from place to place and floor to floor and were offering to deliver his.

He smilingly demurred, and explained he was on his way to consult Mr Hargreaves regarding this particular file. They accepted this, smiled and made for the lift shaft. He climbed two flights and emerged on the sixth floor. He was about to move off in the direction where he thought there may be a fire escape, when Francis appeared with Claudio, the Third Secretary from the Taranganese embassy. They were walking from the direction of the lift towards the rear of the building. Van Ekeren's first reaction was to panic and run but saner counsels prevailed. Where they came from was beyond him, if they had been heading for Francis' office when he saw them in the foyer they should have been there by now.

He slipped the glasses over his nose and proceeded cautiously, praying he wouldn't draw attention to himself by walking into a pillar or tripping over a fire bucket. He paused and examined a notice board in a small alcove which mentioned an internal table tennis competition and an inter-departmental cricket match. The Staff Dance intrigued him, were guests required to leave bugs, guns, cloaks and daggers at the door?

Francis and Claudio had now passed him, he heard odd snatches of conversation, and heard Francis say 'No we haven't seen anything to that effect in the papers but we can't guarantee nothing will leak out. In the meantime, keep the lid on it as we take a serious view.'

He wondered what Claudio had asked, but Francis could have meant anything, the coup, Van Ekeren's impending capture or even the quality of the coffee in the canteen.

Someone else approached, he was about 25 or so, Van Ekeren hastily referred to the file as if checking his bearings.

The print jumped out at him and he nearly went cross-eyed. He started to move off, walked into a water dispenser and some plastic cups, which were loose, fell off. This was in some respects a great relief. He knelt down to recover them, experiencing nausea and dizziness as his eyes re-adjusted.

Three men appeared at the end of the corridor and advanced in his direction. He hastily re-positioned the glasses, peered at the trio over the top of the lenses and clasped the file. He didn't like the look of them, there was a definite security look about them. He was trapped, if he ran, they'd soon catch him, he had nowhere to go.

He took the bull by the horns, he had little option. He walked towards them, glanced into the file from time to time and turned over a page or two. There was an office door between him and them as the distance between them narrowed. Van Ekeren paused by the door, looked at the room number and through the glass, at his file as if confirming his destination, then opened the door. He crossed the threshold into the office area, still engrossed in the file as the three men walked past in the corridor.

'For an ordinary bloke, he certainly knows how to vanish,' was a comment he heard one of them say before the door closed. 'We ought to sign him on when we catch him.'

'McKay said he's a dab hand with a handgun,' said another. 'You go that way and we'll go this.'

Van Ekeren closed the door and heard no more. A young woman was in the reception area, she looked up and gave him a welcoming smile that went straight through his eyeballs and all the way down his spine. It was his best moment for the whole of the past ten days.

'Can I help you?' she asked.

My Oath! Van Ekeren thought, realised he was scanning her all over and hastily averted his eyes. She was aware of his examination but didn't seem to mind.

'I...er ...' Van Ekeren decided to ask if he was in a particular office, and pray that he wasn't. He peered over the top of the glasses and just made out the name on the door. It looked like Kelsey. 'I wanted Mr Hargreaves office, is it here?'

'No, you're on the wrong floor, you want the next floor down.'

'I'm sorry, someone told me it was on this floor,' Van Ekeren turned away.

'That's all right,' she replied. As Van Ekeren went to the door, he saw one of the security types was outside. He returned to her reception desk.

'Er...where's the lift shaft, I've lost my bearings.'

'Oh, a lot of people get confused. It's because of corridors crossing each other outside here. I'll show you.'

She rose to her feet and walked to the door. Her carriage would have rivalled that of a Paris model. Van Ekeren became aware how long it was since he had really looked at a woman and how refreshing a sight it was after being punched, kicked, shot at and roped to trees. Her perfume hit him like a battleship's broadside as she passed by him and opened the door. He followed her obediently, she was chatting brightly and this assisted with diverting the attention of the security man still hovering about outside.

The receptionist's attributes certainly worked in Van Ekeren's favour, the security man's eyes wandered all over her and he ignored Van Ekeren completely. His attention was so intense and concentrated that Van Ekeren half expected all her clothes to fall off. She escorted him to another lift shaft and passed the time of day after she'd pressed a button while they waited. He was thankful for that; someone in animated conversation with a staff member was less likely to be a fugitive. Van Ekeren turned as he stepped into the lift.

'Thanks Alice.'

She gave him another flashing smile. The security man must have heard the exchange and, since Van Ekeren was ostensibly on first name terms with her, assumed all was in order. In any case his attention was still distracted, his eyes travelled up and over her again so thoroughly Van Ekeren was surprised her clothes didn't catch fire. As the lift doors closed, he blessed the name plate prominently displayed on her desk.

He went down one floor, reached the next 'T' junction and broke into a trot. He then heard a shout behind him. He cursed angrily, one sure way to attract attention was to either run or creep around looking furtively over one's shoulder. Somebody had spotted him running and put two and two together. He turned a corner where three doors faced him, he avoided the first that looked like an office, and dived into the second.

He found himself facing a mirror, he was in a toilet. He headed for the nearest cubicle; the one next to it was occupied. As he pushed open the door, a feature of the facility struck him, there were no urinals. The full implication hit him as he saw a machine on the wall, which dispensed items not utilised by the male sex.

The other cubicle flushed, he hesitated with his hand on the door of the empty one, undecided what to do. As the bolt clicked on the other cubicle he panicked, entered the empty one and closed the door. As he slid the bolt home it occurred to him that not only was he being hunted for drug offences and matters affecting the security of the state, he now stood a good chance of having sexual perversion added to his charge sheet.

He heard running water, followed by whirring of a hand

drier before the door opened and closed. He sat on the pedestal and considered his next move. For want of anything better to do he opened the file and examined it. Even that was mundane. Peter Lewkonowicz was not a Russian agent, nor was he an ASIO sleuth, he was the man who cleaned the windows of the building, inside was an account he had submitted for his labours. He must have had the contract for years as the file was bulky. Van Ekeren looked at the beginning of the file and was intrigued to see they had checked his antecedents; even window cleaners needed a security clearance.

He waited for about 15 minutes, then decided to move. He opened the door and crept out, ready to dive back into his refuge if anyone entered. A cursory glance up and down the corridor established the coast was not exactly clear, two men were conversing some distance away, they were both bald headed and were both probably in their fifties.

They had an ordinary look about them, as opposed to the security types so far encountered. He slid into the corridor and avoided the temptation to slink furtively, one of them looked up as he approached but evinced no interest, luckily his glance was too late to note from which door Van Ekeren had emerged. He inclined his head gravely to one side as he approached them and they nodded in response. They parted just as he passed them and one of them entered a lift so Van Ekeren elected to follow suit.

The next floor down two further security types entered, accompanied by a young girl carrying some account books and the same pimply youth previously encountered, still pushing his trolley. The lift dropped down two floors and Van Ekeren realised one of the two security types was eyeing him fixedly so he edged closer to the bald-headed man. He began to perspire as two pairs of eyes bored into him while his hands and knees trembled. He moved the file up and down slowly, hoping the arm movements would possibly stop his hands shaking. He heard one of them clear his throat and felt a challenge was in the offing.

'Was that Hargreaves you were chatting to by the lift?' Van Ekeren asked. The bald-headed man awoke from his reverie and shook his head.

'No...' he had to cast his mind back.' No...let me think...Ah yes that was Bill Shackleton.'

'Oh yes...Bill, of course,' Van Ekeren thought hard back to the other bald man who had been conversing with his companion, grim faced with pressure marks across the bridge of his nose. 'I didn't recognise him without his glasses.'

The bald man chuckled.

'He's not happy; somebody nicked them. He left them on his desk on the ground floor and when he got back...they'd gone.'

Oh God! Once more Van Ekeren felt adrenalin run through him, he had walked right past Shackleton wearing them.

'Who'd ...um...do a thing like that?' with difficulty he resisted the temptation to bring up the file to mask his glasses. He was also forced to view the outside world through the lenses, looking over or around them could arouse suspicion now it was known a spectacle thief was in the building. He became nauseous and dizzy as his eyes struggled to focus.

'People will take anything these days,' commented his companion. 'I lost my fountain pen last week.'

'Tell Bramble that,' Van Ekeren said on the spur of the moment. 'He'll find it for you!' That one really went down well, it brought an instant reaction from the other occupants of the lift, they all guffawed and even the two security types smirked. The bald-headed man was still enjoying the joke as they left at the next floor. Van Ekeren left with him and struck off in the opposite direction with a muffled farewell.

He headed for the staircase and went down at the run, still carrying the Lewkonowicz file. He had great difficulty in focussing his eyes and gauging the distance of the stairs, he fell down the last three before he cautiously opened the ground floor door. He could see the foyer with groups of security types still blocking the only exit.

He went down another flight and found a room with a snooker and table tennis table, it was unoccupied. A door on the other side led into an underground car park. He passed through the door and found he was looking up a ramp. There was a steel door at the far end, obviously opening into the street.

He ran back and climbed aboard one of the vehicles, the ignition key was still in it. He started it up and drove up the ramp, hoping a photo-electric cell would automatically open it. The door didn't budge. He looked around for a plastic card in the glove box but there wasn't one. He got out and tugged viciously at the cables and pulleys, but nothing moved. He thumped the box on the wall that was supposed to take plastic cards, it did no good but it relieved his feelings.

'You bastard!' he said feelingly.

Raging inwardly, he left the car where it was and stalked down the ramp. He was nearly in tears, after thinking he had found a way out of the building he was baulked again. All the time the clock was ticking away, and Lopez, his family and De Souza were becoming more and more vulnerable by the minute.

CHAPTER 32

Van Ekeren shook off his despondency, to feel sorry for himself was a recipe for disaster. He yanked open what he assumed was the door to the table tennis room and stepped into a broom cupboard.

'Bloody Hell!'

He slammed the door and walked into the table tennis room next door before the import of the broom cupboard struck home. He hastened back and examined the contents with interest. There were several mops and buckets, bottles of cleaning fluid and a boiler suit behind the door.

Ten minutes later he emerged from the lift into the foyer wearing the boiler suit, carrying a bucket of soapy water and mop, plus three or four witches' hats. He had wrapped a coloured handkerchief into a band round his head such as footballers wear when carrying on after a head injury. A couple of heads turned as he entered the foyer then turned away, not even the ultra-efficient Bramble gave more than a cursory glance.

He wasted no time before establishing his identity and becoming mentally invisible. He advanced to the far corner of the lift vestibule, strategically placed the witches' hats, put down the bucket and commenced swabbing. He carried out the task scientifically, commenced cleaning at the wall and worked his way backwards. He thought of John Buchan's character Richard Hannay in his novel The Thirty Nine Steps, when he evaded capture in the Highlands by pretending to be a roadmender. He had devoted his entire thoughts to road mending. Van Ekeren did the same, he devoted all his mental processes to cleaning the floor.

Whoever was normally charged with the task had skimped his work, the floor was filthy and the dirt was ingrained. Where Van Ekeren had been working it gleamed markedly. He reached the edge of the vestibule; still nobody paid him any attention apart from getting out of his way or jumping over where he had been. He left the floor in front of the lifts, he didn't want to draw attention to himself by having anybody slip and fall, though it wouldn't have worried him unduly if Bramble, Francis or bloody Claudio twisted an ankle.

The main entrance presented a problem; the architect in his wisdom had decreed that it be covered by carpeting which successfully prevented him working there. He thought back to the cleaning cupboard, had there been a vacuum cleaner?

He had a squeegee; this gave him an idea. He ran the squeegee over the area he had cleaned, picked up the bucket and utensils including the witches' hats and headed towards the doors. There were three men encamped there, they looked bored while Bramble, the one major fear, had temporarily departed for pastures new. He started on the side windows first, and succeeded in making a filthy mess of the first one since he was putting most of the filth from the floor onto it.

He dipped the sponge in the water and tried to swab the muck off the window but it made matters worse. He felt himself go cold as a security man wandered over, plainly unimpressed with his efforts and about to make some caustic comment. To become involved in an altercation or conversation, even a one sided one, was the last thing he wanted. It could draw unwanted attention.

'You're making a fine mess of that!' the security man remarked unpleasantly. 'Do you normally clean floors and windows with the same water?'

'Not normally,' Van Ekeren quelled the tart rejoinder that sprang to his lips. 'I was in a hurry to finish, that's all.'

'Well you'd better get some clean water, what a filthy mess,' the security man wrinkled his nose and Van Ekeren couldn't disagree. He didn't like the fellow's tone of voice either. Did security men have the right to order cleaning staff around? Van Ekeren wondered how the cleaners' union would view that. He decided not to make an issue of it.

With bad grace, he picked up the bucket, with difficulty resisted the urge to empty it over the security man's shoes and made for the lift shaft. As he entered the lift Francis and Claudio exited from it, brushing past him with little more than a cursory glance.

Van Ekeren tipped the water over one of the official cars in the basement, which relieved his feelings. He refilled the bucket, realised he hadn't put any soap in it and had to go back.

The window stood out like a sore thumb, still with grease and filth all over it. The security man still hovered around, he peered closely into the bucket and it took a strong effort of will not to push his face in it. He washed down the mess and applied the squeegee with a circular motion he had seen window cleaners do. He suddenly had an awful thought, what if Peter Lewkonowicz arrived on the scene and saw Van Ekeren usurping his duties.

The security man nodded approvingly.

'Very good' he said.

'Thank you,' Van Ekeren moved closer to him. Francis had re-appeared from outside, having seen the Taranganese official back to his car.

'Better job than the mess you made last time!' the security man remarked acidly, Van Ekeren gritted his teeth and just managed to stop himself from tipping the bucket over the other man's trousers. He wondered if the security man had any friends and doubted it. Maybe this delight in being bloody to people made him an ideal ASIO man, the only ones to appreciate his humour would be his own colleagues or his opposite numbers in the CIA or the Russian SVR.

'Quite so,' Van Ekeren replied but stayed close. Despite his obnoxious presence he didn't want to move away from him. Carrying on a dialogue with one of the hunters was probably the best way of staying invisible and averting suspicion.

'Don't be funny with me!' he snapped, and Van Ekeren's blood froze. The sentiments didn't worry him, he'd received far worse in the past week. What did cause him worry was it signalled the imminent end of the conversation. But Francis was heading for the lift, so exchanging pleasantries, or unpleasantries, was not important now. Van Ekeren looked suitably cowed and attacked the neighbouring window. He did the next three, then walked out through the door.

He resisted with difficulty the urge to throw down all the washing accoutrements and take to his heels. He started on the outside windows and worked his way to the corner of the building. The three remaining security men met in the middle of the foyer and exchanged notes, they had their backs to Van Ekeren so he dropped everything and ran. As he left the building behind, he realised that being outside didn't make much difference to the odds for De Souza, Lopez and Westerman. He still had problems.

*

The first task was to get rid of the overalls. He wasn't sorry to divest himself of them, he still had his normal trousers and shirt on underneath and the addition of overalls made him hot and uncomfortable. He vaulted over a retaining wall onto steps beneath and ran into an expanse of parkland where he dived into a bush, removed the overalls and joined the lunch-time strollers. He picked up a newspaper from a park bench and tucked it under his arm. He headed to the road on the other side of the park, walked along the grass and up some steps, ostensibly reading the paper, but glancing left and right. Two men appeared at the steps on the far side where he had entered the park but he continued reading his paper and walked along the pavement.

He felt naked as he walked; he would have felt better with a hat which would have acted as some disguise. He wasn't certain if he had been seen leaving the building, or whether they had the immediate vicinity patrolled after his disappearance. He left the pavement and strolled into a building where every law-abiding citizen had the right to be...a Post Office.

One of his immediate problems manifested itself. He had no money. Not for the first time he realised how essential money was, even just a little. He recalled his approach to that young child in the small town...what was his name? Johnnie ...that nasty selfish little oik! He remembered his utter helplessness when he couldn't even afford an apple or a bun. He avoided the queue to the counter, no point in joining that, made for a pay phone, picked up the receiver and kept a watchful eye on the door. The dialling tone bored into his ear, it seemed so loud he thought everyone within two metres of him must hear it, and pushed the ear piece into his ear to try and crush the noise.

There were several pay phones in small dome shaped plastic compartments, all were taken. Two people sauntered up and were plainly waiting, and he began to sweat. One of them came and leant against the wall nearby and he could feel perspiration pouring off him. Over his shoulder he saw one of the ASIO security men enter and look around, he recognised him as one of those in the foyer.

Van Ekeren turned his back, reached for the directory and thumbed through it as though searching for a number. He watched the security man out of the corner of his eye. He had a cursory look around, appeared satisfied but didn't leave. He seemed to be struck by a thought and joined one of the queues for stamps. Van Ekeren cursed him soundly — blast the man! Why run out of stamps now? He returned to the phone book and realised it was open at the page relating to international calls. He was idly perusing the page when it hit him.

Good God! He could dial direct to Taranga if he wanted to. If he could find the number of HLL Insurances he could ring Lopez direct. He found the code for International enquiries and dialled it.

'What country?'

'Taranga!' the word seemed to reverberate in the ether, he was sure the security type and everyone in the post office must have heard it.

'What city?'

'Taranga'

'No! What city?'

'Taranga ...it's the same name.'

'I'm sorry I can't hear you'

'Oh f...!' Van Ekeren bit off the expletive before it came out. 'Taranga City,' he whispered hoarsely. The security man had bought his stamps now and was coming nearer.

She asked Van Ekeren to repeat it yet again, then to spell it. He cursed her under his breath and the sweat oozed from him, after all he had been through within the past week it was just his luck to strike a cloth eared operator. It was a toss-up whether he was to be arrested for treason, drug running, or stealing a bucket and mop, with the remote possibility of the brief invasion of a ladies' toilet being added to the charge sheet. He took a grip on himself and repeated it coldly and distinctly, this time she got it.

'Who are you calling?'

He told her.

'Hold the line, please.'

The security man was looking around; he was having a last look around before he departed. Why didn't that blasted operator hurry up?

'Hallo caller.'

'Hallo? Yes?'

She gave him the number, a biro pen was on a string on the shelf. He wrote the number on the directory page and tore off the top of the directory page. He replaced the phone and saw the ASIO man was near the door. He could breathe again.

'Here you, what you think you're doing?'

'Eh? You what?'

'Ripping pages out of the phone book, other people want to use that'.

She was an overweight woman with a grim set to her jaw. She was ginger haired, which looked dyed and she carried a shopping bag. She reminded him of a schoolmistress he had suffered from in the third form at school.

'I think it's disgraceful, utterly disgraceful.'

A man behind a nearby counter looked up and she locked onto him.

'This man was tearing pages out of the directory.'

Her voice was strident and the ASIO man's head turned. Van Ekeren's teeth went on edge.

'Just forget it, will you,' he hissed, trying not to look in the direction of the ASIO man.

'Are you threatening me?'

Great God in Heaven! He was coming over, initially to see the fun, but if he came too close, he would inevitably recognise Van Ekeren as the man they were hunting. Then he did, that much was obvious from his sudden change in demeanour and he began pushing people aside.

'People like you are a disgrace, vandalising directories that other people...Ooooh!'

Looking back, Van Ekeren counted that amongst one of his more satisfying moments since he had been hustled out of Sydney airport. As the ASIO man was reaching out to clamp his hand on Van Ekeren's shoulder, he seized his tormentor and pushed her hard so she fell against him. The ASIO man lost his balance and hit his head against one of the pay phones. The fat lady fell across him and Van Ekeren heard the breath exhale from him as her bulk crushed him onto the hard floor. Van Ekeren turned and ran while her indignant cries echoed across the Post Office, despite the seriousness of the situation they were music to his ears. He hit the main door, stumbled over the pavement and took off.

The ASIO man wouldn't be delayed for long, but it would take him a few seconds to get that damned overweight woman off him. Van Ekeren ran down the alleyway alongside the building and dived into the first door on the right. He was in a vestibule between two doors. He opened the second door and entered the same Post Office from the rear just in time to see the back of the ASIO man as he ran out the front.

Van Ekeren picked up another pay phone and looked busy. He stood there for a couple of minutes before he realised the occupant of the next phone booth was his erstwhile assailant. She had her back to him, he decided to move on as he wasn't keen to renew the acquaintance.

He went to the street door and peered out. There was no sign of the ASIO man. He looked around and saw two possible security types across the street. He exited the door, slunk along the side of the building and entered the one next door. He walked across the foyer and pressed the lift button.

He travelled to the sixth floor and found himself in a general office, the lift opened directly onto the floor and there was a reception desk in front of him. He turned towards a door marked 'Stair' on the right. He cantered down the steps and tried the fifth. Once again it opened directly into general office space; it looked like a shipping company judging by pictures on the walls. He tried the fourth floor, again heads behind desks raised and looked at him curiously. This time the nature of the company was confirmed, "Southern Cross Steamship Line" was emblazoned across the wall behind the reception desk.

'Oh hell!'

It was incongruous! His embarrassment at being in a place where he might be challenged by ordinary, law abiding citizens was greater than his fear of being apprehended by ASIO men or Rivera. Now he thought about it... where the hell was Rivera? Van Ekeren felt his shoulder blades tingle as he half expected Rivera to materialise behind him. As he turned in alarm, he nearly collided with two ladies wheeling a tea trolley. They were both very large ladies and wore uniforms that tried to hide their bulk without success. They halted and were promptly swamped by starving office workers.

This diverted attention from Van Ekeren, one young man who looked as though he was going to either greet or challenge him, changed his mind and headed for the trolley, elbowing one of the office girls aside. Van Ekeren realised he was feeling peckish, so decided to join the queue, not only to defer the pangs of hunger but to attain invisibility.

'You right, mate?'

Van Ekeren realised he had inadvertently stood too close to the young man, he looked as though he had some semblance of authority and was itching to use it, he had that type of face. Van Ekeren was too hungry to panic; he eyed him levelly and nodded in a friendly manner.

'Yes thanks, more room around the trolley than we have on the fifth,' he cast a cursory glance around the walls, there were pictures of ships and cranes, as there had been on the floor above. "A bit like a rugby scrum up there.'

'Ah!' the young man nodded and raised an eyebrow. 'Are you accounts or insurance?'

'Insurance!' Van Ekeren couldn't believe his good fortune. This question and answer placed him on familiar ground and reduced the chances of questions that could floor him. He casually filled a cup from the urn and made some small talk to the tea lady that he hoped established his legitimacy.

'What happened about that claim on the Exmouth?'

Manna from heaven, he could scarcely believe his luck. He had been dealing with some aspects of that marine claim at Harwood's before he left for Taranga. He thought back to the case in question, there had been a collision in the Malacca Straits and much of the Exmouth's deck cargo had been lost, jettisoned to save the ship. What had the cargo been? Machine parts, rubber, some jute, and iron sheets.

'Dicey,' Van Ekeren responded. 'They're still trying ascertain what went over the side, the ship ran aground off Singapore and it's still there.' He skilfully extracted a cream bun from the tray while the two trolley guardians chatted to their customers and plunged his hand into the tin that served as a till. He picked up a $5 note; then dropped it back into the tin as if it had been his all the time and helped himself to some small change, which he made a point of showing to Fat Lady No.1 before pocketing it. 'We're still arguing that with Lloyds.'

Van Ekeren munched steadily at his bun as he left the queue and realised with some trepidation he had nowhere to go as the others drifted back to their desks, so he hung onto the officious young man and chatted about the 'Exmouth'.

'It's not clear why the ship was in Malacca Straits...' Van Ekeren said knowledgeably, '...since she was sailing from Perth to Durban. There was a hint she was gun-running.'

Utter bullshit, but there was nothing like a knowledgeable air about something not quite above board to sound convincing and to arouse interest, in any case he needed to prolong the conversation.

'This gentleman here is from the insurance department,' Van Ekeren heard someone say, and nearly choked on his bun as he looked around for an avenue of escape, but it was too late. A young man with a moustache and carrying a file waylaid him.

'Take this upstairs will you, old chap, it will save my legs. I don't like putting files in the hoist, we lost one last week and it's still somewhere at the bottom of the shaft. It's for Carl Bennett.'

Van Ekeren nodded, he was handed a bulky file and the other man walked away. He finished off his tea and bun, said farewell to the officious type and headed for the lift. He emerged on the fifth floor and headed for the receptionist.

'I have a file for Carl Bennett,' he said. 'Where can I find him?'

'He's not here are the moment,' she leant forward and exposed some cleavage that made his head reel. 'I can take it — who's it from?'

'Mr Johnstone,' he replied, having riffled through it on the way up.

He turned and headed for the lift; his legs were aching with the incessant running up and down stairs, across parks and streets, interspersed with wrestling bouts with fat ladies in post offices. He reached the ground floor and peered across the foyer.

'Damn!' he said feelingly, there were some athletic ASIO types on the pavement outside and they looked alert. He recognised them from the group in the foyer of the ASIO building. They must have the entire street staked out. He pressed the button and went down into the basement, there was bound to be a back entrance ...he hoped. He stepped out into yet another underground car park; with an open roller door at the rear. He walked out into sunshine and turned right, headed up the street at the rear with the water of Burley Griffin Lake appearing occasionally through gaps in the buildings on his left. A group of young men appeared at the next intersection, probably quite innocent and ordinary office workers, but he wasn't taking any chances. He dodged into an alcove at the rear of a building and considered his position.

It wasn't good, wherever he appeared on the street he was bound to be recognised, it was quite possible ASIO had brought the police into the equation. They would have some idea what he was wearing and no doubt were all conversant with his appearance.

Roaming around other office buildings was not an option, he'd been lucky last time, but strangers stick out like sore thumbs and a challenge or a phone call to authority by a suspicious clerk could finish up with the police. That would render him incommunicado and condemn Lopez and De Souza to death.

What was needed was a telephone that would take overseas dialling. Normal offices would have a few phones for overseas dialling and many would restrict interstate phone calls, abuse by staff members had been widespread in Van Ekeren's own offices in Melbourne as STD dialling was so easy, consequently international call dialling was strictly controlled. But ASIO offices would likely have a higher proportion of such phones. So why not get back into their building, where he knew his way about to a limited extent? Further, that would be the last place they would expect to see him now he had broken out and been spotted outside, logic would dictate he would be running around Canberra like a scared rabbit and most of his pursuers would be watching the streets.

He peered around the corner, the coast was clear and he made up his mind. The ASIO building was the second one down; he would enter it and trust to luck. Gaining ingress was easy, there was a delivery platform at the rear and a small truck was unloading, mainly towelling and stationery, with probable additional items such as rubber truncheons or thumbscrews! He peeped around the side of the truck and saw a man seize a roll of towelling then heave it onto his shoulder. Van Ekeren waited until he had entered the rear door, picked up another roll, placed it on his shoulder and entered via the same door.

He walked along a corridor with the roll against his head and face and entered the first gents' toilet he saw. He reached out and pushed the door, it gave easily as someone pulled at it from the inside and he nearly fell in. It opened and two men came out. One of them was Bramble!

CHAPTER 33

If anything proved the point of being in a place where they didn't expect him to be, this was it. Bramble and his companion didn't even look at him as they passed by. Van Ekeren was also assisted by their proximity to each other and the towel roll on his shoulder that wholly masked his face. Nevertheless, as he entered a cubicle and collapsed on the toilet seat, he felt weak at the knees and sat for some minutes flexing his calf muscles. Two men entered, chatted to each other and one of them entered one of the other cubicles.

His next task was to find a phone but he needed another disguise. The towel roll would do for now, if he changed the old one on the rack for the one he was carrying, so much the better, but how far could he progress carrying either a clean or soiled towel roll. He could hardly walk into general offices or individual office areas with a towel roll on his shoulder and try to use a phone, his beat was limited to corridors and toilets.

He sat and wondered, not for the first time, if his course

of action was right. Was Australia right to deliberately turn a blind eye while another nation took over Taranga with expectation of economic advantages to be granted by the usurpers? Was it in Australia's long-term interests that Taranga be swallowed and cease to exist as a separate entity? If Australia came to a tacit agreement for Taranga to be annexed, should Van Ekeren, an Australian, support Australia's policy? Yet was it right to cast adrift, and possibly condemn to death, people like De Souza, Lopez and others, possibly their families, so Australia could strike a more advantageous deal with the island's new masters? Australians may be guaranteed economic advantage, but what of the Taranganese generally, Lopez and his family? Yet Australia had stood by while East Timor had been annexed, and embarrassed when that annexation had been reversed.

Could Australia justify takeover of a smaller nation by a larger one, if it was for financial gain how long would it last? Would that justify the likes of Delgado and Lebak gaining positions of power and elimination of their predecessors?

Would it assist Australia if a large northern neighbour would then be that much closer? Or was Australia better placed with a small, possibly potentially, rich and more amenable island nation acting as a buffer? Van Ekeren thought again of Delgado, Lebak, Rivera and De Ryk. Then he thought of De Souza, his wife, and Lopez. Dry cynical bastard he may be but Van Ekeren now had great respect for the man. He thought of Lopez' wife and daughter, then rose to his feet, his mind made up.

How could he get his hands on a phone? Could he walk into an office and pick one up? True, this building was the last place they'd expect him to be, but how far could he push his luck.

He waited for the man in the next cubicle to clear before he emerged. He decided not to change the towel roll. A used towel roll would be expected to be carried to the nearest rear exit whereas a clean one was a passport to any toilet on any floor.

He wandered over three floors before he found a general office location that suited. He looked around uncertainly after entering and was accosted by a senior clerk who asked where the hell he thought he was going.

'Towels,' he said laconically. 'Where's the gents' toilet?'

'Over there by the lift shaft,' the senior clerk pointed.

As Van Ekeren followed the direction of his finger this confirmed that towels were a limiting factor, more appropriate to corridors or toilets. He needed an office with an open plan where lifts opened directly into it, he was presently limited to walking from elevator to toilet.

He needed something that acted as a passport to an office area. A file, that may work, it had before but that window cleaning file was now down in the basement. Stationery maybe, perhaps a box of it, but where could he lay his hands on one? He pondered on the problem as he exited the toilet where the senior clerk had directed him, still carrying the clean towelling roll. He went down to the next floor, loath to ditch the towel roll until he had a substitute alibi.

He passed three men working on a fuse box in a corridor near the lift shaft, they nodded as he stepped over their tool boxes and carried on working, while Van Ekeren entered the lift and went up two floors. He meandered around aimlessly, hastily entered a toilet with the towel roll on his shoulder when a man who looked like security appeared at the far end of the corridor.

He emerged to find a crowd gathered by the lift shaft, it was clearly lunch-time. This spawned an idea. He went down two flights of stairs to where he had seen the electricians. There was no sign of them, they had knocked off for lunch, their tool boxes neatly stacked against the wall. One of them had left his top coat, with the name of the electrical firm emblazoned across the back, lying over his box. He was likely going to a pub for lunch and didn't want to broadcast his work affiliation, some employers took a dim view of employees drinking on the job.

He looked up and down the corridor, a few people were coming and going but none of them took any notice of him. He picked up the top tool-box and jacket, scuttled into the stairway and peered over the balustrade, the stairs were clear. A fire hydrant cupboard was by the door, he opened it and stuffed the towel roll inside it. He donned the jacket, picked up the tool-box and went down two flights of stairs to the fourth floor. He emerged in a general office area where there was no corridor.

There was an office pen at one corner of the general office. He strode boldly towards it as nobody was on counter duty and picked up a notepad and biro. He found time to shake his head sadly at the lack of security, petty pilfering from offices was rife in Melbourne which caused many insurers to impose heavy excesses on office insurance policies.

He remembered reading an article in the insurance press about a computer and printer theft ring in London. They entered offices in the early morning when only a few had arrived and with a laconic — 'Is that the one for repair?' calmly appropriated it and walked out.

Bearing in mind if you have enough cheek you can get away with anything, he advanced to the door of the office pen with a brief nod to the girl sitting at the desk outside it. There was a plaque on the door which read 'Mr John Holsworthy'.

'Is this Mr Holsworthy's office?' he asked with a winning smile.

'Yes, can I help you?'

'The power point is playing up,' he placed the tool-box on the floor and consulted his pad. Its owner had been a doodler with sexual hang-ups, he hastily turned the leaf over.

'Oh? I didn't know about that?'

He jotted the name 'Holsworthy' name down on the pad, plus a quick sketch map of his office, and marked a cross where he could see the power point through the glass. He flashed it before her long enough for her to see the name and the sketch.

'I'll have a quick look now if I can, where is he?'

'He's gone to lunch, should be back about 1 o'clock'

'Good ...that is...bad ...I mean yes...right!' Van Ekeren picked up the tool-box. 'I'll just look at it. I've got to ring my office as well, just to check in, my mobile battery is flat. I'll do that in there if that's OK?'

'Oh...yes...I suppose so.'

'My God!' Van Ekeren remarked conversationally as he walked slowly past her. 'It's certainly cooler here, we've been on the sixth by the lift shaft most of the morning and it's like a furnace up there.'

She smiled and he entered the office, his heart thumping. He pulled the light plug out of the power point, picked up the phone, gave her a wave and started to dial.

He got the engaged tone!

He dialled five more times, getting hotter and hotter under the collar, it was still engaged. As an experiment, he dialled Harwood Larbalestier & Luck in Melbourne, they were also engaged. He tried three more times with the same result, putting a zero in front of the number.

'Damn!' he cursed angrily. Was Mr Holsworthy not very important if he could only make local calls? He looked up, the girl was looking at him and he gave a sickly grin and started to unscrew the power point. He had removed it and placed the cover on the floor when he realised he stood a good chance of electrocuting himself, it would still be live. He was about to reach for the phone again when there were heavy footsteps, the occupier of the office had returned.

'What the hell?' he was young, very officious with a permanent frown.

'Point was giving trouble.'

'What...it was working this morning.'

'That was this morning, there's a cross circuit with a point on the floor below,' Van Ekeren explained with sweat pouring off him. 'This one was working OK, but the one below was intermittent.'

'How could this one affect a point on the floor below?'

That was the question Van Ekeren hadn't wanted, but he came up with a glib response. He couldn't answer it, so he parried it skilfully.

'It wasn't, this one is in order,' he screwed the power point plate back. 'I'll have to try elsewhere.'

As he put back the screw-driver he noticed an electrical circuit plan in the lower tray of the box, he took it out and perused it sagely. 'Hmmm!' he said thoughtfully. 'It looks as though the trouble is down below somewhere.'

'I should think it damn well is,' Holsworthy snorted angrily. 'I've never heard such nonsense, who is your supervisor?'

Again, Van Ekeren deflected it.

'Is there a point on the other side of this wall?' he asked.

'What? No...I don't know ... yes there must be,' Holsworthy picked up the phone, dialled '9' whereupon Van Ekeren distinctly heard a second, higher pitched dialling tone. He cursed himself angrily, but at least he'd learnt something. He straightened up, but ducked down again in horror as Bramble entered. He dropped on his knees again, unscrewed the last two screws, and then re-commenced screwing them in, slowly.

'Have you found him yet, Bob? Oh hallo, is that Harold?'

Bramble sat down at Holsworthy's desk, half facing away from Van Ekeren, while Holsworthy bent the ear of the unfortunate Harold. Van Ekeren put the two screws back, picked up the tool-box, left the office pen, gave the girl a cheerful smile and vanished behind a filing cabinet. He would have to find another phone, preferably on another floor.

He debated whether to use another office pen on the same floor, but that would be asking for trouble with Bramble in the vicinity. He headed for the lift, after checking for indignant electricians.

He tried the seventh floor and located an empty office. Once more he managed to observe the nameplate by the door and gained ingress by judicious name dropping. With his back to the office pen door he picked up the phone and commenced dialling. Then the door opened and he felt a tap on the shoulder.

'You've certainly given everyone the run around! I had a feeling you'd come back in the building and I'd find you if I looked long enough. I'd say you're under arrest!'

CHAPTER 34

Van Ekeren was escorted through various corridors in the direction of Francis' office with Bramble's hand on his upper arm. The subsequent interview with Francis was something of a surprise, Van Ekeren had expected an angry tirade but he merely upbraided Van Ekeren for the trouble he had caused, mopped his brow and followed it with a brusque 'Take him back to his room and make sure it's locked!'

Bramble did just that, he escorted Van Ekeren to his quarters on the top floor and locked him in. Van Ekeren flung himself onto the bed and slept the sleep of the exhausted.

He was awoken the next morning by Francis, he came in at breakfast time accompanied by Bramble, but they weren't carrying breakfast, one of their minions was doing that. Francis held a newspaper; his face was impassive. He stood and looked at Van Ekeren , then tossed it over, it was that morning's edition of "The Australian".

'You'll find that of interest, Mr Van Ekeren,' then he and

Bramble departed. Van Ekeren opened it out and read the headline.

COUP FOILED IN TARANGA
DE SOUZA RIDES STORM, NOW FIRMLY BACK IN SADDLE!

'*Last night troops under the control of the Taranganese Government raided various offices which included their State Electricity Commission and the Security Police Headquarters, making several arrests. Last night the capital was reported to be in lock down, though there was sporadic small arms fire in northern suburbs.*

Rumours circulated that the Police Minister, Mr Delgado, has been arrested by Government forces, as yet this is unconfirmed.

It is anticipated more news will be to hand later today, a news conference has been arranged for 12 noon Eastern Australian time, today.'

Francis Burton returned later with Bramble, he was still impassive, yet there was something about his demeanour that Van Ekeren could not put his finger on.

'You did this, didn't you, Mr Van Ekeren?' he said. 'How did you do it?'

'How could I?' Van Ekeren protested. 'You put a block on me and your security was such I couldn't contact anybody, even when I went on the run your men were everywhere.'

'Yet you're obviously happy about it.'

'Yes,' Van Ekeren admitted. 'I am.'

'Somebody else was in the know, you had help?'

'Yes.' Van Ekeren knew what he meant but deflected it. He knew it would inevitably come up. 'I had contacts in Taranga who were in the know, they knew something was going on, a man named Westerman was one.'

'Hmmm!' Burton stroked his chin and a brief smile crossed his features before he turned to go. 'Maybe we're better off without a large overpopulated nation too close to us...eh?'

He and Bramble departed and the door closed behind them. Then it reopened and Burton poked his head around.

'After you've had breakfast, you can go. I wish you good day, Mr Van Ekeren.'

Van Ekeren returned the greeting, then a thought struck him.

'Mr. Burton. Why was that man Claudio from the Taranganese Embassy here yesterday?'

'That is a matter of State, I'm hardly at liberty to confide that to you. Why do you ask?'

'Just curious, that's all,' Van Ekeren mumbled as he tucked into the eggs and bacon.

Burton turned to go, then paused.

'I don't suppose it matters now; I may as well tell you. I called him in to administer a reprimand. Conducting shooting wars around Australia is definitely not on, and I told him so.'

'This man is a diplomat?' Van Ekeren asked.

'Ostensibly, yes. In fact...he was...is...one of their security personnel, the same as us. It was a case of like talking to like!'

'You speak to each other then?'

'On occasions when circumstance demands, especially in a situation like this with gunmen rampaging over our countryside, Mr Van Ekeren,' Francis explained. 'We don't do it in their country and we won't tolerate it in ours.'

'What happened about those bastards who were shooting at me...and McKay? I can remember four names, Rivera, De Ryk, Fino and Tara.'

'Don't worry about them, Rivera for one has gone into hiding. We don't know where he is but you'll be in no danger from him. The coup is in the open now and has been crushed. As for De Ryk, the Victorian Police have had outstanding warrants for him on several counts of assault for months. He is currently in Melbourne in a top security gaol. The other two we don't know about, they are loose and probably with Rivera. Again, they should be no threat to you now; they were trying to kill you to keep the coup under wraps, now it's out in the open they'll have no interest in you.'

'I hope you're right.'

'I am right, rest assured,' replied Burton.

'Another point, Mr Burton.'

'You have my ear, Mr Van Ekeren.'

Van Ekeren jerked his head at the glasses on the bedside table.

'Those belong to your colleague William Shackleton. Can you see he gets them, before he walks into a fire bucket?'

To Van Ekeren's surprise Burton dissolved into laughter. He picked up the glasses and handed them to Bramble, who was also grinning.

'See those find their way home, will you Bob.'

He turned on his heel and they both left, Bramble closed the door. Van Ekeren could hear them both still laughing as they walked down the corridor.

Van Ekeren began to wonder whether Francis Burton had been saddled with a policy with which he disagreed. Van Ekeren had empathy with that, he had had many run ins with Flowers on general policy in the brokers' Melbourne office. It had been on the tip of his tongue to tell Burton that Claudio had been one of the conspirators, but he held it back. He decided to impart that to McKay so he could expose friend Claudio and gain some kudos. He owed that to McKay.

Van Ekeren was glad De Ryk was in custody, he considered

De Ryk was merely a mean fighting machine, who wouldn't forgive any assaults on his person even though he had been the initial aggressor. The now public knowledge of the coup would not affect De Ryk's desire to avenge any blows or assaults during the chase across Victoria. He wondered if the police charges would include contaminating the atmosphere with methane.

As Van Ekeren tucked ravenously into breakfast, he was glad he hadn't wholly alienated Francis Burton, it seemed as if Burton thought his task had been satisfactorily completed. He had incarcerated Van Ekeren and there was nothing to indicate he was the one who tipped off De Souza and his government, while McKay would be satisfied that his own aims had also been attained.

As Van Ekeren wiped the fried bread around the plate and gathered up every last morsel, he thought back to the scene in the office after that finger tapped his shoulder as he was dialling Lopez' number...when he had nearly died of fright.

*

'I'd say you're under arrest,' McKay had said softly as he moved across and closed the office door. 'But finish your call first. You know how to dial it, don't you? Dial 9 and you're out? Then dial the international number.'

As Van Ekeren nodded, he continued.

'When you've finished it successfully you may as well get caught, no point in going outside, the police are looking for you, while Rivera may have cottoned on to where you are and there's no point getting killed now. When you do turn yourself in, try and surrender to Bob Bramble if you can, he's not a bad chap...he's a friend of mine the same as Lopez and De Souza appear to be friends of yours...OK?'

'OK!' Van Ekeren said. 'You mean you'll let me finish the call?'

'Yes, and hurry up, Francis Burton is no fool, he's on the ball and they are all over the place, inside the building and out. Francis is not unsympathetic to your stance, but he is employed by the government and when they beckon, he has to jump and so do I. Now I have to go. Good luck!' He was still limping as he went out and Van Ekeren noticed a fresh scar on his hand.

'And for Christ's Sake make sure you've got the right number before you blurt it all out,' was McKay's parting shot as he went through the door. 'Don't dial the wrong number and spill the beans to Delgado! See if you can get something right!'

With that he was gone. The phone at the other end was picked up and a familiar voice said:

'Roberto Lopez.'

'Mr Lopez, this is Douglas Van Ekeren.'

'Ah! Mr Van Ekeren, what an unexpected pleasure. How nice to hear from you again, did you have a good flight back? How are you?'

'Listen, Mr Lopez ...Roberto...I have information for you.'

'Information? Is it about the warehouse robbery?'

'No, not directly. What I have to tell you is vital! Please don't interrupt me, this is a matter of national importance to you and I haven't much time....!'

'I am listening, Mr Van Ekeren.'

Van Ekeren had looked around for McKay but he had long gone. He placed his elbows on the desk and continued speaking.

*

Francis Burton looked up as Alan Kelsey entered his room and signalled him to sit.

'How were things with the Minister?' asked Kelsey.

'Frosty,' responded Burton. 'I've no doubt he holds us

responsible for the leakage, although we concealed the fact that Van Ekeren went missing for a period of time.'

'Good,' grunted Kelsey.

'De Souza appears to be firmly in the saddle and all the conspirators have been rounded up,' said Burton. 'This should give De Souza a clear run from now on.'

'Not entirely,' said Kelsey. 'Dave McKay had words with me last night.'

'McKay?'

'Apparently Van Ekeren overheard a conversation relating to the coup while he was in that house. There is still one conspirator running around free.'

'Oh, who?'

'McKay was informed that Claudio Pécurto was one of the men in that house. He was complicit in the death sentence passed on Van Ekeren, apparently he was in it up to his neck.'

'Was he by God!' Burton rubbed his nose. 'Then we'll have to drop a hint into a ministerial ear. I can't say I'm surprised; he always struck me as a slimy bastard.'

'I'll leave it with you,' said Kelsey. 'Incidentally we've also interviewed that man Westerman who Van Ekeren met in Taranga. Gary Phillips took a full report from him. He took refuge in our embassy when the coup was imminent. Someone tipped him off that he could be vulnerable.'

'Someone tipped him off...? Who the hell...?' Burton looked up at Kelsey, then shook his head. 'Never mind, don't tell me Alan. I don't want to know.'

*

Van Ekeren poured the wine and looked at Val. They were in her apartment; it was late at night and they were having dinner plus a bottle of wine. As she smiled Van Ekeren felt prickles go up his spine, there was something about her that made him feel the whole world was with him when he was with her.

'Here's to us,' he raised his glass. 'And to no more overseas trips.'

'Oh, don't say that,' she also raised her glass. 'I do envy you being able to take trips overseas, they must be fun.'

CHAPTER 35

One aspect of the whole affair had always puzzled Van Ekeren, whenever he thought back over the whole frightening episode and mulled it over in his mind, he consistently came back to the incident that was the lynch pin of the whole business, as it related to his part in it.

This could have remained unanswered for ever; he had no desire to ever visit Taranga again so he could never have known the answer. But enlightenment came some months later when Bill Flowers sent for him.

'We are going to have a visitor from overseas,' Flowers said. 'I thought it would be a good idea if you were responsible for him whilst he's here, in fact he insisted on it.'

'A visitor?' Van Ekeren asked.

'You know we are refinancing and revamping the organisation of the broking company, we're moving into underwriting in addition to broking so we're registering our own insurance underwriting company for certain classes of business.'

'Yes, I knew that,' replied Van Ekeren. 'An interesting development if it's done properly.'

'It will be. The new carrier will transact business in Australia, New Zealand, Taranga and Indonesia. To finalise the Taranganese arrangements, Roberto Lopez will be arriving the day after tomorrow. He will be one of the directors of the Taranganese arm.'

'That's good news.'

'I thought you'd be pleased,' said Flowers. 'I want you to meet him at the airport, and escort him to his hotel. He's bringing his daughter with him, apparently she's secured a university place here in Melbourne.'

*

Three days later Van Ekeren was sitting on the balcony of the city apartment he shared with Val. It overlooked the River Yarra, the city and Flinders Street Station on the opposite bank. Since the disastrous, for him, trip to Taranga and his desperate meanderings throughout the Australian countryside with David McKay, he had gained a lucrative promotion and (almost) a new wife. His divorce had finally come through and he and Valerie were getting married the following month.

Roberto Lopez was in the other chair; they were both puffing on cigars after a very satisfactory meal. Valerie and Maria Lopez, who had taken an instant liking to each other, had decided to pay a visit to the Crown Casino which was within walking distance.

Van Ekeren had not had many opportunities for conversation with Lopez, much of Lopez' time had been taken up with negotiations regarding the administration and financing of the new organisation, when they did have time for social exchanges both Maria and Valerie were present and Van Ekeren couldn't broach the subject.

This was the first time Van Ekeren and Lopez had been alone and now was the time to bring it up.

'One thing puzzles me, Roberto. Can I ask you a question?'

They were now on first name terms; they had had frequent e-mail correspondence since Van Ekeren's Taranga trip and first names through this medium were automatic. Consequently, this form of address had been established as soon as Lopez disembarked at Tullamarine airport. Lopez drew on his cigar and looked quizzical.

'Is it about the new company?'

'No, nothing to do with that,' Van Ekeren replied. 'It's about my visit to Taranga.'

'Please ask.'

'It's about the burglary.'

Lopez sat upright.

'The burglary...at the warehouse you mean?'

'Well, there's no other burglary I can think of offhand,' Van Ekeren said gravely. 'I have been constantly thinking about that since I got back.'

'What intrigues you about it, Doug?'

'There was something funny about it.'

'Funny? You mean strange?'

'Yes, strange. There was the timing of it plus the intruders knew the alarm code. Also, only one of those TI crates was taken, while all the other TI crates were removed the next day. What did it have to do with the Ministry of Internal Security?'

'You ask some strange questions.'

'I have another one. Why the insistence that somebody from Melbourne check out the claim when it could easily have been handled locally. Why did you ask us to investigate?

It was almost within your terms of reference. You could have handled it yourself.'

'I thought it a good idea to enable you, by that I mean Melbourne office, to become involved, and to become conversant with Taranganese conditions.'

Van Ekeren looked at him and was gratified to see that although Lopez held his gaze levelly for some seconds, he eventually looked away to watch a train enter Flinders Street Station.

'It also prevented you from becoming directly involved with any aspect of the theft of those items, didn't it?' Van Ekeren said coolly. 'You didn't want to become involved because of the threat to your daughter.'

That caught Lopez' attention, he turned to face Van Ekeren and raised one eyebrow.

'I don't know what you are...!' he began then broke off and smiled ruefully. 'Yes, I do...!' he corrected himself and laughed. 'You are well informed. Who told you that?'

'It was said at that meeting I gatecrashed that was chaired by Julius Lebak. I had no reason to doubt it.'

'You heard correctly. Yes, that is why I sent for you. And yes, my wife and daughter were under threat. I determined whatever was turned up with regard to that affair had to come from outside.'

'I can see that, but it wasn't only the investigation of the break-in I was referring to.'

'Then what are you asking?'

'Who carried out that break-in in the first place? Who arranged it?'

There was silence, Lopez drew on his cigar and watched the smoke spiral into the still air. Then he turned to Van Ekeren and grimaced.

'I think you know already,' he said.

'No, although I was coming to that,' said Van Ekeren. 'Let me fill in the details. You were involved because imported goods had to come into that warehouse. Did you know what was in those crates?'

'No,' Lopez shook his head. 'Not initially, but when I saw them, I had my suspicions. The man who worked it all out was Gorge Corriea. He broke some of them open to have a look, and briefed me. They were full of rocket launchers and others had AK 47s.'

'What happened after that?'

'I, in my innocence, reported it to the security police in Taranga City. That was a mistake, I had reported the substitution of the crates to the very people who were involved in the conspiracy. I was visited by members of the security police who came under Delgado's wing and was told to keep my mouth shut, and so was Corriea. In view of the threats I had little choice.'

'So, you faked a burglary?'

'Yes,' admitted Lopez. 'Gorge Corriea was responsible for that. He is another Goanese, our families have long been connected and I had assisted him and his family to come to Taranga from Goa. Gorge has had a...hmm...chequered... history, he has many contacts, some of them are...well...let's say questionable, or perhaps I should more politely describe them as unorthodox.'

'Their ethics are open to question?'

'Yes, they are...' they both broke into laughter. 'He arranged for the burglary. We turned a blind eye and those who committed it were allowed to keep what they took; we didn't want to know about it. That is, apart from the TI crate, or alleged TI crate, they removed as well which finished up with

Inspector Hamad, an old friend of mine. You met Hamad at the hotel when your room was broken into.'

'What did he do with it?'

'It was delivered to people he knew were loyal to Juan De Souza.'

'You mean the government knew about the coup?'

'Yes and no,' Lopez shrugged. 'Countries like Taranga, with large neighbours breathing down their necks, are always susceptible to coups d'état; although thanks to you, very much less so now. I don't say a discovery of a cache of arms like this was routine, but it did happen from time to time. The removal of the remainder by the Ministry of Internal Security certainly caused eyes to turn in Delgado's direction, but there was no proof, and he was at that time too powerful to haul in for questioning. Investigations were in hand. It might have led to him eventually but by then it could have been too late.'

'You mean the coup could have come about before you could do anything?'

'You gave us the date, and the proof. Juan moved immediately and the rest you know.'

'What happened to Delgado?'

'In prison and in disgrace,' Lopez said pointedly. 'There he will stay for the time being. He will be placed on trial, which is more than he would have granted to De Souza had his coup been successful.'

'And that disgusting little man Franco?'

'He was shot trying to evade capture, I cannot say I was sorry,' Lopez lowered his eyes. 'He described to me what he would do to Maria if I said anything about that shipment, he was a revolting and disgusting man, but regrettably history is full of characters like him. I never told Maria about it, and I still have not. I'd appreciate it if you never mention it to her.'

'I won't,' Van Ekeren then had another thought. 'What of that young man who was living with you, wasn't he one of them?'

'He was,' said Lopez bitterly. 'He was arrested with the others. I wasn't sure whether he was involved with them or not initially, but Franco made it clear he had a spy within the household and it could only have been him. I was glad to see the back of him. Because of his family connection with me Juan spared him prison, he was sent back to Malaysia.'

'What about Van Elderen?'

'Arrested and deported, I believe he was wanted in The Netherlands for embezzlement. His involvement in the coup was for money, not ideals.'

'What of your employee Toro, I heard he was one of them as well.'

'I sacked him, quite apart from his affiliations he was damned useless anyway.'

'What happened to Lebak?'

'He evaded capture and got away to West Timor, after that he disappeared. No doubt he is fomenting trouble somewhere.'

'Yes, I suppose he is,' sighed Van Ekeren. 'His sort always does!'

The End